End of

Born in Lincolnshire, Alex Gerlis was a BBC journalist for nearly thirty years. His first novel, *The Best of Our Spies* (2012), has been an Amazon bestseller, and is being developed for television serialisation by a major production company. The other books in the Spy Masters series of Second World War espionage novels are: *The Swiss Spy* (2015), *Vienna Spies* (2017) and *The Berlin Spies* (2018). *Prince of Spies* – the first novel in the Prince series commissioned by Canelo – was published in March 2020, followed by *Sea of Spies*, *Ring of Spies* and now *End of Spies*. Alex Gerlis lives in London, is married with two daughters and is represented by Gordon Wise at the Curtis Brown literary agency.

www.alexgerlis.com

Facebook: @alexgerlisauthor

Twitter: @alex_gerlis

www.canelo.co/authors/alex-gerlis/

Also by Alex Gerlis

Spy Masters

The Best of Our Spies
The Swiss Spy
Vienna Spies
The Berlin Spies

The Richard Prince Thrillers

Prince of Spies
Sea of Spies
Ring of Spies
End of Spies

ALEX GERLIS

END OF SPIES

CANELO

First published in the United Kingdom in 2021 by

Canelo
31 Helen Road
Oxford OX2 0DF
United Kingdom

A CIP catalogue record for this book is available from the British Library.

Print ISBN 978 1 80032 260 8
Ebook ISBN 978 1 80032 155 7

Look for more great books at www.canelo.co

Printed and bound in Great Britain by Clays Ltd, Elcograf S.p.A.

Characters

Principal characters:

Richard Prince British intelligence agent, detective superintendent

Hanne Jakobsen Danish police officer, British agent. Married to Richard Prince

Tom Gilbey Senior MI6 officer, London

Sir Roland Pearson Downing Street intelligence adviser

Kommissar Iosif Leonid Gurevich NKGB officer

Friedrich Steiner Gestapo officer, aka 'the Ferret',

Wolfgang Steiner Senior Nazi official, father of Friedrich

Other characters:

The Admiral British Nazi sympathiser

Major Tom Barrow US Counter Intelligence Corps, Munich

Bartholomew MI5 officer

Kenneth Bemrose British Liaison Office & MI6, Berlin

Benoît Officer at Fresnes prison near Paris

Roland Bentley Senior MI6 officer, London

Hauptsturmführer Klaus Böhme SS Officer, Berlin

Martin Bormann Head of the Nazi Part Chancellery, Berlin

Mr Bourne Owner of art gallery, London

Branka Slovenian partisan

Christine Butler SOE agent, Dijon (Thérèse Dufour)

Myrtle Carter British Nazi sympathiser

Peter Dean SOE agent, Enschede (Pieter de Vries)

Edvard Slovenian partisan

Frau Egger Housekeeper in Villach, Austria

Evans Field Security Section, Trieste

Charles Falmer Courier in Frankfurt

Kapitan Leonid Fyodorov NKVD officer, Berlin

Charles Girard Aka Alphonse Schweitzer, Gestapo Paris

Giuseppe port worker in Trieste

Hon. Hugh Harper Senior MI5 officer, London

Captain Wilf Hart Field Security Section, Austria

Paul Hoffman Berlin detective

Joseph Jenkins Intelligence officer, US Embassy, London

Jožef Slovenian partisan

Kiselyov Soviet officer at Hohenschönhausen prison

Willi Kühn Man in Berlin

Major Charles Lean F Section, SOE

Anna Lefebvre Prisoner at Fresnes near Paris

Ludwig Soviet agent working for Gurevich

Marguerite Former resistance fighter, Paris

Marija Slovenian partisan

Frieda Mooren (Julius) Resistance fighter, Enschede

Frau Moser farmer in Bavaria

Orlov Soviet officer at Hohenschönhausen prison

Edward Palmer (Agent Milton) Escaping British Nazi

Kenneth Plant SOE radio operator, Dijon (Hervé)

Franz Rauter former German intelligence officer

Mr Ridgeway Man at art gallery, London

Tim Sorensen US Counter Intelligence Corps officer

Captain Christopher Stephens F Section, SOE

Major Laurie Stewart Field Security Section, Austria

Ulrich Nazi in Frankfurt

Wilson MI6 officer, Paris

Frau Winkler Shopkeeper in Villach, Austria

Prologue

Richard Prince stood nervously in the shadow of the Gothic splendour of Lincoln Cathedral, a flurry of leaves gathering around his feet in a premature burst of autumn. He glanced around uncomfortably and retreated to the canopy of the Judgement Porch, Jesus Christ and the angels looking down on him in a quizzical manner as if wondering what he was up to. He didn't blame them. He wondered that too.

He'd never particularly liked the cathedral: it held a sense of foreboding and he'd always felt that for a place of worship it was too replete with imagery of the devil. As a small child he'd been told the cathedral's grounds had been used as mass burial pits for the city's victims of the Black Death, and the fear instilled then had lasted into adulthood. As a young police constable, he'd dreaded the night-time beat that took him anywhere near the darkened mass of the cathedral.

It hadn't been his idea to get married here. In truth it hadn't been his idea to get married at all: it seemed so rushed and unnecessary, and they'd hardly had an opportunity to get to know each other in normal circumstances. But Hanne was keen, and young Henry in particular was thrilled at the idea. He had no memory of his mother, and the prospect of his father marrying excited him. Only two weeks after Hanne had moved in with them, Prince had overheard his son call her 'Mummy'.

But the person who seemed most keen was Tom Gilbey, his erstwhile boss at MI6. 'You'll be able to make a decent woman of her, Richard.' He only called him 'Richard' when he was trying to flatter him, when he was about to ask a favour or make a demand of him.

'You don't think she's decent enough already, sir? She risked her life for this country – she spied for us in Copenhagen, was arrested by the Gestapo and ended up in a concentration camp. I'd say that's the mark of a pretty decent person.'

'Just a turn of phrase, Prince, you know that. But on balance, perhaps the right thing to do, eh?'

Prince would have been happy with a discreet ceremony in a register office, or if it had to be in a church, then one of the smaller ones dotted around the city would have been fine. But from the first moment Hanne saw the cathedral, she'd been captivated by it, and when he'd told her – in the way one does when showing your home town to a visitor – how in medieval times it had been the tallest building in the world for more than two centuries, she'd announced that that was where they'd have their wedding. Prince had told her it was highly unlikely they'd get permission.

'Ask Mr Gilbey then – he seems so keen on us getting married.'

So he'd asked Tom Gilbey, more in passing than anything else, the question preceded by an 'I don't suppose...'

He ought to have known better, because inevitably it turned out that Gilbey had been at school with the bishop. 'I'll telephone him now!'

Prince had said it seemed quite unnecessary to go to that effort and it was only an idea, but Gilbey said not at all, and within a matter of minutes he was speaking to a man he called 'Bunny', which seemed an odd way to address a bishop. He spoke quietly, so Prince only picked up snatches. 'Heroes, both of them... absolutely... almost died... Berlin... unimaginable... tragic... enormous favour... if anyone deserves it...'

When the call ended, he'd turned round to face Prince, a satisfied look on his face. 'Many congratulations, Richard, you're getting married at Lincoln Cathedral. Apparently you need a special licence to do so, but Bunny said it would be an honour to grant it, and you can even hold the reception in the Chapter House.'

The bishop's office couldn't have been more accommodating, and the dean gave them a choice of chapels for the ceremony. There was some paperwork to sort out, and the Danish Embassy in London was required to come up with a letter confirming that its citizen Hanne Jakobsen was free to marry. They were a bit dilatory at first, but again, Gilbey managed to sort it.

Now, as Prince stood under the Judgement Porch listening to Henry playing with his nanny, he became aware of a silent presence behind him, like a victim of the Black Death risen from the grave where they had lain for six hundred years. He knew who it was without needing to turn round.

'Good morning, Mr Gilbey. I'm surprised to see you here.'

Tom Gilbey was elegantly dressed in a formal black suit, a fawn-coloured cashmere coat folded over one arm and a white carnation in his buttonhole.

'You were generous enough to invite me, Richard.'

'I assumed you'd be too busy, sir.'

Gilbey patted Prince on the shoulder and wished him many congratulations, then shook his hand with a tight grip. 'It's my way of thanking you both.'

The wedding party was preparing to move into the cathedral, and Prince turned to join them.

'I wouldn't mind a few words with you after the ceremony, Richard,' and with that Gilbey moved away.

Prince stopped: he had little doubt what that meant. It would account for why Tom Gilbey had come all the way up to Lincoln for the wedding of two of his agents. It no doubt also explained why he had been so keen for them to marry in the first place.

There weren't many of them, easily fitting into the Soldiers' Chapel in the north transept, where the dean himself performed the ceremony. Prince and Hanne were joined by Henry, who acted as pageboy, his nanny, Prince's elderly father and a few relatives. In addition, there were various colleagues from the police force, a couple who'd been very friendly with Prince and his late wife Jane, and two sets of neighbours. And then of course Tom Gilbey, at the rear of the chapel, as if there to ensure everything was carried out to his satisfaction.

For a few minutes during the ceremony, Prince was calm and at peace with himself. He was marrying a woman with whom he was deeply in love and who until a few months ago he had feared was dead.

Afterwards, they moved into the Chapter House for a buffet lunch. Prince found Gilbey studying a painting of a seventeenth-century bishop whose beady eyes appeared to be surveying the room.

'You said you wanted a few words with me after the ceremony, sir?'

'I didn't mean straight after, Prince. Don't want to spoil your big day.'

'You already have.'

'Come on, now…'

'I know the way you work, sir. You've come here to sign me up for another job.'

Tom Gilbey said nothing as he lit a cigarette and watched his protégé through the smoke.

'Are you taking a honeymoon?'

'No, sir. Henry starts school next week.'

'Come down and see me later in the week, then. Oh, and Prince…'

'Yes, sir?'

'Do bring Hanne with you.'

They left the cathedral an hour later. Gilbey had long gone, and Prince and Hanne walked through the Angel Choir arm in arm, Henry holding Hanne's hand.

'What is that, Richard?' She was pointing to a carving of a strange creature perched high on top of a stone column. A sunbeam piercing through the south transept window caught its face sneering at them.

'That's the Lincoln Imp. He's famous around these parts.'

'And why's he here?'

'According to a fourteenth-century legend, two imps were sent by the devil to cause trouble. They created chaos in the cathedral until one of the angels up there turned this imp to stone while the other one escaped.'

'He looks as if he's alive.'

Prince nodded. 'Apparently it's to remind us that evil is never far away, even in a place as holy as this.'

Chapter 1

London and Dijon, France, November 1943

'No news, I imagine?'

'No, sir: I did promise to let you know as soon we hear anything.'

'I know you did, Forster, but it's getting late and—'

'Why don't you go home, Major Lean, and I'll call you if we hear anything.'

'Remind me how late the circuits transmit these days, Forster?' Lean was speaking from the corridor as if afraid to enter the room. Because of his height – he was taller than the door frame – he bent low to address the man sitting at a desk laden with radio equipment.

'It varies from circuit to circuit: Tractor tends not to transmit as late as some others, but who knows, sir.'

Lean remained in the corridor, glancing hesitantly into the room but without saying a word for a while, instead watching the tiny lights blinking on the equipment in the gloom and listening to the bleeps from the radio, which sounded like dripping taps.

'I tell you what, Forster, I'm going to put up the camp bed in my office. Call me as soon as you hear anything.'

He climbed the two floors to his office, gingerly feeling his way along the darkened corridors of Orchard Court on Portman Square in central London, the headquarters of the Special Operations Executive's F Section. He noticed the lights on in the office opposite his. A man a good decade and a bit younger than him was sitting in an easy chair with his feet stretched out onto his desk. He was wearing a waistcoat, and his sleeves and tie were both undone.

'No news, Major?'

'I'm afraid not, Stephens. How long is it now since we last heard from them?'

'Just over forty-eight hours, sir.'

'Remind me what the message said again?'

The other man closed his eyes as if trying to recall it. 'The decoded version, sir, was that the whole circuit had been compromised and they were expecting to be caught any minute. Hervé used the word "thunder" three times in the one message, sir, which means things are about as serious as they can get.' He shook his head, his eyes still closed.

Neither man said a word. It was just over an hour before midnight and the building was cloaked in silence. Not a sound penetrated from outside. They could have been in the middle of the countryside but for the absence of the calls of wild animals.

'A message like that doesn't hold out much hope, does it, Stephens?'

'I'm afraid it doesn't, sir.'

'Does her husband know?'

'Of course not, Major.'

'Shouldn't he be told?' Even though he was the younger man's superior officer, Major Lean had recently found himself deferring to him. He'd noticed that as the war went on, older men such as himself – those in their mid-forties and beyond – seemed permanently exhausted. The younger ones like Christopher Stephens seemed to have picked up a second wind from somewhere. Perhaps the course of the war invigorated them. And Stephens was so bright: a double first from Cambridge, Lord knows how many languages, and three missions into occupied France to his name. Lean was convinced Stephens would one day end up as his superior. A commission in a Guards regiment and being distantly related to Churchill's wife wasn't doing him any harm either.

'I don't see why we should tell him, sir; after all, we don't know what's happened yet, do we?'

'Surely we have a reasonable idea. I knew we shouldn't have sent a woman.'

Stephens finally opened his eyes and sat up, looking disapprovingly at the major. 'She's the best man for the job, sir. If it wasn't for our female agents, the SOE would struggle to get enough half-decent people to send over. Her French is excellent and she's as brave as a lion.'

Lean sighed. 'She's going to need to be. The thought of what the Germans will be doing to her absolutely terrifies me.'

—

There were a number of things that bothered Christine Butler, or Thérèse as she was now known. 'Annoyances', her mother had called them; *dérangements* in her native French. Her mother's life was accompanied by a considerable number of annoyances. Thérèse knew she shouldn't let these things bother her, because they were proving to be a distraction, and the very last thing a British agent in occupied France needed was a distraction. There was enough to worry about as it was.

The first annoyance was an extremely petty one – it was more of a superstition than anything else. Really it ought to have been the opposite of an annoyance, because it was to do with her journey to France and how well it had gone. They'd left RAF Tangmere in Sussex just before midnight, and it was a perfect flight over the Channel in the Lysander. It hadn't been nearly as uncomfortable as she'd been warned it would be, the landing in a field near Chaumont had been incident-free, and within half an hour of her climbing down from the plane she was safe in a farmhouse, surrounded by the members of the resistance cell she'd be working with. But from an early age her father had instilled in her an irrational notion that the easier the journey, the more things were likely to go wrong upon arrival.

During her three weeks in France, she hadn't been able to get that out of her mind. *Something's bound to go wrong.*

Then there was her radio operator, a man with a Yorkshire accent whose personal hygiene left much to be desired and who she was shocked to find spoke virtually no French, which made his code name of Hervé sound all the more implausible. She had raised this with the Captain, the enigmatic man who ran Tractor circuit, but he'd told her not to worry, and said that in any case, that was why she was there. She was the first to acknowledge that Hervé was a skilful radio operator, quick to encode and decode, fluent in his transmissions and the rest, but he was beginning to get on her nerves. They'd met up near Auxerre, and after a week had been moved south, where they were based in a woodsman's cottage close to the River Brenne near Montbard. They'd remained there for another week, Thérèse doing her best to carry out London's orders and bring some sense of order to the resistance in the area, an awkward mix of urban communists and rural Maquis.

Then came the orders to head south again, an abstemious journey through Burgundy to the city of Dijon. Once Hervé had become aware of their destination, he'd expressed the hope that they'd cut the mustard, which Thérèse acknowledged was mildly amusing, but not when he used the reference as an accompaniment to every conversation.

The final annoyance was a far more serious one. Her training as an SOE agent had been rushed through in a month, but they'd said she was an excellent student, and of course her French was fluent. They'd also said she needn't worry too much because Tractor was a good circuit and most of the resistance cells within it were watertight. That was the word Major Lean had used, 'most'. She had pointed out that 'most' rather undermined the whole business, a chain only being as strong as its weakest link, et cetera, but that condescending man Stephens had told her there was a war on and nowhere was perfect. Once in France, and especially since they'd arrived in Dijon, it was clear that the groups in the circuit were anything but watertight, but when she'd raised this with the Captain, he'd told her there was nothing to worry about, and in any case it was being dealt with, which all seemed to be rather paradoxical.

Fortunately, Hervé – whose real first name turned out to be Kenneth – shared her view, and they decided to split up. Hervé moved south of the city to the village of Fauverney, where the River Ouche forced a path through the trees crowding both of its banks. Thérèse remained in the city, on her own in a stuffy attic overlooking Dijon-Ville station.

After a few days, she was satisfied she'd found a reasonable modus operandi. Every other day she'd go to Parc Darcy, and after circumnavigating it to be sure it was clear would check the benches for the various safety signals the Captain had arranged. Once satisfied, she'd walk through the old centre of the city with its distinctive multi-coloured tiled roofs to Saint-Bénigne cathedral, where she'd meet the courier.

But on one visit to the park something was not right. The park looked fine from its perimeter, but there was no chalk mark on the first two benches she checked, and as she approached the third one, she caught a glimpse of two men looking towards her from behind the bushes. Beyond the bench a couple were embracing in a most unconvincing manner, and past them, at the entrance to the park, she could make out three black cars parked together.

It was a trap, and she realised it was one the Captain must have led her into. She thought of his unscheduled visit earlier that morning.

What time will you go to the park?
What route will you take?

Her only possible means of escape was across the lawn into the wooded area, where she might be able to lose them. For a brief moment she thought of her husband, Nicholas: she had been forbidden to tell him about the mission, and he'd seemed hurt when she'd said she was going away somewhere but he wasn't to worry. She was sure he thought she was having an affair.

She turned onto the wet grass but hadn't taken more than a step or two when she was aware of being surrounded, a dozen men encircling her, none of them saying a word as her hands were pinned behind her back and something reeking of stale sweat was placed over her head.

–

When the hood was removed about an hour later, Christine Butler was in a brightly lit windowless room. She assumed it was in the headquarters of the Gestapo in Dijon, on rue du Docteur Chaussier, which happened to be near the cathedral.

She was tied to a metal chair, the straps around her ankles cutting into her skin. Her wrists were attached to the chair by handcuffs. The man sitting opposite her seemed out of breath.

What is your name?

'Thérèse Dufour.'

Where are you from?

What do you do?

How did you get here?

His French was poor, and he didn't follow up any of her answers.

'You have my handbag: you'll find all my papers are in order,' she told him.

Finally he stood up, and she realised quite how overweight he was. 'Never mind: your interrogation will start soon. You'll soon have the pleasure of making the acquaintance of my friend *das Frettchen*!' He laughed loudly, and was still doing so as he left the room.

She was left on her own, still strapped to the chair. When a gendarme came in to check on her, she asked him who *das Frettchen* was.

'He means the interrogator: *le furet*.' He bent down beside her, his mouth so close to her ear his moustache brushed against it. '*Le furet* has a terrible reputation. Don't resist him.'

When she was once again alone in her cell, she remembered what *le furet* meant.

The ferret.

–

It was a few hours before the Ferret arrived. In that time she'd imagined a man who resembled one, perhaps with a long neck or a pointed nose, maybe beady eyes. She preferred that to an assiduous hunter and an efficient killer.

In fact *das Frettchen* looked nothing like a ferret. He was far younger than she'd expected – perhaps even in his twenties – with blonde hair swept back and bright blue eyes that seemed to twinkle. He smiled at her briefly and spoke to the guards in German, which she didn't understand. She was unstrapped from the chair and taken over to a wooden chair in front of the desk where he sat. A glass of water appeared in front of her, and he gestured for her to drink as if they were acquaintances meeting in a bar. Despite all this, she was mindful of the training she'd had in England on how to handle interrogations, when a man who reminded her of the priest who'd married her and Nicholas only a couple of years before had told her how easy it was to be lulled into a false sense of security. *You have no idea how frightened you'll be. Even someone smiling at you will throw you off your guard. Be alert all the time.*

'Your papers tell us you're Thérèse Dufour from Paris and that you're a schoolteacher with permission to travel to look for work.'

He'd addressed her in French and she was surprised that he used the familiar *tu* for 'you' rather than the more formal *vous*. She nodded and smiled, which he didn't return.

'Which is all of course nonsense!' He was speaking English now and swept her papers off his desk with the back of his hand.

'So please don't waste my time and cause yourself avoidable suffering. Tell me who you really are and what you are doing in France.'

She blinked and felt her throat tighten. He spoke good English and sounded as if he was trying to mimic an upper-class accent. Her training had made it very clear that she should endeavour to hold out as long as possible and not speak in English until it was impossible to avoid doing so. She replied in French.

'I beg your pardon, I'm afraid I don't understand. My name is Thérèse Dufour and I—'

He held up his hand as if stopping traffic. For a few moments he looked carefully at her before standing up, stretching himself and then strolling towards her. He bent down and she noticed he smelt of cologne and toothpaste; he must have nicked himself while shaving, as there were flecks of dried blood on his collar.

'One last time, please: your name, those of everyone you work with and the location of your radio operator.'

She shook her head, which she immediately realised was a mistake because she wasn't meant to understand English. The next thing she was aware of was her chair being kicked, and sprawling across the floor. Her shoulder seemed to take most of the impact. Other people were in the room now, and she was hauled to her feet, dragged over to the wall and pinned roughly against it. The Ferret moved in front of her, a wide grin on his face.

'So they've insulted the great city of Dijon by sending us an amateur, eh?' He thumped her in the stomach and she concentrated hard on not being sick. He stepped back as two of the guards manacled her hands and feet to rings on the wall. Her arms were fully stretched and her toes only just touched the floor.

The longer you hold out, the more time your comrades have to escape. Sometimes you may need to give them real information to buy time.

The fact that he'd asked about her radio operator was a good sign; at least Hervé hadn't been captured yet. He'd get a message to London, and who knows, maybe the resistance would rescue her. She doubted he would be making jokes now about cutting the mustard. She reckoned it was early afternoon, and thought if she could hold out for a couple of hours and then begin to answer in English and give them titbits of information, she could drag things on until night came. By the following morning, the others in the circuit would have escaped and she wouldn't be betraying anyone.

There is no easy way of saying this, but sometimes the physical pain is not the worst part of being tortured. Often the psychological approach is far worse – especially the humiliation.

—

She was ashamed of herself.

She'd been sure she could hold out for longer, but as soon as the humiliation began, she felt she caved in almost without resistance. It wasn't that she wanted to be physically tortured, but she'd been told during her training that the purpose of torture was to get information out of you rather than kill you, and if the pain was too bad the body would shut down, by which they meant become unconscious.

Once she'd been manacled to the wall, the Ferret ordered the guards to undress her, which they began to do. She immediately spoke in English, falling back on her emergency cover story far sooner than planned.

'My name is Audrey Manson, from Bristol. I was arrested a year ago for committing fraud and was facing a long prison sentence. Then they discovered I spoke fluent French – my mother was French – and made me an offer. If I came to France on a secret mission then the charges against me would be dropped. Otherwise I would go to prison for ten years. I very reluctantly agreed. I must tell you I'm not in favour of this war. I think there should be peace between our countries so we can fight the real enemy, the Soviet Union. I was flown to France and landed by parachute north of Dijon and made my own way into the city. I rented a room near the station and was told to go to Parc Darcy, where someone would give me a package and instructions on what to do next.'

The Ferret looked as if he was unsure what to make of her. He hesitated, and then went to his desk, where he made notes on a sheet of paper. The only parts of her story that were true were that she was from Bristol and that her mother was French. She thought that was what they would concentrate on. She would tell them her mother was from Nice; it would take them a few days to check that out. The city was still in chaos apparently after the Italians had left it.

'I don't believe a word.' He was lounging back in his chair, his feet on the desk. He continued to stare at her as he lit a cigarette. 'Do you know how much we pay for information about the resistance?'

She shook her head.

'It depends on the quality of the information, of course, but for a British agent we pay up to one hundred thousand francs. We paid a bit less for you. We know you landed by Lysander near Chaumont around three weeks ago and made your way to Auxerre before arriving here a week ago. You're helping to run the British circuit operating in the area. The British, I can assure you, don't send over thieves, however good their French is.'

She was sure the Captain was the only person who knew all that information, so she decided to tell them about him, embellishing considerably to imply he couldn't be trusted by anyone. She even went off at a tangent about how he had been a bank robber in Lyons – she had no idea where that came from, but she hoped it sounded plausible: Lyons was after all a centre of resistance activity. She described the stuffy attic near Dijon-Ville station and told them she'd been trained at a country house near a town called Harpenden in Hertfordshire, going to great lengths to describe it, right down to a damp basement and an extensive herb garden. The house had been used by the SOE and closed the previous month after a security breach, and she'd been advised to tell them about it so she knew she was on safe ground. As for the radio operator, she wasn't sure what to say. It wouldn't be credible to deny his existence, so she told them he was Belgian, from Liège, she understood, and she had no idea how to contact him because he was always the one to find her. He had bad hygiene, she added, and a poor sense of humour.

From that point on it was a series of horrendous events, one after another. The Ferret laughed and told her he didn't believe a word and announced he'd now lost patience with her, at which point he himself removed the rest of her clothing, which was humiliating enough, but then the cell filled with a dozen or so men who'd clearly been invited in to have a look, and they laughed and leered at her, a couple of them pawing her as if she were at a livestock market.

When they left, it was just her and the Ferret. He said she had one last opportunity to tell him the truth, and she did try to, but she found herself unable to speak, such was her state of shock. Her lips moved, but no words came out of them. She would have told him anything he wanted to know; she'd even have betrayed Nicholas. If only she'd had the words.

What happened next was too dreadful to recount, but when it was over, she lay on the cell floor in a pool of blood and tried to speak, anxious to tell him everything in case he was minded to start again: Major Lean, the man called Stephens, the woodsman's cottage near Montbard, Hervé, otherwise known as Kenneth, the village of Fauverney. She couldn't take any more.

She must have drifted into unconsciousness, and was woken by shouting in the corridor. It was in German, and by the sounds of it someone was telling her interrogator off. Soon after that, she heard two gendarmes speaking. *He had a real go at* le furet, *told him it wasn't his job to kill prisoners!*

A doctor came to see her that night and said she needed to be in hospital. She was taken on a stretcher to Dijon prison on rue d'Auxonne, where there was a rudimentary infirmary. She was aware of little for the next day or so, but when she came round, an orderly told her she was lucky to be alive.

Le furet has such a terrible reputation... Apparently you told him nothing and he got even angrier than usual. Take this medicine and pretend to be unconscious. With some luck they'll take you to Fort d'Hauteville.

'What's that?'

It's a prison just outside the city and they have a proper hospital there. After that they'll take you to one of their camps... not nice places, but at least you'll be away from le furet.

The orderly returned the next day, whispering urgently as he cleaned the floor around her bed.

They've arrested so many résistants... now they're looking for the rest. They found an Englishman down in Fauverne... Apparently he managed to get a message out and destroy his transmitter and then burn all his code pads before killing himself. So brave...

—

The following night, she woke with a start: in the gloom she made out a man in a large coat standing silently at the foot of her bed, arms folded. She asked in French who was there, and when a nurse turned a light on, she saw it was the Ferret.

'No one,' he hissed, 'gets the better of me.' He snapped his fingers and two orderlies appeared with a stretcher, which she was bundled onto. Pain seared through her body and she felt the bleeding start again. She was carried into the prison yard, where a warder stopped them. From his uniform he looked quite senior.

'Not here, sir, please not inside the prison.'

'Who says?'

'There'll have to be an inquiry.' He was wringing his hands.

'Very well.' The Ferret snapped at the orderlies: 'Take her outside and put her on the pavement.'

Her main regret was not having written to Nicholas. She'd thought about that in the hospital, but was too weak, and also worried what would happen to him if they found the letter. It was agony when the orderlies dumped the stretcher on the pavement before hurrying away. She watched as the Ferret removed a revolver with a long barrel from his coat and pointed it at her. It was a strange way to end one's life, she thought, lying on a wet pavement in a foreign country hoping the man who was about to kill would hurry up.

An annoyance, as her mother would have said.

Un dérangement.

Chapter 2

Nazi-Occupied Netherlands, May 1944

Het ongeluk was how the work of the Dutch section of the SOE was described around Baker Street.

Het ongeluk – the disaster.

In fact by late 1943, some senior officers in the Special Operations Executive were of the view that to describe N Section as a disaster was a serious understatement. It was less a disaster, more like a catastrophe.

De catastrophe.

And they had good reason for forming this opinion. Over an eighteen-month period, the SOE network in the Netherlands had been so thoroughly penetrated that every agent parachuted into the country – more than fifty of them – had been captured. By late 1943, operations there had been suspended.

It took the SOE until the spring of 1944 to work out the extent to which its activities in the Netherlands had been compromised. They realised that the Germans had discovered all the British codes and ciphers, and that N Section radio operators in London had inexplicably failed to pick up a series of secret security checks in the radio transmissions of captured agents.

But by April 1944, the SOE was satisfied that matters had been rectified and they could once again resume operations in the Netherlands. They were still wary, though, so much so that SOE headquarters decided to send in an agent of which N Section was unaware.

They'd found Peter Dean by chance. When he'd tried to enlist in the Royal Navy, he'd mentioned in passing to a recruiting officer that he was born in the Netherlands and spoke fluent Dutch. His details ended up with MI6, who passed them on to the SOE – though fortunately not its Dutch section.

Peter Dean's Dutch name was Pieter de Vries. He was originally from Rotterdam but had lived in England since his family had emigrated when he was ten. Despite his age – he was now fifty-one – he turned out to be good agent material: an intelligent man, physically fit and he passed all the rigorous security checks. They decided he should use his original name and place of birth: Rotterdam had been so badly bombed that they were able to give him a home address in a street that no longer existed.

Pieter de Vries travelled across the North Sea by trawler to a rendezvous point just north of the West Frisian Islands, where he transferred to a Dutch trawler that took him on to the port of Harlingen, from where a trusted resistance cell transported him to Enschede in the south of the country, close to the German border.

There was a resistance cell in the city that had survived because London had managed to suspend its activities just in time. Now they wanted to revive it and gather what intelligence they could from the area. Pieter de Vries arrived in Enschede with instructions to meet up with the leader of the group, who went by the code name Julius.

Julius turned out to be Frieda Mooren, a resourceful woman in her early twenties, and for a few weeks the group flourished. They amassed intelligence from across the border on all the transport links in the area, and particularly on the airfield, which was a target for the RAF.

De Vries was adamant the group should be highly disciplined. Its members were to keep a low profile, lead their lives as normal and do nothing to draw attention to them. They all adhered to this, apart from one member: a retired schoolteacher called Johannes, who cycled round the city in the same shabby suit whatever the weather. Johannes had a neighbour, a man who openly collaborated with the occupiers and was widely believed to have betrayed a Jewish family hiding in the town. For over a year Johannes had developed a seething hatred of this man but was powerless to do anything about it. Now the group was becoming active once more, he saw his opportunity.

De Vries was unaware of this. In fact he was so satisfied with the group that he sent a message to London informing the SOE that they were ready to move on to the next stage of their operation.

Two important railway lines passed through Enschede: one to the west that led to Amsterdam, Rotterdam and The Hague, and a separate line going east into Germany, both lines vital to the German war effort. De Vries's instructions were to blow up both lines simultaneously.

The RAF dropped a consignment of weapons and explosives in Overijssel, to the north of Enschede, and de Vries started to prepare the team. The arms drop had included a dozen handguns – Spanish Llama pistols – and he gave one to each member of the group.

The night before the planned sabotage, disaster struck. As far as de Vries could gather, Johannes had gone round to the collaborator's house and shot him with the pistol he'd just been given. The collaborator's wife had managed to raise the alarm, and Johannes was arrested. It didn't take the local Gestapo very long to break him, and within hours of the shooting they'd begun to round up other members of the group. One person they failed to find, however, was Frieda Mooren. She'd managed to slip out the back of her house and had gone straight round to where de Vries was living. They left immediately and went to the farm just outside Enschede where they'd stored the explosives.

The word from the city was that the hunt for the two of them was gathering pace: extra troops had been drafted in, along with a senior Gestapo officer from Amsterdam. They decided to attempt to blow up the railway line heading west. After that, they'd go north, to Amsterdam.

Because of the concentration of troops searching for them in the area, de Vries decided to sabotage the railway line further away from Enschede, close to Tusveld, north-west of the city. The farmer drove them to the area one morning on his way to market, stopping outside a small wood for the two of them to climb out of the back of his truck. They hid in the trees until the very early hours of the morning, when darkness wrapped itself around the countryside and not a sound was to be heard. De Vries whispered to Frieda that it was time to move, and began to crawl out of the undergrowth where they were hiding. She placed a hand on his back to stop him.

'Something's not right.'

'What do you mean?'

'Listen.'

'I can't hear a thing.'

'Exactly. It's unusual to hear nothing in the countryside: this is too quiet.'

They waited another half-hour before de Vries said it had been long enough and they needed to move. Half walking, half running in a crouched position, they hurried out of the woods and across the field leading to the railway line. They were just feet from the bank dropping down to the line when night turned to day, and when their eyes finally adjusted to the searchlights trained on them, the field was swarming with troops emerging from the hedgerow.

Both de Vries and Frieda sank to their knees and held their hands high above their heads. A young man in a Gestapo regulation trench coat had just climbed up from the railway line and was walking towards them, a pleasant smile on his face and his hand outstretched as if greeting old friends. He shouted in German for the pair to be separated and followed de Vries as he was dragged to a waiting truck.

'What kept you? We've been waiting so long – I'm chilled to the bone!' He smiled pleasantly once more and threw back his head, his blonde hair falling into place. He spoke surprisingly good Dutch. De Vries didn't reply, trying to work out who could have betrayed them. He wondered about the farmer.

'We are going to Amsterdam,' the German said, rubbing his hands together as if he was looking forward to the outing. 'What is your name?'

De Vries said nothing, pursing his lips in case he uttered anything involuntarily. The German shrugged as if it didn't terribly matter.

'Ah well, there'll be plenty of time for you to tell me when we get there, eh? I've not introduced myself, have I?'

Another smile as he edged closer to de Vries, who picked up a strong smell of cologne. 'I'm known as *das Frettchen*. Do you understand German?'

De Vries shook his head.

'In Dutch, it's *de fret*, but I don't know if you prefer English. It translates as the Ferret.'

–

In the normal course of events the Ferret would have been punished after managing to kill the British agent in Dijon the previous November without extracting any useful intelligence from her. He'd ignored instructions to bring her back to Paris, where there were plenty of people at 84 Avenue Foch perfectly capable of doing the job for him.

It was his last chance: his combination of an explosive temper and sheer incompetence was not ideal for the Gestapo, which liked to pride itself on efficiency and discipline. The Ferret had arrived in Paris with a bad reputation, and it never improved. His bosses were also bothered by what was described to them as 'psychopathic sexual behaviour'. It wasn't that they cared about the well-being of French citizens, but they were concerned when such behaviour impeded his ability to function effectively.

Of course the Ferret would never have been in Paris in the first place had it not been for the influence of his father, a senior party official who was part of what was known as the Österreichisches Clique – the Austrian clique.

After the death of the British agent in Dijon, the Ferret was banished from Paris. His superiors there rather hoped he'd be sent to the east, where he'd do less damage and might even learn a lesson or two. He *was* sent east, but only as far as Amsterdam, thanks to his father's intervention with two more members of the Österreichisches Clique: Arthur Seyss-Inquart, who as Reichskommissar was effectively the ruler of the Netherlands; and Obergruppenführer Christian Winkler, who ran the Gestapo there.

For a while the Ferret behaved. He spent most of his time keeping his head down in the Gestapo headquarters on Euterpestraat, just about smart enough to realise that a period of avoiding trouble was advisable. Out of hours was a different matter, when he frequented the brothels around the canals, always looking for the youngest prostitutes and always doing his best to avoid paying.

By the end of April, he was told that he needed to impress with some cases of his own. He hadn't broken any Dutch resistance cells yet, or caught any British agents. Perhaps he'd like to get a move on. So when he heard about a resistance member being arrested in Enschede after trying to kill his neighbour, he headed straight down there and much to the chagrin of the local Gestapo took over the interrogation.

He seem to be vindicated, as the elderly schoolteacher called Johannes broke down under torture and gave the names of the other members of the group, even revealing that they'd recently been joined by a British agent. He also admitted – though he only revealed this minutes before his death in unimaginable agony – that the British agent and the woman called Frieda had explosives and were planning to blow up the railway lines east and west of Enschede.

Once Johannes died, however, it became clear that this pair had gone to ground, and now Amsterdam was on the Ferret's back: how could he have allowed a prisoner to die before he'd extracted the information they needed?

But then he had a stroke of luck. A farmer was arrested after his truck tried to turn round as it approached one of the many roadblocks round Enschede. There was nothing on the truck, and the farmer's story about returning from market seemed plausible enough, but evading the roadblock was suspicious and there was no question that the man was particularly nervous. The Ferret insisted on conducting the interrogation himself, and even he had to admit it was hardly the most difficult of tasks. The farmer was clearly not cut out for this: in return for a promise of freedom the Ferret had no intention of keeping, he told them everything: where the British agent and the woman were hiding, and the exact stretch of railway line they intended to sabotage.

And now the Ferret was back in Amsterdam with the two prisoners in cells in the basement on Euterpestraat. It was suggested that a more experienced officer should conduct the interrogations, but he was having none of it, appealing directly to Obergruppenführer Winkler: he'd sorted out the mess in Enschede, he'd been responsible for capturing the group and stopping the sabotage; he'd be the man to do the questioning.

–

His first mistake had been to underestimate the young woman and he certainly didn't believe Johannes' claim that she was the leader of the cell, giving little credence to the possibility that a seemingly meek young woman could be in charge of such a group. His interrogation got nowhere. She revealed nothing and he couldn't work out whether this was because she knew nothing or was unexpectedly obdurate.

His senior officer suggested they should at least allow the Gestapo's most experienced interrogator in Amsterdam to have a session with her, and as Obergruppenführer Winkler was away, the Ferret felt he wasn't in a position to refuse. He did think about telephoning his father in Berlin and asking him to speak with Reichskommissar Seyss-Inquart in The Hague, but he didn't want to try his father's patience, which even he recognised was wearing thin.

He decided to sort things out himself before this could happen. He went back to Euterpestraat at midnight and ordered the guards to bring the woman to the man's cell. There he held a pistol to her head and forced her to kneel in front of de Vries, who was ordered to reveal everything. She started sobbing and shook her head. When the Ferret pulled the trigger, she moved so the first shot only grazed her skull. He was so angry it took him another three shots to finish her off.

Only then did he realise that the British agent was slumped in the chair he'd been strapped into. When he pulled his head back, it was evident something was wrong: the man had turned grey and wasn't breathing. The medic confirmed he was dead.

When Obergruppenführer Winkler returned to Amsterdam, he found it hard to conceal his anger.

'I see you managed to kill two birds with one stone?'

The Ferret muttered something about the woman trying to escape, and the Obergruppenführer told him to shut up. 'I've spoken with your father: you're being moved again. Fortunately you'll be many hundreds of miles from here.'

The Ferret stared at the ground. He felt tears well in his eyes and his throat tighten. They'd send him to the east. He'd only been trying to do his best. He bit his lip so hard it started to bleed.

Chapter 3

Germany, March 1945

The young SS officer was waiting in the doorway of Wolfgang Steiner's outer office, unsure exactly where he should stand. It was lunchtime, which had traditionally been a quiet period of the day, but that had been when life was normal, which it was now anything but. Indeed, the very notion that people would take a lunch break was a fanciful one: for a start, Wilhelmstrasse had been so badly bombed there was nowhere to go, and then there was the added complication of there being precious little to eat.

Steiner beckoned the officer in. He was an *Obersturmführer* and seemed nervous, which was also something new: SS officers, even younger and more junior ones, had always manifested a confidence bordering on arrogance, even when dealing with an official as senior as Wolfgang Steiner. But this *Obersturmführer* forgot to greet him with the Heil Hitler salute as he entered, and apologised profusely. As he moved in front of Steiner, the light fell on the man's face, one side of which was badly scarred. Steiner wasn't surprised; there were very few fit SS officers of that age and rank in Berlin. The city was being run by old men and invalids.

'What is it?'

The young officer saluted again. 'I have come straight from the Führerbunker, sir.'

Steiner nodded and waited for the man to continue. When he turned his head to reveal the part that wasn't burnt, he looked younger than Steiner's own son.

'Yes, and?'

'I have a message for you, sir, from the Reichsleiter.'

Wolfgang Steiner felt a sensation in his stomach. Although he got on well enough with Martin Bormann, he was always nervous about any dealings with Hitler's deputy. For a couple of years they'd worked very closely in the Nazi Party headquarters – Bormann's office had been just across the corridor from his – but for the past few months Bormann had spent most of his time in Hitler's bunker, and Steiner hadn't heard from him in a while. The rumours were that Bormann was more or less running the country.

'Perhaps you'd like to give me this message?' He held out his hand.

'There is no letter, sir: a car will collect you from the front of this building at nine o'clock tonight and take you to a meeting with the Reichsleiter. He asks that no mention is made of this to anyone.'

Even allowing for his propensity to worry, Wolfgang Steiner realised this sounded ominous. Rather typically, too, he was bothered about a minor detail. 'How will I know which car?'

'I will find you, sir. Heil Hitler!'

–

Wolfgang Steiner's secretary had brought him a plate of herring and a few slices of proper black bread, but he had no appetite that afternoon. He picked at the bread and sipped some water and wondered about having a schnapps or two but decided against it because these days once he started he'd never stop, and Bormann wouldn't appreciate him turning up in any kind of drunken state.

He did think about whether he should leave the city – it was over seven hours, after all, before the car would be coming for him – but quickly decided against it. His plan had been carefully constructed and he wasn't ready yet. It would all be a rush and something was bound to go wrong. And he knew how shrewd

Bormann was: he had informants and confidants throughout the Parteikanzlei. He wasn't even sure about his own secretary; she fussed over him unnecessarily, always wanted to know what he was up to and where he was going.

By the middle of the afternoon, he'd decided that if he was in trouble, then Bormann would hardly have left him alone in the Party headquarters; he'd have been pulled in straight away. But on the other hand – there was always an 'on the other hand' with Wolfgang Steiner – it was a rather formal summons. He and Bormann were on first-name terms after all, and Bormann was in the habit of sending hand-written notes. Using an SS officer as a messenger seemed to be making a point.

He'd been so careful and so meticulous he'd be amazed if Bormann had any evidence against him. As nine o'clock approached, a strange calm fell over him. Whatever was going to happen would happen, he told himself. Berlin would fall soon anyway, so it wasn't as if the future looked especially bright. His only concern was Friedrich: his son wouldn't cope.

Always his only concern: Friedrich.

The *Obersturmführer* was waiting in the reception area and led him to a black Daimler waiting with its engine running in front of the building on Wilhelmstrasse. Steiner was relieved to see that the curtains in the car weren't drawn, and nor was there any kind of escort other than the officer and the driver, who greeted him with a 'sir', which boded well.

The Daimler headed south on Wilhelmstrasse and then west along Tiergarten Strasse. Steiner tried not to pay too much attention to the route, not least because that could mean very little these days. Berlin had been so badly damaged, it felt as if the city was being dismantled brick by brick – a neighbour had remarked to him that it seemed as if the roads were being pulled up like carpets, before he realised that he sounded disloyal and apologised profusely.

They carried on heading west, through the southern part of Charlottenburg, along Kanstrasse, before turning south, pausing by the roadside as the first Allied bombers of the night passed overhead. It didn't surprise Steiner when they arrived at the Kleiner Wannsee, the smaller and more exclusive section of the lake. The whole area was dark, but he could tell where they were: a quiet stretch on the southern shore with some of the most expensive houses in Berlin. The Daimler pulled into the driveway of one of them, and the gates closed behind it.

–

It was a small villa, but perfectly appointed and decorated in exquisite taste. The walls were covered in a silk material with a modern print, and the rugs on the polished parquet flooring must have been worth a fortune. There was no doubt the design and decor were Bauhaus – that was apparent from the exterior, with its flat roof, bold curves and clean lines. Despite the regime's disapproval, it was notable how the Bauhaus influence prevailed in Berlin. Steiner had little doubt this was one of the many Wannsee villas taken from Jewish owners; for a while he'd hoped he might be allocated one – looking out over the water would have been wonderful for his nerves – but was told they were reserved for families.

The *Obersturmführer* led him through the house to a lounge on the first floor that Steiner assumed looked over the lake. The large windows were covered in modern-looking blinds. Sprawled in a leather armchair was a beautiful girl in her early twenties wearing what appeared to be a cocktail dress with nothing underneath. She ignored Steiner but smiled sweetly at the young officer and waved her long cigarette holder in front of her like a conductor's baton, appearing to beckon him towards her.

Martin Bormann bustled into the room and told the girl to go, patting her on the backside as she brushed past him. He ordered the officer to pour two cognacs – *Not that bottle, you fool, that's German brandy: I said cognac!* – and then told him to leave and close the door behind him.

He'd already indicated that Steiner should take a seat on a large sofa; now he sat opposite him in the leather chair the young girl had been in. Over the years, Steiner had got to know most of Bormann's mistresses, some of whom were quite sweet. They saw him as some kind of father figure, and he'd had to arrange abortions for most of them. He didn't like Bormann's main mistress very much but still felt obliged to ask after her.

'And how is Manja, may I ask, Herr Reichsleiter?'

Bormann shrugged and pointed to the door through which the girl in the cocktail dress had recently left. 'Not as lively as her.'

'What's her name?'

'How the hell should I know?'

'And Frau Bormann and the children?'

'What do you think, Wolfgang, the whole fucking—' He stood up shaking his head in despair, and brought the cognac bottle over. 'I'm sorry, Wolfgang, I've hardly been in the Parteikanzlei in recent months. The Führer barely leaves the bunker these days and he relies on me more and more. With the way the war's going, he doesn't trust the generals any more. He hardly trusts anyone.'

'I understand; in fact I—'

'He was never the most trusting of people, which in many ways is one of his strengths, but now – you understand I'm speaking frankly with you, Wolfgang – now he's not in a good state. Some would say he's paranoid: he shouts and rants, and God knows what drugs he's taking. He only listens to Eva, and she's in a pretty bad state herself. The party won't survive this. In fact,' he leaned towards Steiner and a grin appeared on his face, 'you could say the party's over! Do you get it, the party's over!'

He stood up and paced the room, laughing at his own joke until tears formed in his eyes. 'The party's over... I must remember that. I'd use it in the bunker if there was anyone there with a sense of humour, but it's full of Bavarians and Austrians.'

Steiner stared at the floor. He'd never seen Bormann like this. He was normally a calm man, always in control; now he was bordering on the hysterical. And he'd aged, too. He was in his mid-forties and had always taken care over his appearance, but now he looked nearer sixty.

'I'm sorry, Wolfgang, I forget you're Austrian.'

'Don't worry, sir, I wasn't offended.'

'And how are you keeping?'

Steiner felt relaxed and allowed Bormann to fill his glass. It was clear this was a social occasion and his concerns had been misplaced. He muttered something about these being difficult times for everyone, but hopefully... He stopped because he could tell Bormann was staring at him but no longer smiling.

'I understand you've been making arrangements, Wolfgang?'

Steiner hesitated, puzzled at what Bormann was getting at, and at the sudden change in mood.

'I beg your pardon, sir?'

'I said I understand you've been making arrangements.'

He realised he must have looked as shocked as he felt. This was clearly no longer the social occasion he'd thought it was. There was an undoubted air of menace in the room, as if one of the windows had been opened and the wind was blowing in from the Wannsee.

'What kind of arrangements do you mean, sir?'

'That is what I very much hope you are going to tell me.'

The room was so quiet he could hear the *crump crump* of artillery in the distance. Just a few weeks ago he'd been impressed at people who could tell the difference between incoming and outgoing artillery fire – it all sounded the same to him. Now even he could tell this was incoming. Most of it was these days.

'I really... I really don't know what you...'

'Let me help you, perhaps, eh? What I mean is that I understand you have made arrangements to escape from Berlin. That is correct, is it not?'

Steiner hesitated, unsure how to reply. 'No, sir – I intend to remain at my post until the last possible moment, at which point of course it would be improper for me to remain in Berlin and surrender or be captured or…'

Bormann held his forefinger to his lips. 'Let's not beat about the bush: I know you're making plans to leave Berlin well before the battle for the city is over. Don't forget, I have eyes and ears everywhere; how else do you think I've got to the position I'm in now in this nest of vipers? I know everything. I know you're smart and I know you've been photographing documents at the Parteikanzlei and taking the film home, and I've picked up reports of you being seen in the Rott Valley. So don't treat me like a fool, Wolfgang.'

Steiner found himself unable to respond. It was as if he was hypnotised, but was brought round by a heavy slap to his thigh.

'But it is no more than one would expect of you, you crafty Austrian bastard, eh?' Bormann was smiling. 'Not only do I want you to continue with your arrangements, I want to be part of them!'

'I'm not sure I understand…' Steiner was convinced he'd stepped into a trap.

'For so many years, anyone who was anyone wanted to be in Berlin. In a matter of weeks, anyone who's anyone will want to be anywhere but here.'

'But, sir, I—'

'Stop, Wolfgang, please. Anyone not making arrangements to leave the city is a fool, as long as they're being discreet about it, of course. Who wants to hang around for the Russians, or to be arrested by the Allies? There are escape lines being set up, some of them quite sophisticated, I'm told. My problem is who to book my passage with: I don't trust anyone.'

Bormann leaned back in the leather armchair and smiled at Steiner.

'Apart from you, of course, Wolfgang: I'm counting on you.'

Chapter 4

Germany, July 1945

When Wolfgang Steiner realised he had no choice but to take his son to a psychiatrist, he was careful to choose one of the few in Vienna who didn't appear to be Jewish. The last thing a prominent Nazi needed in 1935 was to have a Jew analysing his son's problems.

Steiner had been most reluctant to admit that twenty-one-year-old Friedrich had a problem. For years he'd attributed his behaviour to adolescence, and then to the excesses of youth: girls seemed attracted to him, and he liked a drink, and Wolfgang Steiner couldn't see what the problem was with that. If Friedrich did sometimes go a bit too far, Wolfgang blamed himself: his own low moods and frequent absences had probably been the cause of his wife's alcoholism, which in turn had led to her death when Friedrich – their only child – was just fourteen.

But recently matters had become increasingly hard to ignore. The boy had sexually assaulted two maids at the Steiner family home in Alsergrund, the city's smart 9th District. In the case of the second girl – a sweet young thing from Carinthia – Wolfgang had had to arrange an abortion and then pay a considerable sum to her family to keep matters quiet. Then there'd been an incident in a bar in the 4th District that resulted in Friedrich beating up a man; again Wolfgang had had to pay a large sum in compensation to avoid a criminal case. Inevitably the police had become involved, and the sympathetic senior officer who agreed to drop the case warned him that unless he did something about it, his son was bound to end up in prison.

Christian Gruber might have had a decidedly Austrian name, but as far as Wolfgang Steiner was concerned, the psychiatrist looked suspiciously Jewish, with his dark complexion, black hair with eyes to match, and a nose that while not classically Jewish could certainly not be described as typically Aryan either. He was also extremely perceptive, perhaps almost too much so. After two sessions with young Friedrich, he asked to see the boy's father alone. It was with some reluctance that Wolfgang went to Dr Gruber's consulting rooms on Burg Ring, with the Parliament building framed through its neat window.

'You have heard of manic depression, Herr Steiner?'

He replied that he had, but wasn't too sure of what it meant. Dr Gruber explained that manic depressives typically suffered from extremes of mood: excitable mania on the one hand – which could present as a form of psychosis – and periods of depression, sometimes very severe, on the other.

'So are you saying Friedrich is a manic depressive?'

'Actually, no – in fact I'm struggling to make an accurate diagnosis, to be frank with you, Herr Steiner. He certainly suffers from very elevated moods, which would explain the psychotic behaviour you describe – the attacks on women, for example, his temper. He told me about his mother.'

Wolfgang nodded but shifted uncomfortably. The more he saw of the man, the more he believed Dr Gruber could well have Jewish blood, and the last thing he wanted to do was discuss his family with a Jew. He made a mental note to have Dr Gruber's background checked.

'Friedrich described your moods and believes they may have contributed to his mother's drinking. Is it true you suffer from low mood, depression perhaps?'

It was as if Dr Gruber had put him in a state of hypnosis, because against his better judgement, Steiner found himself opening up to the psychiatrist. He told him how he'd always suffered from anxiety – depression, indeed – and at times felt overwhelmed by it. He'd never experienced the manic episodes

Dr Gruber had described, and he felt his moods were just something he had to live with. Early on in his life he'd found that if he kept busy, then he could cope. He'd studied hard as a student and made a successful career as a lawyer. He decided not to mention his political activities.

'Are you and Friedrich very close?'

'We are, yes. We only have each other.'

'It seems to me, Herr Steiner – and this is hardly even a hypothesis yet – that your combined behaviour is a good example of manic depression: you suffer from the depressive side of that behaviour, while your son suffers from the manic side. I may be completely wrong about this – it's just a thought – but I would be interested to have more sessions with both of you; together you present as fascinating subjects.'

Steiner replied that he really wasn't sure about this; he was more interested in what could be done to help his son – to control his behaviour. He most certainly didn't want to be analysed himself.

Dr Gruber replied that he needed to realise that his son suffered from a potentially serious psychiatric condition, one that could certainly not be cured by medication. He needed more sessions of analysis and then a course of therapy; perhaps a period in a residential clinic he often used in the Vienna Woods, one where discretion and privacy could be assured.

Wolfgang Steiner became quite angry at this point, bitterly regretting having revealed matters about himself to the psychiatrist. He told him his son was not that ill and he certainly didn't need to be locked up. It wasn't as if he was mad.

He ended the consultation and went to the secretary's office to pay. As he prepared to leave, Dr Gruber came of out his room. 'I apologise if I upset you in any way,' he said. 'It is often the case that patients, and their families in particular, find what psychiatrists have to say very difficult, sometimes too difficult.'

Steiner nodded. He continued to put on his gloves, anxious to leave.

'However, Herr Steiner, as unpleasant as it is for you to hear this, I would be negligent if I didn't tell you that I consider your son to be quite unwell. Unless he is treated, I think his tendency towards psychotic behaviour could escalate and have very serious consequences.'

–

After an uncertain start, Wolfgang Steiner ended up having a good if unspectacular war. Apart from a few favourable mentions in the Nazi Party newspaper, the *Völkischer Beobachter*, he kept a low profile, which he had determined best served his own interests.

He was on the fringes of the influential Österreichisches Clique, whose members occupied so many important positions in Berlin and throughout the regime: fellow Austrians like Ernst Kaltenbrunner, Arthur Seyss-Inquart, Odilo Globocnik, Adolf Eichmann and of course Adolf Hitler himself.

He'd moved to Berlin in the spring of 1938 after the Anschluss. Part of the idea had been to give a fresh start to Friedrich, who'd predictably continued to get into trouble in Vienna and only stayed out of prison thanks to his father's growing influence once the Nazis came to power. Soon after arriving in Berlin, he met Martin Bormann, Hitler's personal secretary, and when in 1941 Bormann became head of the Parteikanzlei – the Party Chancellery – he asked Steiner to join him. It suited him perfectly: an important job with a lot of influence but not necessarily a high profile, and one fitting his capacity for hard work. He began to develop an influential circle of acquaintances, people he was assiduous at keeping in touch with and doing favours for. He'd hesitate to call them friends; few people in Berlin were trusting enough of others to regard anyone as such. But Bormann had shown faith in him and afforded him status and respect, and he worked hard to repay that. Bormann was often described – though not to his face – as Hitler's shadow, and soon Wolfgang Steiner became known as

Bormann's shadow. He recognised that as the fortunes of war began to turn against the Reich, being seen as the shadow's shadow was a good reputation to have.

The enduring unfortunate aspect of Wolfgang Steiner's life was his son, Friedrich. No one knew of his reputation when they arrived in Berlin, and he was sufficiently in awe of his surroundings at first to behave in an acceptable way. In 1939, he joined the SS; though he had failed the initial selection, his father knew who to speak to and he was given a second chance.

He only lasted a few months. A senior officer – a fellow Austrian, naturally – had a quiet word with Wolfgang: Friedrich was selective about which orders he chose to obey. Indeed, he even occasionally tried to give orders to his superiors. The officer suggested it would be less embarrassing all round if he left the SS before he inevitably faced a court martial.

Fortunately, Wolfgang had done a number of favours for the head of the Gestapo, Heinrich Müller, and he was persuaded to recruit Friedrich. After a spell at the Gestapo headquarters in Prinz-Albrecht Strasse, the young man was sent to Norway, a move engineered by his father, who felt it was a posting where he could do least damage.

It turned out to be a disaster. After a brawl with a local policeman, Friedrich was transferred – again thanks to his father's intervention – to Denmark, where he served for just over a year and didn't blot his copybook, assuming one ignored the unsolved murder of a fifteen-year-old girl found in an alley close to his apartment in Copenhagen.

Next Wolfgang managed to arrange for him to be transferred to Paris, the most desirable posting for any German officer. It wouldn't be enough to stay out of trouble there; he'd also have to impress the Gestapo bosses, and that meant catching Allied spies and breaking up resistance groups.

From what Wolfgang Steiner could gather, his son was better behaved in Paris, but as a Gestapo agent he was useless, failing to solve any of his own cases and annoying colleagues by muscling in on theirs and trying to take the credit for them. One task entrusted to him was to recruit a network of informers; he was given funds to help him with that, but as far as his bosses could tell, he spent all the money in the brothels and bars around Boulevard de Clichy. Prostitutes and their pimps, he was told, made notoriously unreliable informers.

Matters reached a nadir when a resistance cell in Dijon was broken and a British agent arrested. Friedrich hurried to the city, where he insisted on conducting the interrogation of the British woman. He raped her so brutally she had to be taken to the prison infirmary, from where he took her out and shot her dead. What most bothered the Gestapo was that he'd failed to extract any useful intelligence from her.

It was around this time that Wolfgang discovered his son had a nickname – *das Frettchen* – which he apparently revelled in. He was sure the nickname was not meant to be as flattering as the young man clearly thought it was.

Friedrich even used it to introduce himself when he was back in Berlin. The name accompanied him to his next posting, in Amsterdam: the Netherlands seemed to be run by Austrians, and Wolfgang assured them he was close enough to be able to keep an eye on his son there. Amsterdam, he told Friedrich, was his very last chance. He had no more favours left to call on.

This turned out to be not entirely true. Once again, his son's heavy-handedness led to the death of a British agent, in Enschede. But by now, Wolfgang's star had risen high in Berlin: his network of contacts and his quiet influence was almost unrivalled, and he used every scrap of influence he could muster to stop his son being thrown out of the Gestapo. He agreed to a transfer somewhere so remote he'd had to look it up on the map. Surely even Friedrich couldn't cause too much trouble there.

–

One of the symptoms of Wolfgang Steiner's low mood was a pervasive pessimism and a propensity to worry all the time. As the war went on, he began to see this as a blessing: it was as if he finally had something genuine to worry about so he no longer had to worry about being worried. This didn't mean his anxiety was unfounded, but it did mean he could be realistic. While most of Berlin struggled to contemplate the possibility of defeat, for Wolfgang Steiner it was something he'd long expected and indeed prepared for.

After the defeat at Stalingrad in February 1943, he had no doubt Germany would lose the war, though this was a senti-ment he never voiced to any other person. From that moment he began to prepare for defeat and do everything he could to ensure his own survival. His innate pessimism ensured he had no intention whatsoever of hanging around Berlin. As he saw it, he couldn't be accused of desertion: he'd wait until the battle for the city was all but lost. He was quite clear in his own mind that he would do more good for the Reich by leaving rather than remaining like some obliging fool to be killed or arrested by the Russians.

He had access to thousands of records in the Nazi Party Chancellery: not just those relating to party members, but also the records of senior military officers, criminals, scientists, civil servants and members of the SS. In his safe he kept a Leica 35 mm camera, which he knew was a risk, but one he mitigated by ensuring there was never any incriminating film in it. He was often one of the last to leave the office, giving him ample opportunity to photograph important files, especially those that were revealing or incriminating.

His influence went beyond his ability to organise and be indispensable. He became adept at finding important people in Berlin who were experiencing difficulties and helping them. He gained a reputation as someone people could confide in when they were desperate, and who could help them in a practical manner, whether that be arranging an abortion for a mistress or sorting out a debt. He had discovered a large but little-used fund at the Party Chancellery intended for the welfare of Nazi Party members and their families. He became a trustee of it and used it for medical treatment, paying off blackmailers and a variety of other claims.

And he kept notes – of illegitimate children, of senior officials with sexual interests so unusual he needed to look some of them up in the Parteikanzlei library, of others who had a Jewish skeleton – or a communist one – hidden deep in the recesses of a wardrobe.

And it was in another wardrobe – this one in his bedroom, a large walnut one with a concealed base – that he hid the notebooks in which he'd written up what people were up to, and this was where he also stored his rolls of 35 mm film.

But the notebooks and rolls of film didn't stay there long.

He'd found another hiding place.

This was a farm in the Rott Valley, near the small Bavarian town of Eggenfelden. He'd got to know the area when stopping there overnight on his journeys back to Vienna, a trip he preferred to do by car, and had sensed the farm would fit perfectly with his plans. It was owned by a Frau Moser, whose husband was listed as missing in action on the Eastern Front, presumed dead. She was struggling to keep the farm going and was most open to the proposal of the gentleman from Berlin.

He arranged for two Czech slave labourers to work at the farm and gave her a regular sum of money. In return, she agreed he could store items in the cellar and could assume the identity of her husband, though she only agreed to this once she'd been assured he was not interested in any other aspect of matrimonial life.

Back in Berlin, it was a simple matter for someone in Wolfgang Steiner's position to alter Andreas Moser's records, though for the time being it was an identity he wouldn't use. Every couple of months he'd hide notebooks and rolls of film in his Daimler and stop overnight at the farm, where he'd secrete them in the cellar before continuing his journey to Vienna.

After meeting Bormann, Wolfgang Steiner waited until the third week of March 1945 before leaving Berlin. At the beginning of the month, Friedrich had paid a final visit to the city and his father had taken him aside and insisted he listen carefully to what he was about to tell him. If he did exactly as he said, he'd have a chance of evading capture.

An argument followed in which Friedrich insisted Germany could still win the war, but Wolfgang could see that even his son realised it was a hopeless case.

'If you do as I say, then after two or three years it should be safe enough for both of us to come out of hiding and assume new identities. In any case...' he hesitated, unsure how to broach this with his son, 'I have a plan. If it works out, then you and I ought to be safe. It will just require you to do exactly as I tell you and for you to curb your excesses.' He then gave his son the new identity he'd created for him and told him where to go. At one stage he'd thought about bringing him to the farm near Eggenfelden, but had decided that might be too rash.

It was a Thursday morning when he slipped away from his house in Charlottenburg. He told his elderly housekeeper – he'd made sure not to repeat the mistake of employing a young one – that he'd been called to Munich on urgent business and would be away for a few days. He telephoned a colleague at work to say he was unwell but expected to be back at his desk first thing Monday morning.

He took a train to Nuremberg and from there to Passau. He was travelling light, just a briefcase and a small case. He couldn't be sure what would happen when he arrived in Passau – he had no idea whether there'd still be rail services heading west – but he was in luck: the last train to Neumarkt-Sankt Veit was departing in half an hour. He bought a ticket to its final destination but got off at Eggenfelden, leaving the station through a side exit and making his way east out of the town towards the farm. It lay in a dip in the fields; above it was a small copse where he waited until darkness fell. Then, satisfied that there was no danger, he walked down to the farm.

–

The first three months at the farm were extremely difficult. On his first morning there, Wolfgang Steiner knew he had to undertake what was going to be a most unpleasant task. The two Czech labourers were too much of a security risk – it was hard to imagine that when the war ended, they wouldn't tell someone about the man who'd come to live on the farm, and there was also the danger they'd run away.

He found the two of them resting at the rear of the cowshed after their early-morning chores, their backs to him as he approached. He shot the taller of the two first, hitting him in the shoulder. The other one turned round, which made his shot easier, catching him high in the chest. He finished them both off with another bullet each and stood over them to make sure they were dead.

Frau Moser was in a terrible state after that, convinced she'd be arrested, and then worrying about who'd do the farm work. For a few weeks she clearly regretted letting the gentleman from Berlin into her life, spending much of the day sobbing and exhausted from all the extra work she had to do.

It turned out she had no close neighbours or friends and no family other than a sister near Munich who she'd not seen for years. They agreed that if anyone asked, she'd say her husband had returned unexpectedly from the war but had become a recluse and refused to see people.

–

The Americans arrived in the middle of May. The man who came to collect the milk each day had told Frau Moser they were in Eggenfelden and would soon be visiting all the farms. They turned up a few days later, four men in a jeep who checked the place out and then looked at their papers. They seemed satisfied, and registered them and issued new documents.

After that matters, began to get easier. Wolfgang persuaded Frau Moser to employ someone to work on the farm for a few hours each day, during which time he'd stay in the house. She was less exhausted and slightly calmer.

He spent his days in the cellar, logging the rolls of undeveloped film and reading through the notebooks. The more he thought about his plan and the more he refined it, the more confident he was about it.

By the time they got to July, life seemed easier. No one ever bothered them and Wolfgang found the physical work had a positive effect on his mood. He felt fitter – mentally and physically – than he'd done for years.

Of course he still worried. Someone might discover he wasn't Andreas Moser after all. And then there was his plan: as good as it was, it could still go wrong. His biggest worry, though, was his son. He had little idea what he was up to and whether he was doing as he'd been told.

The farm did have a telephone – he'd gone to some trouble to have it installed – and his only link with the outside world was Ulrich, a comrade in Frankfurt with an impeccable network of contacts himself, whom Wolfgang trusted implicitly to keep an eye on Friedrich. Once a week he'd telephone him to check whether there was any news.

Is Mother well? When do you think it would be a good time to visit the cousins?

And Ulrich's replies would be the same.

Mother is well, you're not to worry. No, now is not the right time for you to visit the cousins.

But in late July, his response was far from reassuring.

Mother is not good, actually: her old condition is playing up.

Wolfgang felt the air turn cold around him.

She was taken ill in Munich. I'm not sure what to do. One of the cousins appears to have found out about her.

Wolfgang said Ulrich was to find out more and he'd call back the following evening. In the meantime, perhaps he'd best go and visit Mother in Munich?

He told Frau Moser he felt under the weather and wouldn't join her for dinner that night. He went to sit in the farmyard, thinking about what to do.

Ulrich had told him that Friedrich was in trouble, in Munich. As for the cousins, they were the Allies – an integral part of his plan.

Chapter 5

Wolfgang Steiner arrived in Munich using the identity of Andreas Moser, the farmer from the Rott Valley. He'd had no intention of leaving the farm near Eggenfelden, where he felt safe and hoped to remain until the time came to put his plan into action.

But he'd not taken into account his Achilles heel, his son Friedrich. Ulrich's initial warning on the telephone had been heavily coded, but when they'd spoken the following evening, he'd provided a bit more detail.

As far as Ulrich could tell, Friedrich had left the safe house his father had found for him in the Tyrol because he was bored, and travelled north to Munich of all places. The Bavarian capital was occupied by the American army and was the last place you would go if you were hiding from them. It was also a place where even the American troops not garrisoned there gravitated to when they had some free time. Despite the fact that the city had been half destroyed, it hadn't taken long to dust itself down and start providing places where the American troops could spend their money.

Once in Munich, Friedrich had quickly begun to revert to his normal behaviour. He did at least use the new identity his father had gone to some trouble to supply him with, but he might as well have not bothered: in every other respect his behaviour was utterly reckless. If people asked where he was from – wondering about his accent – he'd happily volunteer that he was Viennese, and when the subject of the war came up, he'd give a knowing wink and would sometimes even take out his metal Gestapo identity badge, carefully allowing whoever he was showing it to a glimpse of the Reich symbol of an eagle on top of a swastika on one side, then quickly showing the reverse, with the words *Geheime Staatspolizei*. The only precaution he'd take was to cover his identity number with his thumb.

He hung around the area south-east of the main railway station, where every other building seemed to be a bar of some sort or the other. Some of them consisted of little more than a trestle table in a damaged building, the clientele having to take care not to lean on walls liable to give way at any moment. The area was the centre of the black market, and Friedrich was able to do some wheeling and dealing. He'd brought a dozen watches with him and used the money from selling these to fund a hedonistic lifestyle, albeit one edged with the danger of a fugitive.

But what most attracted him to this area was the brothels that had sprung up like a rash once the Americans had taken over the city. Almost every taste was catered for by women – and men – who'd never ordinarily have contemplated prostitution. But desperation had forced hundreds of them onto the streets, and Friedrich found it was a perfect outlet for his appetites.

Eventually he rented a room near the Theresienwiese fairground, where the Oktoberfest was held every year. He'd become particularly attracted to a fifteen-year-old girl he'd bought from her Polish-German pimp for a whole night in return for a watch. He'd become rather friendly with the pimp, Emil, who seemed to specialise in younger girls and, it had to be said, boys – though this was something Friedrich preferred not to think about. Emil told him that he'd done what he called 'specialist work' in Poland during the war; as far as Friedrich could tell, this involved helping to run and then clear the Jewish ghettos.

Friedrich was impressed, and felt he could confide in Emil. He showed him his Gestapo badge and then told him he'd been almost single-handedly responsible for defeating the resistance throughout Europe. 'In fact, so good was my reputation, they called me *das Frettchen*!'

It was true the girl – her name was Gisela – seemed to have been forced into prostitution, but Friedrich found himself thinking more and more about her, and when he took the room by the Theresienwiese, he decided to move her in, ignoring Emil's protests. Things began to go wrong after that. Gisela turned out to be neither as obliging nor as grateful as Friedrich had assumed she'd be. Nor could she cook. She spent so much time hunched on the edge of the bed crying, jumping whenever he came near her, that she got on his nerves, and her behaviour didn't change after he started beating her.

But far worse was to happen. He was drinking at a bar north of the station one afternoon when he found himself surrounded by Emil and two of his associates.

Where is Gisela?

Friedrich said he had no idea whatsoever, and pulled out his knife and threatened one of Emil's associates. The brawl that followed was broken up by a squad of passing American military policemen. Friedrich, whose English was good, told them the men had attacked him because he'd criticised Hitler, and the policemen escorted him out of the bar.

But as they did so, Emil addressed them in equally good English. Far from being an anti-Nazi, did they realise the man they were taking away was a Nazi criminal?

The policemen stopped to listen, and rather than laughing it off, as he later realised he should have done, Friedrich shouted at Emil and called him a fucking liar, and said he'd tell them what he'd been up to.

'If you don't believe me' said the Pole, standing very calmly at the bar, 'he told me he's a Gestapo officer known as *das Frettchen*. I'm sure you'll find him somewhere in your files.'

The captain in charge of the military police squad was happy to let Friedrich go once they were away from the bar, and he headed back to Theresienwiese and Gisela. He was unnerved by what had happened: he should never have trusted Emil and told him his nickname; it just went to show you couldn't trust a Pole. But at least it seemed no harm had been done. He didn't even think the Americans had been listening properly to the accusations.

But one of the Americans *had* been listening. A young sergeant, he was surprised his captain hadn't wanted to take the matter further. When they returned to their base later that day, he checked the extensive watch list containing the names of thousands of Nazis wanted for war crimes and other offences.

And there he found the following entry:

> *Das Frettchen*: translates as the Ferret. Known in France as *le furet* and in Holland as *de fret*. Wanted for crimes against British agents and resistance fighters. PLEASE CONTACT MAJOR LEAN, F SECTION, SOE, LONDON WITHOUT DELAY.

–

Even before the war ended, it had become a matter of honour in the Special Operations Executive that every agent they'd sent into occupied Europe should be accounted for. The SOE demanded that justice should be sought for every one of the many who'd been killed, and that all agents who'd disappeared should be traced.

Major Charles Lean of F Section of the SOE – the non-Gaullist French section – had been haunted since December 1943 by Christine Butler's murder. He'd recruited her personally, though at first she'd not seemed to be SOE agent material. She was in her mid-forties, relatively recently married and working as a secretary in the RAF. But a senior officer had discovered that her mother was French, and she was fluent in the language. All the background checks on her were excellent, so Major Lean arranged to meet her at St Ermin's Hotel to see what he made of her, and by the end of their meeting he was highly impressed. She was a determined woman who felt under-used and unappreciated in the RAF and had a passionate desire to do what she could to help France. Despite her age, she was physically strong: she spent as much of her free time as she could hill-walking, and she sailed through her medical examinations.

Her husband, Nicholas, was a nervous man, medically exempt from conscription because of a breakdown a few years earlier, and it was agreed by all concerned that he shouldn't know of his wife's recruitment to the SOE. Christine Butler was given a few weeks' training – Lean had to admit they were rushing them through these days – and sent to Dijon, where she was to link up with a British radio operator and sort out the Tractor circuit, which had been operating with very mixed results.

But the mission had not gone well from the start. The Captain – the man who ran the Tractor circuit – had insisted she be landed near Chaumont, which Lean felt was too far north of Dijon, and then they'd seemed to meander through Burgundy before reaching the city.

She'd not been there long when the message came through from Hervé, the radio operator: the word 'thunder' used three times, which meant everything had gone wrong. As far as they could gather, Christine had been arrested by the Gestapo and taken to their headquarters in rue du Docteur Chaussier. After that, communications ceased and it seemed Hervé had either been caught or killed.

A few days later, a report came through from another agent who'd been sent to Dijon from Lyons to find out what had happened. According to this, Christine Butler had undergone a brutal interrogation and torture at rue du Docteur Chaussier at the hands of a young Gestapo officer from Paris. It seemed that this officer had raped her so violently that she was sent to the infirmary at Dijon prison. According to a friend of someone who knew someone who worked in the infirmary, her internal injuries were probably fatal, but before her condition declined to that point, the same Gestapo officer who'd raped her turned up at the prison and had her carried out to the pavement, where he shot her dead.

According to the report, the agent was known by his nickname: *das Frettchen*.

The Ferret.

It fell to Major Lean to travel to the tiny terraced house in south London to inform Christine Butler's devastated husband of her fate. For the first time in many years, the poor man had found a degree of happiness, and now all that was being taken away from him. Lean told him that his wife had been working for the RAF in Scotland and had been killed in an air accident. Sadly, no remains had been found. When he asked if there was anyone he could let know – maybe family or friends who could come round – Nicholas Butler shook his head and said there was no one. No family, no friends.

Major Lean added the Ferret's details to all the watch lists, including an internal SOE one, and wasn't terribly surprised – though he was horrified – when N Section contacted him the following May to say that a man matching that description, and with the same nickname in Dutch, appeared to be responsible for the death of an SOE agent called Peter Dean in Enschede, along with a woman called Frieda Mooren who ran the local resistance group.

Later, he also learned of other atrocities committed by this young, rather presentable Gestapo officer, possibly with an Austrian accent, who answered to the nickname 'the Ferret'.

The SOE agreed that Major Lean would be the officer responsible for tracking him down.

–

In August 1945, Charles Lean was enjoying his first holiday in nearly four years when the receptionist at the hotel in north Devon handed him a message. A Christopher Stephens had called: please could he call him back on this number? Apparently it was urgent.

By the time Lean had incurred the considerable wrath of his wife and returned to London, Captain Stephens was ready to brief him. A man matching the Ferret's description had been briefly detained by American military police officers after a bar brawl in Munich. There'd been some kind of argument and insults had been exchanged with a group of men, one of whom told the policemen that the man was in fact a Gestapo officer known as *das Frettchen*.

'And you say he was released?'

'Unfortunately, but a sergeant checked his name out and found him on our watch list. Fortunately the system appears to have worked sufficiently well for us to find out about it, what… three days later?'

'We need to get someone out to Munich, Christopher.'

'I'd like to volunteer, sir.'

'I need you here.'

'Why, sir? The war's over and we're not running agents any longer. I speak German and I know the case – and I've worked in Europe on clandestine missions: this one ought to be much more straightforward.'

Later, Major Lean reflected that Stephens had sounded a bit too complacent, too careless of the danger that still existed in Germany despite the Allied victory. But by then it was too late.

Captain Stephens arrived in Munich two days later. The American military police were somewhat chastened by their failure to detain a man identified to them as a Gestapo officer, and did what they could to help.

The young sergeant from Chicago who'd found the Ferret's details on the watch list was assigned to help the captain. He took him to the bar north of the station where the fight had taken place, and eventually they traced one of Emil's friends. Emil himself had left town, but the friend told the British officer what he knew: that the man who said he was known as *das Frettchen* was from Vienna, that he carried a Gestapo identity badge and had stolen a young prostitute from Emil, a girl called Gisela.

It was only when he was threatened with arrest that he revealed more. *It's only rumours, but Emil told me he'd heard this Austrian was living with Gisela near the Theresienwiese.*

For the next few days Christopher Stephens hung around the bars of central Munich, and especially those near the Theresienwiese, asking people if they knew a young Austrian – maybe from Vienna – known as *das Frettchen*. He was generous with whoever talked to him, buying drinks and promising rewards if they could help him find the man.

But he wasn't careful enough. He forgot that this was Munich, the city where the Nazi Party had started and that could still be regarded as its heartland. One man who overheard Stephens in a bar became suspicious and didn't believe the story about the young Austrian owing him money. He mentioned it to a friend, who told someone else, a man who'd been an SS officer and was now living under an assumed identity. This man contacted someone he knew who'd been in the Paris Gestapo, and fairly soon word reached a man in Frankfurt who said not to worry, he'd take care of matters.

–

Ulrich and Wolfgang Steiner had first met in late 1943, and instinctively trusted each other. It was immediately apparent to Steiner that they could not be more different: one a working-class Protestant from Lower Saxony, the other a middle-class Catholic from Vienna. Ulrich had joined the SS as a private and worked his way up through the ranks, gaining a reputation for being especially ruthless. He'd lost an arm at the Battle of Kursk, and after that was based in Berlin, where the two men had got to know each other. Sometime in late 1944 Steiner provided Ulrich with an excellent new identity, and in return, Ulrich – who was very well connected in the SS – promised to act as a point of contact for both Wolfgang and his son.

Now they were in a café on Munich's Promenadeplatz, where the windows had been replaced with planks of wood. Ulrich looked carefully around before he spoke.

'He called me.'

'When?'

'Just before I left Frankfurt – and after I got word that someone was looking for him.'

'Did he say where he was?'

'Here in Munich, but he didn't say where. He admitted he was having trouble with a man called Emil, but I don't think he's aware people are searching for him. I told him to lay low and meet me in two days at a grocery shop I know on Türkenstrasse, near the Wittelsbach Palace – the owner's husband was a comrade. In the meantime...'

'...we need to find who's asking about him!'

It didn't take them long.

They put the word out that someone who knew the whereabouts of *das Frettchen* and was most interested in the reward would be at a bar on Ludwig Strasse opposite St Ludwig's church at eight o'clock the following evening.

Sure enough, the man turned up. His German was good, but he clearly wasn't a native speaker. And his story about *das Frettchen* owing him money was less than convincing. When Ulrich asked him where they'd met and for other details, he seemed hesitant. Ulrich, worried that they might be scaring him off, asked about the reward instead.

It turned out to be a generous one, and they agreed he'd pay half now and half when he found the man, which would be very soon, as Ulrich assured him *das Frettchen* was living just round the corner.

That was when it all went drastically wrong for Captain Christopher Stephens. He'd arranged for the American military police sergeant and two of his men to be waiting outside in civilian dress and in a German car. His plan had been for them to go with him to arrest the Ferret. But Ulrich insisted he leave with him through the rear of the bar, where he found himself in a small yard. Two men held him against the wall while an older man stood in front of him and asked him who he was and what he wanted.

Stephens' only hope was that the Americans had realised what was going on and would come to look for him – he had said something to the sergeant about giving him ten minutes, and more than ten minutes had passed. He tried to buy time by saying that maybe there'd been a misunderstanding, and he wasn't sure what the fuss was all about – he'd known the man called *das Frettchen* in Paris and they'd become friends; in fact – he gave a conspiratorial wink – they'd worked together in Avenue Foch. He owed his friend some money and had heard he was in Munich and wished to repay it; that was all.

'I thought you told me *he* owed *you* money?'

Stephens realised he was shaking violently, and his mouth had turned dry.

'You're not German.'

'Unfortunately not, no – I'm from Luxembourg. I feel unable to return there because of my... activities.'

'I don't believe you.' The older man had produced a knife.

Stephens shouted – a loud shout in English, hoping the Americans were looking for him and would hear – 'I'm here... help me!' He repeated it and tried to kick the man with the knife, but it was too late. One of the others had plunged a blade into his side.

When the Americans found him a few minutes later, the surface of the small yard was coated in the Englishman's blood, like a pond unexpectedly appearing in a forest.

Friedrich Steiner turned up as instructed at the grocery store on Türkenstrasse. He told the woman behind the counter that he never wanted to see another potato again, and when he asked if she had any cauliflower, she ushered him into the back of the shop. His delight at seeing his father ended when his father slapped him repeatedly round the face.

What on earth do you think you're up to?

Did I not give you very strict orders?

Why have you been volunteering information about yourself here in Munich?

Did you know an Englishman was sent here to find you?

Friedrich sank to the floor and started sobbing. He said he was so sorry, but he couldn't stand it in the Tyrol and thought he'd be safer in a city. He'd only told one or two people about himself, and then it was because he knew they were good Nazis like him, and never – on his mother's memory – had he told anyone what his real name was, so really things weren't that bad. And he was a reformed character, he assured his father. His behaviour had improved – he didn't lose his temper as often – and he'd found himself a woman. 'In fact, she lives with me.'

'You're not marrying her, are you, Friedrich?'

'I don't think she's old enough, Father.'

Wolfgang Steiner shook his head. 'You've obviously not learned your lesson. Tomorrow you will go to Frankfurt with Ulrich. He'll arrange your escape from there: fortunately, I've made some arrangements. You're to do what he says, do you understand?'

'But Father—'

'Listen to me! It's not just your safety, it's mine too. You will stay with Ulrich until the morning and then leave for Frankfurt.'

'Can I go to my room?'

'No, it's too dangerous – let me have the address, though.'

When Wolfgang Steiner went to the address near the Theresienwiese the following morning, the place was deserted. A neighbour told him the girl had left the previous evening, and said there were bruises all over her face. Steiner thought it was ironic how close she'd come to being killed without realising it.

In the short time he'd been in the building, the rain had turned from a light shower to such a heavy one it was bouncing off the pavement. He waited in the dark entrance, smoking as he watched people hurrying by, all hunched and avoiding looking at anyone else. One man did glance towards the building, and for a brief moment Steiner thought he looked familiar, so he stepped back further into the shadows.

Europe was like this now: everyone seemingly on the move, journeys born out of desperation, destinations unclear or a secret, and an all-pervading sense of mistrust. A shudder ran down his back as he wondered whether he had either the energy or the courage for all this, for this escape from a life that not so long ago had been so assured.

His only hope was to trust that Ulrich would somehow lead Friedrich away from this nightmare.

His son would now be a traveller on *der Fluchtweg Falke*.

The Kestrel escape route.

Chapter 6

London, September 1945

They were on the early-morning train from Lincoln to King's Cross and Prince was trying to explain to his wife of less than a week why Tom Gilbey's suggestion that the two of them come down to see him was a 'summons'.

'So it's an order?'

'Not as such, no.'

'An invitation, then?'

'Somewhere between an invitation and an order, but closer to an order.'

'I don't understand. Until I came to live here, I thought my English was very good, but...'

'It is good, Hanne.'

'But there's so much I don't seem to grasp. You call it nuance, don't you?'

'We do, though actually I think nuance is a French word originally. But I know what you mean. English is full of subtle meanings. We're very good at understatement – for instance, if someone asks "How are you?" a response of "I'm not too bad, thank you" could either mean that you're fine or that things aren't good.'

Hanne shook her head and stared at the English countryside flying past. 'So how do you know what they mean?'

'You get used to it. An accompanying facial expression can make all the difference, and it also depends very much on who says it. You asked me the other day about the British class system, didn't you?'

'I asked you which class I'm now a member of.'

'And I said middle class: my parents owned their own home, I – we – own ours, I have a senior job and I went to a grammar school. Tom Gilbey, on the other hand, belongs to what we'd call the upper class, and—'

'Is that the highest class?'

'Not as such; he's not aristocracy, which is a whole different matter.'

'So the king and queen – they're upper class?'

'This is where it gets very complicated, Hanne. They're probably regarded as being in a class of their own.'

'I don't think I understand.'

'Probably best not to try to: you'll get used to it. But the point I'm trying to make is the fact that Tom Gilbey belongs to the upper class goes a long way to explaining how he treats people like us. Are you all right, Hanne? You look uncomfortable?'

'I'm all right. These seats are hard to sit on, though.'

'I know. But you're not feeling too tired today?'

'I'm feeling so much better, Richard. On days like today it feels as if I never had typhus. Carry on, you were telling me about Mr Gilbey's class.'

'The upper class tend to be from well-established families: they live in houses – especially in the country – that have been owned by their family for generations, and they would expect to pass them on to their children. They go to the same schools as each other and they benefit enormously from a network of acquaintances and friends from their school days. There's something called the old boy network that tends to help them in their careers – as do family connections.'

'It sounds corrupt.'

'I suppose that's just how it is. When Gilbey told me he'd been at school with the bishop, it didn't surprise me in the least. The upper class marry people from similar families, and their lives are intertwined. They go to very select clubs that are in many ways an extension of their schools, right down to the food they eat in them. And more importantly, they live their lives through a sense of obligation: an obligation to maintain the status quo and to ensure good order in society, not least because they benefit so much from it. It's as if society has been designed with them in mind, therefore they have a stake in defending and promoting it.'

'But this is wrong, isn't it, Richard? Surely people's position in society should be based on their ability – that's what happens in Denmark. You seem to just accept the situation.'

'Perhaps one just gets used to it, darling. In any case, now that we have a Labour government, things may change, who knows?'

'The new prime minister...'

'Clement Attlee.'

'...what class is he?'

'I imagine he's middle class. We're not too far from London now, Hanne; you'll see the city building up around us.'

'What is that building?'

'That's Alexandra Palace. As I was saying, this sense of obligation extends to other people, the people the upper class would regard as being of an inferior class, although they'd never express it in those terms. They would consider it wrong, for instance, to be rude to people: they regard themselves as having obligations towards us and us as having obligations towards them. Have you heard the French phrase *noblesse oblige*?'

She shook her head.

'Essentially it means that the nobility, the gentry and the upper class have an obligation to behave decently and properly. It recognises that their position in society comes with certain responsibilities.'

'Just two words mean all that?'

Prince nodded. The noisy brakes indicated that the train was slowing down.

'It wasn't a phrase the French prisoners used at Ravensbrück.'

'I wouldn't imagine they had much cause to – I don't think *noblesse oblige* applies to Germans, in any case. But it does go some way to explaining how Gilbey, for example, treats me: perfectly properly, probably somewhat patronisingly, but he has an expectation of how I should behave. He sees it as my – our – obligation or duty to serve this country, just as he does. He doesn't need to order me to come and see him, but it is bred into him to ask in such a way that there's an expectation I will.'

'And what do you think he has in mind, Richard?'

'I have no idea. The war's over, after all.'

'So we can always say no.'

Richard Prince looked at his wife as if she was being naïve. 'I suppose we can,' he said in a resigned manner, 'in theory.'

—

Tom Gilbey couldn't have been more charming. His manner was effortless and he came across as utterly sincere as he greeted Prince and Hanne like they were his own children returning after a lengthy absence.

In turn, they thanked him profusely for the Royal Doulton dinner service he'd given them as a wedding gift, and Gilbey responded that it was the least he could do, but perhaps best not let young Henry play with it, and the three of them laughed, which went some way to relieving the tension not too far below the surface. Gilbey dutifully asked how Henry was, and Hanne said he was very sweet and she was pleased they'd decided to keep his nanny on as he needed continuity in his life, and he then asked how she was, and she replied that she was much better, thank you.

'Probably not my business, Hanne, but now you've married an English police officer, what do you intend to do?'

Prince bridled. It was indeed none of Gilbey's business, but he'd managed to ask the question in a charming way, and Hanne said something about getting to know her new husband and his son, and that after more than two years in a concentration camp she didn't want to rush into anything, and Gilbey said of course, of course in an almost apologetic manner.

There was a period of silence as a tray of tea was brought in and Gilbey somewhat awkwardly poured it out. 'And you, Richard: enjoying being back on the beat?'

'I'm hardly on the beat, sir. There's some talk that I may be promoted to chief superintendent next year. I may get the Lincoln division if the wind's in the right direction.'

Gilbey said jolly good and passed round a plate of biscuits. 'I have a job for you two, if you're interested.'

Hanne smiled politely and looked at her husband, who remained impassive. Gilbey coughed nervously, and when he spoke again, it was in a louder voice, as if making an effort to sound confident.

'It would require you going to Germany, for a week or two at the most. The brief is to find a German fugitive who's wanted for murdering British agents and others in France and Holland.'

He paused and looked at them with raised eyebrows as if expecting an answer.

'I think you may need to tell us more, sir.'

'I was about to, Prince. Hanne, excuse me if you are already aware of this, but there is an organisation called the Special Operations Executive, or SOE. It grew out of MI6 – our overseas intelligence service – with a brief to conduct espionage and coordinate resistance in Nazi-occupied Europe. It's been a remarkably successful organisation: mixed results in some countries, outstanding in others. It sent many hundreds of agents into Europe, and now it's being wound up, but not before it accounts for all those who've gone missing. It is regarded as a matter of honour that we find out what happened to all our agents and where necessary mete out justice to the people who either betrayed them or harmed them. Are you sure you wouldn't like a biscuit?'

Hanne didn't reply. Her head was bowed.

'I say, are you all right, darling?'

When she looked up, her eyes were filled with tears. 'I knew some of those agents.'

'Really – in Denmark?'

'No, no – in Ravensbrück. Three women, British agents, were executed there. I remember their names: Violette Szabo, Denise Bloch and Lilian Rolfe. They were extraordinarily brave. One of them managed to talk to another prisoner and told her they worked for the British and that they'd been dropped into France by parachute.' Tears streaked down her cheeks and Prince noticed that Tom Gilbey had placed a knuckle between his teeth in an effort to control his own emotions.

'Fritz Suhren, the camp commandant, supervised their executions himself.' She pronounced the name through gritted teeth. 'If you ever catch him, I shall be a witness.'

Gilbey nodded, then continued. 'One agent we flew over was a woman called Christine Butler. She was sent to France in December 1943 to organise the resistance in the Dijon area. Her group was betrayed and most of them were arrested. As far as we can ascertain, she was interrogated by a young Gestapo officer from Paris, who tortured her and – I'm sorry to have to say this, Hanne – raped her so badly she had to be transferred to the infirmary at Dijon prison.

'He then turned up there and had her carried on a stretcher to the pavement outside the prison, where he shot her dead.'

Gilbey paused and sipped his tea.

'We have a good physical description of the chap, which I'll let you have, but what we don't have is his name: he was apparently only known by his nickname – *das Frettchen*.'

'The Ferret.'

'Indeed: a nasty, mean little animal, a close relation of the weasel and the polecat – we had no end of trouble with weasels on my in-laws' estate. My father-in-law took it personally, but then he takes everything personally. Anyway, we understand that after Christine Butler's murder, the Ferret was transferred to Amsterdam, where he was involved in the death of an SOE agent and a young woman who ran the resistance group there. We don't know what happened to him after that: he was transferred elsewhere, but we lost track of him. The man responsible for finding him is an old school chum of mine, Charles Lean... Did you say something, Prince?'

'No, sir, it just seems that you went to school with an awful lot of people.'

'It's a large school, Prince. Charles ran agents for one of the SOE's French sections and was the man who recruited Christine Butler. As the first officer to lose an agent to the Ferret, he has overall responsibility for bringing him to justice – that's the way it works in the SOE. He put the Ferret's details on a watch list, and lo and behold, a couple of weeks ago the American military police in Munich contacted him to say the man was in the city.

'Charles had a jolly good chap working for him, a Guards officer called Christopher Stephens who served in Europe during the war – rather like you, Prince. Stephens volunteered to go to Munich and bring the Ferret back, but I'm afraid it all went dreadfully wrong.'

'What happened?'

'As far as Charles can gather, Stephens was lured to a bar by a man who told him he knew where *das Frettchen* was. Clearly, he failed to take the right precautions: he had some Americans waiting on the street outside the bar, but he ought to have had cover inside and also made sure they were watching the back of the place. When the Americans found him in the yard behind the bar, he'd been stabbed to death. One doesn't want to criticise a dead man, but I can't believe he was quite so... incautious.'

'It's the end of the war, sir.'

'What do you mean, Prince?'

'I experienced it myself, sir, on my last mission – both in this country and in Germany. On my previous missions, when the war was still going on, my alertness and concentration were constantly operating at one hundred per cent. Not once did I relax or take my eye off the ball. But when the war ended, I reckon my concentration level dropped slightly, and maybe it was the same with this chap Stephens.'

'It sounds as if you're interested…'

'We've not said yes as such, sir.'

'Let me tell you something first about Charles. I mentioned I was at school with him?'

'You did, sir.'

'We were quite close chums actually: same year, same form and house – for a while we even shared a dorm. We've remained friends. Charles was a bit different from a lot of us: not terribly ambitious, and not sporty at all, bullied quite a lot when he first went there. He loved nature and was forever going on rambles and finding all these insects. Matron used to get furious. For a while his ambition was to be a country vet, but I don't think his science was quite up to it, and he ended up working at his uncle's stockbroking practice in the City. He wasn't terribly happy there, so he joined the army, which I suppose is one way of seeing nature. Look, are either of you two going to have this last biscuit?'

It was already in Gilbey's hand, and he eagerly bit into it as his guests shook their heads.

'Good enough career, and well placed when the war started. Was never going to make colonel, but his French is decent so he went to work for the SOE. It had two main sections covering France: RF, which was linked to de Gaulle, and F section, which Charles worked for, the non-Gaullists. The point I'm trying to get to is that the war has been a bloody strain for him, and I'm afraid it's all got on top of him now. He was responsible for sending over dozens of agents, and many of them didn't make it. Now that the war's over, he's beginning to find out what happened to many of them – a number of them were betrayed, tortured, killed… it's dreadful. Of course, Charles is no exception. I've sent over agents and lost some of them, and nearly lost others, like you, Prince.'

'And Hanne too.'

'Of course! It's a bloody strain, but we all react differently. Charles has taken it very badly, and I think losing Stephens like that was the final straw. On top of it all, his son was killed at El Alamein in late '42 – he was in the Eighth Army – and Charles had what I suppose was a bit of a breakdown: not one of those where you shout at neighbours and then end up in one of those awful hospitals, but still, he's not coping awfully well. So he's asked me to help, and just as the SOE owes a debt of honour to its dead agents, so Charles and I have a responsibility to each other.'

'Couldn't someone else at the SOE take over the case?'

'They could, but for better or worse, Charles thinks they'd see that as a sign of weakness and it would count against him. He wants to stay in the forces for a few more years and doesn't want to blot his copybook. So we've come up with a perfectly plausible tale that I too have an interest in the Ferret and have asked to take the lead on it, and the SOE seem happy enough with that. Charles meanwhile has gone off to Scotland to have a good rest. This file here is everything we know on the Ferret – description, dates, places, the deaths of the agents. You need to get over to Munich as soon as you can. I think with you two on the case, we ought to have this wrapped up in a week or two.'

Gilbey stood and walked over to the window, his hands thrust deep in his pockets. 'Europe's changing by the day; it's increasingly hard to know what to make of it, to be frank with you. The Soviets seem to know what they're doing, and the Americans too, but I'm really not sure we do. There's certainly a role for MI6 over there: we need to know who's who, who's on whose side, where the power is – the usual meat and drink of intelligence – but I fear we've not adapted to that new world as yet. We've been a bit slow off the mark. You two going out there could be useful for me – help me to establish contacts and start some kind of network. And the place is still teeming with Nazis: we've rounded up a number of the more prominent ones, but there are still thousands of nasty types we need to get our hands on. I believe this could be our way in, so to speak.'

'I'm confused, sir. Do you want us to find this chap whose name we don't know, or set up a network for you?'

'Your mission would be to find the Ferret, Prince. But what I'm saying is that that ought to give you an entrée into the world of escaping Nazi war criminals, which would be useful for me to plug into. Everyone here at the Service is talking about what job they'll be doing now the war's over: this could be a role for me. The younger chaps are learning Russian; I fear I'm too old for that.'

'I think it will take us more than a week or two to find this Ferret,' said Prince.

'And in any case, it doesn't make sense…' Hanne was shaking her head as she spoke.

'I beg your pardon?'

'Going to Munich makes no sense.'

'In what way, Hanne?' Tom Gilbey had turned to face her.

'If this man is on the run and was caught in Munich before being released, then surely the last place in Europe where he'll now be is Munich? He'll know it's too dangerous for him.'

Both Gilbey and Prince nodded.

'I see your point, but I thought if you rode into the city and let your dogs have a good run around the place, then sooner or later you're bound to pick up his scent.'

Prince turned to his wife. 'Mr Gilbey is using hunting metaphors. I'll explain later. In any case, sir, I agree with Hanne: we might not only be wasting our time in Munich, but given the nature of the city, we could alert people that we're searching for this man's real identity. Odd to have nothing but a nickname to go on – maybe it's an indication of how important he is.'

'You said the last place we know where he was during the war was Amsterdam: is that right?'

67

'Yes, Hanne. You could go there.'

'And before that it was Paris?'

Gilbey nodded.

'Maybe if we start off in Paris… There are bound to be plenty of people there who'll be able to help us.'

'Don't overestimate the gratitude of the French, Prince.'

'I still think that will be a more productive place to start.'

'Fair enough, and I suppose you do have a perfect cover story, don't you?'

'What's that, sir?'

'Your honeymoon!'

—

'You look confused, Richard – as if you're not sure.'

They were on the train back to Lincoln and had a compartment to themselves. Before they left, Tom Gilbey told them that as they were now on a new mission, they could start claiming expenses, so they'd decided to travel first class.

'I'm not confused. I just thought we'd want time to think about it. We've got Henry to consider too, remember. And also – well, I am surprised at how keen you are to go. After all, we've only been married for a week, and what… four months ago you were in a concentration camp. I'd have thought running round Europe after Nazis would be the last thing you'd want to do.'

'But that's the point, Richard.'

'What is?'

'That I was in a concentration camp until May. I nearly died. I saw suffering and cruelty I could never have imagined – the way prisoners were shot for just looking at an officer, and the dreadful medical experiments. I suffered terribly myself and yet I was one of the lucky ones. Before the war, and for part of it, I was a senior police officer in Copenhagen, as you know. Although I knew I was taking a risk when I became a British agent, I never envisaged I'd see what I did. I'm haunted by what I encountered and I know I'll continue to be unless I do

68

something about it – and this is my opportunity. That's why I am so keen to go on this mission. We are both highly experienced agents, Richard. You know we can catch this Ferret. And it will be an opportunity for revenge.'

'Revenge is not necessarily the best motivation.'

'Ha!' She waved her hand dismissively. 'It's the best one I can think of. At my lowest points in the camp I would motivate myself by thinking of what I would do to those bastards after the war. I lost count of the number of women whose hands I held as they slipped away, with me promising them that they wouldn't be forgotten and their death would not be in vain...'

'Yes, but...'

'...and this is my opportunity to be true to my word.'

Chapter 7

He'd been released from prison at the end of 1943, though for six months after that he'd been obliged to stay at a boarding house in south London, just down the road from the police station where he was required to report once a day.

The duty sergeants were invariably hostile to him, making it clear they knew who he was and what he'd been imprisoned for. They'd make him wait for up to an hour, alongside the filth, the cheap criminals and the strays of the district. Most days he'd hear the words 'traitor' or 'Nazi' and look up to see heads turned in his direction. And it was quite common for them to use his rank when they loudly called out his name, the word 'Admiral' laced with as much sarcasm and malice as they could muster. Often as he approached the desk the sergeant would remark, 'Defence Regulation 18B, are you?' and then no one would be in doubt as to who he was: a person of 'hostile origin', as the hateful regulation called it, 'concerned in acts prejudicial to the public safety or the defence of the realm...'

More than once he'd been followed from the police station, and it was only his guile that kept him out of trouble. But he'd avoided the pubs and cafés in the area and spent most of his time in his tiny room, which smelt of gas and mice, marking off the days on a cheap calendar, just as he used to do at boarding school, a constant draught whistling in through a cracked window pane.

One July afternoon in 1944, a letter was grudgingly thrust at him when he checked in, and he was instructed to open it there and then. It told him he was now free to return home: once there, he'd have to report to the local police station twice a week. There was a list of various other restrictions, which he began to read, but the sergeant told him to sign the form agreeing to the conditions before they changed their minds.

His large Victorian house in the country was unchanged. His man had stayed on and kept the house and its grounds in reasonable enough order, and he greeted him as if he'd just returned from a round of golf rather than a few years in prison without trial.

Of course they watched him all the time, and he didn't doubt his letters and telephone calls were being monitored, so for the rest of 1944 and the early part of 1945 he did nothing. It was a strange existence; one that reminded him of being back at sea on one of those voyages where one would sail hundreds of miles from land for weeks on end with the weather unchanging, and a torpor settled on the ship that led to strange behaviour, particularly among younger officers, who became prone to making wrong decisions, such as altering course for no reason.

He began to spend days sitting in his library, staring out of the long window as the changing light altered the colour and shape of the lawn and the trees bordering it. He became like Coleridge's Ancient Mariner:

Day after day, day after day,
We stuck, nor breath nor motion;
As idle as a painted ship
Upon a painted ocean.

But around February, he realised he needed to snap out of his torpor. He began to make contact with the remnants of his own organisation, scattered around the country like survivors from a shipwreck. He entrusted his man with letters, giving him strict instructions on how he was to post them from the town he visited on his day off, never using the same postbox. The letters would instruct the recipient to call him at a telephone box at a given time, to hang up if he didn't answer, to never use their own names and certainly not his. He would slip out of the house at dusk, confident he wasn't being followed, making his way under the cover of the high hedgerows common in those parts to a telephone box at the crossroads of a country lane and a larger road.

That was how he made contact once more with Myrtle Carter, and with Bourne and Ridgeway. It was how he heard about the murder of Arthur Chapman-Collins, who had been one of the few people he could really rely upon. And it was how he found out about Agent Milton, perhaps his greatest success. He was astonished that Edward Palmer was not only alive but still free and active as an agent. He'd half expected to encounter him on a landing at Brixton prison. Instead, he was operating from the heart of the British War Office.

When he found out about Palmer, he realised that he once again had a purpose. All was not lost. That purpose intensified when one morning his man brought him his breakfast tray and on it was an envelope with his name neatly typed on the front. His man explained he'd found it in the porch when he'd come down that morning. It hadn't been there when he'd locked up the night before.

The Admiral waited until the man left the bedroom before opening the letter.

Somehow Wolfgang had managed to contact him, which was quite remarkable.

He read the letter three or four times, and once he was sure he'd memorised it, he carefully placed it in the fire and watched it disintegrate.

First Palmer, now Wolfgang.

He most certainly had a purpose now.

He was no longer becalmed.

The man hath penance done,
And penance more will do.

Chapter 8

Paris, September 1945

'Tom said I'm to help.'

The man on the other side of the table was avoiding looking at them, concentrating instead on sawing through his steak. Much to the horror of the waiter, he'd insisted on it being *bien cuit*, and it seemed as if the chef had taken revenge for this insult to France.

Prince and Hanne glanced at each other, and she raised her eyebrows. Tom Gilbey had assured them Wilson would do all he could to help, but his attitude could at best be described as grudging. They were in a small restaurant on Avenue Carnot, close to the hotel on Avenue de la Grande Armée where Prince and Hanne were staying. It had indeed felt like a honeymoon until now.

'By the way...' Wilson was still chewing a piece of steak as he spoke, jabbing his fork in their direction, 'I presume you're on expenses?'

Prince said they were, and Wilson said in that case there was a very decent Côtes du Rhône on the wine list, and would they mind terribly if he ordered a bottle?

'I suspect the Germans shipped the best wines back home,' he continued, still chewing as he spoke. 'Hardly a decent bottle to be found in the city, but for some reason they appear to have left the Côtes du Rhône. Odd, eh?'

They agreed it was odd, and Hanne said something about how maybe they'd poisoned them, and Wilson looked unsure if it was a joke. When the bottle arrived, he insisted on pouring: a large glass for himself, a slightly smaller one for Prince and a half-glass at best for Hanne. He looked annoyed when Prince picked up the bottle and topped up their glasses.

'Is your hotel all right, by the way?'

'It's perfect, thank you.'

'Jolly good – had to pull a few strings to get you a decent room. Tom tells me you need to find someone. Care to tell me more?' He was using his steak knife to dislodge a piece of meat from between his teeth.

'I'm not sure how much he told you…'

Wilson was helping himself to another glass of wine, ignoring theirs. Gilbey had told them he could come across as somewhat brusque, but that he'd had a decent war and had managed to get into Paris before the liberation. Since then he'd been based at the British Embassy in rue du Faubourg Saint-Honoré, helping to establish the MI6 station there. 'He's got a bloody good network of contacts.'

'Start at the beginning. I say, is your steak a bit tough?'

Prince gestured to Hanne, whom Wilson had ignored until now. She placed her cutlery carefully on her plate, sipped some wine and began; her Danish accent barely noticeable. 'In December 1943, an SOE circuit in Dijon was broken up by the Germans—'

'Yes, Tractor I think it was. Chap known as the Captain seems to have betrayed them. He's on my "must find" list. Carry on.'

'An SOE agent called Christine Butler was captured; she was using the name Thérèse Dufour. Her radio operator was either killed or killed himself. A Gestapo officer came down from Paris to interrogate her, but she was so badly injured by him she was taken to the infirmary at Dijon prison. A couple of days later, the same Gestapo officer ordered her to be carried out of the prison, where he shot her.'

'Did he get anything from her?'

'Nothing of any use to the Germans, no. We need to find this man. Other than his description, the only thing we know about him is that his nickname was the Ferret, and that a few months later he was based in Amsterdam, where he did something similar to what happened in Dijon. A network was captured in Enschede, and he turned up and killed the head of the local resistance. Another of our SOE agents died in his custody.'

'And you think he's here in Paris?' Wilson waved his knife above his head to indicate the city and wiped his face with the large serviette.

'We don't know. We do know he was in Munich in August, when the Americans let him slip out of their grasp. I'd be most surprised if he'd returned here, but we think Paris may hold the clue to his real identity.'

'Tom didn't go into too much detail, but he did say you were both first-class agents and had spent a considerable amount of time behind enemy lines.'

They both nodded.

'This place sometimes feels like it's still occupied at times.' Wilson leaned forward as he lowered his voice. 'It's bloody difficult working here, to be frank with you. Not easy to know who's in charge. At first it was the resistance calling all the shots, though now de Gaulle seems to have a firmer hand on the rudder, but it all feels rather anarchic at times. Hardest thing from our point of view is knowing who the hell to believe. Everyone claims to have been in the resistance, but the truth is there was an enormous amount of collaboration: for a long time the German occupation was relatively trouble-free, and the reason for that is the number of French people who went along with it. I call them the passive collaborators – the more active ones were the traitors. I say, do you mind if I order another bottle?'

When the wine arrived, Prince told the sommelier to fill all three glasses, and Wilson looked somewhat put out.

'Since the liberation, we've experienced what the French are calling the *épuration*. You've heard the word?'

Both Richard and Hanne shook their heads.

'It translates as "purge", and there are two versions of it – the state purge of collaborators, or *épuration légale*, and the unofficial version of it, *épuration sauvage*. That's what I mean by anarchy. The country has turned on itself to settle scores, and the result is utter chaos. It's quite unedifying. A French chap I know told me it's as if the French people resent collaborators far more than they ever did the occupying German forces. The prisons are full of collaborators awaiting trial, and plenty of them are being dealt with unofficially. The resistance groups are still active, and most nights collaborators are taken from their homes and found dead in a ditch the next day. So if you want to know the Ferret's true identity, you just need to pray that anyone who was aware of it hasn't been killed yet.'

'What about the Germans – the Gestapo?'

'They fled: the general strike in Paris started on the fifteenth of August last year, and the uprising four days later, so they had plenty of opportunity to get out before von Choltitz surrendered the city on the twenty-fifth. Ten days seems to have been ample time for them to destroy any records they were leaving behind and bugger off, if you'll excuse my language. I think your best chance is to find French citizens who worked for the Gestapo.'

'Were there many of them?'

'Enough. Does that surprise you?'

'It does, actually,' said Hanne. 'In Copenhagen, it was almost entirely Germans who worked for the Gestapo.'

'Well then, this isn't Copenhagen, is it? Though many of the French citizens who were known to have worked for them and were arrested at the time have since been killed. Do you know where your Ferret worked when he was in Paris?'

'For the Gestapo.'

'Yes, yes, I'm aware of that, but they had two main offices here. Their headquarters was in rue des Saussaies in the 8th arrondissement, not far from our embassy actually and close to the Élysée Palace, but they also used 84 Avenue Foch, at the other end of the Champs-Élysées, which in many ways was better known – notorious may be a more accurate way of describing it. It was the SS headquarters, and the Gestapo had the sixth floor, I think. A lot of their interrogations were carried out there. If we had some idea of where the Ferret worked, it would help.'

Again they shook their heads.

'And you say you have a description of him?'

Prince opened a small black notebook he had by his side. 'Here we are... late twenties – this was at the end of 1943, remember – thick blonde hair and bright blue eyes.'

'And that's really the best you can do? Hardly narrows it down, does it! Never mind, I'll come up with something. Meet me at noon tomorrow: there's a bar on rue de Duras called Pierre et Fils; it's near the embassy but also round the corner from rue des Saussaies. One question, though: there are two routes open to us, the official one and the unofficial one. Which one would you prefer?'

'I'm not sure what you mean.'

'The official one is rather like the *épuration légale* – it will mean putting in a request to the French authorities, asking them to start an investigation, et cetera. The unofficial one will be more like the *épuration sauvage*.'

'Which one would you suggest?'

'I think you know the answer to that.'

–

'This is Marguerite.'

They were at the rear of the bar on rue de Duras, sitting in a high-backed banquette with what they assumed were fading ancestors of Pierre and his son staring down at them from the wall. The woman who'd come in with Wilson was perhaps in her mid-thirties; slightly younger than Prince and Hanne. There was some brief chat about the weather as they waited for the coffees to arrive, and Marguerite confirmed she was happy to talk in English. She spoke to the waiter, and soon afterwards, an opened bottle of cognac appeared on the table. She poured some into all their cups without asking.

'*Santé!* You need help, I'm told?'

Hanne repeated the story she'd told Wilson the previous evening.

'We'll see what we can do. Let me tell you briefly about myself first.' Marguerite paused as she drank some of her coffee, then topped the cup up with cognac before taking a packet of Gitanes from her handbag and offering them round. She took time to light her own, and soon the group was wreathed in a cloud of the strong tobacco.

'The Germans occupied Paris on the fourteenth of June 1940: before then, I led the classic life of a bourgeois wife. My husband ran his family business, which manufactures and supplies paper products, and we lived in Saint-Germain in the 7th arrondissement in a beautiful apartment with views over the Champs de Mars. Two or three days a week I helped a friend out in her boutique on Avenue de Friedland.

'In truth, the occupation did not make a great deal of difference to our lives, although of course we all shook our heads and said how appalling it was. But in our case we were fine. We'd never been political, and my husband's business prospered considerably, as he gained contracts from the Germans for supplying paper and stationery products. You see, what you must understand is that most people could just continue with their lives and ignore the reality of the situation so long as it was not affecting them directly. But as the war went on, people began to find they needed to come off the fence — is that the correct phrase?'

The others nodded.

'For me, that happened in July 1942, when more than thirteen thousand Jews were arrested in Paris and taken to deportation centres and from there to Auschwitz — it was known as the *grand rafle*. Tens of thousands more were to follow them, and of course we now know that hardly any returned. From that point on it was impossible to ignore the situation.

'Now my husband – his name is Eugène, by the way – had an accountant based in rue Saint-Lazare in the 9th, an old established practice that the business had used for a long while, though Eugène felt they were too old-fashioned for him and was looking to get out of their arrangement.

'One morning he arrived early for a meeting at their offices and a junior employee let him in. While he was waiting, he went to look for the bathroom but got lost, and to cut a long story short – he recounted it to me in great detail, I promise you – he opened the door to a room where a family was hiding. As he said, it was obvious they were Jews. The accountant pleaded with him to keep it quiet – he said the father was his optician and he was hiding them until the resistance could get them out of Paris – but Eugène ignored him and reported it to the authorities immediately. He said it meant he could kill two birds with one stone: he got rid of more Jews and he was able to get out of his arrangement with the accountants.

'When he told me this over dinner that evening, he was very pleased with himself, but I was appalled and decided that I had to do something. My younger brother's in-laws were socialists before the war, and I suspected some of them might be involved in the resistance. After a few weeks of sending messages and meeting one of them, I became involved too. The organisation I belonged to was Les Mouvements Unis de la Résistance – a group linked with the Armée Secrète. I became active in the unit that covered the 9th arrondissement – they always tried to put you in a unit in a different area from the one you lived in. I delivered messages and money, liaised with other groups and helped people to evade the authorities. I never carried out any actions, but I did take weapons and explosives to people who did. I remained with my husband the whole time, because it was perfect cover, and in any case, by then he had a contract with the German military high command, which was based at the Hotel Majestic on Avenue Kléber. He would often have copies of the material he printed for them in his study, and I was sometimes able to take documents and pass them on to the resistance.

'Since the liberation, I have maintained my contacts: my main motivation is to ensure that people who collaborated with the Germans should not get away with it.' She stubbed her cigarette out in a metal ashtray and poured more cognac into her cup.

'And your husband?'

She laughed bitterly as she lit another Gitanes and began to smoke it as if she was in a hurry. 'Yes, my husband. He had no idea, of course, about what I'd been up to – he was so arrogant that he assumed I was just another loyal Parisian wife, in awe of him and with no opinion of her own. When the city was liberated, he was terrified – he spent days trying to destroy documents and coaching me on how we were to account for ourselves during the occupation. I arranged for some of my resistance comrades to come to our apartment one evening a week after the liberation. Before they were due to arrive, I sat him down and told him what I'd been up to – how I was so angry at his informing on the Jewish family that I had joined the resistance, and how active I'd been. He was beyond shocked, and pleaded with me to help him, and then, as arranged, my comrades arrived.' She paused, holding her cigarette in front of her face and watching the smoke spiral towards the ceiling.

'And?'

'They took him away.' She shifted in her seat and tipped some more cognac into her cup. 'I guess you want to know what happened to him? *Le épuration sauvage*: he was handed over to a group of Jewish resistance fighters who were specifically looking for people who'd informed on Jews, leading to their deportation. They made him write a full confession.'

'And has he been put on trial?'

'There's a French saying: *manger les pissenlits par la racine.* How would you translate?'

'It means to eat dandelions by the root,' said Wilson.

She paused, looking at the others for a reaction. 'It means he's dead. Thank God.'

She smiled sweetly as she opened her handbag, removed her lipstick and proceeded to apply it. 'That's my story, so to find someone who knew *le furet* will be a pleasure. I will make some calls this afternoon and speak to people. Let's meet back here at eight o'clock tomorrow morning.'

–

Paris had continued to feel like a honeymoon. On Wilson's recommendation, they dined that evening at Fouquet's on the corner of the Champs-Elysées and Avenue George V. They both had caviar and duck and agreed that after what they'd both been through Tom Gilbey would find it hard to deny this meal on their expenses. They toasted Gilbey with a champagne cocktail, and Prince explained how the talk was that Gilbey's family had set up one of the most famous gin distilleries in England.

When they turned into rue de Duras just before eight o'clock the next morning, a heavy drizzle had made the cobbles slippery and a black Citroën was waiting outside the bar, its engine running. As they approached it, the passenger door opened and Marguerite gestured for them to get in the back. She turned round as it pulled away.

'I think I have had some luck – maybe. We're heading to Val-de-Marne, it's about half an hour's drive south of Paris. There's a large prison there called Fresnes. The Germans used it as a place to imprison and torture many of our resistance comrades. Now it's full of collaborators – we're interested in one of them.'

'But if they're a prisoner, won't this all need to be official?'

'You don't need to worry about that. The resistance still carries considerable moral authority. Last night we arranged for the prisoner to be moved to a section that is under the control of one of our former comrades. The only thing I ask is that you don't speak until we're in a room with them. Meanwhile, enjoy the journey. Do you like this car?'

'It's magnificent!'

'One of the fleet of Citroëns the Gestapo had in Paris. My group borrowed them.'

–

An hour later, they were in a small office in the basement of the prison. The car had driven through a side entrance, passing through three security barriers until they reached a small cobbled courtyard, where a tall, strikingly handsome man in a black uniform was waiting for them in an open doorway. He shook their hands, introduced himself as Benoît and told them to follow him.

He led them into a room in the basement and closed the door. 'I have made sure my most trusted guards are on duty today. They'll bring the prisoner in and then wait outside. I can give you a maximum of forty-five minutes with her. Marguerite, you have the file there on the table. I'll give you a few minutes to read it, and then they'll send her in.'

Prince and Hanne sat either side of Marguerite at a metal table as they studied the file together:

Name: Anna Lefebvre
Age: 47
Residence: Sarcelles
Date of arrest: 17 July 1945

Alleged offence: the prisoner Anna Lefebvre was employed by the German occupying forces from October 1940 as a clerical worker. From November 1941 she worked for the Gestapo at 11 rue de Saussaies in the 8th arrondissement. We have specific information from three sources that after a period as a records clerk in January 1943, Lefebvre transferred to a section of the Gestapo that comprised French citizens who undertook surveillance on other French subjects. See appendices to this file for details of cases she worked on, which include infiltrating a resistance group and informing on hidden families. Lefebvre is understood to have been an active member of this unit until July 1944, when she left Paris ahead of the liberation. In July this year, acting on information received, she was arrested in Blois, where she had been living under the false identity of Eugénie Paquet. She claims she was forced to work for the Gestapo and says it was only ever as a clerk.

Action: trial of prisoner Anna Lefebvre scheduled for November 1945 at Fresnes.

When Anna Lefebvre was led into the room, she looked surprisingly defiant. Despite her prison clothes, she had a certain elegance. The collar of her prison blouse was turned up, and she appeared to be wearing make-up. She held her hands out in the expectation that the guards would remove her handcuffs, which they did, and sat down before being asked to do so.

Marguerite spoke. This was part of the investigation into Lefebvre's case, she said; part of the preparation for her prosecution. There was a possibility that significant cooperation on her part could help reduce the seriousness of the charge against her, which at present was one of treason, carrying the death penalty.

Anna Lefebvre sat impassive, looking at Prince and Hanne as if trying to work out who they were. Even when Marguerite said the words 'death penalty', she didn't flinch. She ran her fingers across her hair to make sure it was in place.

'Are you prepared to answer some questions?' Marguerite asked.

Lefebvre shrugged. 'Depends if I know the answers – I doubt it, though. I keep telling you people, I was no more than a clerk at the Gestapo. The cleaners would know more than I did.'

'According to this file, there is evidence that you were more than a clerk – you were part of a Gestapo unit spying on citizens. There are witnesses.'

'Ask those witnesses whatever questions you have then. It's all right for you, with your posh accent and your airs and graces, but a poor woman like me didn't have any choice. I had an elderly mother and no job; we'd fallen behind with the rent and were about to be kicked out of the room we shared. The first job I got was in a police station – that's hardly collaborating, is it? Then I was ordered to go and work at rue de Saussaies, and I could hardly refuse that, eh?'

'Plenty did.'

'Well good for them. They probably knew where their next meal was coming from. Look, I know that everyone now claims they were in the resistance and those of us forced to work for the German were collaborators. But it really wasn't as simple as that. The whole country collaborated, in the sense that the vast majority of people passively went along with the occupation. You people see everything as being black and white, whereas in truth most of us were forced to live in an uncomfortable grey world in between.'

'I want to ask you about one person, Lefebvre, a German who worked for the Gestapo here in Paris. We're not sure when he arrived here, but we know for sure he was here in December 1943 and left Paris sometime in early 1944. According to the description we have, he'd have been in his late twenties, and had blonde hair and what are described as bright blue eyes.'

'Are you serious? You're describing the majority of Germans who were here! Have you not heard of the Aryan race? Most of them in Paris looked like pretty good examples of it.'

'His nickname was the Ferret.'

Both Hanne and Prince picked up on her reaction, perhaps before Marguerite did. Between them they must have interrogated hundreds of suspects, and both knew there was a point in an interrogation when someone was asked a question they knew the answer to but were reluctant to give it. It might be some information that would incriminate them, or they might be too scared to answer, or they might just want to keep quiet and see how much their interrogator knew. But the reaction was invariably the same – a momentary look of surprise, perhaps a pursing of the lips or a twitching of another facial muscle, accompanied by an adjustment in their seating. And the answer would always be a bit too quick to be convincing.

'I have no idea who you're talking about.'

'Think about it very carefully, Lefebvre, because your life could depend upon it. I promise you if you give us his name then this will count in your favour and the charge against you will be reduced.'

Anna Lefebvre leaned forward, as if she was interested but trying not to show it. 'Could I have one of your cigarettes?'

Hanne lit one for her and passed it over. Lefebvre looked closely into her eyes as she did so, still trying to work out who she was. She smoked the cigarette for a few moments and then pointed it towards them. 'These two – do they speak?'

'These two, as you call them, are the people who can decide whether you live or die. Think about it, Lefebvre, a Gestapo office matching that description who was nicknamed the Ferret. I find it very hard to believe that if you worked at rue de Saussaies for all that time, you never came across him or heard the name.'

'Ask her about Dijon.' It was the first time Prince had spoken, and Lefebvre raised her eyebrows.

'Ah, yes – he was involved in a case in Dijon where he raped a British agent and then shot her dead.'

A slight narrowing of the eyes as if this had rung a bell, but still Lefebvre said nothing as she finished her cigarette.

'Let me say this.' Prince was speaking in a friendly manner, smiling at her. 'I think I understand your situation. You may well have been junior in the Gestapo, but I find it very hard to believe that in the nearly three years you worked for them, you never came across that nickname.'

Lefebvre shrugged. Hanne lit another cigarette for her.

'But you are probably wondering whether we're telling you the truth – whether if you give us the information, we really will ensure your charge will be reduced. Is that the case?'

Lefebvre nodded.

'You're not exactly in a position to bargain with us. If you know anything, tell us and we can assess how helpful it is. After all, your life is at stake – why should you risk it to protect a Gestapo officer who's probably living it up somewhere?'

Anna Lefebvre ran her fingers through her hair in a more agitated manner and sighed as she looked up at the ceiling. 'He didn't work at rue de Saussaies.'

'So you had heard of him?'

'I heard this nickname but I don't know his real name. He had a reputation for being both violent and incompetent. I think when he first came to Paris he was based at Avenue Foch, but then he was moved. As you know,' she looked at them, 'or maybe you don't, each of the twenty arrondissements in Paris has its own town hall, a *mairie*. The Gestapo had an office in each *mairie*. If my memory serves me correctly, this Ferret character was based in the *mairie* of the 15th arrondissement. That is all I can tell you.'

Marguerite started to speak, but Hanne placed a hand on her arm to stop her and whispered in English, 'Tell her that's not good enough. She's no fool. She's obviously holding something back.'

'Did you understand that, Lefebvre?'

The woman nodded her head.

'We need something more than that.'

Her shoulders dropped as if in resignation.

'Ask Charles Girard… and give the bastard my regards.'

Chapter 9

No one in the *mairie* of the 15th arrondissement admitted that they'd heard of a Charles Girard or come across a blue-eyed blonde German who answered to the nickname of the Ferret. No one even knew about a Gestapo bureau in the building.

There was much shaking of heads. *Try rue de Saussaies – number 11.*

'No, we understand this man worked here, in the *mairie*.'

Of the 15th? Not possible.

'Are you certain – we were told the Gestapo did have an office here: perhaps a small one?'

More shaking of heads. *Avenue Foch – that was Gestapo too, have you tried there?*

They'd driven straight to the *mairie* from Fresnes after meeting Anna Lefebvre. It was a large building, stretching from rue Blomet on one side to rue Lecourbe on the other, and it took them the best part of two hours to work their way through it. Eventually Marguerite said they were wasting their time, they'd have to think of another way to find Charles Girard. She'd told the driver to park the Citroën further down rue Blomet, and they were walking back towards it when a young woman pushed between them as she hurried along the pavement. She paused to apologise before adding urgently that they should follow her and say nothing.

She turned into rue Gerbert and then continued on towards a church. The building was dark and empty apart from an elderly woman dressed in black dusting the pews in front of the altar. The young woman led them into a small side chapel that smelt of damp.

'We'll be safe here for a while. Hardly anyone comes in between masses. My name is Irène.' She shook their hands formally. She was thin and pale and probably still in her twenties, though her face was lined and her long dark hair had flecks of grey in it. 'It's strange being in here again, in a clandestine manner: this church is Saint-Lambert de Vaugirard, and we used it during the war. The priest was very helpful.'

'We?' Marguerite looked suspicious. 'I think you need to tell us who you are, Irène.'

'I work in the *mairie*. I heard the questions you were asking and saw how reluctant people were to help you, which doesn't surprise me. I think I can help. You ask what I meant by "we". I was FTP.'

She paused and looked at them carefully. Marguerite addressed Hanne and Prince in English. 'The FTP was – is – Francs-Tireurs et Partisans. It was the communist resistance. You were in it throughout the war?'

Irène nodded. 'I speak good English if that helps. I studied it at university.'

'Hang on.' Marguerite sounded suspicious. 'Let me ask you some questions first. Which unit were you in?'

'Grenelle.'

'So near here?'

'Very near.'

'I know about Grenelle: where did you meet?'

'At first we met in an apartment in rue Violet, at number 41. Then we used the school across the road. The caretaker was a sympathiser and allowed us access to the basement: we stored weapons there too.'

'Who recruited you?'

'I only ever knew him as Major Marcel. He was arrested by the Nazis in March 1943 and tortured in Fresnes and then executed. For a while our group was dormant until we were sure Marcel had not divulged anything about us. That's when we moved our base to the school.'

'And give me the name of the person who commanded the group after that?'

'Well actually we merged with another group – the idea I think was to move from small cells to larger ones. The group we merged with was based around Gare Montparnasse.'

'That was commanded by Captain Edouard, right?'

'No, there was no Captain Edouard. It was a woman: Germaine.'

Marguerite nodded. 'How come you joined the FTP: are you a communist?'

Irène shrugged, as if she'd not really thought about it. 'Maybe… I was married to one, though. My husband, David, was a Polish Jew who'd moved here when he was a boy, and he was a party member. When the occupation started and the restrictions on Jews came into force, he insisted we get divorced so as to protect me. I didn't want to, but he was adamant. I hoped we could escape from Paris, maybe head south, but it became impossible. I was working at the *mairie* here and continued to do so throughout the war. David moved around Paris and we met whenever we could. In July 1942, he was living in a room in the 9th, and that was when he was arrested in the *grand rafle*, the round-up of Jews. He was taken to the Vélodrome d'Hiver, and when I went there to find out what had happened to him, a police officer – a French police officer – told me he'd gone home to Poland and laughed.'

'Auschwitz?' It was the first time Hanne had spoken.

Irène nodded.

'I was at Ravensbrück,' said Hanne, taking the French girl's hand.

'You're Jewish?'

'No: I'm Danish. I was a British agent – with Richard.' She turned to Prince and smiled. 'So I understand, a little.'

89

Irène was lost in her thoughts for a while. 'That was when I joined the FTP – a friend of David's arranged it. I'd avoided being active before that because I didn't want to do anything that could compromise David. After he was deported, I had nothing to lose. Because I worked in the *mairie*, I was able to access information that was useful to the resistance – addresses, that kind of thing. Now, you need to understand that most of the people you encountered today worked there during the war. They weren't collaborators as such, but they were close to it, if you get my meaning. By working in the *mairie* they indirectly helped the Nazi occupation, so it's no surprise that they feel sensitive about it now, which would explain why they're reluctant to help you. They're certainly reluctant to admit there was a Gestapo office there.'

'So there was one?'

'Of course! The Gestapo had a presence in all the *mairies*; it was the best way of checking on people, getting addresses, accessing local information. They used them for the rounding-up of Jews and then carried on throughout the war. It was only a small office, but it was there on the third floor, overlooking rue Lecourbe.'

'And Charles Girard – and the German, the Ferret?'

'Ah – that is where I can help you. The man who ran the office went under the name of Charles Girard and he was something of an enigma. For a start, that was not his real name – this is not in itself unusual: many French collaborators used different identities. But it was hard to work out what nationality Girard was – his French was fluent and sounded like that of a native, but he also sounded like a German too. He was more like an office manager at first – and there were always one or two German officers based there. For a while, one of them was the man you describe – he was only ever known as the Ferret.'

'When was that?'

'Hard to say, but perhaps towards the end of 1943 – maybe early 1944. I used to have to go into that office quite often, because I work in the finance department and Girard often needed help sorting things out to do with money. Because I was always looking to gather intelligence, I pretended to be friendly with him. One day he was complaining about the Ferret, who'd apparently taken a large sum from the cash box, and Girard had to find a way of accounting for it. He said this man was making his life very difficult; he was constantly creating problems and didn't do what he was told. He said he couldn't do much about it, as the Ferret's father was an important official in Berlin. When I asked him what his real name was, he said he couldn't tell me – he said he'd be in trouble if he did.'

'So Charles Girard knows the Ferret's real identity?'

Irène nodded and pulled her raincoat tight round her.

'And does the name Anna Lefebvre mean anything to you? Apparently she worked for the Gestapo at rue de Saussaies, their headquarters. There seems to be some connection between her and Girard.'

'She was there sometimes. I think she may have had some type of affair with Girard: there were rumours she'd had an abortion because of him. Later on, Girard became far more active – as a Gestapo agent. He seemed especially interested in communists; it was as if he was obsessed with them – far more than with Jews actually, which was unusual. He put all his energy into finding them – he'd come across an old list of party members from the 15th arrondissement, and he spent hours trying to track them down and arrest them. The worst thing he did was arrest the parents of one of the senior party members who'd fled to Moscow before the war. As I understand it, the parents weren't even communists, but Girard shot the father and then had the mother sent to Auschwitz. He kept this behaviour up until the middle of June last year – then, about a week after Normandy, he disappeared.'

'What – altogether?'

Irène shrugged, and then waited as an elderly couple shuffled past the chapel towards the front of the church.

'Certainly from the *mairie*, but he may have gone to work at Avenue Foch or rue de Saussaies. He was certainly in Paris at the start of 1944.'

'How can you be sure of this?'

'My aunt runs a bar on rue de Vignes, on the right bank of the Seine, and sometimes I help her out there. I was working there on New Year's Eve at the start of 1944 and to my horror, I noticed he was there with a group of friends and they were all speaking an odd German dialect. When I asked my aunt about them, she told me they were Alsatians; she said they behaved like dogs too. People from Alsace can appear to be both French and German at the same time – you are no doubt aware it's on the German border and many of its residents would see themselves as German rather than French, which would explain much about Girard.

'I didn't want him to see me there, so I asked her if I could work in the kitchen for the rest of the shift. According to my aunt, his real name is Alphonse Schweitzer. I think he must have felt safe because the name Girard was his collaborator identity, if you see what I mean. No one would have realised that Schweitzer and Girard were one and the same.'

'If only we knew where is now.'

'Aha – I can tell you! When the Communist Party leaders returned from Moscow, I told the man whose parents had been caught by Schweitzer exactly what had happened, and he was put on a wanted list. It took the FTP a while to find him, but I'm told they eventually tracked him down a few months ago in Colmar, which is a city in Alsace, on the border with Germany. They handed him over to the Russians.'

'Why to the Russians?'

'They're good communists.'

'And where is he now?'

'Berlin. During the war, Alsace was annexed into the German Reich, so the Russians claimed that the proper course of action was to try him in Berlin.'

Prince and Hanne looked at each other and nodded. 'If we go to Berlin, we can question him and find out the true identity of the Ferret,' said Prince.

'If Schweitzer's still alive,' said Irène. 'Last month there was a report about his trial on the front page of *L'Humanité*: they'd sentenced him to death!'

Chapter 10

'Berlin, you say?'

'Yes, sir.'

Tom Gilbey shook his head and didn't look nearly as pleased as Prince and Hanne did sitting in front of him. Shafts of late-morning sunlight caught their faces, enhancing their bright demeanour.

'It's always complicated, isn't it? This is what I meant when I said how Europe is changing so fast and we don't appear to be keeping up with whatever's going on. I rather hoped that once the bloody war ended, life would be somewhat more straightforward, but instead it feels as if the rules have suddenly changed in the middle of a game. Now we have the Soviets to worry about, and Europe is still teeming with Nazis. It's like the game's over and now we're into extra time. We had a games master at school who used to do that: kept adding on time to a match if his house was losing.'

He paused and held up his hand in apology, aware that he'd been rambling. He pushed his reading glasses down from his forehead and once again scanned the report they'd submitted on their return from Paris the previous day.

'So it all seems to hinge on what this Irène woman says, eh? Seems rather tenuous, if you ask me.'

'Marguerite checked her out and she is genuine. She was a member of a communist resistance group operating in and around the 15th, and supplied valuable intelligence from inside the *mairie*. Her husband was deported to Auschwitz and murdered there. Marguerite couldn't find anyone who had a bad word to say about her, which is saying something in Paris.'

'There is no question she's telling the truth.' Hanne had rested her hand on her husband's arm. 'Remember I spent more than two years in a concentration camp. There you have to rely absolutely on your instincts as to who you can trust and who you can't. You learn to spot the stooges and know who's telling the truth and who's lying, and more to the point, you also learn to know when people are telling the truth for good reasons but exaggerating, telling you what they think you want to hear. Irène was genuine.'

'Let me get this straight then – and you'll no doubt correct me if I get something tangled up along the way. Wilson has a contact in the resistance...'

'Marguerite.'

'...yes, yes... who found there was a woman in Fresnes prison called Anna Lefebvre who told you that a chap going by the name Charles Girard might know the identity of the Ferret. So you visited the *mairie* and—'

'It's all there in the report, sir. We met Irène and she told us Girard's real name is Alphonse Schweitzer and he knows the real identity of the Ferret.'

'Yes, thank you, Prince, I can read, though I'm not convinced these damn spectacles help. And Schweitzer is a guest of the Soviets in Berlin.'

'Yes, sir, if he's not been executed yet.'

'I'm still not clear why he allowed anyone in Paris to know his real identity.'

'Nor are we, sir, but he'd obviously been leading a double life for some time, and perhaps he became a bit too confident.'

'I think,' said Hanne, 'that we need to go to Berlin – it's urgent we find Schweitzer before he's executed.'

'Well I agree that's preferable to seeing him after he's executed, but I'm not sure we can have you two gallivanting all over Europe, can we? It's not as if you're on the Grand Tour. We have liaison chaps in Berlin who can take this up.'

'With respect, sir, I'm not sure how good an idea that is.'

'Really, Prince?'

'I know Berlin, and—'

'Under the Nazis.'

'But that's the point, sir, not just under the Nazis. On my last mission, when I was working for Hugh Harper, I was in Berlin after the Red Army captured it. I know my way around and I have an excellent contact there with whom I have a good relationship. He could be of enormous help. If it wasn't for him, I doubt I'd have found Hanne alive.'

'And who is this contact?'

'Iosif Leonid Gurevich,' said Prince, as if he was announcing the man's arrival. 'He's a senior officer in the NKGB, which is their security organisation, and…'

'I do what the NKGB is, thank you, Prince.'

'…and he's a *podpolkovnik*, which is like our lieutenant colonel rank.'

Gilbey looked impressed.

'And of course, sir, I did file a contact report when I returned.'

'Naturally.'

'So if I – we – can get over to Berlin as soon as possible?'

'We'll need to see how—'

'The RAF have taken over an airbase at Gatow in the south-west of the city, sir. I've already made some calls, and we can get on a flight there first thing in the morning if you approve it now.'

'Both of you?'

'Yes, both of us,' Hanne said. 'My German's far better than Richard's.'

'Very well then. Let's hope this isn't going to be something I end up regretting, eh?'

The Dakota of RAF Transport Command left RAF Northolt at seven in the morning, landing at RAF Gatow in Berlin nearly four hours later. A tall man wearing a trilby and a long gabardine raincoat was waiting for them at the bottom of the aircraft steps. Hanne gripped Prince's hand as they descended.

'Is that the man?'

'I imagine so.'

'He looks like Gestapo.'

'I doubt Gilbey's employing former Gestapo officers, but we'll soon find out.'

The man was called Kenneth Bemrose and was the best Gilbey could find at such short notice. He wasn't MI6, but he had some kind of civilian role in the British Liaison Office, and most importantly he had security clearance. Almost as importantly – certainly as far as Prince was concerned – he also had use of a car, a khaki-coloured Humber Snipe with Union Jacks painted on the two front doors. Bemrose sounded rather put out when he explained he'd not been able to get hold of a driver so would be doing the honours himself, as he put it.

'Here are your papers.' He handed them a large brown envelope. 'Not much, I'm afraid, but hopefully enough to get you through the checkpoints. They'll impress our side more than theirs, but then that's always the case. Where is it you want to go?'

'Behrenstrasse. I'll tell you which building once we're there.'

'I'm not terribly good at finding my way round the Soviet sector.'

Prince said not to worry, he'd be able to navigate.

They crossed the border at Potsdamer Platz, where the NKVD Border Guards officer in charge seemed unimpressed with their papers. He explained very slowly in basic German that it was most unusual to let people across if it was not a routine visit or if they didn't have an appointment. He shook his head, and Bemrose muttered something about having told them so and whistled something jolly from a musical.

Hanne then spoke in Russian: it wasn't very fluent, with a lot of pauses and gesticulating, but she smiled as she spoke and when the officer – clearly impressed – asked her something, Prince distinctly heard the word 'Ravensbrück' in her reply.

She turned to him. 'Remind me of the name of the man we're hoping to see?'

'Iosif Leonid Gurevich, Podpolkovnik Gurevich: NKGB. We want to go to his office on Behrenstrasse.'

The officer straightened up and shouted orders to his men, and the barrier was raised.

'I didn't know you spoke Russian?'

'We had Russian prisoners at the camp; I picked up a few words and the odd phrase from them. He seemed impressed when you mentioned Iosif.'

'Let's hope he's there.'

Since his last visit in June, the NKGB headquarters had been smartened up. Bemrose seemed annoyed when Prince told him to wait outside. They explained who they wanted to see and were shown to some seats, but less than five minutes later, there was a shout of joy and Prince looked up to see Iosif Gurevich bounding across the entrance hall towards them. The Russian grabbed him by the shoulders to look at him properly, and then enveloped him in a warm embrace, slapping him on the shoulder when he eventually released him. As he did so, he spotted Hanne.

'Is this really you?'

She promised him it was, and tears streamed down his face. He kissed her on both cheeks and told her he'd done many good things in the war – along with one or two bad things, of course – but helping find her was undoubtedly the best.

'Please, come with me. I imagine you want some favour?'

'Why would that be the case, Iosif?'

'Because why else would you come to this shithole?'

Iosif Leonid Gurevich occupied the same office where Prince had first met him, but he had some news, which he recounted with an air of considerable pride.

'I've been promoted, my friends.'

'Congratulations – to what?'

'I'm now a commissar – a one-star commissar,' he said, tapping the gold epaulettes on his green uniform.

'Which means you're a…'

'A general! It was a big promotion, I didn't expect it. They're very pleased with how things have gone in Berlin. There have been some problems with discipline among our troops here and I've been effective in dealing with it; I seem to be able to get my way with you British especially – the Americans too. The French are more difficult, but… Imagine, after everything, a Jewish general in charge here in Berlin!'

The three of them laughed and Gurevich opened a bottle of German brandy and handed it round. They toasted his promotion, followed by a toast to peace between their nations, and when they told him they were now married, he poured more brandy and toasted that before going over to a wall piled high with boxes, oil paintings stacked alongside them.

'Please, you must choose a wedding present.'

Eventually they got down to business. Speaking in German but dropping in the occasional word or phrase in Russian, Hanne explained everything. When she'd finished, the Russian nodded gravely and glanced at the notes he'd been making. 'So this Alphonse Schweitzer is a prisoner of ours?'

'Have you not come across him?'

'Ha! Do you know how many Nazis we have in custody – thousands of them, literally thousands. We're running out of prison space. If I'm honest with you, not all of those we've captured have gone through the system, so to speak. Many of them have been dealt with in a summary manner, much as they treated our troops they took prisoner. We're processing the rest as fast as we can and sending most of them to camps in Siberia, so I wouldn't know about an individual such as this. You're certain he's in Berlin?'

'Yes.'

'And remind me where he was arrested?'

'Colmar – it's a French city in Alsace, but it was annexed into the Third Reich.'

Gurevich nodded. 'Very well then: give me an hour and I will have some information. You say you have a driver waiting for you?'

'He's outside.'

'Send him away: I'll look after you. I'll tell my aide to get you something to eat.'

–

Bemrose was dozing in the Humber when Prince tapped on the window. He seemed annoyed at being woken up, and even more so to be told he was no longer needed. He said he was going to tell Mr Gilbey that he wasn't a chauffeur.

An hour later, Hanne and Prince were back in Gurevich's office.

'I've found him!'

'Alphonse Schweitzer?'

The Russian nodded and looked pleased with himself as he opened a box of cigars and clamped one between his teeth. 'Being a commissar unlocks many doors. I just have to ask a question and people fall over themselves to answer it. He's in Hohenschönhausen.'

'Where's that?'

'Here in Berlin – in Lichtenberg, to the east of Mitte. We've constructed a large prison camp there where we process prisoners before they're sent to the Soviet Union. It also acts as a prison for people convicted here. Schweitzer faced a People's Tribunal last month and was found guilty of being a Nazi agent in occupied France and of pursuing a campaign of vengeance against comrades from the French Communist Party and their families. He was sentenced to death.'

'And did he plead guilty?'

'Our People's Tribunals perhaps work in a different way from your courts, my friend. He made a statement, and from what I understand, he said he was forced to work for the Gestapo. He claims he helped people, but... we had evidence, including that of the woman you mentioned.'

'Irène?'

'That's right. Look, I only know this from a telephone conversation. We will go now to Hohenschönhausen.'

They drove north through Mitte and Prenzlauer Berg and then along Landsberger Allee into Lichtenberg. It was a slow journey: whereas Mitte was largely deserted and the roads were more or less clear, it was a very different matter once they left the centre. From then on the roads and pavements were still littered with rubble and dotted with potholes and bomb craters, and at times it was impossible to get through and they had to try another route. They were both shocked, not so much by the devastation around them but more by the atmosphere and the way the population moved around.

Despite the warm weather, most people were wearing coats and hats, many with blankets round their shoulders as they shuffled along. They looked nervous, doing their best to avoid the ubiquitous Red Army troops as they carried battered cases or bags, many pulling carts or pushing prams loaded with possessions. From almost every ruined building – and most of the buildings were damaged in one way or another – plumes of smokes rose high into the sky. On the pavement, people were cooking on piles of rubble, while others waited in long queues at what appeared to be makeshift shops selling a few vegetables with the odd tin here and there – usually little more than planks of wood balanced on chairs serving as a counter.

At one stage Hanne wound down the window, but she soon put it back up: the smell was overpowering. Each time the car stopped, people would gather around it, the frightened eyes of emaciated children gazing at them as they pleaded for food. At one point a boy reached up to tap on the glass, and for a moment Prince thought it was his son Henry.

'They did this to themselves,' said the commissar, indicating a group of people fighting over something in a gutter. 'Save your sympathy for their victims.'

'I don't have any sympathy for them,' said Hanne.

'Not even for the children?'

She shrugged and took her husband's hand.

Gurevich pointed ahead of them to an enormous complex rising to their left high above the ruined landscape: Hohenschönhausen. Their progress was halted by a cart being pulled along the road in front of them. The driver sounded his horn, but it didn't move out of the way. Gurevich said something to him in Russian and he edged forward, knocking the cart over. The two old ladies who'd been pulling it stood with their heads bowed as the car drove on.

Inside the prison they were directed to one of the few brick buildings and escorted to an upper-floor office where two uniformed men were nervously waiting for them. There was a long conversation, the two men seeming to defer to Gurevich, who eventually spoke in German to Hanne and Prince, gesturing at the men.

Comrade Orlov was the governor in charge of Hohenschön-hausen, he said. Orlov looked old and tired, his head completely bald and his eyes red as if through lack of sleep.

'And this is Comrade Kiselyov; he is in charge of the block where Schweitzer is held. Comrade Kiselyov speaks German. Maybe if we all sit down, he can tell us about the prisoner. I've told him you need information from him about a German fugitive.'

Kiselyov's hands trembled as he spoke, all the time looking at a sheet of paper on the desk in front of him. His voice was surprisingly high-pitched.

'Prisoner Schweitzer was arrested in May in Colmar in France, formerly an annexed zone of the Nazi Reich. He was arrested by a unit of French communists and eventually handed over to the Soviet Union. Under the special wartime provisions of section 117, subsection 48 of the Penal Code, he was eligible to be tried in Germany as someone who committed war crimes on German territory during the war against fascism.'

He paused to cough and gratefully sipped from a glass of water the governor passed to him. He glanced anxiously at the commissar to check all was in order before continuing.

'The specific charges against Prisoner Schweitzer are that in the period from June 1940 to June 1944 he was an active agent of the Nazi Gestapo organisation, in which capacity he assisted the Nazis in carrying out war crimes and conducted war crimes himself, specifically but not exclusively a vendetta against members of the Communist Party of France and their relatives and associates. In terms of—'

'Maybe get on to what happened when the prisoner arrived here, Comrade?'

'Of course, Comrade sir, my sincere apologies. Prisoner Schweitzer arrived at Special Camp Number 3 Hohenschön-hausen on Wednesday the first of August and appeared before a People's Tribunal on… Apologies, Comrade, I need to find the date…'

'Don't worry, Kiselyov, you're not on trial here!'

Kiselyov looked up, shocked, before continuing. 'Here we are: Thursday the ninth of August was the date of the tribunal. Prisoner Schweitzer was found guilty of all charges. In a statement he said he was forced to do the work, but of course, all the evidence…'

'Of course, Comrade. Perhaps you'd now tell us about his sentence and when it is due to be carried out?'

'Yes, Comrade: he was sentenced to death on… here we are… Tuesday the fourteenth of August and the sentence was confirmed by Comrade Orlov on the third of September.'

'Why the delay, Comrade?'

'The governor said he was sorry but there was a backlog and he'd been in Moscow for a meeting and—'

'Don't worry, my friends here will be pleased you didn't execute the prisoner straight away. But that was over three weeks ago, and he's still alive?'

It was Orlov who replied. 'There is always a two-week period between my confirming the sentence and it being carried out. During this time the prisoner has the right to make an appeal, though an appeal will only be considered if it is based on a factual error in the conviction. In the case of Prisoner Schweitzer, he claimed it was a case of mistaken identity, and it took us some time to get further evidence from Paris. His execution has now been scheduled for Monday the first of October.'

'And the prisoner knows this?'

'Of course, Comrade.'

Gurevich had been translating what the two officers said into German. Prince said they'd need to question Schweitzer urgently. 'He's the only person we are aware of who knows the true identity of the Nazi we are looking for.'

Orlov had an owl-like demeanour: his head remained quite still but his eyes darted around, taking everything in, and he came across as wise and unhurried. He said nothing for a while as he removed a cigarette from a packet on his desk and lit it, all the while without taking his eyes off his visitors.

'I would say no.'

'I beg your pardon?'

'I would strongly suggest you don't question the prisoner on this topic.'

'But Comrade,' said Gurevich, 'I have the authority to order it and I—'

'Yes, Comrade, of course I know that. What I mean is I would not recommend it. Prisoner Schweitzer is typical of the non-German Nazis we see here – they tend to be more fanatical and stubborn than the Germans. If you go in now and question him about the man you're after, it will be counter-productive. He won't say anything. What do you think, Kiselyov?'

Kiselyov looked nervous again but sounded confident in his reply. 'I would agree: I would say Prisoner Schweitzer is no fool. He knows he's about to be executed so why should he tell us anything?'

'Because he has nothing to lose?' Hanne sounded as if she was negotiating.

'But he hates us – he hates communists and is still a committed Nazi. If you ask him about the man you're hunting, he'll just clam up.'

The room fell silent. The governor lit another cigarette and Gurevich drummed his fingers on the arm of his chair. Through the open window came the sound of orders being shouted and large numbers of people moving. In the distance a fighter plane flew low over the northern suburbs.

'There is another possibility,' said Gurevich, leaning back with his eyes half shut as he spoke, 'but we need to buy some time. Remind me when you said Schweitzer is due to be executed?'

'Monday morning, Comrade sir. The executions always take place at dawn. We use a firing range at the barracks to the north of this complex.'

'We must delay that.'

'He'll suspect something.'

Gurevich said nothing for a minute or so and then nodded his head. 'Who is the most senior Soviet official in Moscow, Comrade Orlov?'

'Marshal Zhukov, of course, sir.'

'That's right: so how about you wait until Sunday and then offer Prisoner Schweitzer the option of applying for a… what shall we call it... a petition to the Soviet commander? How does that sound?'

'I'm afraid I've never heard of it, Comrade sir.'

'Of course you haven't, Comrade Orlov! I've just made it up, but it will buy us time and will enable us to find a way of getting the information out of the prisoner. Don't look so worried, I'll square it with Marshal Zhukov's office.'

'This way of getting the information we need.' Prince was looking worried. 'Did you have something in mind?'

'I have an idea actually.' Hanne stood up and walked over to the window, where she gazed at the parade ground below. When she turned round, she was silhouetted against the late-afternoon sun. 'I was thinking about it because we were asked the other day about Irène – about whether we trusted her. I said I did, that my time in Ravensbrück had taught me how to spot a stooge.'

'I'm not sure I understand.' Gurevich had leaned forward, curious.

Hanne returned to her seat. 'We find someone we can trust but who will also be someone Schweitzer instinctively trusts.' She paused while Gurevich translated into Russian for the governor. 'And that person tricks Schweitzer into revealing the name.'

'Ah – I understand you. In Russian we have a word for this type of person; we call it a *provokator*! Well done, Hanne, that is a very clever idea!' Gurevich clapped his hands, and for the first time the governor looked animated and allowed himself a smile. 'Of course, we need to find this *provokator*; we don't have long.'

'Actually,' said Prince, 'I think I know the ideal person.'

Chapter 11

In the minutes approaching midnight on Sunday 30 September, the block containing the condemned cells at the Hohenschönhausen prison complex in Berlin was as silent as anywhere in a prison housing thousands of inmates could ever be.

It took a while for the sound of the footsteps of two men as they marched across a courtyard and into Block D to become apparent. The silence was disturbed by a series of doors being unlocked and then secured again, and the same footsteps moving along the stone floor until they reached an office on the second floor.

Kiselyov, the officer in charge of that section, was waiting nervously when the two men walked in. He stubbed out his cigarette and stood to attention, but the governor told him to sit. Kiselyov recognised the other man, the commissar from the NKGB headquarters in Mitte, no less, the man who'd turned up a week earlier with the two visitors who were neither Russian nor German.

'How is he, Comrade?'

Despite the invitation to sit, Kiselyov had remained standing, his hands clasped tightly behind his back. 'Prisoner Schweitzer spent the evening writing his final letters, Comrade sir. He was checked by the medical officer at six o'clock and then his evening meal was brought to him, but I'm told he didn't eat any of it. I can't say I blame him, I—'

'Get on with it, Kiselyov.'

'Yes, Comrade! He asked to see a Roman Catholic priest, but this was refused. The guards monitoring him in his cell say he has been agitated all evening, pacing up and down, crying and hitting the wall on occasion. He has been sick a number of times. In accordance with your instructions, he was given a mild sleeping draught about one hour ago, and when I checked with the guard five minutes ago, I was told that he is now asleep.'

'Good, all as planned.' The governor turned to Gurevich. 'Are you satisfied, Commissar?'

'I think so: you know what to say to him?'

'Yes, sir, but what if he declines the opportunity?'

Gurevich helped himself to a cigarette from Kiselyov's desk and raised his eyebrows in surprise. 'Do you think he's mad, Comrade Orlov? Five hours before he's due to die? Come on, let's go.'

–

The cell door burst open at the same time as the main lights were turned on, and Kiselyov shouted to the prisoner to wake up. Alphonse Schweitzer woke with a start and sat bolt upright on his narrow prison bed, letting out a yelp of fear as he did so. His shirt was undone and stained, and he stared at Kiselyov, the governor and the two guards in absolute terror.

'Surely it's not time, is it? Please… it must be too early… I asked to see a priest.'

Kiselyov told him to stand in the presence of the governor. Orlov nodded at one of the guards to handcuff the prisoner, who was now shaking so much it seemed as if he was having convulsions, while at the same time making a whimpering sound. He was trying to hold up his trousers and not succeeding. In the few days since the governor had last seen him, he seemed to have shrunk to half his size and looked twice as old.

'You need to listen very carefully, Schweitzer, do you understand?'

The prisoner nodded frantically, gazing at them in a pleading manner.

The governor spoke slowly in Russian, pausing every sentence or two for Kiselyov to translate. 'Prisoner Schweitzer, you have been found guilty of war crimes under the special wartime provisions of section 117, subsection 48 of the Penal Code. You have been sentenced to death and your appeal has been dismissed.'

Schweitzer was weeping now and shaking his head.

'Shut up and act like a man! Your execution will take place,' Orlov looked carefully at his wristwatch, 'in just over five hours.'

After Kiselyov had finished translating that last sentence, the governor paused. 'However, Prisoner Schweitzer... I have been informed this evening that as of the first of October, all prisoners who are neither German nor Soviet citizens are able to make use of a petition to the Soviet commander requesting clemency.'

He managed to look resentful at having to impart this good news. The prisoner stared at him in amazement and asked him to repeat what he'd just said, and if possible to explain further.

'What I mean is that you may have been very lucky, Prisoner Schweitzer. The new regulation comes into force tomorrow, whereby the Soviet commander of the occupied zone of Germany will review all death sentences scheduled to be carried out on prisoners other than German or Soviet citizens. Personally I was of the opinion that this did not apply to prisoners sentenced before the first of October, but others took a different view.'

The prisoner mumbled something that sounded like a prayer.

'However, for this to happen, you have to request it by signing this form – here, read it first by all means.'

The prisoner was weeping tears of joy, which dripped onto the sheet of paper as he read it and signed. *Thank you... thank you... thank you...*

'Well, let's see, Prisoner Schweitzer, your thanks may be premature: who knows what Marshal Zhukov will decide when he considers your case? But it could take up to a month for him to make his judgement, so tomorrow you'll be moved to another cell.'

Thank you… thank you… thank you…

'You're a lucky bastard, Prisoner Schweitzer.'

When Orlov and Kiselyov left the cell, they noticed the commissar leaning against the wall, just out of sight of the man within. He said nothing as they walked back to the office on the second floor, but when they got there, he took a bottle of Armagnac from his briefcase, along with a wooden box of cigars, and placed them on the desk.

'You have both handled this very most impressively. It will not go unnoticed, I promise you.'

The two men looked almost as grateful and relieved as the prisoner had minutes before.

'Now we need the next stage to work. However, I do know that my friends have found someone who should make an excellent *provokator*.'

–

In the end, they moved the terrified Alphonse Schweitzer to another cell late on the Monday evening. Since the governor and Kiselyov had turned up in his cell the previous night and announced a temporary reprieve, he'd not slept. At first he was overcome with joy, relieved beyond words at his stay of execution. Then he worried the whole business might be a cruel trick by the Russians – he wouldn't put anything past those bastards – or worse still, a trick of his own imagination.

He'd stayed awake all night: dawn came and passed, and the first Monday of October, which was a day he'd been fated never to see, was spent in his cell. The guards constantly checked him and Kiselyov came in two or three times to assure him he was about to be transferred to another block, but that was still being sorted and he should be patient.

He'd begun to doubt it would ever happen, but then at eight o'clock that night, the cell door opened and Kiselyov told him to get a move on. He was handcuffed and shackled and led through Block D, by which time of course the other prisoners had been locked down and the lights in the corridors and halls dimmed. When they came to the entrance to the block, he was told to wait and a hood was placed over his head; he was convinced this meant they were about to shoot him, or worse still, hang him, which he considered a far worse fate. As he was hurried across a courtyard and along a rough path and then into another block, he wondered why they needed to go to all this trouble if they were going to kill him.

The cell they took him into was the least unpleasant of the half-dozen or so he'd been in at Hohenschönhausen. It was quite large, with a toilet and a sink in one corner, which made a welcome change from the bucket and bowl he'd been used to. It also contained two beds, and to his surprise, a man in prison uniform was sitting on one of them.

'Reinhard Möller.' The other man had waited until the guards had locked the door and turned off the light before getting up and shaking Schweitzer's hand in a friendly manner. He apologised for not being very talkative but said he was tired. 'I'll introduce myself properly in the morning.'

–

Three days earlier – on the Saturday morning – back at RAF Gatow in the south-west of Berlin, an irritated Bemrose was waiting outside in the Humber Snipe, muttering that he still resented being treated as a chauffeur but that when he'd complained to Mr Gilbey, he'd been told how important this job was.

In the arrivals area, Hanne and Prince watched as the RAF Dakota landed somewhat awkwardly, bouncing on the runway as it was buffeted by a cross-wind and then taxiing towards the apron.

The two men they were waiting for greeted them warmly. Tom Gilbey said he couldn't believe the destruction he'd seen as the plane descended over Berlin. The other man said he could. 'It's far worse on the ground, I can tell you – remember, I was only here five months ago. I lived through the Battle for Berlin!'

The conversation in the car from the airport to the safe house Bemrose had organised in Wilmersdorf was restricted to the weather and the areas they were driving through. The German who'd arrived with Gilbey apologised. 'I could give you a guided tour, but it's so hard to recognise places.'

Hanne watched the man carefully. Prince had told her all about him. Franz Rauter was a former Abwehr spy master who'd run a successful spy ring in London. When Prince had found him in Berlin at the end of the war, Rauter had undertaken to cooperate in return for a promise that he not be treated as a prisoner. It was agreed that after he'd helped the British, he'd be allowed to return to Germany. Prince had told her it hadn't been a difficult promise to keep. Rauter was pleasant man, a professional intelligence officer and certainly not a Nazi; it had even been suggested to Tom Gilbey that he might be able to use him as a British agent once he was back in Germany.

Rauter himself was keen on this: he was clearly an Anglophile, and the promise of a new identity appealed to him. Although he'd worked in Berlin for a number of years, he was originally from Hamburg. Somewhere nice in the British zone of western Germany would suit him fine.

Neither he nor Gilbey had imagined his return to Germany would happen quite so soon. Gilbey had received an urgent phone call from Prince on the Thursday evening.

'We've found Alphonse Schweitzer.'

'Good.'

'The Russians don't think he'll cooperate.'

'I'm sure he will in time, Prince.'

'We don't have time, sir.'

'Why ever not?'

'He's due to be executed first thing Monday morning.'

That was when Prince explained the plan he, Hanne and Gurevich had come up with. Alphonse Schweitzer would be told about a stay of execution and moved to a cell in another block while his sentence was allegedly reviewed by no less a person than Marshal Zhukov. He would share the cell with a stooge who'd hopefully get the information from him.

'And Schweitzer's bought all this?'

'He doesn't know about the stooge, sir.'

'Obviously, Prince, don't treat me like a fool. I meant about his case being reviewed at the last minute by Zhukov?'

'Apparently he was so relieved he'll believe anything.' It was then that Prince had suggested they use Franz Rauter as the stooge. He expected Gilbey to find a good reason why not and was ready to make the case: they needed a German, someone who understood the Gestapo, who was credible and who they could trust. But Gilbey was surprisingly amenable to the idea. So much so that he said he'd bring him over himself.

'As soon as possible, please, sir.'

They spent the weekend and all day Monday in the safe house in Wilmersdorf briefing Rauter: *Schweitzer is the only person we're aware of who knows the true identity of the Ferret, and we'd like you to get him to tell you.*

They came up with a plausible cover story, and by the Monday afternoon Rauter was ready.

Reinhard Möller was about to become an inmate of Hohenschönhausen.

–

Alphonse Schweitzer was so relieved at his stay of execution that he was more than happy to chat with the man he shared his cell with, especially someone as like-minded and sympathetic as Reinhard Möller – that was, as the man insisted on pointing out, Möller with an 'ö' rather than Müller with a 'ü'.

On the first day, Möller allowed Schweitzer to tell his own story, a typically self-serving account of a fanatical and committed Nazi who was anxious to blame everyone else for the predicament he found himself in and who was now desperately clutching at the unlikely straw of being reprieved by Marshal Zhukov.

'Have you heard of this petition, Reinhard?'

'Of course: apparently the British and Americans wanted the Soviets to observe more of a judicial process.'

'And what do you think?'

'What do I think about what, Alphonse?'

'About my chances of being reprieved?'

'Quite good, I'd say: look, they're hardly going to waste Zhukov's time with someone they were going to execute anyway. I only wish I was eligible for this – but you know, being German...'

It wasn't until later on the Tuesday that Möller opened up about himself. He was from Dortmund, he'd joined the party in 1934 and become a Gestapo officer in 1938. From the summer of 1941 onwards, he'd been based at their Amsterdam headquarters on Euterpestraat. He'd managed to escape at the end of the war, but for some mad reason had headed east rather than west... a woman in Leipzig, he must have been crazy... and here he was.

Schweitzer seemed impressed, especially when Möller told him he'd been responsible for finding communists and socialists in the Netherlands, and recounted in some detail how many he'd caught and how many he'd killed with his own hands. Schweitzer had already explained how he himself had worked for the Gestapo in Paris, 'though I wasn't as important as you, Reinhard'; the other man told him not to be so silly and of course he was important, and Schweitzer said please not to tell Marshal Zhukov, as then he'd definitely be executed.

They both laughed, and then Reinhard Möller mentioned casually how he'd worked with a Gestapo officer in Amsterdam who'd been transferred from Paris.

'I can't for the life of me remember his name, Alphonse – I don't know what's happened to my memory. He was a young chap, quite good-looking. Austrian, I think. We knew him by his nickname, the Ferret. I don't suppose you ever came across him?'

Alphonse Schweitzer slapped his new friend's thigh. 'Of course I did! He worked with me at the *mairie* for a while. Difficult chap, very arrogant; father was a big cheese here in Berlin. As I recall, while he was based in Paris, he completely screwed up an investigation. They wanted to throw him out of the Gestapo, but his father arranged for him to be transferred to Amsterdam – quite a lot of the senior officers in the Netherlands were Austrian, and I think the father used that connection.'

'That would have been when?'

'Early 1944, I guess.'

'That's right – your memory's so much better than mine. I don't suppose you remember his name?'

'I do, as it happens. His name was Friedrich Steiner, and I even recall his father's name: Wolfgang.'

–

When Kiselyov came into the cell the following morning, Reinhard Möller asked him if the date for his hearing had been fixed, the agreed code to indicate that he had the information he needed.

An hour later, Kiselyov returned and told him his tribunal had been arranged and he was being moved.

The two prisoners shook hands and wished each other luck, Schweitzer managing a whispered 'Heil Hitler' just before his new friend was led out.

Franz Rauter was taken to Orlov's office, where Hanne and Prince were waiting for him. He greeted them both and gratefully accepted a glass of cognac and a cigarette from the governor.

'The Ferret's real name is Friedrich Steiner; he is the son of Wolfgang Steiner, who was a Nazi Party official here in Berlin. Funnily enough, his name rings a bell, but I never met him – as you know, I didn't mix in those circles.'

Prince said how pleased they were, and Rauter finished his cognac and allowed the glass to be refilled, then asked whether they'd be leaving straight away. 'The sooner I'm out of this place, the better.'

'The governor thinks it would be safer if you're kept here until after Schweitzer's execution. If he somehow catches wind that you're no longer around, he may suspect something and somehow get a message to his fellow Nazis. I know that's unlikely, but it's not impossible: this place is full of Nazis on the lookout for anything.'

'And I should add that when he's taken out to be shot, he will get to see a Catholic priest. You never know what he might say. It's going to be safer to let you go after he's been executed.' The governor was speaking slowly, allowing Kiselyov to translate.

Rauter looked disappointed. 'I'm not keen on staying here: this isn't my idea of a holiday.'

'Don't worry,' said the governor. 'This afternoon I'll tell Prisoner Schweitzer that his petition to Marshal Zhukov has been denied and he's being executed in the morning. We'll move him straight back to Block D. Once he's dead, we'll have you out of here.'

–

It was a mistake no one could have foreseen; a coincidence more than anything else, something that happened by chance and could be put down to sheer bad luck, though it was to have dreadful consequences.

Prince and Hanne left the brick building by a side entrance and paused in the doorway to say goodbye to Franz Rauter. They joked that this time tomorrow he'd be enjoying a fine lunch in the best restaurant in Berlin, and Rauter said they'd be lucky to find any restaurants left. There was much slapping of shoulders and laughter as he finished his cigarette and then allowed the guard to put him in handcuffs prior to the walk back to the block.

Watching all this from his cell window was a young SS major awaiting his tribunal, where he fully expected to be sentenced to death. Hauptsturmführer Klaus Böhme had been an aide to SS-Brigadeführer Walter Schellenberg when the latter had taken control of the much-distrusted Abwehr in July 1944. He had been appalled at the attitude of many of the Abwehr officers, some of whose loyalty he seriously doubted.

One of those had been Franz Rauter, a bright and well-regarded Abwehr career officer who was running a successful spy ring in England and was therefore protected from the purges towards the end of the war. The rumour was that he was now helping the British.

Now Klaus Böhme observed a man who looked very much like Franz Rauter chatting amicably with a man and a woman in civilian clothes, neither of whom appeared to be Russians. After a friendly farewell, he was put into handcuffs and led towards his block.

As he queued for supper later that afternoon, Böhme spotted the same man ahead of him on the landing. He heard a guard address him as Möller, but when the man turned his head, Böhme had absolutely no doubt. If Rauter was here – under an assumed name – it was because he was a traitor. Böhme knew what his duty was, and it wasn't as if he had anything to lose. They might even put him out of his misery sooner.

He collected his supper and walked towards the man, whose back was towards him. 'Hey, Franz – Franz Rauter!'

Instinctively Rauter turned. In the brief moment before Böhme plunged the knife deep into his heart, he recognised the young man who'd called his name but couldn't for the life of him place him.

His memory was so bad these days.

Alphonse Schweitzer was unaware of all this. He was still in Block D. The governor had come to his cell that afternoon and informed him Marshal Zhukov had reviewed his case and denied his petition.

'What does that mean?'

'What do you mean, what does that mean? It's obvious, isn't it? You're going to be executed after all – at dawn tomorrow. You'll be transferred to the death block now.'

Schweitzer was dragged crying from his cell at dawn the next morning. The guards were disgusted at having to handle the terrified prisoner, who'd soiled himself and kept vomiting. He was thrown in the back of a truck and driven the short distance to the barracks, then dragged to the firing range.

A white-faced Catholic priest was allowed to spend a few seconds with him, but Schweitzer couldn't hear what he was saying and nor did he care.

As he was strapped to a post, he felt his legs give way. At that moment a tall man in a commissar's uniform strolled over to him. The man – who looked suspiciously like a Jew – smiled as he instructed the guards to gag the prisoner but not to bother blindfolding him. 'Let him enjoy everything!'

Once he was trussed up like a pig, the commissar leaned over and spoke clearly in his ear. 'I really must thank you, Schweitzer: you've no idea how helpful you've been!'

–

When Hanne and Prince met with Commissar Gurevich in his office in Behrenstrasse later that morning, the mood could not have been more sombre. Prince had listened to the Russian's account of Schweitzer's execution without showing any reaction, and simply shrugged when informed that the prisoner had been told how helpful he'd been just before he was shot.

'Are you not pleased, my friend?'

Prince said he supposed he was, but he was more devastated at Franz Rauter's death. 'I don't know how that could have been allowed to happen.'

'It wasn't allowed to happen; from what Comrade Orlov tells me, it was sheer bad luck – he was in the wrong place at the wrong time. The man who killed him – Prisoner Böhme – knew him from the RSHA and guessed he was a traitor, don't ask me how. When he realised he was using an assumed name, he concluded his guess was correct. If it's any consolation, Prisoner Böhme was shot later that day.'

'It's no consolation actually. I think we should have pulled Franz out of Hohenschönhausen once he'd told us the Ferret's identity. It was risky to—'

'Hindsight, my friend, hindsight. It could also have been risky to pull him out immediately. We weren't to know Böhme would spot him; it was a chance in a million, sheer bad luck. And at least he's dead, which means no one will make the link with the Ferret. Do you want some news to cheer you up?'

'Go on.'

'I did a check yesterday, and we do have a Wolfgang Steiner on our watch list. He was a Nazi Party official at the Parteikanzlei, just a few minutes' walk from here. We don't know a lot about him, but he was known to be an associate of Martin Bormann, Hitler's personal secretary, who is someone we certainly want to arrest – he's one of the most senior Nazis whose whereabouts we know nothing about. As far as we know, Wolfgang Steiner left Berlin in late March and has disappeared.'

'He got out early,' said Hanne, 'before your main assault on the city.'

Gurevich nodded. 'Obviously smart – and the fact that he got away then means he's probably more important than we realised. I'll make a note on his file. But what I don't quite get is the son – Friedrich. He was a young Gestapo officer who murdered people. I'm afraid that was not unusual. So why are you going to these lengths to find him – surely there are more important war criminals?'

'Because, Iosif, two of the people he murdered were our agents, people who'd been sent over from England, and there's a view in London that we have a responsibility to bring the person who killed them to justice.'

'But it sounds as if there may be a reason why he's so hard to find – why someone was murdered in Munich when they tried to track him down. I can get Friedrich Steiner's name added to our watch lists – I'm sure you'll be doing the same with yours.'

'It's already been done.'

'Good. There is something, though.' Iosif Gurevich hesitated, as if unsure whether to carry on. He drummed his fingers on his desk and then held up a hand – *wait* – and walked over to the door. He opened it and appeared to look up and down the corridor before closing it again. Then he pulled up a chair and leaned forward.

'There are escape lines for Nazi war criminals operating across Europe, and from what we gather, they're far more prevalent in the American, British and French zones than in ours. We want to know more about these escape lines: we want to know who's on them and where they end up. We think Italy is the main destination, because there are plenty of people there who'll help them, and they can also then escape through the Italian ports. Friedrich Steiner may well be on one of those escape routes – if you can find out anything about them, it could help us track him down.'

'You mean you want us to supply you with intelligence?' Hanne had raised her voice slightly, and Gurevich indicated that she should lower it.

'I'm suggesting we share information. To show you evidence of my goodwill, there is something about Wolfgang Steiner I didn't mention. Please be careful about how you use this intelligence, though. Come closer.'

They shifted their chairs so their knees were almost touching.

'This is in Wolfgang Steiner's file. You won't be able to read it, as it's in Cyrillic script, but it says "possible link with RLB and *der Fluchtweg Falke*", followed by the letters FFM, V and T.'

'*Fluchtweg* would mean escape route, I think,' said Hanne, 'but I'm not sure what *Falke* means – is it a kind of bird?'

'It's a shortened form of the word *Turmfalke* – a kestrel. I'm not sure who added that note to the file; officers pick up scraps of intelligence and just include them, when really they should be putting in more detail, like where they got it from, and then identifying themselves… but this goes on all the time. People are so busy. My guess is that whoever put that in got it from an interrogation and was in a hurry. I'm trying to track down the officer. My supposition is that this is a reference to an escape line – that's what *der Fluchtweg* would mean. Kestrel is probably its code name.'

'And the initials?'

'FFM almost certainly stands for Frankfurt am Main: those initials are often used to differentiate it from the smaller Frankfurt, which is on the River Oder and is usually abbreviated to FFO. My guess is that the Kestrel escape line starts in Frankfurt, and the V and the T are the initials of places it goes to, but where those are is anyone's guess. I have no idea what RLB stands for.'

'If you say these escape lines end up in Italy, then the V could be Venice,' suggested Prince.

'And the T – Turin, possibly?'

'I think Turin is more than possible. True, it isn't a port, but it's near Genoa, which is the main port the Nazis are using. Look, I think we're guessing, Hanne, but let's hope this helps you find him. All I ask is that you share with me what you discover about the escape line. In the meantime, I'll try and find the officer who made that note on the file.'

–

Tom Gilbey had reluctantly remained in the safe house in Wilmersdorf. He'd thought about coming to the east of the city to meet Gurevich but decided it wasn't worth the risk of exposing himself. He was as upset as Prince and Hanne were at the news of Franz Rauter's death, but soon turned his attention to Friedrich Steiner.

'At least we now know who the Ferret is, so we should be able to pick him up soon enough. Now that his name's on our watch lists, it should only be a matter of time before we find him.'

Both Hanne and Prince looked surprised at his optimism.

'What do you make of the note on the file about the Kestrel escape line?' Prince asked.

'May be something in it – but then where on earth do you start?'

'Frankfurt? That seems to be the first place mentioned. Perhaps we should…' Prince stopped himself.

'Perhaps you should what?'

'Nothing, sir, just a thought.'

'Which was?'

'I was going to suggest that maybe Hanne and I ought to go to Frankfurt; there might be some kind of clue there about Steiner and the Kestrel escape line.'

'I think that's a good idea.' Hanne looked interested. 'We came over here to find the Ferret: I never like leaving a case only half investigated for someone else to solve.'

'Very well then: you can go to Frankfurt – but only for a few days, and then that's it. I'd imagine you'd want to be getting home anyway, eh?'

Chapter 12

'How much longer am I expected to remain in this prison?'

'It's hardly a prison, Friedrich – how many prisons have carpets, and pictures on the wall? Before the war this was a smart guest house.'

'So you keep telling me, Ulrich – and one frequented by Jews: I imagine you chose it as some kind of joke?'

'I know we had to get you out of Munich in a hurry, and Frankfurt didn't feel much safer, to be honest, but this place does. And it's ideal: it's set apart from the neighbouring houses, so no one can see what's going on, and because of the damage to the roof, the Americans won't requisition it. Can you please take your feet off that table? People eat from it.'

The younger man gave the older one a dirty look, clearly resentful at being told what to do. 'People! What, you're planning to hold a dinner party, eh? At least I'd then have someone else to talk to. Maybe you could even invite a woman. Apart from you, I've not seen a soul for weeks.'

Ulrich asked Friedrich to light him a cigarette: it was an action he still struggled over with one arm. Friedrich lit one for himself first and took a few drags from Ulrich's before passing it to him.

'I keep telling you, Friedrich, you don't appreciate how ideal this place is. Even though we're just, what, ten, twelve miles north of Frankfurt, no one's going to think of looking for Nazi fugitives here in Königstein. These Taunus mountain resorts have a reputation for being quiet and healthy.'

'Great – so I can go and enjoy the town then, take a bracing walk maybe?'

'Yes, wander round the place and visit bars just like you did in Munich. And while you're at it, don't forget to tell whoever's listening that you were in the Gestapo, and that you were known as the Ferret: I'm sure they will admire you all the more.' Ulrich paused and pointed his cigarette at the younger man. 'I don't think you have any idea how dangerous things are for us now in Europe. We are all at great risk. Just because the Americans and the British aren't quite as brutal as the Soviets doesn't mean the situation is any less perilous. They may not rape our women, but… Why are you laughing?'

'Because it sounds as if they've made rape legal. Maybe there's something to be said for them after all!'

'For heaven's sake, Friedrich, you're impossible. I was trying to explain that we're still in great danger here. If you're caught, they'll throw the book at you. I doubt your father will be able to come to your rescue then. You don't appreciate how fortunate you are that he's sorting out an escape line for you. Very few are able to get on one of those. You need to be grateful he's made arrangements. And you need to be patient too.'

Friedrich walked over to the window and opened the shutters to peer onto the quiet tree-lined avenue in front of the house. The previous day had been notable because five vehicles had driven past during the morning. Today he'd heard none. He closed the shutters and returned to the sofa, determined to be more conciliatory with Ulrich. He lit another cigarette for him and poured a beer; it was the only alcohol Ulrich would allow him to have, and even then he restricted him to three bottles a day.

'I've been here how long now, Ulrich – at least two months? And nothing's happened. I'm going to be forgotten about. I thought you were meant to be making plans – I mean, does my father know I'm still here?'

'Of course he does, and yes, I am making plans, but these things take time. I have to be very careful – it's not something we can rush into.'

'But in Munich I heard all these stories about organised escape routes from the Reich.'

'I'm afraid the Reich no longer exists.'

'You know what I mean – escape routes through Europe into Italy. I met a man in Munich who told me he was an SS *Obersturmbannführer* and that he was going to Genoa, from where a boat would take him to South America and—'

'I very much doubt that a genuine SS *Obersturmbannführer* would confide in a stranger like that, in Munich or anywhere else for that matter.'

'He told me in confidence, Ulrich.'

'Even if it's true, *Obersturmbannführer* is a very senior rank. The escape line that exist are for senior Nazis – SS, party officials, people suspected of major war crimes… To be blunt, Friedrich, you don't qualify on any of those grounds, which is why you're so lucky your father's sorting something out for you. What's the highest rank you reached in the Gestapo?'

'*Obersturmführer*, but I was due to be—'

'Well there we are then – a lieutenant. Look, you're not the only one in this position. I ended up as a *Sturmbannführer*, and even I'm not deemed important enough. I'm fortunate your father has asked me to look after you; that's my chance of escape.'

'So you owe me then?'

'Don't be so cocky.'

Friedrich fell silent and for a while appeared to be uncharacteristically reflective. 'So when?' he said eventually.

'Hopefully soon. The most pressing thing we need is money – we're running out of funds – but some will be arriving any day now.'

Charles Falmer was a long way from being the best qualified person for the job, but then it wasn't as if those who'd recruited him were exactly spoilt for choice.

For a start, it had to be someone they trusted, which certainly narrowed it down, and then they needed to be able to move around Europe, particularly Allied-occupied Germany, and that narrowed it down even further, so much so that they'd drawn a blank. Then Ridgeway remembered that his nephew Charles was working for the Royal Army Pay Corps in Cologne, and there was a lively discussion about how easy it was to get from Cologne to Frankfurt.

'It's around a hundred miles: shouldn't be difficult.'

'Yes, but one's in the American zone and the other's in the British: you need all kind of permits to move around.'

'But we're on the same bloody side; it's not as if we're expecting him to crawl under barbed wire!'

The discussion then turned to whether nephew Charles was up to it.

'Didn't you mention before that he was asthmatic and a rather nervous type?'

Ridgeway said that yes, he was asthmatic and generally not someone who enjoyed the best of health – he always seemed to have a stomach problem of one kind or another – but he was sympathetic to the cause and in any case who else did they have?

There was a bit of an argument at that point until the woman, who'd remained silent until now, said to stop acting like children and obviously it would have to be Ridgeway's nephew because there was no one else, and they'd just have to hope his stomach didn't play up. In any case, she said, she'd discussed the matter with the Admiral and he'd approve: the priority was to get the package to Germany, and he took a dim view of how long this was taking.

At first it had gone rather well. Falmer had managed to grab a few days' home leave, and once in London he came to collect the package and his instructions. It was larger than he'd anticipated.

'What were you expecting, Charles – a cheque?'

'No, but I thought maybe… an envelope?' They were in the tiny office in the West End art gallery, and his uncle and his business partner and the woman were all smoking, which he worried was going to trigger his asthma, but he didn't like to say anything. He stared at the package on his uncle's desk. It was just over a foot long and possibly nine inches deep; certainly not the kind of thing you could slip into your pocket. It was wrapped in brown paper and secured with string and tape. On the front was the stamp of a pharmacy in London, and the word 'medicine' was written on the front and the back in English and German.

No one had so much as glanced at it when he took it back to Cologne, where he kept it in a case under his bed at night and carried it round in his briefcase all day, every day, until he managed to get a pass to go to Frankfurt for the weekend. The officer who issued the passes gave him a knowing wink and said if he had any plans – another wink – to take care, and if he didn't take care then to enjoy it, but remember to see the medical officer as soon as he returned.

By the time Falmer arrived in Frankfurt, he was in a terrible state. He'd not slept for two nights and his stomach was playing up quite badly. As sympathetic as he was to the cause, he wasn't sure he was the right man for this job. The journey to Frankfurt had been painfully slow. The bus had had to negotiate its way through the damaged streets of the city, stopping frequently as carts carrying rubble moved out of its path. It stopped at the railway station, or at least what remained of it, and when Falmer asked an American soldier where the nearest public toilets were, he laughed at him and said about a hundred miles away.

He walked from the station to the small hotel on Allerheiligenstrasse that was reserved for Americans and other Allied officials. It was the only building in the street that appeared unscathed, and seemed pleasant enough. As he was checking in, an American officer told him that as long as he had dollars, there were a couple of decent cafés near the remains of the main post office, and gave him directions.

The handover was planned for ten o'clock the following morning, the Sunday. As Falmer washed in the stained basin in his room, he wondered what to do with the package in the meantime, eventually deciding to take it with him in his briefcase.

His downfall came in a small bar in an alley opposite the post office. He was in the alley because of what had been on his mind since a colleague had told him that the whole of the centre of Frankfurt was a red-light district, due to the fact that people were so desperate. 'It's about the only way they can earn dollars – women and men, even children!'

The first bar was noisy and full of American troops and women old enough to be their mothers, and the second felt so menacing he only glanced into it from the doorway. He spotted the third bar down a cutting off the alley, and it was just what he'd had in mind. It seemed much quieter, and more to the point, it had only men in it. As he edged nervously to the bar, teenage boys began to gather around him. *Are you American, sir? Do you have dollars? Buy me a drink, I will let you have whatever you want…*

He wasn't sure what to do. He felt intimidated and thought he ought to leave, but on the other hand… It was at that moment that a large man wearing a vest and smoking an enormous cigar sidled up to him. 'This is my place: you give me five dollars and choose a boy, then you go upstairs. When you're in the room, you pay the boy.'

Falmer looked at the boys watching him, all smiling expectantly. He was now wishing he wasn't there; he'd not expected it to be so blatant and so sudden. He'd somehow assumed he'd have time to assess the situation and make up his mind; he'd been hoping for something more discreet. Another couple of boys had gathered round, including one who looked no older than twelve. The man pushed up against him and spoke in a menacing tone.

'You choose a boy now and don't waste my time: five dollars.'

'I'd like to leave now... please.' Falmer was doing his best to sound authoritative, but he was aware he came across as anything but. He pushed past the man and headed towards a door he assumed was an exit, but instead found himself in a narrow corridor with a staircase at one end.

'To leave now, you pay ten dollars.'

He couldn't remember exactly what happened next and in what order, but he did recall the briefcase being wrenched from his grasp and his wallet being taken from his jacket pocket, and then being punched in the ribs as he was dragged to the exit and pushed onto the wet cobbles, which were so slippery he felt as if he were sliding on ice. He picked himself up and realised he wasn't hurt, but when he turned round, the door of the bar was shut. At that moment, half a dozen American troops appeared and he blurted out what had happened.

They told him not to worry and to wait outside. He heard much shouting from inside, and watched as everyone in the bar was thrown out and sent on their way. One of the Americans emerged carrying the briefcase.

The relief that swept over Charles Falmer didn't last long.

He was asked whether this was the briefcase and he said yes, and then the American opened it and peered inside.

'This is definitely your briefcase?'

Falmer said it was and he was terribly grateful, and it was only then that he noticed that the American – an officer – was looking at him suspiciously as he angled the briefcase for him to peer into. The parcel had been torn open and the case was full of American dollar bills and pound notes. He was so shocked that when the officer said you'd better come with me, Charles Falmer said yes, of course.

Frankfurt hadn't started well for Hanne and Prince. The Americans had taken over the IG Farben building off Fürstenbergerstrasse as their headquarters – it was one of the few large buildings left standing, and the rumour was that the Allied air forces had avoided hitting it so they'd have somewhere to use as a base.

Hanne and Prince went from office to office, from department to department and from floor to floor looking for someone who'd help. But no one had heard of a Friedrich Steiner, nor of *der Fluchtweg Falke* or anything to do with kestrels or any other bird, or of Nazi escape lines for that matter.

After two days they were inclined to give up, and telephoned Gilbey, who told them he was confident they'd get Steiner sooner or later and felt they'd done their best so should return to England. When they managed to telephone Henry that evening, he sounded upset, worried that his father wouldn't be coming home. They found the British liaison office in the building and arranged to get on a flight that was leaving in two days from RAF Wahn, just outside Cologne. The liaison officer – he'd introduced himself as Gibson – couldn't have been more helpful. They told him about their mission and how they'd hit a dead end in Frankfurt and couldn't find anyone to help them. He walked to the window, looking over the ruined landscape, then turned and spoke quietly.

'Something you said just then…'

'About the German – Steiner?'

'No, about Nazi escape lines: what was it?'

'We think Friedrich Steiner could have a possible connection to something called *der Fluchtweg Falke* – the Kestrel escape line.'

'This could be a total coincidence, of course, but a couple of days ago, the Americans arrested an Englishman found in a bar with a briefcase containing nearly one thousand dollars and five hundred British pounds.'

'That's an awful lot of money,' said Prince, 'but I'm not sure I see the connection with what we've been asking about.'

'His name is Charles Falmer and he's a clerk with the British Army in Cologne. As far as I can tell from our chaps there, he's not very important and wouldn't be earning much – probably no more than a hundred pounds a year. The only explanation he offered was that he was in Frankfurt for a weekend off and this was his spending money, which as explanations go was about as unconvincing as you can get. You've seen this place – who'd come to a bombsite like this to relax? With that amount of money he could have bought half the city. They asked us to have a word with him. According to the Americans, he was caught in one of those bars where men go to meet other men, and at first I thought that was why he was so reluctant to tell us anything, but it still didn't explain the money.

'The Americans were minded to charge him with currency violation – they're very anxious about their zone being flooded with dollars from the black market – and once I explained to him that this was a serious crime, he changed his tune and came up with a complicated story about how his uncle is an important art dealer in London and had given him the money to buy a painting from a man in Frankfurt. He said he was to meet the man in a small square called Elsa-Brändström-Platz, on Guiollettstrasse, where they have a flea market.'

Hanne and Prince looked at each other, still unsure of the point of the story.

'Frankly, his tale sounded ridiculous, like some cheap detective thriller: he said he was to meet a one-armed man who'd answer to the name "Kestrel". To be honest with you, I assumed he'd made it up. My commanding officer said we were wasting our time with him and we should allow the Americans to confiscate the dollars and then send him back to Cologne and let our chaps there deal with him. But when you mentioned Kestrel, I put two and two together, though I could be wrong, of course, it could just be a coincidence.'

Prince had been making notes in his little black book. 'Remind me of his name?'

'Charles Falmer, last name spelt with an "l".'

'And where is he now?'

'He's in the American cells in the basement: would you like to meet him?'

–

Before they were due to meet Falmer, Hanne and Prince had a row. She felt their investigation was too chaotic and Prince asked her what on earth she meant.

'In Berlin, I think we relied too much on the goodwill of the Russians.'

'But they're our allies, Hanne. I trust Gurevich; if it wasn't for him, you—'

'That's the point – you trust him too much, you see him as your friend. I agree he's very charming and I realise that if wasn't for him I'd probably be dead, but the fact is, we're not on the same side as them any longer, are we? I think we ought to have made more effort at the prison – we should have insisted on interrogating Alphonse Schweitzer once he'd given Rauter the Ferret's real name, and then we should have asked the Russians not to shoot the man who killed Rauter.'

'Klaus Böhme?'

'Yes, they shot him the same day: surely he ought to have been interrogated? Maybe he could have told us something. I think we need to stop wandering around Europe being grateful for the opportunity to ask a few questions here and a few questions there. We need to treat this like a serious criminal investigation. Remember, I worked in the major robbery unit at Norrebro when I was in Copenhagen. I'm experienced in dealing with complex crimes, and that's how I think we should treat this case. With respect, Richard, I know you're a senior detective, but maybe this is more my kind of crime, so please do let me take the lead when we question Falmer.'

Charles Falmer – Charles Denton Falmer, according to his papers – appeared at first to be grateful to see them, as if he believed they'd come to help him. It was an impression reinforced by the way Prince began the questioning, speaking in a friendly manner and checking Falmer's details – name, date of birth, address in England, where he worked in Cologne and the facts surrounding his arrest. More than once he said 'we ought to have this sorted in no time', and each time he said it, Falmer seemed to relax a little more. He appeared not to have shaved for a couple of days and was stroking his stubble, still unused to the novelty of it.

'And you understand why the Americans had to confiscate their dollars, do you, Charles? They have very strict regulations on how much of their currency they allow to be in circulation in their zone.'

Falmer nodded, and smiled at Hanne, who had still said nothing.

'And before you return to Cologne, it's likely the English money will be confiscated too.'

Falmer nodded again, more hesitantly than before, but both Hanne and Prince guessed he was thinking this might be the end of the matter.

'It's an awful lot of money, Charles – the five hundred pounds sterling alone is close to two decent annual salaries. What the hell were you doing with all that?'

Falmer shrugged and muttered something neither of them could hear.

'I beg your pardon?'

'I said my uncle runs an art gallery in London and gave me the money to purchase a painting. I told them that and they seemed satisfied enough.' He sat up straight in his chair and tossed his head back in a 'so there' manner, as if the explanation was perfectly reasonable.

Neither Prince nor his wife said anything as they watched the man in front of them. It was the familiar pose of someone who was frightened and worried but was concentrating a bit too hard on giving the impression that all was fine. They'd talked about this before, how suspects all too often put their efforts into appearing innocent rather than focusing on the subject matter of what they were being questioned about.

As the silence continued, Falmer appeared increasingly agitated. He moved around in his chair and ran his fingers through his thinning hair. According to his papers, he was forty, but he looked older, with a gaunt appearance and a pockmarked face. He fiddled nervously with his watch strap and adjusted the cuffs of his shirt. He was well-spoken, though with a voice as thin as his features, and Prince had noted that his background did not seem to match his status as a clerk in the Army Pay Corps.

At last Hanne leaned forward and nodded at her husband: *my turn*.

'I think you're talking nonsense, Mr Falmer!'

'I beg your pardon?' Charles Falmer looked both aggrieved and confused, not least at Hanne's accent. He gave the impression that he wasn't used to being spoken to like that, least of all by a woman and certainly not by one who sounded foreign.

'I – we – don't believe you. How about you tell us what happened, from the beginning?'

'I thought I'd already done so. I had the impression our meeting here was to sort out my return to Cologne. Surely having the money confiscated is going to be ample punishment?' Falmer addressed his remarks at Prince, ignoring Hanne.

She repeated her question, and they both noticed Falmer's air of defiance leak away as it dawned on him that this was a more serious business than he'd thought. He'd come to terms with being discharged from the wretched Pay Corps, and though he knew he'd have to face his uncle's wrath, his mother would ensure her brother wasn't too harsh on him. She'd tell him he had no right to send his nephew on such a ridiculous errand.

His hands started shaking and he clasped them together to keep them still as he started to tell his story again.

'My uncle is an art dealer in London, and when I was back on leave recently he said he was in touch with a chap in Frankfurt about buying a painting and would I mind popping down from Cologne to pick it up. He gave me some money wrapped up in a parcel so I had no idea how much it was – I never opened it, you see. I had it in my briefcase and when I went out for a meal on the Saturday night, I took it with me. I'd been told there were some decent restaurants near the main post office and I saw a bar on the way so I thought I'd stop in for a drink, and that's when someone tried to steal the briefcase – for all I know, they could even have put the money in there!'

'That's not how thieves tend to operate – in my experience they take money *out* of a bag rather than put it in.'

Falmer shrugged and again looked at Hanne as if he believed she had no right to speak to him like that.

'Your uncle the art dealer...'

'What about him?'

'I'd like his name and address, please.'

Falmer started to say something, but stopped and was now looking quite flustered. 'I'm not sure what the relevance is of—'

'The relevance, Mr Falmer, is that you're claiming the money came from your uncle in London who's an art dealer, so it is perfectly reasonable for me to ask his name.'

'Donald Ridgeway.'

'And his address?'

Falmer's foot was tapping hard on the floor. 'He's a partner at Bourne and Sons in Cork Street in the West End of London. I can assure you it's a very well-established and respectable business. I would imagine...' he paused to allow a weak smile, 'you are not familiar with the art market. If you were, you'd know it is perfectly common for paintings to be purchased from contacts in such a manner.'

'Buying a painting on the black market in Germany doesn't sound like the height of respectability to me, Mr Falmer. One can only imagine where the painting was looted from. Tell me, please, about how you were going to obtain it?'

'I was to go to a square off Guiollettstrasse, if that's how one pronounces it, at ten o'clock on the Sunday morning. There is a flea market of sorts there, and a one-armed man – which I know may sound somewhat clichéd – would be selling a painting of a kestrel. I was to give him the package and he'd give me the painting. It's as simple as that.'

'What is the man's name?'

'I have no idea – Hans, I would imagine, they're all called Hans, aren't they?' He laughed nervously and then stopped abruptly, as if he'd said something wrong.

–

'And you're sure you're telling me the truth, Ulrich – this isn't another excuse?'

Friedrich Steiner was pacing up and down the lounge of the safe house in Königstein like an angry animal, glaring at Ulrich as if he'd just challenged him to a fight and was awaiting his response. He paused by the window and pushed open the shutters, ignoring the other man's warning to be careful. He pulled hard on his cigarette and flicked the ash onto the floor.

'Will you please calm down and come and sit here,' Ulrich said. 'You're making me nervous walking around like that. I told you, it's just a setback.'

'For how long?'

'I don't know, I need to speak with your father. Maybe a few weeks. We needed the money the courier was bringing – without it, we have problems.'

'I really don't see why we need all this money.'

'Because, Friedrich, we're setting up a proper escape line for people like you and me. We need to pay for safe houses like this one, to arrange transport, buy false papers and bribe people. It's a very expensive business, far more so than you'd think. These people were meant to be helping us.'

'And the man who was meant to give you the money – do you think he ran off with it?'

'Sit down, Friedrich, and listen. He was arrested – wait, just listen. All he knew was to go to Elsa-Brändström-Platz, approach a one-armed man and ask how much the painting of the kestrel was, and that's how I'd get the money. We think he was arrested the night before. But he didn't know my name and he certainly doesn't know about this place, so it's not nearly as calamitous as it could be. There's something else, though...'

Friedrich was silent, sitting quite still as he stared at Ulrich through the smoke from his cigarette.

'We have a contact in Frankfurt, the IG Farben building off Fürstenbergerstrasse: it's the building where the Americans have their headquarters. A man and a woman – British, we think – were there to question this courier.'

'But you said he doesn't know about us.'

'Not quite, Friedrich. Apparently they were asking about *der Fluchtweg Falke* – and I'm afraid they also asked about you by name.'

Chapter 13

Germany, October 1945

'You seem somewhat shocked, Mr Falmer.'

'Do I?'

'Yes: I'd say you appear to be taken aback.'

'I would say I'm surprised rather than shocked: pleasantly surprised, though. I'd not expected that outcome.'

'Well as I say, Mr Falmer, you are fortunate that both the American and British authorities accepted your explanation that the money found in your possession was intended to be used for the purchase of paintings. We checked out your story, and there is indeed a market on Elsa-Brändström-Platz off Guiollettstrasse where paintings are traded, as well as an art gallery called Bourne and Sons in Cork Street. Furthermore, the American administration have consulted their lawyers, who are of the view that they handled the matter improperly from the outset, in that you were the victim of an alleged crime and therefore should not have been treated as a suspect in another crime.'

Prince stared at Charles Falmer, daring him to believe what he was telling him. It wasn't proving to be too difficult: Falmer looked pitifully grateful.

'Personally, Mr Falmer, I have to say I think you're most fortunate: the money is not being confiscated for procedural reasons more than anything else.' Hanne was managing to look aggrieved as she spoke. 'But there we are. My advice is to return to Cologne. A report will be passed to your superior officer, but he will be advised that no further action is being taken.'

There was a pause as an incredulous Charles Falmer smiled and glanced first at Hanne, then at Prince.

'Well, thank you very much indeed. I presume I'm free to leave now?'

They waited as he was led away to another office, where his briefcase was returned to him, and then stood at the window to watch his diminishing figure leave the building and walk across the rubble towards Fürstenbergerstrasse.

'Do you really think he believed us?'

'I hope so, Hanne. Don't you?'

'I'm not so sure. Yesterday we were telling him he'd committed a serious crime, and twenty-four hours later we inform him he's free to go, and by the way, here's all that money we apparently had such a problem with yesterday.'

'That's true, but don't forget he wants to believe it. That counts for an awful lot. You and I have enough experience of interrogating suspects to know how biddable they are.'

'What do you mean?'

'That they're easily persuaded: if you tell a suspect you believe he's innocent or admit there's no evidence against him, he's hardly likely to argue with you, is he?'

'That's true.'

'Anyway, even if this is something of a long shot, it's the only way we're going to have a chance of finding about Kestrel. Those two chaps following Falmer – see them there?'

Hanne nodded.

'They must be the Americans Gilbey sorted out – and there are more of them too, apparently. Let's hope they're as good as he says they are.'

–

They'd pulled more strings than there were in a large orchestra.

After interviewing Charles Falmer the previous day, both Hanne and Prince had agreed there was no question he was a link to the Kestrel escape line, and through that to Friedrich

Steiner. But now that he was in custody and the money confiscated, that lead appeared to have vanished.

They needed to find a way of restoring it.

They managed to get a call through to Tom Gilbey in London, and he in turn contacted the senior OSS officer in the IG Farben building, who promised to do what he could. The man from the Office of Strategic Services turned out to be as good as his word, not least in promising the services of an officer called Tim Sorensen.

That night, the three of them hatched a plan. Falmer would be informed – with a degree of ill grace that would hopefully make it appear more credible – that the case against him was being dropped on technical grounds, and that not only was he free to go – with the money – but that he should also consider himself a very lucky man.

'You don't think he'll be spooked?' Sorensen seemed keen to help but was struggling to conceal a degree of scepticism.

'In what way, Tim?'

'What I mean is, one minute he's being told he's committed a serious offence and is losing all that money, and the next he's being told he's free. In those circumstances don't you think the first thing he'll do is get the hell out of Frankfurt and go back to Cologne – or indeed, just disappear? With all that money, I'd be tempted to.'

'There is a risk of that.' Prince was nodding thoughtfully.

'I don't agree.' Hanne looked annoyed. 'He's a weak man. I have experience of dealing with criminal organisations; Falmer is probably fairly low down in this one and will feel accountable to the people above him. He's more likely to be spooked, as you put it, Tim, by the thought of what will happen if he leaves Frankfurt with the money. I believe he'll have come with instructions about what to do if the first rendezvous didn't work. It's inconceivable there wouldn't be a backup plan.'

They agreed that following his release, Charles Falmer would be followed. If he headed for the Hauptbahnhof and back to

Cologne, then the gamble would have failed. But it was a risk worth taking.

–

There was something close to a spring in Charles Falmer's step as he left the American headquarters. He couldn't relax completely, of course, but the worst part of the nightmare was over. His stomach no longer felt quite as wretched as it had done over the past few days, and he paused for a minute or two to breathe in fresh air.

It wasn't quite as fresh as it had first seemed. There was a definite early-winter bite to it along with the ubiquitous smell of burning. That was what he'd noticed in Cologne too: everything was being burned – wooden beams, ruined furniture, and some kind of filthy coal that exuded thick brown smoke and stuck to the back of the throat.

Falmer had asked the American officer who'd escorted him from the building for directions to the station, and he'd very helpfully pointed the way: *just over a mile south-west of here but probably longer given the detours you'll need to make.* He'd indicated a ruined building in the distance that seemed taller than the ones around it, twisted metal beams pointing accusingly at the sky. *Head for that, the station's nearby.*

Falmer walked slowly, mindful that most of the pavements were impassable and the roads could be dangerous, with the few vehicles on them not appearing to be subject to any kind of Highway Code. It wasn't an easy journey – not so much because of the detours the American had mentioned, but more due to the absence of many of the street signs. He paused on a street corner to buy a packet of cigarettes from a young girl and allowed himself a minute or so to gather his thoughts and get his breath back, although the acrid smell didn't make that easy.

He'd certainly been lucky, as the Englishman and the woman with the odd accent had repeatedly told him, though he considered that to an extent he'd been responsible for that luck – they ought to have at least acknowledged that. After all, he'd stuck to his story, and what he'd told them was, by and large, true. He was surprised they'd allowed him to have the money back, though, but then the Americans had been so heavy-handed, he wasn't altogether surprised they'd breached their own rules.

The little girl who'd sold him the cigarettes was pestering him to buy another packet, and in a rare moment of goodwill, he chucked a couple of coins from his pocket in her direction and watched in amusement as half a dozen children emerged from the rubble to scrap over the money.

He could head straight back to Cologne, but the consequences of that would be too serious. He just wanted to be shot of the money and put the whole sorry business behind him. Never again would he allow his uncle, or indeed anyone else, to talk him into something like this, no matter how much he agreed with the cause. Apart from anything else, his health wasn't up to it.

He'd memorised the instructions about where he was to go if the first rendezvous didn't work out, and reckoned he was now around five minutes' walk from his destination. He looked around to check that no one had followed him, but he needn't have worried. There were no Americans in uniform; just a few civilians shuffling along, all wearing more layers than usual of filthy clothing, heads bowed to avoid sharing their shame with someone they might know, and in case they should be fortunate enough to spot a cigarette end or some other treasure on the ground.

It took him longer than he'd anticipated to reach Kaiserstrasse; once there, he had to turn away from the direction of the station, so he waited in the doorway of a building that no longer existed and took time to light another cigarette, watching people walk slowly by. There was more of an edge to this area: it was the heart of the black market and there were signs of business being carried out deep inside the ruins and in the street – furtive conversations as an item was slipped from one pocket to another, money being palmed in the opposite direction. He moved along until he came to the junction with Moselstrasse, and was briefly thrown by the fact that the road ran in both directions off Kaiserstrasse, but then he spotted the sign he'd been told to look out for, crudely painted in black on what looked like the headboard of a bed.

Kartoffeln

Under the sign stood a cart piled high with potatoes, many of which appeared half rotten. Inside the remains of the building was a crudely built brick oven in which potatoes were being baked.

There's a woman on the stall, she'll be wearing a light blue headscarf. Ask if she's Gertrud.

'That's me. What do you want?'

Tell her you want two baked potatoes to take with you for your train journey.

'Of course: where are you travelling to?' She was paying him a bit more attention.

Karlsruhe.

Gertrud's bushy eyebrows lifted slightly. She'd now know he needed to contact the man called Ulrich, the one he'd failed to meet at the market on Brändström-Platz.

'Sure, no problem, I'll put two good ones on for you. Come over here, look at these – tell me if you think they look nice.'

She beckoned him closer, and as he leaned in to look at the potatoes, she spoke loudly in his ear, well above the volume of a whisper, her breath hot and flecked with spittle. 'Go round the block into Elbe Strasse; there's a stall there that sells soup. There's always a long queue, which will fortunately keep you occupied. Come back here in forty minutes, you understand that? Not before then. When you return, I'll take you to the back: Ulrich will be waiting there.'

'And how long ago was that?'

'Ten minutes ago. Two of my guys followed him into Mosel-strasse, where he headed straight to a stall selling potatoes. They saw him talking to a woman there. One of the team thinks he heard her telling him to come back: he was looking at his watch the whole time, still is.'

'And where is he now?' Hanne hadn't taken her eyes off the map of Frankfurt. Her finger was running along Moselstrasse.

'Seems he's in a queue in Elbe Strasse. There… the street behind.'

Her finger traced the map to Elbe Strasse. 'And they're watching him?'

'Of course.'

They were in the control room in the building on Fürsten-bergerstrasse as the messages came through intermittently from Sorensen's team following Charles Falmer.

Subject is still queuing for soup on Elbe Strasse, appears nervous.

Subject has purchased soup and is drinking it in a doorway, keeps looking at watch.

Subject on the move and…

The last message had broken up: the radio operator said it was distorted and they'd have to wait. The room filled with the sound of static, and Hanne stared at the operator as if it was his fault. It was five minutes before the messages resumed.

Subject is now back in Moselstrasse: has returned to potato stall.

Subject has moved into building behind potato stall: no longer in sight.

'They're going to lose them. Shouldn't they move in?'

'Be patient, Richard.' Hanne placed her hand on Prince's arm. 'They have the building covered.'

'But with the cellars… he could slip away.'

Sorensen assured them no one would slip away from his team of watchers and remained calm as Prince paced the room and

Hanne glared at the map and the radio operator in turn. The tension was broken by a burst of static followed by a deep voice.

Subject is leaving potato stall and now on Moselstrasse – following.

Subject now on Kaiserstrasse and heading west in direction of Hauptbahnhof.

Sorensen instructed the radio operator to tell them to keep watching the potato stall too.

Subject now crossing Hohenzollern Strasse and about to enter station.

Man carrying a rucksack and wearing a leather jacket and a woollen hat now leaving stall. Appears to have just one arm: request instructions.

'Did I hear him say it was a one-armed man?'

'Yes.'

'In that case, we have to follow both him and Falmer.'

'That's just what I was about to tell them.'

–

Ulrich had been shocked when he received the telephone call to tell him the courier had turned up at Moselstrasse. When he had failed to appear as arranged on Elsa-Brändström-Platz, he'd assumed that was it, and when he heard he'd been arrested by the Americans and was being held at IG Farben, he'd feared the worst.

Not in a month of Sundays had he expected to hear from the Englishman, but now here he was on Moselstrasse giving the correctly coded messages. Gertrud had told him to hurry: the man would be back soon.

Now he was waiting in the cellar of the building next to the potato stall, reflecting on how fortunate it was that he was in Frankfurt that morning. The ceiling had been destroyed, exposing the room to the rest of the building, but it had been patched up with boarding, and enough of the rubble had been swept away to accommodate an incongruous patch in the middle containing a rug and two dusty armchairs.

The Englishman was in a bit of a state when he climbed awkwardly into the cellar. He didn't look well, for a start, and there was a fresh soup stain down the front of his coat. He was carrying a small suitcase and a briefcase, which he clutched tightly to his chest when he sat down.

He said nothing as he glanced around anxiously, his eyes narrowing to adjust to the dim light. He had clearly forgotten his instructions.

'And you are…?'

He apologised profusely and said in quite reasonable German that his name was Michael and he was still interested in purchasing the painting of the kestrel.

Ulrich replied that that was no problem, that it was indeed still for sale but he would require the money first, and although the Englishman hesitated, he did open the briefcase, though with a degree of reluctance.

'It should all be there, but I'm afraid it's been rather messed up, what with one thing and another.'

Ulrich took the money out, not bothering to count it as he folded it into rolls, which he secured with string and placed in his rucksack, before handing the briefcase back to the Englishman. 'Thank you.'

'That's it?'

'That's it.'

'I don't need the painting?'

'An unnecessary touch.'

'But what if I'm stopped again?'

Ulrich shrugged as if he didn't really care. 'I'm sure you'll think of something to say. Tell me, what happened with the Americans?'

The Englishman told him it was nothing: they'd been concerned at the amount of US dollars and British money he was carrying but were satisfied with his explanation.

'That's all?'

'That's all. Perhaps I ought to leave now. I'm going to try and catch the train to Cologne.'

'I heard you were also questioned by the British?'

'Well, yes, after a fashion – but they must have been satisfied with my explanation too.'

'What did you tell them about meeting me?'

'I just told them I was buying a painting from a man at that market.'

'Did you give any details about me or the painting?'

The Englishman hesitated for far too long and shifted awkwardly in the armchair.

'I don't believe I did, no.'

'So how come they've been asking around IG Farben about Kestrel, and specifically about a man called Friedrich?'

The Englishman looked shocked. 'I really have no idea.'

Ulrich stared at him for a while. He didn't like what he saw and he certainly didn't like what he was hearing. The man was naïve and complacent at best. He didn't trust him when he said he'd revealed little detail about the market. On the other hand, as far as he could tell, the man hadn't been followed to Moselstrasse, and most importantly, Ulrich now had the money.

Wolfgang would be delighted. He could get the escape line working again and move Friedrich on.

He looked up: the Englishman was wringing his hands and had a sheepish grin on his face as if aware he'd done something wrong.

'May I go now?'

'I think you better had.'

After he had left, a man appeared from the shadows where he'd been hiding. He brushed the dust from his coat and hair and glanced at Ulrich, who looked relaxed in the armchair.

'You heard all that?'

The man from the shadows nodded.

'So you know what to do?'

He nodded again and left the cellar.

Sorensen's team followed the one-armed man in the leather jacket and woollen hat as he walked up Moselstrasse, crossing Kaiserstrasse before turning right into Taunus Strasse. Walt, the senior member of the team following him, said the man was a professional, increasing his pace without it being obvious and using classic techniques to be sure he wasn't being followed.

'I'm going to cut radio contact for a while. I'm worried he's heading for some kind of transport. I'll see what we can do.'

It was an hour before they heard from Walt again, during which time even the unflappable Sorensen began to appear agitated.

'He headed to Landstrasse, where there was a motorbike waiting for him: fortunately we'd pulled both our cars up by then and were able to follow him. He headed north-west out of Frankfurt and up into the Taunus mountains.'

'Where are you now, Walt?'

'A spa resort called Königstein; it seems really nice and peaceful.'

Sorensen arranged for a car to take the three of them to the town. The building Ulrich had been dropped at was a former guest house set in a quiet road with the mountains looming behind it. They met Walt diagonally opposite the house in an abandoned building he'd taken over.

'The roof's damaged, but as far as we can tell, the building is inhabited. We've been watching it for an hour now, maybe a bit longer. The ground floor seems to be very secure, and there is some movement on the first floor. The windows are shuttered, but we're working on the assumption that they can see what's going on outside. I've got three men watching the rear and the sides, and two at the front.'

'I don't suppose you have any idea of how many people are inside?'

'My guess is at least two. We watched the one-armed man go in, and there was definitely someone moving around the first floor when he arrived.'

'Is there any reason why you can't call for backup and move in?' Prince was watching the house through binoculars.

'No,' said Hanne. 'We want to find out what we can about the Kestrel escape line. Going in like that could mean everything ending in chaos. Let's wait and see what happens. They may have other visitors after all.'

Sorensen decided that they'd watch the house overnight and into the following day, and if nothing had happened by the late afternoon – by which time the one-armed man would have been inside for twenty-four hours – they'd move in.

They didn't need to wait that long.

It had been dark for an hour when a side door opened and two figures moved furtively along a path from the house towards the quiet road in front of it.

The instructions had been that in the event of this happening, they should be allowed to move clear of the house before being challenged. Somehow word hadn't got through to everyone, because no sooner had the two figures emerged than there was a shout, an order in German to halt, then another shout, followed by a volley of pistol shots. Prince heard Sorensen bellow orders over the radio to move in and stop them. 'We need to keep the perimeter secure!' But it was too late: the two figures had ducked back into the house, and were now firing from a ground-floor window. It was then that Prince heard the crack and whistle of a shot, and Hanne screaming behind him, followed by the searing pain in his shoulder.

He was aware of feeling light-headed and nauseous, and felt Hanne's arm round him as she told him to sit down. Across the road, the Americans were still trying to force their way into the house. Suddenly Hanne shouted out and pointed to what appeared to be the same two figures emerging from the shell of a house two doors along.

But in the chaos, no one heard her, and they could only watch as the two figures hurried to the roadside, reaching it just as a jeep pulled up, the men jumping in as it sped away. By the time, the Americans realised what was going on, it was too late. A couple of them opened fire at the jeep, but its taillights were already dimmer than the stars above them.

–

Dusk was descending on Cologne as the train from Frankfurt finally pulled into Köln Hauptbahnhof. It had been a long journey, delayed because of speed restrictions, or damage to the track, or for no apparent reason at all.

Two of Walt's team had followed Charles Falmer onto the train. Prince had made it clear that they should leave him for as long as possible: they needed to see where he went and what he did. The train was crowded, and Walt's men watched as Falmer found a place in an eight-seater compartment towards the front. They split up, one of them positioning himself at the front of the carriage, the other at the rear.

The train emptied slowly in Cologne, the two Americans waiting for the Englishman to leave so they could follow him. But soon the trickle of passengers dried up, and Charles Falmer had certainly not been among them.

They found him apparently asleep in a corner seat by the window, the brim of his trilby tipped low over his face, his briefcase wedged between him and the side of the carriage.

The two Americans looked at each other. One of them shook him by the shoulder as the other checked his pulse. Both shook their heads. They knew that whatever happened, this would reflect badly on them. They checked him over for any clues. The body was still warm and the blood that had seeped onto the seat from where he'd been stabbed in the back was still bright red and not yet too sticky.

'It must have just happened,' one of them said.

The other nodded. It was hardly much of a consolation.

Chapter 14

'Sir Roland is in the library if would you care to follow me, Mr Gilbey.'

Tom Gilbey assured the steward he knew where the library was, thank you very much, but the response was a fleeting smile and a slight bow of the head as the man stepped towards the stairs, indicating that the visitor should follow.

They found the ample figure of Sir Roland Pearson on the first floor, wedged into a high-backed club chair positioned between two tall dark oak bookcases of Victorian literature that cast him in a valley of gloom. A brass and green glass lamp threw some light in his direction. He waved a leather-bound volume at Gilbey by way of greeting. A shaft of sunlight caught the small cloud of dust from the book.

'*Our Mutual Friend* – one of Dickens' finest and most underestimated novels; I must reread it. My maternal uncle Wilfred made a point of reading it twice a year, every Easter and Christmas. "And O there are days in this life, worth life and worth death."'

'Pardon, Roly?'

'It's a quote from the book, part of a passage I had to read out at his funeral. I'm afraid I rather blubbed at the time. Thankfully it was a sparsely attended event – Wilfred didn't marry, you know; bachelorhood is something of a family tradition, one I'm afraid I've followed.'

Sir Roland was gazing out of the window, the autumn afternoon's weak sun catching his watery eyes. He blinked and turned to face his visitor, inviting him to speak.

'From what I hear, Roly, you now have all the time in the world to catch up on your reading.'

'Is this visit business or pleasure, Tom – I'm presuming the former?'

Gilbey nodded and Sir Roland slowly stood up. 'There's a room along the corridor where we can have a private chat. I'm never too sure what one should drink at three o'clock in the afternoon; it's one of those neither-here-nor-there times, don't you find?'

The steward had followed them and was standing expectantly in the doorway.

'We'll have two large whiskies, Barker, and a jug of water, please. The club's own malt is terribly good, Tom.'

'I didn't know you were a member of Boodle's, Roly.'

'There's a lot you don't know about me.'

Gilbey laughed briefly and the two men sat in the dusty silence for a while as the steward poured their whiskies.

'It's not on my file then, Tom?'

'What isn't, Roly?'

'That I'm a member here.'

'It would be the Security Service who'd hold it rather than us. They've probably got a file on me too.'

The two men laughed and wished each other good health, and Gilbey asked Pearson what he made of the new prime minister.

'Too early to say, Tom: he's hardly had time to unpack his overnight bag. Looks a bit like Trotsky, don't you think?'

'I think you may mean Lenin.'

'You're quite right: let's hope that's the only similarity, eh? He had me out of Downing Street soon enough.' There was a distinctly resentful tone to Pearson's voice.

'Well he would do, wouldn't he, Roly? You were Winston's appointment as his personal intelligence coordinator or whatever your title was. You can hardly blame Attlee for that.'

'Nonetheless, one does feel rather cast out – nearly six years I worked for Winston, hardly a day off, and then just to be sent packing… but hey ho. This is where one rather realises being married would help. They tend to push you, do they not, Tom?'

'In what sense, Roly?'

'Well, you're married, so you'd know better than me, but from what one gathers, wives are rather ambitious for their husbands – they don't like them to become complacent, eh: not keen on them sitting around and moaning.'

Gilbey nodded and muttered, 'Maybe.'

'Winston asked me if I'd like an embassy after the war – he even went so far as offering me Brussels, and I foolishly turned it down. A wife would have made sure I took it.'

'I remember, Roly: you asked me if I'd be interested.'

'Flemish rather put me off. It's like having to speak backwards, like that funny made-up language we used in prep school. By the time the war ended and Winston lost the election, I was exhausted and complacent, which a wife would have soon seen to. Hadn't given much thought to what I'd do after it. So now I spend my days here at the club drinking malt and getting emotional over books.'

'Something in the City, maybe?'

Pearson scowled at him.

'How is Winston these days?'

He shrugged his shoulders. 'Licking his wounds at Chartwell – they've bought a rather nice place in Hyde Park Gate, though. He's talking about writing a history of the war: I told him he needed a decent agent.'

'I understand he has one already. So you do see him?'

'Went down last weekend. Hardly saw Winston, as he was busy painting clouds or something, but I did have lunch with them. He barely said a word; just sat there brooding. I think it was Clemmie who really wanted to see me.'

'Why's that?'

'A cousin of hers – second or third, something rather distant in any case – was killed in Munich in August. She wanted to know if I knew of anyone who might know something about it. Whole thing's shrouded in mystery and is rather hush-hush, but then she told me he was SOE and I thought, well, yes, of course it's shrouded in bloody mystery. Didn't say that to her, of course. Promised I'd ask a few questions. Didn't realise the SOE was still going.'

'They're tying up loose ends. Is the cousin Christopher Stephens?'

'Yes, that's the chap: he must be one of the loose ends.'

'F Section?'

'So I believe.'

Gilbey turned round to check the door was closed, then leaned forward. 'Actually, Roly, it's in connection with that case that I wanted to talk to you.'

The other man's eyebrows lifted, and for the first time a hint of smile crossed his face. 'Really, Tom?'

'Yes, Roly. I have a job that may be just up your street. It will get you out of this place, at any rate.'

–

A few days before Tom Gilbey met with Sir Roland Pearson, he'd had an awkward session with Prince and Hanne in his office in St James's.

'And are you both well?'

They'd looked at him somewhat incredulously. Prince gingerly held up his arm, which was still in a sling. 'Well, if you discount being shot in the shoulder, sir, and everything else…'

'I'm told it's barely more than a graze?'

'I'd hardly describe it like that, sir: the doctor said it was just inches from an artery.'

'One doesn't want to play down the fact that you were shot, Prince, and I'm no anatomist, but surely anywhere in the human body is just inches from an artery?'

In the silence that followed, he clapped his hands and mumbled something along the lines of 'but well done anyway', then came round from his desk to sit in an easy chair close to theirs.

'Apologies if I appear to be flippant. I understand Frankfurt had mixed results.'

Prince shifted in his chair and his wife coughed. Gilbey gestured for her to speak. She explained patiently how they'd been getting nowhere in Frankfurt until a British officer there told them about the Englishman who'd been caught with a bundle of cash, and the fact that he was due to give it to someone in exchange for a painting of a kestrel.

'*Fluchtweg Falke.*'

'Exactly, the Kestrel Line. His account was confused: he'd initially told the Americans the he was meeting a man called the Kestrel, but he told us that the painting he was to buy was of a kestrel – no doubt he was nervous, hence the confusion. But as you know, Tom, we felt this was a lead – we know there's a link between Friedrich Steiner's father and the Kestrel Line, and Charles Falmer appeared to be something to do with Kestrel too.'

'Remind me how much cash he had on him?'

'Five hundred pounds, sir, along with a thousand American dollars.'

'Good Lord… to buy a painting that may or not be of a kestrel at a street market in Frankfurt? Was it painted by Rembrandt?'

'We believed that if the money was returned to Falmer, there was a chance he could lead us to the Kestrel Line, and we are grateful for your help with getting the Americans to agree to that.'

'But it didn't quite work out?'

'Yes and no.' Prince leaned forward as he spoke, wincing with pain. 'Charles Falmer was followed by the Americans and he appeared to have headed to a fall-back rendezvous point, which we hoped he would do. When he left this place – a potato stall – he was followed to the station. The Americans also spotted a man with one arm, whom they followed to a small spa town just outside Frankfurt called Königstein. We went up there with an American officer called Sorensen. I'm afraid the Americans didn't handle matters terribly well.'

'So I hear: the Germans escaped?'

'Turns out the cellar of the guest house was linked to the cellars of neighbouring houses, and they got out that way. They must have made a telephone call, because they escaped in a stolen American army jeep.'

'And one of them shot you, Prince?'

'Yes, sir.'

'Do we know whether one of the two was Friedrich Steiner?'

'We know one of them was definitely the one-armed man who was followed from Frankfurt – Sorensen's team had a good view of him. Hanne saw the other chap better than I did, sir.'

'I spotted them when they emerged from the other house. They were across the road, so all I can say is that one of the men had one arm and the other was quite young, possibly late twenties or early thirties.'

'Similar age to Steiner.'

'Yes, sir. I had to look after Richard because I didn't know how badly injured he was, and also I didn't have a gun. If I had, I could have got closer to them.'

'So it's a fair assumption it was Friedrich Steiner?'

'In so far as we established a link to the Kestrel Line, yes, sir. It's not proven, of course, but if I were investigating this as a crime, I'd say he was a likely suspect.'

'And he got away?'

'Yes, sir, I'm afraid so. The jeep was found abandoned the following day in a town called Bad Kissingen, which is about fifty miles due east of Königstein. No sign of them after that.'

'The Americans let stolen jeeps drive around their zone, do they?' Tom Gilbey shook his head and then let it rest in his hands as he closed his eyes in thought, before standing up and walking over to the window, looking out of it as he spoke.

'The problem I have is whether we can afford to carry on with what may well be a wild goose chase.' He paused and turned round to face them, looking down at the carpet, his hands thrust deep into his trouser pockets. 'I fully appreciate that I told you hunting down the Ferret was regarded as a debt of honour by my friend Charles Lean, and that I had assumed the obligation on his behalf, and you have done terribly well to establish that the Ferret is this Friedrich Steiner. But whether it is right to have you two continuing to run round Europe looking for him, I'm not sure…'

'But he's a war criminal, sir, surely?'

'He is indeed, but I'm afraid Europe is teeming with them. There are literally thousands of former SS and Gestapo officers who did the most dreadful things, many if not most of them far more senior than Friedrich Steiner. Now, my superior, Roland Bentley, has caught wind of this, and while he fully understands my involvement, he does wonder if…' He trailed off and turned back to the window.

'Are you suggesting we drop the case?'

'We have Friedrich Steiner's name. It's on our watch lists. Sooner or later we're bound to find him. I'd love to get stuck into these Nazi escape lines, but I fear it's not a priority at the moment.'

Prince nodded, but Hanne shook her head angrily.

'You're forgetting a possible British connection – what about Charles Falmer? I know he was murdered on the train and the money wasn't with him, but surely that all points to something going on here.'

'That would be a matter for the Security Service or Special Branch.' Gilbey had returned to his seat alongside theirs. 'Richard knows all about that – your last case involved Nazi sympathisers in this country.'

'Yes, sir, and I have to say I believe Hanne is right, actually. There certainly seems to be a very strong case to be made for saying that Falmer was probably a courier, bringing money from London to help fund the Kestrel Line. If that's true, then surely there's an obligation to investigate further – after all, we know about this art gallery, don't we? If we find out what's going on here, it could open up the Kestrel Line for us.'

'I suppose I could argue that as we came across this intelligence while on an operation overseas, we can justify continuing the investigation here. After all, we don't want to be presenting gifts to the Security Service after we've done all the hard work, do we?'

Hanne and Prince both said they agreed.

'We'd better keep you chaps out of it at this end – Prince, you're known from your last investigation, and in any case it's possible that word about you may have got back here from Germany, you never know. You go back to Lincoln; I imagine you'll be wanting to see your boy, won't you? If anything crops up and it's worth reopening the case, I'll be in touch. You have my word.'

He leaned forward and shook hands with both of them rather formally.

'And who will investigate matters here, sir?'

'I have just the man in mind.'

–

There was a certain confidence in Sir Roland Pearson's step as he turned from Old Bond Street into Burlington Gardens. For the first time in weeks, the fog of lethargy that had hung over him was lifted.

Sir Roland took the view that his life was unquestionably made up of more achievements than setbacks, though he was aware that one of his failings was to dwell far too much on the latter, and he'd certainly been doing plenty of that recently.

Early in 1940, Winston Churchill had appointed him to his staff at Downing Street, where his role was to coordinate the activities of the various intelligence and security agencies. It was a job that was hard to define and even harder to get right, but he very quickly proved to be indispensable. He was in many ways an invisible man: no one outside Whitehall and the intelligence agencies knew of him, but for those who did, he was all-powerful. He had, as people would say, 'Winston's ear'.

But when Winston lost the election, he had nowhere to go other than his apartment overlooking Birdcage Walk, and his club. It was from Boodle's that Tom Gilbey had rescued him with the offer of the mission he was now embarking on. He had done his homework and it all sounded rather fun.

From Burlington Gardens he turned into Cork Street. He made sure he took his time, strolling along without any apparent care in the world and visiting at least three other galleries before finally coming to Bourne and Sons. Only two days previously, one of Gilbey's men – something of a know-all on art by all accounts – had visited the gallery and written a most helpful brief for him.

A bell rang uncertainly at the back of the small gallery as he entered. It was darker inside than he'd have expected, though there were lights above some of the paintings. His shoes echoed loudly on the wooden floor and the room had a musty smell. For a moment or two he was alone, though he did hear some movement at the back. He soon spotted what he was looking for and made sure he was studying it when a figure appeared at his side.

'May I be of assistance, sir?' What Sir Roland noticed wasn't so much the accent, more the tone of voice, the keen-to-oblige, very slightly servile tone, one that wanted to assure the listener that the speaker was of a certain class.

'I beg your pardon?'

'I was wondering if I could help you, sir?'

Sir Roland Pearson was now Anthony Hawke – Hawke being his maternal grandmother's maiden name. He'd decided that Hawke should be not nearly as clubbable as Pearson, so he muttered something unintelligible and continued to stare at the painting as he removed his spectacles and put them on again. Then, without looking at the other man, he pointed at it and nodded approvingly.

'A Richard Wilson, I see.'

'Indeed, sir: the father of English landscape painting.'

Hawke shot him a questioning look. 'Wilson was Welsh.'

'Indeed, sir, but very much the father of the early English school of landscape artists.'

'If one disregards Gainsborough,' said Hawke. He laughed and the other man gratefully joined in, then asked his visitor's name.

'Anthony Hawke: Hawke with an "e".'

'You certainly are most knowledgeable, Mr Hawke. One does so appreciate meeting a connoisseur.'

'And may I ask your name?'

'It's Ridgeway, Donald Ridgeway. Are you by any chance interested in the Wilson?' Ridgeway was fidgeting with his cuffs and clasping and unclasping his hands in a hopeful manner.

Hawke didn't reply, but moved deeper into the gallery, where he spotted the painting Gilbey's man had briefed him about.

'I say, is this a Joseph Wright of Derby, by any chance?'

'It is indeed, sir, very well spotted if I may say so. The signature is hard to decipher, but we do have full provenance, I can assure you.'

'I do so admire Wright's bold use of light and dark: his landscapes are quite exquisite. This is a fine example – the hills almost seem to move. May I ask...?'

'The price, sir? Yes, of course: it is two hundred and thirty guineas, but I'm sure…'

His voice tailed off as Hawke nodded in a manner to suggest disappointment. 'My brother-in-law paid a hundred guineas for a Wright of Derby landscape before the war.'

'Before the war indeed, as you say, sir, and if I may mention, quite a number of landscapes are attributed to Wright of Derby rather than being certified as having been painted by him.'

Anthony Hawke said he quite understood and went back to look at the Wilson. After a few minutes, he asked Ridgeway if he had any George Lamberts.

'No, sir, but I may be able to find one if you're interested. You are an admirer of landscapes, I see.'

Anthony Hawke said that indeed he had a weakness for English landscapes, and Ridgeway said yes, but did he have the wallet for them, and chuckled before apologising, but Hawke said no, not at all.

He paused and moved back to the Joseph Wright and decided now was the time. It was a small oration Sir Roland Pearson had very much enjoyed preparing, and he spoke quietly with just the slightest catch of emotion in his voice as he told Ridgeway how English landscapes in particular evoked for him the true essence of England, of a country and a time fast fading like a watercolour, along with its traditional values and its… morals. He apologised for being sentimental and said he wondered what on earth we'd just wasted the best part of six years fighting a war for when… then hesitated before adding, 'Can you really call it a victory?'

Ridgeway had moved closer to him, shuffling from foot to foot but remaining silent.

'I'm terribly sorry; I'm probably speaking out of turn,' Hawke continued. 'My wife does warn me to bite my lip, but when one sees what is happening in Europe and one is told by those who are running matters to accept what is going on, one does really question the outcome.'

He coughed and walked over to a portrait of a man in eighteenth-century dress. Ridgeway had dutifully followed.

'I'm pleased to see you have nothing by the likes of Pissarro.' He phrased it as a question and looked at Ridgeway for an answer.

Ridgeway shook his head. 'We make a point of not selling paintings by Jewish artists – nor indeed Soviet ones, not that there are any!'

Sir Roland smiled but didn't reply: he'd gone as far as he dared. Ridgeway came uncomfortably close and grasped Hawke's hand in his own, which was bony and slightly moist. He shook it enthusiastically, taking too long to let go.

'It's a great honour, Mr Hawke, to meet someone of your standing with whom one so clearly agrees. I too feel that maybe...' He stopped and looked at the door and then towards the back of the gallery. It was clear that he wanted to be certain they were alone and was unsure whether to continue.

'You feel what, Ridgeway? I'm sure we can be frank with each other, eh?'

'There are like-minded people I'm sure you would enjoy meeting: people who view the world in the way you and I do and who endeavour to do something about it.'

Anthony Hawke stepped back. 'I say, Ridgeway, I hope you don't think I'm some kind of collaborator?'

'Good heavens no, sir – quite the contrary. I'm talking about patriots. If you care to come back this time the day after tomorrow, I'd be more than happy to explain further.'

Chapter 15

Germany, October 1945

They arrived at the Moser farm in the Rott Valley late at night, four days after escaping from Königstein.

Wolfgang Steiner was expecting them, though it had to be said with a feeling of dread: for a father-and-son reunion it was marked by a noticeable air of tension, one bordering on hostility. The first Wolfgang had heard about the events in Königstein had been a coded telephone call two days before from Nuremberg.

I have two bull calves for you. I need to deliver them as soon as possible.

His heart had sunk. He'd told Ulrich very clearly that he didn't want him anywhere near the farm, and he especially didn't want his son anywhere near it. He regretted having given Ulrich the address: he'd told him it was only to be used in extreme emergency: *bull calves*. He'd replied that he'd changed his mind and didn't want the calves after all, thank you very much. He was sure there were other farms who'd happily take them.

I have to deliver them quickly – there is no other option.

'Perhaps take them to Austria and then head south?'

Not possible, but don't worry, they'll be transported with great care.

He'd felt his chest tighten and Frau Moser had given him a quizzical look as she passed through the hall. 'In that case, deliver them after dark.' He'd paused, realising he needed to give more explicit instructions. He couldn't afford to risk things going wrong. 'There's a small wood above the farm: wait there until nightfall. Only come down to the farm when you see a light go on in the upstairs room facing the wood.'

He'd explained to Frau Moser that two comrades of his were coming to visit and she wasn't to worry, they'd only stay for a day or two and they'd remain in the cellar. He'd rather she didn't get into conversation with them. They didn't arrive that night, but the following night he'd only been waiting inside the open barn for a few minutes when two figures emerged from the pitch darkness and walked uncertainly into the farmyard. Wolfgang whistled for them to come over to the barn.

'Are we staying in here? It's fucking cold – I was hoping for somewhere warm, along with a bath and a decent meal.'

'Is that the way you greet your father?'

Friedrich Steiner shrugged and mumbled some kind of apology, then asked for a cigarette.

'I trust Frau Moser, but the less she knows the better, so we'll talk out here. Tell me what happened.'

Friedrich began to speak, but Ulrich interrupted him.

'The Englishman didn't turn up at Elsa-Brändström-Platz on the Sunday and nor did he come to the fall-back point on Moselstrasse the next day. However…' he paused to inhale deeply from the cigarette Wolfgang had given him, 'I then heard he'd been arrested because of currency violations and was being held in the IG Farben building on Fürstenbergerstrasse. In addition, a pair of British officers – a man and a woman – had turned up there and were asking about *der Fluchtweg Falke* and about Friedrich.'

'It's not funny, Friedrich – why on earth are you smiling?'

'I'm not saying it's funny, Father, but it's like I'm famous!'

'You've not learnt your lesson, have you? Continue, Ulrich.'

'To my surprise, a couple of days later the Englishman arrived at the potato stall on Moselstrasse with all the right codes, and so I went to see him: he still had all the money, so I took it and sent him on his way to Cologne.'

'Really?'

'Not quite. I couldn't allow him to stay alive, not with him having met me and with all those questions... I had a man follow him and made sure he didn't arrive in Cologne.'

'Good. I presume it was made to look like a robbery.'

'I hope so.'

'Because the last thing we want to do is alienate our friends in England. They may stop being so generous.'

'But I thought you said they need us as much as we need them?'

'Well, let's see. Tell me what happened after that.'

'Your instructions were that once we had the money we must start out on our journey, so I called the comrade who was going to take us on the next stage. He was going to pick us up outside the house, but when we came out, there were Americans waiting for us: I fear they may have followed me to Königstein. Fortunately we had our revolvers drawn and we were smarter than them. Friedrich hit one of them, and we managed to get back into the house and from there through the cellars into another house. The comrade picked us up outside that one. I don't suppose you have a drink?'

'You'll get one inside – I want to hear what happened first.'

'The comrade was very good, Wolfgang: he'd picked us up in an American jeep, and after a few miles we pulled into a farm and he left the jeep there. We waited until dawn, when he drove us to Würzburg in another car. He then returned to the jeep and left it in Bad Kissingen to put them off our scent.'

'Very thorough – as I would expect.'

'We stayed in Würzburg with the widow of a comrade for a day and then took separate buses to Nuremberg.'

'From where you called me.'

'The priest who looked after us in Nuremberg – he kept asking for more money and I felt I had to give it to him. He seemed very nervous, and when I told him he was supposed to arrange our journey on to Salzburg, he said he didn't realise that.

I said of course you did and he asked for even more money, and that's when I became very concerned: I wasn't sure I trusted him and I thought the safest thing was to come here. The money's all in that rucksack – apart from what I had to use.'

Wolfgang took them into the house, where they sat silently in the kitchen as Frau Moser served them a stew, eyeing them suspiciously as she fussed nervously around the table. Friedrich grumbled as they were shown into the cellar, but his father told him to shut up. He'd sort something out, he said, but it would take a few days. They were only to leave the cellar when told to do so.

They weren't allowed out until later the following afternoon, once the milk had been collected and the farm labourer had left. While Friedrich had a bath, Wolfgang took Ulrich into the cowshed.

'You know that this was the last place on earth I wanted Friedrich to come, don't you?'

'Yes, sir, you told me, but the priest worried me and I felt you'd be furious if anything happened to us, and to the money, of course, and—'

'Very well. Just listen, Ulrich – listen carefully and calm down. I don't want you to misunderstand me. I love Friedrich very much and I want to ensure that he's safe, and that's why he's on the Kestrel Line and I'm doing what I can for him. But I also have to recognise that he's prone to – how can I put it? – to irrational behaviour at times. He can be wayward and irresponsible. That's why I didn't want him here – I wanted him south of the Reich as soon as possible. And there's a more important reason too.' He paused and looked around him: they were alone in the cowshed, the cattle shuffling and snorting around them. 'This farm... I have to ensure it is kept secure. You know who this place is for, Ulrich?'

Ulrich shook his head, and Wolfgang beckoned him closer. As they leaned on the rails, they were just inches from the head of a cow, which looked quizzically at them, surprised to have been allowed in on the secret.

'The purpose of the Kestrel Line and this farm – and all the money – it's for a special person. Helping you, Friedrich and the others, that's a secondary part of it. Originally I found this place as a refuge for me, but it evolved: now the main aim is to help one man.'

'Can I ask who it is?'

'If you tell a soul, you'll be killed. Friedrich in particular must never know. No one else must know. I'm telling you because I trust you and because you need to know why you have to move on from here. Put that cigarette out, you shouldn't smoke in here... It's the Reichsleiter.'

Ulrich stepped back in shock and gripped the rail. The cow nuzzled his hand.

'He's alive?'

'I'm not sure, Ulrich, I'm really not sure... I've not heard anything for months, but we do know he hasn't been captured, and no one has announced that he's dead, so that must give us hope. My guess is he's still alive and hiding in or around Berlin. He may have found somewhere safe and doesn't want to risk putting his head above the parapet: that's what I'm hoping anyway. If we can get him out of Berlin and down here, and then move him along the Kestrel Line... You do understand the importance of this, don't you, Ulrich? If we can rescue him and get him somewhere safe, then who knows what the future holds. People would take heart that he is alive, and he would become our new Führer!'

'But how will you find out where he is?'

'I'm going to have to go to Berlin, God help me.'

–

Wolfgang Steiner was taking a risk he wouldn't have taken for anyone else, apart from Hitler himself.

The Reichsleiter had been his mentor, ensuring his successful career at the Parteikanzlei. But after that night back in March at the Bauhaus villa on the Kleiner Wannsee, he owed him an even bigger debt. It was then that Bormann had revealed he knew all about his plans to escape and hide in the Rott Valley, and the fact that he'd been photographing documents. At one stage Steiner was convinced the Reichsleiter was about to pronounce his death sentence; that at any moment the door would burst open and he'd be carted away to Prinz-Albrecht Strasse, or even shot there and then and dumped in the Wannsee. But instead, Bormann had been quite amenable, even friendly. He'd told him he wanted to be part of his arrangements; that he knew many people in Berlin were making arrangements to escape, but he trusted very few of them. 'Apart from you, of course: I'm counting on you, Wolfgang,' he'd said.

They'd spoken long into the night, about how Steiner should get out of Berlin as soon as possible and go to the farm to ensure it was secure and that no one knew about it. Bormann wanted him to set up his own escape route from there, one that would have nothing to do with the others being organised at the moment. This would be for the Reichsleiter's exclusive use, its security not compromised by allowing others to use it.

'You're one of the few people I know and trust who has the skills and the attention to detail to set up something reliable. The only matter to be resolved is when I leave Berlin.' He'd paused at that point, leaning back and shutting his eyes, wisps of cigar smoke rising above him. He seemed to be lost in his thoughts for a long while, and when he spoke again, it was in a quieter voice, the tone less upbeat. 'When I was younger, I went hiking in the southern Alps, in the eastern Tyrol. Did you go hiking in the Alps, Steiner?'

'No, I'm afraid not – my asthma, you know.'

'Really? I thought all Austrians loved the Alps – this was a particular range called the Gailtal Alps. I was with my friend Klaus, but he twisted his ankle on the second or third day so I was on my own, but that was fine. One afternoon I was on a difficult climb and reached a point where I could rest, so I leaned against the rock face and had a drink. The air was so pure I felt it could nourish me, there was no wind, it wasn't cold, the sun shone on me and there was utter silence. It was an almost perfect moment, but then I became uneasy. I was convinced I was being watched and I looked around but couldn't see a thing. It was the strangest feeling. You know me well enough, Wolfgang, to appreciate that I'm a straightforward man: many people in our movement believe in darker forces, but I've never been one of them. Then I looked up and saw a kestrel hanging in the sky just a few feet above me, its beady eyes staring at me as if trying to work out if I could be prey.

'It's like that in the bunker: beady eyes looking at you all the time. Everyone does it – I probably do it too. So I have to be careful, Wolfgang. I will have to leave the bunker at the last possible moment; to do so before that would be suicide. But if I know that you are making arrangements for me, that my fate is in your hands, I will feel more confident. That will help sustain me during the difficult times ahead.'

They'd discussed the route of the escape line and how Bormann would contact him. Steiner gave him the telephone number of the farm and they agreed a code – a message from Jens, a cousin in Essen.

'Make a note of these contacts in Berlin, Wolfgang: it may be easier for us to make contact through one of them.'

Once Bormann was satisfied that Steiner had memorised the details, they agreed they needed a code name for his escape.

'Kestrel would seem appropriate in more ways than one, Reichsleiter, what with your connection and the route.'

They agreed. It would be the Kestrel Line.

Der Fluchtweg Falke.

–

The night before he left for Berlin, Wolfgang Steiner took Ulrich and Friedrich into the barn. They sat facing each other on bales of hay, a bottle of schnapps on the floor between them.

The light of the full moon flooded the barn in an ethereal blue light.

Wolfgang said they were to listen very carefully and not interrupt him – he looked pointedly at his son as he said this. 'I don't know when I'll be back, but it will be at least three days, probably longer. I want you to be gone long before I return. Do you understand that?'

They assured him they did.

'Wait for twenty-four hours after I've left and then get on your way. The journey to the next point in the Kestrel Line will not be an easy one. You remember all the details about where you're to go and how to get there?'

Once again they assured him they did, and he said they ought to; they'd been through it often enough.

He left early the next morning, embracing his son in the knowledge that he might never see him again. For a moment as he held him by the shoulders, he could see Friedrich's mother's profile and her deep blue eyes – even the shape of her ears – and this brief resurrection of his late wife took him aback. He pulled the boy towards him and held him tight as the tears welled in his eyes.

Back in February, he'd prepared an identity for just this eventuality. He knew he was taking an enormous risk, but he'd calculated that once the war was over, such an identity would carry a certain cachet to it, if that was the right word. He hoped it would afford him a degree of privilege, with people understandably unwilling to question him too closely.

Max Stein was a man similar in age to him from the Berlin district of Reinickendorf. Because of his situation, Stein wouldn't be expected to have much in the way of paperwork, which was part of his appeal. There was a dog-eared identity card, though, stamped with a red 'J' to show he was Jewish.

Stein and his family had been among more than sixteen hundred fellow Jews on Majestic 33, the thirty-third transport from Berlin to the Auschwitz death camp. According to the records Steiner had found, the family had assembled at the old people's home on Grosse Hamburger Strasse on 3 March 1943 before being taken to Putlitzstrasse station in the Moabit. They'd reached Auschwitz the following day, and all had perished within hours of their arrival.

Max Stein's story would be that he alone of his family had in fact survived. After a series of death marches in late 1944, he'd ended up at Buchenwald and had been there when the camp was liberated. Steiner was counting on people feeling it was not right to question Stein too closely: the poor man had been through hell as it was.

He avoided shaving for a couple of days, and his shabby clothing was two sizes too large for him. He thought he looked credible to a degree, though he doubted the identity would hold up to concerted questioning.

He left the farm early on the Thursday morning. The man who collected the milk gave him a lift in his lorry and dropped him near a bus stop. Once he was sure no one was around, he went into a wood and changed into his Max Stein clothes, then caught a bus to Passau. He decided that his best bet was to take the most direct route to Berlin, so he headed due north, entering the Soviet zone south-west of Chemnitz. The identity held good in Dresden; he'd planned on staying the night there, but so little of the city was left, he decided to move on. An obliging Red Army officer gave him a lift to Leipzig and told him how his own family had perished at one of the camps. He even arranged for him to stay in a school the Red Army had taken over, one of the few large buildings still standing in the city.

The next day, he took a bus to Berlin, but at a checkpoint on the edge of the city, an NKVD officer was a bit too diligent.

What was your address in Reinickendorf?
Give me the names of some neighbours.
Which synagogue did you attend?
Where did you work?

Explain your presence in the Soviet zone.

Steiner worried he'd been more hesitant with his answers than he ought to have been, and decided he had to take matters into his own hands.

'How dare you question me like this – don't you think I've been through enough? The Nazis murdered my family and now I'm returning home to try and see if there's anyone I know who's alive, and you behave like one of them!'

He'd raised his voice, and the officer appeared taken aback and apologised: he hadn't meant to upset Herr Stein, but he hoped he understood...

Max Stein said he didn't understand. He certainly didn't understand why he was being treated like a bloody criminal, and he shouted so loudly that a senior officer came over and asked what on earth was going on. He was most apologetic once things were explained to him.

'You say your home is in Reinickendorf – you realise that is in the French sector?'

Max Stein asked whether that mattered.

'Is that where you want to go?'

'I want to find some family – maybe my brother's family, my wife's sister may still be alive, cousins perhaps: I doubt it, but I need to know.'

The officer said he had the perfect solution. 'You know the old synagogue on Oranienburger Strasse?'

Max Stein said that of course he did. 'My uncle used to worship there.' The officer was being so pleasant to him, he wondered if he was Jewish himself. He'd heard the terrible rumours that half the Red Army officers in Berlin were Jews. That was all he needed.

'It's where Jewish refugees go. We'll take you straight there.'

It was the last place Wolfgang Steiner wanted to be, and as he self-consciously entered the building, he worried that people were looking suspiciously at him. He asked to be shown to the toilets, and further down a corridor found a side door that led to the street. It was mid-afternoon but getting dark, and a bitter wind whipped around him. He wondered whether he should have stayed for a few minutes to get a warm drink and something to eat, and maybe some papers, but he decided to hurry away from Oranienburger Strasse. At least he was in Mitte, which was not far from his destination.

The destruction of Berlin was quite beyond anything he'd imagined. He'd seen what the bombing had done to Munich and Dresden, but as bad as that was, those were cities he was unfamiliar with. Berlin was different: it had been his home for seven years and he'd grown quite fond of it. In many ways he'd felt it had more soul to it than his native Vienna, lacking the latter's suffocating formality.

Now it felt as if it wasn't just the city's buildings that had been destroyed but its heart too. There was no atmosphere; it was as if the remains of the place had been transported to an alien landscape.

The destruction was so bad he had trouble finding his way round. He'd got to know the city very well: during the curfew, he'd enjoyed strolling around it in the dark, enjoying the privilege of being able to do so thanks to his rank. But now it wasn't just the street signs that were missing; it was the streets themselves, and the buildings and other landmarks that had helped identify them. He was reluctant to ask other pedestrians for directions: no one seemed to be in a mood to talk.

Eventually his instinct led him in what he hoped was the direction of Prenzlauer Berg. The house he was looking for was in Grenadier Strasse, just off Horst-Wessel Platz. But along with the name of the square, the house was missing too, as were half its neighbours. The street was like an old man's mouth: foul-smelling, half open, with unsightly gaps between the teeth.

He spotted an old woman watching him from the doorway of a nearby house.

'Frau Schulze…'

'What about her?'

'Do you know where she is?'

The woman was chewing something black, and her teeth were stained the same colour. She leaned forward and peered at the gap where the house had been. 'She seems to have popped out!' This was followed by a bitter laugh and a bout of noisy coughing. When she had recovered, she asked him why he wanted her.

'I was a friend of hers.'

'You don't look like one of her friends.'

'Do you know where she is?'

Another cackling laugh, followed by more coughing. She pointed to a high pile of rubble blocking the end of the street. 'Somewhere in there, I imagine, what's left of her. Her house took a direct hit. What's your name anyway?'

He thanked her and hurried away. He hadn't asked Bormann how he knew Frau Schulze, though the connection seemed strange. She wasn't his kind of contact, not beautiful or an obvious Nazi. She was just an ordinary woman, a war widow with two sons on the Eastern Front. Maybe that was why he'd chosen her: because no one would suspect her of a connection with a prominent Nazi.

She was one of four contacts Bormann had set up across the city.

If I manage to leave the bunker, Wolfgang, and can't get out of Berlin and down to you, I'll try to leave a message with one of these people. I may even be able to hide there – or at least tell them where I am. That way you will know where to find me.

Steiner had had his doubts about the plan but couldn't think of anything better. The idea had been to find contacts in different parts of the city, thus increasing Bormann's chances of getting a message to at least one of them. As well as Frau Schulze in Prenzlauer Berg, there'd been a man called Köhler who ran a cobbler's in Neukölln in the south-east of the city; a schoolteacher called Kühn who lived in a smart apartment with stunning views of the Tiergarten; and an elderly woman – Frau Vogt – in Schöneberg.

For two days Max Stein walked the city, his identity card getting him through checkpoints easily enough and the dollars in his wallet enabling him to buy a bed for the night. The cobbler in Neukölln was horrified when he entered the shop and asked whether the pair of dark brown hunting boots he'd brought in to be re-soled months ago were ready… name of Graf. Köhler said he knew nothing – absolutely nothing, nothing whatsoever – and he was to leave. *Please go!* He pushed him out of the shop.

Frau Vogt's apartment in Schöneberg was still there, but Frau Vogt wasn't. As he knocked on the door of her apartment, he spotted neighbours watching him from every doorway.

She's dead.

Steiner said he was sorry to hear that – how did it happen? he wondered.

The Russians raped her: they raped all of us. She bled to death.

A notice on Herr Kühn's door in Tiergarten said the apartment had been requisitioned by the British, and that he was staying with his daughter in Wedding, her address helpfully added.

'Let's go for a walk,' Kühn said after Steiner had identified himself: *I was wondering if you'd heard from my friend Graf – he was a former colleague of yours, I understand?*

They walked silently onto a patch of wasteland – there were plenty to choose from – and sat on two chairs incongruously placed in the middle. Kühn insisted Steiner should call him Willi.

'Look, I don't know where Martin is and I've not had any contact with him.' He was looking around nervously. 'But I can tell you what I heard, though it's third-hand, from someone who says he got it from another man who spoke to Axmann – I presume you know him?'

Steiner nodded. Of course he did: Artur Axmann, head of the Hitler Youth.

'According to them, Axmann left the bunker on the first of May, the day after Hitler committed suicide. He was in a group that included Bormann and an SS doctor called Stumpfegger. They escaped through a U-Bahn tunnel as far as Friedrich-strasse, and then tried to cross the Spree on the Weidendammer Bridge to reach Lehrter station along the railway line, but because the Soviets were so close they decided to split up. Axmann was on his own and escaped, but it's not clear what happened to Bormann and Stumpfegger.'

'Where's Axmann now?'

'This man said he's hiding in the Lübeck area, I've no idea if that's true.'

'So Bormann could still be alive?'

'It's certainly possible.'

The two men were walking back across the wasteland. 'Can I ask how you knew the Reichsleiter?' Steiner said.

'Our mothers were great friends back in our home town in Saxony, and he and I grew up together, so when we both found ourselves in Berlin, we kept in touch, though increasingly less frequently. It was a relationship based on nostalgia, I guess. I'm not a political person, but when Martin approached me in March, I felt obliged to help an old friend.'

'Of course.'

'You're Wolfgang Steiner, aren't you?'

He stopped abruptly. 'Martin told you?'

'He confided in me – I got the impression he wanted to unburden himself. He even told me about the Kestrel Line and—'

'He told you all that?'

The other man nodded, and Steiner said it would be best if he didn't mention a word of this to anyone.

'And where are you based now, Wolfgang – in case Martin turns up and wants to find you?'

For Steiner, that was one question too many. He wasn't sure about this urbane schoolteacher who knew far too much.

'Martin will know.'

'But what if he contacts me and needs to get hold of you urgently?'

'Memorise this telephone number, Willi – and don't give it to anyone else, you understand? Only use it if there's a message from Martin.'

It was not as much of a risk as it could have been. When he'd had the telephone installed at Frau Moser's farm, he'd made it untraceable by ensuring all records of it were destroyed.

They came to Gericht Strasse and shook hands as they prepared to go their separate ways.

'So you have no idea where Martin is?' Kühn asked.

Steiner shook his head. He'd rather been counting on the schoolteacher to tell him.

Chapter 16

'Good Lord, Roly, you are being serious!'

'Well of course I'm being serious, Tom. If one is to have some credibility with these people, then one needs to purchase... Look, Roland, perhaps you'd care to back me up here?'

Roland Bentley was Tom Gilbey's superior in MI6, an enigmatic man skilled at the art of standing above any dispute until the last possible moment. He had recently been knighted, and the gossip was that he was about to become the head of a Cambridge college. He looked up at Gilbey and Pearson, the two men sitting either side of him.

'Perhaps if we calm down just a little bit, eh? Roly, how much did you say the painting is?'

'The asking price is two hundred and thirty guineas, but I'm of the view—'

'I'm sorry, but I've never heard of Joseph Wright of Derby. Have you, Roland?'

'Wright of Derby? Of course I have, Tom: he is an outstanding painter, perhaps not with the reputation he deserves — at least not among the general public.' Bentley managed to make the word 'general' sound as if he meant uncultured.

'As I was saying, I'm of the view that two hundred and thirty guineas is something of a bit of a try-on. I have bought fine art before and I'm sure a price nearer to two hundred guineas would be feasible. The point I was endeavouring to make is that if my new persona of Anthony Hawke is to be taken seriously so that I can find out what they're up to, then his interest in art must be demonstrated to be a genuine one through the purchase of a painting.'

'If it helps, Tom, the money need not come from your budget; I'm happy to cover it from central funds. After all, it's not as if Roly's going to keep the painting, is it? Once this is all over, we can sell it. We may even make a profit.'

They all laughed, and Gilbey said in that case maybe he could see the merit of the idea, and he'd have a word with their man at Coutts and ensure there was an account opened that afternoon in the name of Anthony Hawke.

'You'll have a chequebook by lunchtime, and then you can head off to Cork Street. We only had time to give you a fairly basic backstory, as you know, so one hopes they don't dig too deeply. I doubt they'll be up to that, though – certainly as long as you give them no cause for concern, eh?'

'And our objective?' It was a classic Roland Bentley pronouncement: straight to the point. Both he and Pearson looked at Gilbey.

'To see whether these fellows are involved in funding the Kestrel Line. If Roly believes they are then he'll say he wants to make a small donation and we can see how matters develop from there. No heroics, please, Roly: I'll have a couple of chaps outside the gallery just in case.'

'I'm not sure what you think I'm going to do, Tom. I sense they may indeed want to me to make a donation to their cause – that's the most likely outcome, wouldn't you have thought? In which case you'd better make sure there are sufficient funds in the Coutts account.'

'How much did you have in mind?'

'Twenty-five pounds should open a door or two: plus the cost of the painting, of course.'

Sir Roland Pearson's return visit to Bourne and Sons did not start well. He was shocked as he approached the gallery on Cork Street to see a silver-grey Jaguar sports saloon parked more or less outside the building. It was obvious to him that the two middle-aged men in the car – both reading newspapers – were Gilbey's 'chaps', as he called them, there 'just in case'.

He hoped they were not as obvious to other people.

When he entered the gallery, there was no sign of Ridgeway. No sooner had the bell rung as he opened the door than a man appeared from the rear. He was shorter than Ridgeway and about the same age, wearing a black suit with a grey waistcoat and a bow tie.

'May I help you?' He sounded more confident than Ridgeway, less servile. Pearson said he had met a Mr Ridgeway here two days earlier who had suggested he return around this time.

'And for what purpose, may I ask, sir?'

Pearson hesitated. He had no idea who this man was. 'I was interested in purchasing a painting, actually: the Wright of Derby landscape.' He'd moved in front of the painting, admiring it once again. It was actually a fine piece, one that would look good in his study. Maybe Bentley would let him have it at a discount once this was all over.

'An excellent choice, sir, a very good example of Wright's work, and I have little doubt a painting like this will appreciate considerably in value. You will of course understand that its excellence is reflected in its price.'

'Of course.'

'We are asking two hundred and thirty guineas for it, sir. May I know your name?'

'Hawke – with an "e". Anthony Hawke.'

'Ah yes, indeed, Donald did say you had shown interest in this particular painting and might be returning. Are you by any chance related to the Dorset Hawkes?'

'No, Westmorland actually, though my wife and I are in the process of moving to the North Riding. We're rather between the two at the moment.'

'The Pennine Hills, then?'

'I beg your pardon?'

'The Pennine Hills – they're between Westmorland and the North Riding.' The man chuckled in a self-satisfied manner.

'Oh, I see, yes – jolly good.' Pearson was bending down to study the painting in closer detail, trying to remember that Anthony Hawke was not meant to be jovial. 'I'm sorry, but I'm not sure I caught *your* name?'

'I do apologise, I ought to have introduced myself: Charles Bourne – as in Bourne and Sons.'

'One of the sons?'

'Grandson, actually.'

Pearson nodded and stepped back from the painting, frowning as he looked at it. He caught a movement at the window and was sure it was one of Gilbey's men peering in, which was really not good enough. 'I think I would consider anything above two hundred guineas to be too steep.'

'Perhaps if we were to suggest two hundred and twenty, sir?'

He was concerned that in the absence of Ridgeway this would turn out to be a futile visit, but he could hardly leave now. 'Would two hundred and fifteen be agreeable to you?'

Bourne said it was, and enthusiastically rubbed his hands as he removed the painting from the wall and carried it over to a large table. He said he'd wrap it and prepare the provenance and the invoice.

Ridgeway looked around and lowered his voice, 'Donald said you spoke most movingly of your love for England when you were here before.'

Anthony Hawke grunted as he removed his Coutts cheque-book from his pocket. 'I make the cheque out to Bourne and Sons, I presume?'

Bourne said indeed, and added that he very much shared the sentiments he understood Mr Hawke had so admirably articulated to his colleague.

'There we are, Bourne.' Hawke passed the cheque across the table. 'One of course has one's views on where this country is going and how the war turned out, and I do rather despair, but I very much doubt there's very much one can do about it.'

Bourne paused and wondered whether Mr Hawke would join him in his office so they could finalise the paperwork? Hawke said of course, and Bourne apologised as he led him to the back of the gallery, explaining that the office was not as tidy as perhaps it should be but he blamed his grandfather for that.

It was only when he sat down in an ancient chair that he was unsure would hold his weight that Sir Roland noticed a woman sitting in the corner of the room, her slim legs crossed and her hands resting on her lap. Bourne said she was a colleague and someone who could absolutely be trusted – 'Perhaps even more than me!' Pearson was intrigued by her: she was perhaps in her mid-fifties, a remarkably elegant woman with a face he'd describe as pretty. In her day she must have been quite beautiful. She nodded her head in his direction but otherwise remained impassive as Bourne completed the paperwork and placed the cheque in a small safe.

'You said, Mr Hawke, that you doubted there was much one could do regarding the way the country is going.' He coughed and paused as he considered what he was about to say. 'There are those of us who take the view that that is not necessarily the case. We have long believed that this country has been perhaps… misguided in the allegiances it formed and in whom it sought to protect and those it chose to oppose.'

He paused and turned round to the woman, who said nothing but nodded: *carry on.*

'A number of us are seeking to support those in Europe who may have hitherto been seen as the enemy but who we regard as the last defenders of Christian Europe against the communists – and the Jews, of course.'

The room dropped into silence and Anthony Hawke half nodded.

'Support them in what way, Bourne?'

'Perhaps I could explain.' The woman had uncrossed her legs and was smoothing her skirt. 'What Charles is trying to say is that there are Germans who are being hunted as war criminals when they did no more than fight for their country. We are of the view that these people are in the vanguard of defending Europe's traditional values. To this end, a number of them are seeking to assume new identities and leave Europe, so that they are in a position to resume their cause. We are assisting one particular group in a practical manner, specifically by providing funds to enable their passage. There are also people in this country we wish to send on the same... route.'

Anthony Hawke nodded, trying to appear impassive. 'I despise this government and I had considerable doubts about the course and aims of the war, but I'm a patriot – I'm not a Nazi, you know!'

'But don't you think, sir,' Bourne looked down as he spoke, 'that the enemy of my enemy is my friend?'

'So are you asking me for money?'

Bourne turned to the woman again, who said that indeed, anything would be most appreciated.

Hawke removed the chequebook from his jacket pocket again. 'I wouldn't want to be... embarrassed by this.'

'Of course not, sir: what we can do is treat it as a purchase. We have some Victorian sketches of doubtful provenance that are really worth very little, but it would ensure everything appears above board. May I ask how much you intend to give?'

'Twenty-five pounds is what I had in mind.'

'That is most generous, sir, thank you very much.'

'How do you get the money over to the Continent?' Hawke was looking down at the chequebook as he spoke. 'I don't imagine you send them cheques, eh?'

'Strictly cash,' said the woman. 'We send it by courier. We had one courier who went out a few weeks ago, and there's another we hope to send soon.'

'Yes,' said Bourne, chuckling. 'Killing two birds with one stone!'

The woman coughed, and when Sir Roland looked up, he noticed a furious look on her face.

–

Two days later, Sir Roland Pearson was sitting in Tom Gilbey's office with the Wright landscape propped up on a chair next to him. Roland Bentley was also present, as were Hanne and Prince, summoned back from Lincoln.

Pearson gave a lengthy account of his two visits to Bourne and Sons. When he had finished, he rubbed his hands together and pointed to the painting, as if its purchase had been the purpose of the exercise.

'The objective of Sir Roland's mission was to establish whether there is a link between this art gallery and the Kestrel Line. Is that not correct, Tom?'

Gilbey told Bentley that it was.

'And it would seem that such a link has been established through this visit?'

'To an extent, yes.'

'What do you mean, Tom?'

'Don't get me wrong, it was a successful visit, but the evidence gained from it is circumstantial rather than direct. I'm sure our police officer friends here appreciate the difference – I assume Danish law is similar in this respect?'

Prince and Hanne both nodded.

'Without in any way seeking to diminish what you achieved Roly, we only have what Mr Bourne and Mr Ridgeway have said, along with the more explicit statement of the unnamed woman.'

Pearson had opened his notebook and now read out loud, as if giving dictation: "'…a number of them are seeking to assume new identities and leave Europe, so that they are in a position to resume their cause… We are assisting one particular group in a practical manner, specifically by providing funds to enable their passage." I ought to add that I made these notes more or less contemporaneously: I pride myself on my recall.'

'And you gave them a cheque for twenty-five pounds, I believe it was. To whom was it made out Tom?' Roland Bentley's fountain pen was poised as he waited for an answer.

'To Bourne and Sons, sir: we've already been through this. Obviously it's a pity it wasn't made out to another account, as then it would have been easier to trace.'

'They were hardly going to ask me to make out a cheque to the Nazi Escape Fund, were they?' Pearson looked pleased with his remark.

Hanne looked up, shocked, unsure whether this was a joke.

'I think there is undoubtedly something to this – a possible link between Bourne and Sons and the Kestrel Line has now become a probable one. Nonetheless, we need more evidence. Prince, you had a decent relationship with Hugh Harper at MI5 when you worked with him on that last mission, didn't you?'

'Yes, Mr Gilbey, sir.'

'I've asked him to help; this end of things is really their game. They've already got someone looking at the Bourne and Sons bank account to see if we can spot any interesting transactions. I suggest you and Hanne try to see what you can find out too.'

'There is something else.' Pearson hauled himself into a more upright position in his chair. 'This may be nothing, but nonetheless I made a note of it, and I see I put an asterisk alongside it. After the woman talked about the funds, she said… where are we… ah, here… "There are also people in this country we wish to send on the same route." Then she mentioned having already sent out one courier…'

'Which was presumably Charles Falmer.'

'If you say so… and she added they hoped to send another out soon. Then Bourne made a joke along the lines of killing two birds with one stone. She looked furious with him when he said that.'

'Whatever does all that mean?'

'I have no idea, Tom.'

'What more can you tell us about this woman?'

'Very assertive, I would say, Prince. I got the impression that she was calling the shots somehow.'

'What did she look like?'

'Very attractive, if I might say. Pretty face and good legs; had a refined air about her.'

'Age?'

'Difficult to say, but if you pushed me, I'd say early to mid-fifties.'

'And he didn't use a name?'

'No.'

'Any accent?'

'Nothing discernible.'

'You look as if you think you're on to something, Prince?'

'As you know, sir, in my last case I infiltrated a group of British Nazi sympathisers in an attempt to break the German spy ring we were investigating. There was a woman – an Englishwoman – I came across in Gerrards Cross who was part of that group. I next encountered her when she identified me at a pub in east London. As far as I'm aware, she's never been traced.'

'And your point?'

Prince shrugged. 'Hard to say, sir, but the description Sir Roland gave sounds like her. And remember too, the main purpose of that case was to identify the Nazi spy known as Agent Milton. We established that he was Major Edward Palmer, but…'

'…he disappeared too.'

'Exactly. So when this woman said there are people in England that they want to help escape – you never know, she could have been talking about Palmer.'

The atmosphere altered as the room descended into silence, everyone in it absorbed in their thoughts. It was as if the temperature had dropped by a few degrees.

'Good Lord,' said Bentley, not normally a man given to such expressions. 'I do think you may well be on to something here.'

Chapter 17

After years of blaming other people for his lowly status and what he saw as a run of constant bad luck, Kenneth Bemrose had come to realise it was up to him to pull himself together and do something about it.

Learning Russian was a case in point: he enthusiastically volunteered for Russian lessons and applied himself as hard as possible. He studied in his free time and sailed through the beginner's course with such ease that one of the MI6 officers running the course asked him whether he'd be interested in the intermediate course, and would he also like to be considered for what he called 'special duties'?

Bemrose said of course, and only two days ago he'd been asked to go to the fifth floor of the building where he worked, where one of the guards actually saluted him. He was then taken into a windowless room where a man who never actually gave his name said they were very impressed with his progress, and if he was prepared to sign up to staying in Berlin for another five years and continue to the advanced-level Russian course, he would be promoted to officer status and become a MI6 member of staff. It was only when the man stood up to indicate that the meeting was over that he mentioned – more as an aside than anything else – that Bemrose might be interested to know that he'd also passed through another level of security clearance.

No longer would he be a mere clerk, or even a chauffeur as he had been when that couple had come over from London in

September. At last he would have some standing: it would mean he would qualify for better accommodation, perhaps even in one of those very pleasant blocks in Charlottenburg. And Peggy – the pretty WRAF girl at RAF Gatow who walked with a bit of a limp – might even be interested in him now, despite the fact that he was quite a few years older than her.

His boss had said he could use the Humber Snipe over the weekend, so on the Sunday morning he drove over the Havel to Grunewald. He'd telephoned Peggy on Friday and Saturday and left messages for her: would she be interested in accompanying him? He could collect her and drive her back. In fact, to his slight embarrassment – he hadn't wanted to come across as desperate – he'd actually rung four times on the Friday and twice more on the Saturday, but he imagined someone had failed to pass on the message – or that Peggy was busy.

Once he'd been walking in the forest for an hour, though, he was grateful she hadn't joined him. He doubted she'd have managed the rough terrain with her limp, and it would have been an awfully long time to keep up a conversation. He was enjoying the tranquillity of the place, the strange silence afforded by so many trees so close together.

He was wary of losing his way, so avoided going too deep into the forest and made sure the path to his left remained just in sight. It was then that he noticed the couple walking along the path, seemingly keeping pace with him. He didn't think much of it at first, but after a while, he was unsettled by their presence – not because there was anything suspicious about them, but because it made him feel inhibited: when he was sure he was completely out of anyone's earshot, he liked to talk to himself or sing out loud. He didn't want these people to think he was odd.

He decided to move a bit deeper into the forest, out of sight of the path, and continued like this for a while until he heard twigs snapping behind him and turned round to see the couple just yards from him, smiling apologetically as if they'd disturbed him. They seemed to be in their seventies, both short and smartly dressed as if on their way to a social engagement. The man had a fine head of silver hair and a well-tended beard. He looked like an academic. The woman had a gold brooch on the lapel of her coat and wore a pair of smart leather gloves.

'We are terribly sorry to bother you, Mr Bemrose.'

Bemrose's first thought was that from now on – if there was to be a now on – he would make sure he always carried a pistol. Someone in the office had mentioned it, and he hoped his failure to do so wasn't something he'd regret, though of course it might be too late for that.

'Please, Mr Bemrose, don't look so shocked. We are here to give you a message, that is all.'

The man had addressed him in English with a Mittel-European accent.

'Are you sure you've got the right person?'

'You are Mr Bemrose, yes – a British official?'

Bemrose said he was, but he was sure he was one of many, and in any case how on earth had they found him here? He was wondering about heading back towards the path when he noticed the man – to his horror – reaching into his inside jacket pocket. He held his breath until he produced a silver cigarette case and offered it to him. He eagerly took one.

'In September, Mr Bemrose, you looked after an Englishman and his wife who visited Berlin on official business. Please… do let me finish. They had reason to go to the Soviet sector of Berlin, where they had dealings with Commissar Iosif Gurevich.'

Bemrose started to say that he really couldn't recall it, but the man held up his hand.

'This isn't a question, Mr Bemrose: I am stating matters of fact. This is a message from Iosif Gurevich: you are to contact the couple urgently and tell them he needs to see them in Berlin as soon as possible.'

'Well, I suppose—'

'It is also essential that you add it is in connection with Kestrel. They'll understand. Perhaps you'd care to repeat the message?'

Bemrose did so, and then the couple said it had been very nice to meet him and shook his hand, slightly bowing their heads as they did so. Would he mind, they asked, if he waited where he was for ten minutes or so to give them time to make their way back?

–

The investigation in London had been going badly. Hugh Harper at MI5 gave the impression of being very put upon. He complained that he'd lost most of his influence and half his team, including the Disciples, as his elite team of watchers and followers led by the redoubtable Bartholomew was known – were being dismantled. He was wondering how long he had left in the Service, he told Prince.

Nonetheless, he had managed to secure the services of three officers – 'all qualified accountants, would you believe' – who specialised in investigating financial matters. 'It sounds rather tedious, Prince, but these chaps insist that in investigations like this, money is the key to everything. They look at bank accounts and work out where the deposits have come from and where money paid out goes. They have had some very encouraging results. Let's give them a fortnight: they're confident they ought to dig something up.'

Despite their confidence, they didn't manage to dig anything up. Bourne and Sons turned out to have two business accounts, one with Martins Bank and the other with the Midland Bank. MI5's investigators looked at both accounts going back to the start of 1944: all the deposits by cheque or from other accounts were above suspicion, as was the money paid out. They'd then turned their attention to the personal bank accounts of Bourne and Ridgeway, the former's with Midland Bank, the latter's with

National Provincial. Again they were unable to find evidence of any suspicious activity.

'Other than cash,' said Harper when he met up with Prince and Hanne at the end of the investigation. 'The accountant chaps – though one's a woman, believe it or not – say there's a higher level of cash deposits and withdrawals than one would expect, but then of course one can't trace cash, so that in itself is suspicious.'

'So no one paid money in by cheque? I thought that when Anthony Hawke donated money to them, he did so by cheque?'

'As payment for the purchase of an artwork... these chaps are quite clever. But the evidence of significant amounts of cash going in and out of the account probably means we should persist with this.'

The gallery on Cork Street was watched for a fortnight, and Bourne and Ridgeway were followed, but no clues emerged. Prince said they were especially interested in the woman – the one who'd been at the meeting between Bourne and Hawke and whom he suspected was involved in the Nazi spy ring – but there was no sign of her.

Hanne told him in no uncertain terms that she felt the investigation was ridiculous. 'Like that sport you play – cricket. It's slow and pointless. There seems to be no sense of urgency. Surely we should be getting warrants to search the gallery and their homes and bringing them in for questioning.'

Prince said he had to agree, and he arranged a meeting with Tom Gilbey. *MI5 are rather dawdling, sir, I think we need to up our game...*

But before the meeting could take place, a message came from Berlin, from Bemrose. *Gurevich wants to see you. He says it's urgent – it's to do with kestrel.*

–

'We've found him!'

Commissar Iosif Gurevich clapped his hands and stood up. There was a wide grin on his face and a shot glass of vodka held high above his head as he prepared to deliver yet another toast. Slightly confused, and beginning to feel the effects of the vodka they'd already been obliged to consume, both Hanne and Price slowly stood too before sipping their drinks.

It was late in the morning in Gurevich's new office on the top floor of the building on Behrenstrasse. This one had sweeping views of what remained of Berlin and felt more like a dining room than an office, with its highly polished furniture and expensive-looking rugs. Hanne and Prince were exhausted from their overnight flight from London: they'd hoped for some time in Berlin to rest before their meeting, but Bemrose had insisted they travel to the Soviet zone immediately.

'You found Friedrich Steiner?'

Gurevich shook his head as he topped up his glass.

'His father, then?'

'No, not yet – but hopefully very soon. You recall the file I showed you last time – this one here?'

He angled a folder on his desk so they could see it better. 'This is Wolfgang Steiner's file and it gave us a link between him and the Kestrel Line, if you remember. We assumed FFM stood for Frankfurt, which from what you tell me was probably a correct assumption, but we had no idea what the other initials – RLB, V and T – stood for, though we thought T must be Turin. I said at the time that these were notes added to the file after an interrogation, and that the officer who made them had failed to include his initials – that he was most probably in a hurry. I also said I'd try and find that officer.'

Minutes later they were joined by that officer. Kapitan Leonid Fyodorov looked improbably young – perhaps in his mid-twenties – with a mop of unruly hair, and black eyes that watched them suspiciously. He also spoke good German.

'I have assured Kapitan Fyodorov that he has done nothing wrong,' Gurevich began. 'This is not a disciplinary matter in any way. I understand that he made these notes at a time when he was interrogating maybe a dozen Nazis a day. His oversight in failing to add his initials and not making the notes more explicit is therefore quite understandable.'

Kapitan Fyodorov nodded, and allowed a thin smile to cross his young face.

'Perhaps, Fyodorov, it would be best if you explained everything in your own words. Would anyone like some more vodka first?'

Hanne and Prince both said they were fine, thank you very much, and Fyodorov didn't respond as he opened the file and his notebook. Before he spoke, he stood up and shook hands with the two visitors, looking them both in the eye. He seemed intrigued by them. Prince wondered how Gurevich had explained their presence.

'Since July, I've been working at Hohenschönhausen prison in Lichtenberg.' He nodded to the window, presumably in the direction of Lichtenberg. 'My job was – and still is – to interrogate Germans whom we suspect of being involved in war crimes or who held senior positions in the regime. On the twelfth of July, I was told to interrogate a prisoner who'd actually requested to speak with us, which was most unusual. His name was Paul Hoffman, and he was a *Kriminaldirektor* with the Kripo – the Kriminalpolizei, essentially the detectives in the regular police force, though they came under the Nazi security structure. Hoffman was reasonably senior – a *Kriminaldirektor* is probably equivalent to your rank of major, which is why he was held in custody.

'You understand that by then I had interrogated hundreds of men and all claimed they'd never been Nazis, and I can honestly say that Hoffman was the first one I believed and who I actually found likeable. He told me he'd been based at the police station in Wedding and ran the department investigating serious crimes. He said he had nothing to do with anything political or to do with Jews, and I believed him, because such matters weren't handled at that police station.

'He also told me that not only was he not a Nazi, but he was actually a communist.' Fyodorov paused and looked at Hanne and Prince to see if they reacted. 'I know this sounds remarkable, but according to Hoffman, he'd been a member of the KPD.'

'The KPD?'

'Kommunistische Partei Deutschlands – the German Communist Party. He said he'd been a member in the 1920s, and although he'd joined the police in 1929, he'd retained his party card until the organisation went underground in 1933. That was not unusual: many of our comrades did likewise. Many also joined the Nazi Party and—'

'Perhaps it would be best to stick to the story, Fyodorov.'

'Of course, sir. Hoffman insisted that he had done what he could to help people, including Jews and party comrades, and gave me many examples. He said he thought some people would still be alive who could vouch for him. As it happens, he mentioned one senior comrade who'd gone to Moscow in 1932 and who returned here when we liberated the city, and this man was able to confirm that Hoffman had indeed been a member of the KPD.

'However, we still needed to investigate him; to be sure he'd not been involved in serious crimes. Then he told me a story he admitted was hard to verify but he felt I ought to know about it anyway. He said he had a contact who lived in Tiergarten, a schoolteacher called Willi Kühn. Kühn had also been a KPD comrade, though he'd left the party in 1930, and because of his profession his membership had been under a false name, which I understand was not uncommon: Hoffman used an assumed name too.

'In April, Hoffmann bumped into Kühn in the Tiergarten and they had a coded conversation, the type where one tries to ascertain which side the other is on. Hoffman said that once it was clear they were both anti-Nazis, Kühn told him this story. He said that he had grown up in a small town in Saxony and one of his childhood friends was the son of his mother's best friend. When he moved to Berlin, he met up with this friend and was horrified to discover he was now a prominent Nazi, but he said he allowed the friendship to continue because he never knew when it would come in handy. Sure enough, in 1941, Kühn almost lost his job because some pupils at his school informed on him and said he made negative remarks about the war and displayed no enthusiasm for Hitler. He contacted his old friend, who interceded on his behalf. Because this man was so important, he says not only was his job safe, but he was even promoted!'

'I think you omitted to tell them the name of this prominent Nazi, Comrade.'

'Have you heard of Martin Bormann?'

'Yes, wasn't he...'

'...effectively Hitler's deputy.' Gurevich nodded. 'He was his private secretary and head of the Nazi Party machinery. He had the rank of *Reichsleiter* – so RLB stands for Reichsleiter Bormann. Do you realise how important he is?'

Hanne nodded for Gurevich to tell them.

'*Reichsleiter* was the second highest rank in the Nazi regime, after that of *Führer*, and by the end of the war there were only around twenty of them left. More to the point, Bormann is perhaps the most senior Nazi unaccounted for. Hitler committed suicide, of course, as did Goebbels and Himmler. Rudolf Hess had fled to Britain during the war, as you know. Other senior Nazis like Göring, Streicher, Jodl, Kaltenbrunner, von Ribbentrop, Keitel and Seyss-Inquart are awaiting trial. There are plenty of senior Nazis at liberty, especially from the SS, but of the leadership – those who ran things here in Berlin – Bormann must be the most important one. Carry on, Comrade Kapitan.'

'When Kühn met Hoffman in the Tiergarten in April, he said he'd recently been summoned to see Bormann, who told him he was making plans to escape from Berlin, "should the eventuality arise". The escape would depend on how matters turned out, because he would have to take his chances if and when they arose – you understand I'm reading from my notes here. Bormann said that his main concern was getting out of Berlin – he believed that would be the most perilous part of any escape – but he'd made plans for once he was away from the city. He told Kühn that he had set up or was involved in something called the Kestrel Line, which was an escape route that would take him south and from there hopefully to South America.'

'Hang on.' Hanne was leaning forward, a frown on her face. 'This Hoffman is seriously asking us to believe that one of the top Nazis in the regime divulged his secret escape plans to a schoolteacher?'

'If I may answer, Hanne,' said Gurevich. 'You are right to question this, but we need to consider what the situation was like in Berlin in April. It must have been hell: we were throwing everything we had at the city, and the RAF was bombing it too. After being assured this was a thousand-year Reich, most people realised it would do well to last another thousand hours. Bormann himself would have known how bad things were and was probably grateful to have an old friend he trusted he could talk to.'

Fyodorov nodded in agreement. 'Also, Comrade Kommissar, he probably thought Kühn owed him after he saved him in 1941. Kühn said Bormann asked for two favours. One was to act as a conduit for messages: if he received a message from an Else, he was to know it was from Bormann – that was the name of Bormann's half-sister, whom Kühn knew. And if someone approached him asking about a friend called Graf, then he would know he should pass any message on to them. But no one ever approached him – no message from an Else or anyone asking about Graf. He mentioned a Wolfgang Steiner who was a senior Nazi Party official: Bormann told Kühn he was to trust him if he ever contacted him.'

'And the other favour?'

'Bormann gave him some papers and some American dollars. Kühn said the papers were identity papers for Bormann to use, and he thinks the dollars were counterfeit. He says that as soon as the Red Army entered the city, he was terrified they'd find these things on him, so he burnt them. When the British moved into West Berlin, they commandeered his apartment, so he went to live with his daughter in Wedding. We released Paul Hoffman, because he was clearly no Nazi, and in fact he is now working for our police service in the Soviet sector. When I closed his file, I also made those notes on Wolfgang Steiner's file – it showed he was also unaccounted for. I apologise that they were not more extensive.'

'And you didn't think to report this intelligence about Martin Bormann?'

'I did think about it; in fact I sent a note to be placed on his file, but I understand it got lost. With hindsight, I should have perhaps reported the matter to my superior, but I was so busy I—'

'And the other initials?'

'FFM stands for Frankfurt am Main; RLB, as you know, is for Reichsleiter Bormann. The V, according to my notes, stands for Villach, which is a town in the south of Austria and is apparently a stop on the Kestrel Line. But the T – Hoffman says Kühn couldn't remember what that stood for, other than it was the final destination on the escape route: from there they go to South America, so our assumption is that it's Turin.'

'And that's it?'

The young NKVD officer shook his head. 'When Comrade Kommissar Gurevich contacted me, I got in touch with Hoffman to check that my notes were correct, and he said that Kühn had recently been leaving messages that he wants to see him urgently – he seems to have news, but he's in the British sector and doesn't want to leave it, and now that Hoffman is working for us, he's reluctant to travel there.'

'I'm sure that's something we can sort out,' said Prince.

–

'Kühn is a bag of nerves and doesn't trust anyone.'

Paul Hoffman paused and looked up at Hanne and Prince, though it was clear he was paying more attention to Hanne. He was an elegant man who seemed to have adapted very easily to his new role as an officer in the Soviet-organised German police force. He was wearing a smart coat and an expensive-looking pair of spectacles, and when he moved his arm, there was a flash of gold on his wrist. The transformation from Nazi policeman to a communist one had evidently not been too onerous.

'I saw him on and off during the war, and like me he felt he was living on borrowed time.'

'You'd better explain.'

'Of course. I can understand how he felt, because to a great extent I was in the same position as him. Remember, we'd both been in the KPD: in my case I'd remained in it for a longer period of time, but I had found the KPD Prenzlauer Berg branch records in 1934, I think it was, and removed any details to do with me, even though I'd used a false name. And I was a police officer too: not quite above suspicion, but certainly in a more favourable position than a schoolteacher – especially one whose behaviour had been as rash as Kühn's had in the early part of the war. Now the war is over, the last thing he wants is to be mixed up in Nazi escape lines.'

'So how come he's been in touch with you?'

'You're both police officers, I understand?' He looked from Hanne to Prince. 'So you'll understand what people can be like under what I would call the pressure of having to conceal some-thing: it's human instinct to want to talk, to share confidences. It's a way of unburdening yourself. Often you want the person you're confiding in to say you're not to worry.

'I think if Willi Kühn was told he was meeting someone from British intelligence, or Soviet officials, he'd run a mile.

May I suggest I set up a meeting and...' He paused, looking directly at Hanne and smiling charmingly. 'Let me put it like this: ever since I've known him, Willi has been something of a ladies' man. He cannot resist a pretty face, and if I may say so, I'm sure you will win him over.'

'Well I'm not sure that's—'

Hanne put her hand on Prince's arm. 'How will you introduce me?'

Hoffmann thought for a moment. 'Your German is very good.'

'I spent two years in one of your camps.'

'I'm sorry – but you're not English, are you? The accent sounds...'

'I'm from Denmark.'

'I will introduce you as a colleague, and if he asks, we can say you're from Schleswig-Holstein; the accent is very similar.'

'Which is hardly surprising given that it used to be part of Denmark.'

'Maybe that is for another day,' said Gurevich. 'Hoffman, make arrangements for you and Hanne to meet with Kühn.'

–

Bemrose had sorted out a room above what had been a café on the Kurfürstendamm in the west of the city. Willi Kühn was ten minutes late, and when he came in, he looked uncertainly at Hoffman.

'What is she doing here?'

'She's a colleague of mine, and you can trust her, Willi, I promise you.'

Hanne walked over and shook Kühn's hand, then took his coat. She led him to an armchair and asked him what he'd like to drink.

'She's a waitress?'

'I said she's a colleague. She has been working on this case.'

'Which case?'

'Come on, Willi, don't be so difficult: she's working on Nazis who escaped from Berlin – she knows about the Kestrel Line.'

Kühn nodded his head and said very well then, but what was said in this room should stay in this room, and both Hoffman and Hanne said of course.

He began without preamble. 'The other week – out of the blue – Wolfgang Steiner turned up asking if I know where Martin is.'

'I didn't know you knew Steiner?'

'I don't, but Martin had told me about him, and from the way he asked me questions, I assumed it was him. I just asked him straight out and he admitted it; I think he was a bit taken aback. I also told him I knew about the Kestrel Line – I thought that would somehow reassure him, but I fear it had the opposite effect.'

'In what way?' Hanne asked.

'He seemed uncomfortable. I asked him where he was based, because Paul told me that if anyone came asking about Martin, I ought to find out what I could, but his reply was just "Martin will know". That's what he said – "Martin will know".'

'So that was the extent of your conversation with him?'

'No – you see, I had heard rumours about Martin and I told Steiner what I knew. I'd heard he'd escaped from the bunker on or around the first of May in a small group that included Artur Axmann. The source of my story was someone who'd heard it from another person who'd got it from Axmann himself. I reckon if it was second or third hand and I'd heard it, then Steiner would have heard it too, but apparently not – he seemed surprised.'

'And what is the story?'

'I'm sorry, dear – yes, where was I?' He smiled at Hanne and shifted his chair closer.

'Axmann?'

'That's right: according to this account, the group escaped from the bunker and emerged somewhere near Friedrichstrasse station. Axmann last saw them by Weidendammer Bridge trying to get to Lehrter station along the railway line. Martin was with one other person: they went in one direction, Axmann in another. He said there were explosions all around them: they may have been killed, they may have got away.' He held out his hands to indicate that that was it. 'This all came as news to Steiner. He'd obviously hoped I'd have more concrete news. He left soon after that.'

'May I ask you a question, Willi?'

'Of course you can, dear. Where are you from – your accent…?'

'Near Flensburg.'

'I spent a pleasant holiday in Schleswig-Holstein many years ago.'

Hanne smiled patiently. 'When you first told Paul about Kestrel, you said Bormann gave you some details about the route of the Kestrel Line: is that correct?'

'It is, yes.'

'Which I think starts in Frankfurt am Main and then goes to another important point: Villach in Austria?'

'I seem to recall that, yes.'

'And according to what you told Paul, the final destination before South America begins with T?'

She noticed that Kühn was staring at his legs, and it was a while before he looked up. 'Yes, I think you're right – it did begin with T.'

Hanne leaned forward, placing her hand on his knee. 'What does T stand for, Willi?'

He patted her hand and smiled before his face creased into a frown. 'Now that is a good question. Do you know, I can't for the life of me remember.'

'Was it in Italy?'

He frowned again. 'I'm not sure: it could be – or maybe Spain?'

'Turin, perhaps?'

'Now you mention it, yes – I think it was.'

They went through his story one more time before it was time for Kühn to leave. He paused in the doorway, turning round as he buttoned his coat. 'There is something I meant to tell you that may be of help. I asked Steiner how I should contact him if Martin got in touch, and he gave me a telephone number to memorise. I wrote it down as soon as I got home.'

'Do you still have that number, Willi?' Hanne had moved closer, close enough for Kühn to smell her scent.

'Do you know what? I accidentally used it to light my pipe that same evening!'

'No!'

He burst out laughing and put his arm round her waist, giving it a squeeze. 'I joke, of course, my dear. I have the number on a piece of paper here in my wallet.'

Hoffman and Hanne stood at the window watching Willi Kühn as he emerged from the building and pushed his way past two beggars before hurrying up the Kurfürstendamm, glancing behind him as he did so.

'So there you are,' said Hoffman, adjusting his gold watch as he spoke. 'Now you're on the trail of the most important Nazi still at large.'

Chapter 18

England, November 1945

'You do realise you can't stay here for ever, don't you?'

Edward Palmer began to respond, but stopped himself. Actually he saw no reason why he couldn't stay there for another few months at least, if not a lot longer – possibly until late 1946 or maybe even into 1947. Hopefully by then the baying of the hounds would have faded in the distance and the police and security services would find other people to hunt.

In his more fanciful moments – not that he allowed himself too many of those, it had to be said – he imagined that sooner or later they'd forget about him altogether. But in truth he knew this was so unlikely as to not be worth wasting his time thinking about: it was no more than a fantasy. He considered himself too much of an outsider to be regarded as a pillar of the establishment, but that was just his opinion. No one else would see him as an outsider, other than those who'd been astute enough to spot it when they recruited him as a German spy some twelve years before. Then he'd been a student at Cambridge. By the time he went on the run earlier this year, he was a major in Military Intelligence, based at the War Office and probably Germany's most productive spy in England.

They'd always be hunting for him. He'd always be looking over his shoulder.

So he'd not replied about how long he hoped he could stay there, because she was in one of those moods when her gaze was fixed on a point either side of him. She was also smoking: she could go days without touching a cigarette and then furiously smoke one after another, as if in a competition to see how quickly she could work her way through a packet.

Life was like this with the woman he knew as Myrtle – utterly unpredictable. He'd first met her in December 1938, a largely silent but very passionate encounter that had lasted for two days, at the end of which she'd confided in him that it had taken place because 'they wanted to be sure there wasn't anything untoward about you', which apparently there wasn't. She'd then told him how much she admired him – 'if only there were more men like you' – and assured him that if he ever needed her help, he was to go to an art gallery in Cork Street called Bourne and Sons and ask if they had any paintings by an artist called Myrtle. But he was only to do this, she said, if it was a matter of life and death.

In the third week of April, he'd realised the security services were closing in on him and the Nazi spy ring he'd been so carefully if reluctantly drawn into had all but collapsed. His career as Agent Milton was about to end. He calculated that as Major Edward Palmer of the Directorate of Military Intelligence at the War Office, he was enjoying his final hours of freedom, so he'd fled London and moved around the north of England.

In Manchester he'd acquired the identity of Harold Hamilton, and then spent a few weeks working on a farm in Lincolnshire before he remembered Myrtle – he was surprised he'd not thought of her before – and reckoned his predicament now unquestionably qualified as a matter of life and death.

And from there it had all somehow worked out. From the art gallery he'd been sent to Marylebone station, and thence to Gerrards Cross. When he'd left the station he'd followed his instructions and kept walking.

Don't look for Myrtle – she'll find you.

Five minutes later, she'd sidled up to him as he'd passed a chemist's, slipping her arm through his and asking how his journey had been, and turn right here, that's my car over there, the dark blue one – maybe you should smile.

It was a small snub-nosed Standard Flying Eight with noisy brakes and a window on the passenger door that rattled in a worrying manner. They headed north for about thirty minutes: despite the war being over, there were still an absence of road signs and he knew better than to ask their destination. Soon after crossing a railway line, they turned off the road and headed up a long farm track, open fields to their left and woods to their right. Just before the track came to a dead end, she pulled up alongside a gate and told him to open it and then close it once the car was through. From there it was about a quarter of a mile along rough ground before they came to a small house, set back among the trees rather as he imagined the setting for a cottage in the Black Forest in a fairy tale.

And that was where he'd remained. She told him they were in the Misbourne Valley in the Chiltern Hills and that was as much as he needed to know. He wasn't to leave the house without her permission; he was to make sure no one saw him, though in his whole time there he'd never spotted another living soul.

Edward Palmer – he preferred his true identity to that of Harold Hamilton – became a nocturnal creature, free to move around the house at night and walk in the woods surrounding the house, often for hours at a time. The house had two bedrooms: Myrtle slept in the larger one, and when the mood took her, she would summon him to join her. They would share the bed and each other's bodies until such time as it was made clear he was no longer required.

When Myrtle was in a good mood, life in the house could be quite agreeable: the atmosphere was pleasant and she would be attentive and interested in him. She was not exactly forth-coming about his predicament – how long he'd be staying there, what the plans were – but he put that down to her being unsure herself.

But then for no apparent reason she'd change, becoming resentful at his presence, looking past him when she spoke, preferring to be on her own in the kitchen, staring through the window at the trees, all the while smoking.

Once or twice a week she'd leave the house, usually returning with shopping. Sometimes she'd be away for a couple of hours, other times for most of the day.

One day in October, she'd arrived back later than she'd ever done before. It was pitch dark by the time she returned, and as much as he enjoyed the solitude, Palmer was relieved to see her: he hadn't even been able to light a fire, and the early-autumn chill had penetrated the house. She was smoking when she came in, which was always a bad sign, and ordered him to join her in the lounge. She checked the curtains were closed and told him to light the fire and bring her a cup of tea.

'We may have a problem.' She paused to sip the tea and pulled a face indicating it wasn't quite to her liking. 'I went to London – to the gallery.'

'Oh yes?'

'A man called Anthony Hawke was there earlier in the week, and from what I can gather, he sounded very sympathetic to our cause and arranged to return today to purchase a painting. The Admiral considers Ridgeway to be far too trusting and instructed me to be there today with Bourne to see what I made of the man.'

She lit another cigarette, carefully watching the match as it faded. 'I found him rather plausible, and in fact when I raised the subject of the cause and our need for funds, he was most sympathetic and gave us a cheque for twenty-five pounds. My instincts about people are usually very acute, as they were with you. But it was only afterwards that I said to Bourne that I wondered if I too had been too trusting – seduced by his generosity, if you like. On reflection, there was something about him that could have been too good to be true.'

'Did he give an address – surely he can be checked out?'

'Our ability to do these things is limited, Edward, I keep telling you that. We are very few in number now: we have to be extremely careful. The Admiral is adamant we do nothing that arouses suspicion. Checking this man out could do just that. We're struggling as it is to get money over to the Continent, and that has to be our priority.'

'So when you say we may have a problem...'

'I'm being cautious. I told Bourne that for the next few weeks both he and Ridgeway are to keep their heads down: they're not to meet with anyone, no cash withdrawals, nothing to arouse suspicion. I'll not go into London for a while.'

Her announcement that he couldn't stay there for ever came three weeks after that. He wasn't sure whether it was apropos of anything in particular, so he left it, but two nights later she called him to her room. In the morning, he made her a cup of tea and brought it back to bed. He noticed that she nodded approvingly as she sipped it, so decided to raise the matter.

'I was wondering what caused you to say I couldn't stay here indefinitely?'

She turned to look at him, weighing up whether to answer. She finished her tea and plumped her pillow. 'We heard from Germany, from someone in Frankfurt. You remember I told you about the English couple who turned up there?' She moved closer and placed her hand on his stomach. 'Well, it seems that the man is almost certainly the same one who was hunting for you earlier this year, and who so nearly found you. We think his name is Prince.'

'The one you encountered in Gerrards Cross?'

'Yes – and who I identified at the pub in London. If he's involved in this case, then there could be a problem.'

'So what is going to happen?'

'The Admiral is of the view – which I share – that it's too dangerous for you to remain in this country. We can get you on the Kestrel Line and away from Europe, and you'll be able to take money over with you.'

He edged away from her. 'But how will I get there... and when?'

'I'm sorting things out at the moment, Edward. I'll probably travel with you.' She was talking as if they were planning a Sunday-afternoon outing, and now she pressed her warm body against his colder one.

–

'That's rather put the cat amongst the pigeons, hasn't it, Tom?'

'In what sense, Roly?'

'Oh do come off it… A few weeks ago you were all for giving up looking for this Friedrich chap, ready to file it under "too much trouble", but now – judging by this august gathering – it would seem to be a matter of the utmost urgency.'

Sir Roland Pearson swept his arm round to indicate all the people present, like a conductor preparing his orchestra. They were in a secure room in the basement of the MI6 offices. Roland Bentley was there, along with Hugh Harper from MI5 and a man called Bartholomew. Prince and Hanne were sitting at the end of the table.

'I think one has to recognise that the rules of the game have rather changed,' said Gilbey. He was looking in the direction of Prince and Hanne. Prince glanced at his wife. He could sense she was confused by the language and the unspoken tension in the room.

'Prince, perhaps you and Hanne would care to give us your assessment of the situation,' said Bentley. 'We need to know how seriously we ought to take this Bormann business. If we believe it is true, then we need to up our game. Because of the gravity of the matter, I have referred it to the very highest levels, and I can tell you, the view of His Majesty's Government is that because Bormann is arguably the most prominent Nazi apparently still at liberty, capturing him should be regarded as a priority.'

Prince looked at Hanne and gestured for her to speak. The others in the room seemed surprised.

'I think the truth is we cannot be certain about what happened to Martin Bormann: I think we should regard him as unaccounted for rather than being at liberty.'

'Nonetheless—'

'My personal view is that had he been killed, we would have known about it by now. Commissar Gurevich, with whom we've been dealing, does not seem to think Bormann is dead. Through him I met Willi Kühn, who told me how Wolfgang Steiner had recently been to see him. I – we – think that the people running the Kestrel Line believe Bormann is still alive and are therefore anxious to help him escape. Who knows – it is possible Steiner found Bormann after he met Kühn: we just don't know.'

'You agree, Prince?'

'Of course I do, sir. Until we have proof that Bormann is dead or captured, we must assume he's alive and pursue this. I think we must keep up the hunt for Friedrich Steiner: find him and we'll find Bormann.'

'And how would you propose we go about that?'

'If I may say, I think we are messing around.' Hanne sounded annoyed. 'Since I have been in this country, I notice how many meetings you have – meetings to decide everything. Meetings take up too much time and get in the way of an investigation. We know from Willi Kühn that Villach in Austria is a key place on the Kestrel Line. We ought to be there now rather than wasting our time talking about whether we think Bormann is alive or not.'

'Hanne...' Prince had placed his hand on his wife's arm.

Tom Gilbey looked angry and started to speak, but Roland Bentley stopped him. 'I don't know what you were about to say, Tom, but I happen to very much agree with Hanne. We should be showing a far greater sense of urgency in pursuing Bormann. It would be an enormous feather in this country's cap if we're the ones to capture him. We wouldn't want the Russians to have that honour, would we?'

'Or the Americans.'

'Absolutely, Roly.'

'Or the French.'

'I'd have thought that's highly unlikely, Tom.' There was a ripple of laughter around the table. 'You two need to get to Villach as soon as possible. I find it hard to believe two agents as experienced as you won't pick up the trail. Do we know whose zone Villach is in?'

'Ours, sir.'

'Jolly good – there ought to be a FSS in the town. Tom, have a word in the right ears to make sure they cooperate – remember it's them working for us, not the other way round.'

'Can I ask what FSS stands for?' Hanne asked.

'Of course – Field Security Section. They're part of our military intelligence: we put them into areas we're running. Tom, we'd better get a move on with getting these two out there, hadn't we?'

'May I ask about the London end of things – this art gallery: is that still of interest?' Hugh Harper gave the impression he was hoping he'd be told the services of MI5 would no longer be required.

Gilbey turned to his two agents at the end of the table. 'We've not got anywhere on that, have we, Prince?'

'No, sir, we haven't. With the help of Mr Harper and Bartholomew, we've been watching the gallery and keeping an eye on Bourne and Ridgeway, but so far nothing.'

'And nor did a thorough look at their various bank accounts turn anything up, other than evidence of a higher-than-normal incidence of cash transactions' said Harper. 'We've got telephone-tapping and mail-opening warrants, but no joy there either.'

'Well perhaps it was a long shot anyway,' said Gilbey. 'Let's concentrate on Austria, eh?'

'I think that would be a mistake.'

'I beg your pardon, Roly?'

'I think it would be a mistake to concentrate on Austria and forget about this end of things. Remember, I'm the one who went into the gallery: I've met both Bourne and Ridgeway, and the woman too. There's little doubt in my mind that there's something fishy going on there, and we know for a fact that they were the ones who sent Charles Falmer over to Frankfurt with all that money, which was almost certainly for the Kestrel Line. We simply cannot afford to ignore that.'

'So your point is…'

'My point is we should still watch the gallery: it may give us a lead to the Kestrel Line and thus to Bormann. Do remember, the woman in Bourne's office admitted they were providing funds and said that there are people in this country they wish to send on the same route too – that was the phrase she used, if I recall correctly.'

Hugh Harper said he could still have Bartholomew watch the gallery, but Prince said he foresaw a problem with that.

'From everything Sir Roland has said, I'm sure the woman at the gallery was the same one I saw in Gerrards Cross and at the pub. My instinct is she's probably more important than Bourne and Ridgeway. But I'm the only one who can identify her.'

'And you can hardly be both here and in Austria.'

'Not at the same time Mr Gilbey, no.'

'In that case' said Gilbey 'perhaps the best thing would be for Hanne to go over to Austria and Prince to stay here? That way we could cover both bases.'

Chapter 19

Austria, November 1945

'This really isn't a matter for discussion, Wilf – it's an order. It came from the War Office in London to Eighth Army headquarters, and from there to me, and now I'm passing it on to you. I would add that as orders from London go, this one is notably unambiguous. Is there any part of it you're unclear about?'

Wilf Hart rolled his eyes and replied in a resigned manner. 'The woman flies into Klagenfurt later this afternoon and I'm to escort her back to Villach, where I'm to afford her every assistance in an operation I've yet to be told about.'

Major Laurie Stewart leaned back in his chair, contemplating not for the first time whether he should replace the man sitting in front of him. Stewart commanded the British Army's Field Security Sections in Carinthia in southern Austria, and Captain Wilf Hart ran the FSS unit in Villach. If it wasn't for the fact that he was actually very efficient and spoke good German, he'd certainly move him elsewhere. Hart was somewhat older than his commanding officer, and Stewart had long detected a degree of resentment from him. He was now detecting that resentment over the orders he'd just been given.

'That is not quite true, though, is it, Wilf? I told you the woman is an MI6 agent with what I'm told is an outstanding record of service during the war. Her mission is to be regarded as your priority and you're to do as she requests. She's on the trail of escaping Nazis and is acting on information that some may be in or passing through Villach.'

'I've not picked up so much as a hint of that.'

'Which doesn't mean it's not happening, does it? In my experience, MI6 aren't in the habit of dispatching agents around Europe on a whim.'

'Oh, I don't know…'

'What is the problem, Wilf? Is it that I'm asking you to take orders from a woman?'

Captain Hart appeared uncomfortable and avoided looking at his commanding officer.

'Not in so many words, sir. You said she isn't English – one wonders…'

'*I'm* not English, Hart.'

'I meant British: I would have thought that was self-evident.'

'I can move you back here to Klagenfurt if you prefer: you'd no longer be running your own little unit, but we do have a building full of captured documents here, and going through them would keep you more than busy.'

Captain Hart apologised and said no, of course not, he was sorry for any misunderstanding, and maybe the exhaustion was getting to him. 'Not stopped since Italy, have we, sir?'

–

Hanne Jakobsen was met at Klagenfurt airbase by both Major Stewart and Captain Hart, the former assuring her of the full cooperation of the Field Security Section. When he finished shaking her hand, he introduced her to Hart, who was very polite and said it would take a little over an hour to get to Villach.

Hanne said in that case they'd better get a move on, and thank you very much but she could carry her own case.

The Field Security Section had taken over a building on Hauptplatz in the centre of Villach, halfway between the Drava river and St Jakob's church. It served as their base and their living quarters, and when Captain Hart came down for breakfast the following morning, the Danish woman was waiting for him, clearly impatient to get started.

She asked him what the Field Security Section actually did. Captain Hart explained that their primary function was to run the denazification process, to interview people who'd been prominent in the previous regime, to look at documents and to assist with intelligence that could help the British forces in Austria.

'Very well – and have you found many Nazis?'

He paused as one of his men brought in a cup of tea and a plate of toast. He placed his cigarette in the saucer and drank the tea, looking at Hanne as if he was unsure of what to make of her. His first impression was that she was very calm and organised.

'The trite answer would be no – very few people in Austria will admit to having been a Nazi, and those we can prove were members of the Nazi Party tell us they were obliged to join it otherwise they'd lose their jobs. It's remarkable, actually: Carinthia was one of the most loyal regions of the Reich, yet somehow the whole place has gone rather quiet. People here insist Austria was as much a victim of the war as other occupied countries: they don't seem to understand why we're treating them like the Germans. So the long answer to your question is that we get remarkably little cooperation. We've sent a few prominent local Nazis to Klagenfurt, and at the moment my main priority is keeping an eye on whoever returns to the town.'

'Meaning...?'

'Meaning that many men from the town served in the German forces, and some of them are beginning to come home, especially those claiming to be Wehrmacht conscripts. We interrogate each and every one of those, just to be sure no SS chaps are slipping through the net. You'll have seen when we drove in yesterday that the town was quite badly bombed, lots of buildings destroyed and two or three hundred civilians killed by all accounts. It doesn't make them terribly well disposed towards us – when the Eighth Army captured the town, there wasn't much bunting out, I can tell you. Anyway, how we can help you?'

Hanne explained that they were searching for a Gestapo officer originally known as the Ferret whose real name was Friedrich Steiner. With the help of the Russians, they'd found out that his father, Wolfgang, was involved in organising an escape route called the Kestrel Line. They knew precious little about it, she said, other than that Friedrich was on it and that it started in Frankfurt and Villach was a stopping point.

'You're sure of that?'

She said she was reasonably sure.

'No other clues?'

She shrugged. 'He may be accompanied by a one-armed man – he was with him in Frankfurt when he escaped – but that's about it. There is something else, Captain… I think if we were just searching for one Gestapo officer, we would have given up by now, but we believe Wolfgang Steiner was organising the Kestrel Line not primarily for his son but for a very prominent Nazi, for whom he worked in Berlin. His name is Martin Bormann.' She was about to ask whether he'd heard of him, but Hart let out a long whistle and his eyes widened.

'Really?'

'He is certainly connected with it, but we don't know where he is. We know he hasn't been captured, and if he's dead, no one has claimed it. So there's good reason to believe he's on the Kestrel Line. It should be easier to find Friedrich Steiner, and he could lead us to Bormann.'

Captain Hart frowned. 'I can see how important this is. I would suggest we interrogate prominent people in the town, and most especially the Nazis—'

Hanne shook her head. 'No, no, no – that won't work; in fact it could just alert them. I doubt many Nazis in a place like this would know anything about the Kestrel Line, and if they do, they're not going to say anything. I have a thought, though. Have you come across anyone here who you are certain wasn't a Nazi – who perhaps has strong anti-Nazi credentials?'

Hart laughed and pushed his chair back. 'If there was anyone like that, they wouldn't have survived through the war, I can tell you that. Remember, the Nazis came to power in Austria in early 1938. No anti-Nazi we could trust would have stayed free for seven years. But even if we found such a person, what would they know?'

'They may have heard a rumour or picked up some gossip, you never know.'

Hart said nothing for a while as he closed his eyes and tilted his head back, slowly nodding it, deep in thought. 'I wonder... I wonder...'

'What is it?'

'Now that I think about it, one of my corporals – Harcourt – did meet a Jewish gentleman... Let me call him in.'

Corporal Harcourt seemed pleased that his advice was being sought, and yes, of course he remembered the gentleman. 'He turned up in early August – he wasn't registered in the area and his papers weren't in order. When he told our chaps he was originally from the town but had fled the Nazis, they brought him here and I interviewed him. Would you mind if I sat down, sir?'

He pulled up a chair and angled it to face Hanne.

'The gentleman was in his fifties, I would say, and really rather charming. His name was Mayer, and he was brought up in Villach but left when he went to university and hadn't lived in the town since then. His parents had a clothes shop near the station, which is on the north bank of the Drava. When they died in the early 1930s, he inherited the shop and the apartment above it, both of which he rented out to a couple called Winkler. He'd return to the town once or twice a year to check on his property, and was last here in 1938, just after the Nazis came to power. He described the Winklers as good tenants and decent people. They knew what was going on and agreed he could sell the property to them for a very modest amount to prevent it being seized by the Nazis: the understanding was that after the war they would return the property to him, and they even exchanged documents to that effect, which was most unusual.'

'And Mayer obviously survived the war?'

'He managed to get into Switzerland and remained there for the duration of the war. Now he was back and needed us to verify his identity so the ownership of the property could be transferred back to him. Herr Winkler had died early in the war, but Frau Winkler had kept the shop going and lived in the apartment. It was untouched by the bombing and she told him the bombers must have known it was a Jewish property. Mayer said she readily signed back the property to him and asked him to take rent she owed, which he wouldn't do. He said she could not have been more decent: not only was there not a hint of anti-Semitism about her, but she was very anti-Nazi.'

'Well, they all are, aren't they?'

'Mayer said she and her husband always were like that: in 1938 it would have been easy for them to claim the property by saying a Jewish landlord had treated them badly, or she could have destroyed her copy of the papers that showed the property would be returned to Mayer.'

'So it seems we could trust her, Corporal?'

'Absolutely, yes.'

'But would she know about anything clandestine going on in the town now?'

Corporal Harcourt shrugged. 'Why don't we go and ask her?'

—

They'd wanted to bring Frau Winkler to the FSS base on Hauptplatz, but Hanne suggested she go to the shop near the station on her own. It was dimly lit and dusty, with women's clothes crammed on one side of a narrow aisle and men's on the other. Most of the shelves were taken up with hats and gloves, and the rails with jackets and coats. At the end of the aisle Frau

Winkler sat behind a raised counter, surveying the shop like a schoolteacher watching her pupils.

Hanne explained that she was working for the British authorities, at which point she noticed Frau Winkler pale and grip the side of the counter. She told her not to worry, she was not in any kind of trouble; in fact Herr Mayer had told them how decent she'd been, and would it be possible to ask her some questions?

Come back in forty minutes when I close for lunch: we can talk upstairs.

The apartment was as crammed as the shop below it: dark furniture adorned with ornaments and framed photographs, many of them by a bay window draped in an ornate net curtain. Frau Winkler sat nervously on the edge of her seat and gave a series of polite but sparse answers to Hanne's questions.

Yes, Herr Mayer was a fine landlord and a decent man as his parents had been… All this dreadful talk about Jews, they were the most decent people in the town… The arrangement was a very fair one… There was no question we would honour our agreement to return the property to him after the war… No, my husband died in 1941 – from cancer…

At that point Frau Winkler indicated a silver-framed photograph of a man in what Hanne assumed was the uniform of the Austro-Hungarian army, smiling at it fondly.

We were always opposed to the Nazis; we considered ourselves social democrats… We were very private people… never wanted any trouble, you understand… but what the Nazis were up to was appalling, especially to the Jews…

She explained how she and her husband had resolved they would do nothing to help the regime, but nor would they do anything to draw attention to themselves. 'If someone had come and said their life was in danger, I hope I would have helped. But here, in this town, that situation never arose. After dear Klaus died, I was too occupied with keeping the business going by myself. Many shops were destroyed by the bombing, but this one was spared. Nonetheless, I was a coward. I'm ashamed of myself.'

She was wringing her hands, looking down at the rug that lay between her and Hanne, tilting her head as if following the pattern. Her distress was quite sincere, and it was at this point that Hanne decided she could trust her.

'Ashamed in what way?'

'I feel I should have done something: maybe Klaus and I felt that promising ourselves we would return the property to Herr Mayer was enough, but other people in other places in Europe, one hears about how brave they were...'

Hanne assured Frau Winkler there was nothing someone like her could have done. 'But perhaps you can help me now. Do you know about any Nazis who were in the town – I don't mean so much during the war, but perhaps people who've been active in the six months since the war ended? Maybe you're aware of something suspicious?'

Frau Winkler moved back in her seat. She was a tiny woman, and the armchair appeared to envelop her. She shook her head and frowned, and Hanne wasn't surprised. She hadn't really expected this widow in her late sixties to know anything, and she couldn't blame her. Avoiding trouble was almost an act of resistance in itself.

'I did have a friend, though, Frau Egger – perhaps friend is the wrong word. I've known her for years, in fact we were at school together, but she is a most unpleasant woman. She loves gossip and she loves using people, and she also loves a bargain: she expected a generous discount in the shop. I tolerated her before the war, no more than that, but once the war began, she became an active member of the Nazi Party, and in fact was the *Blockleiter* in this area – you know what that is? A *Blockleiter* was a Nazi who kept their eyes and ears open in a particular area, sometimes just a street or an apartment building. I encouraged her to believe we were good friends because I reasoned that one day I might need her: you never know, someone might have asked questions about me – that kind of thing happened all the time. Fortunately that need never arose. Since the end of the war, the foolish woman has been devastated: she comes into the shop and tells me how terrible everything is, and I take some pleasure in no longer allowing her the discount I felt obliged to give her during the war. I tell her times are hard – she understands that.'

Hanne nodded politely and wondered how she could explain that she needed to leave soon without appearing rude. Frau Winkler was clearly unable to help: she just wanted to talk.

'Frau Winkler, maybe I—'

'Hang on, my dear, please... You asked me if I've been aware of anything since the war ended, and that's what I'm coming to. You see, in the middle of September, Frau Egger came into the shop and was in a far better mood than she had been for a while. She was very upbeat and chose a fine pair of leather gloves for the winter and didn't even ask for a discount. She told me she had a job – a very important one, she said, a reward for her loyalty to the Reich. She said she'd been approached by a man from Vienna who'd heard she was a good Nazi and a *Blockleiter* and that her sons had been in the Waffen SS. He told her he'd bought a house overlooking the Ossiacher See, which is a lake about five miles north-east of the town – you may have seen it. He wanted Frau Egger to work there as a housekeeper, going in to clean every day and doing the cooking when people stayed there. She found it hard to contain herself: she said very important people stay at the house, though usually only for a day or two. She also said there was an armed guard there. She said she'd been sworn to secrecy but knew she could trust me: she was beside herself with excitement. It had quite clouded her judgement.'

'Did she give any names?'

'No.'

'And the man from Vienna?'

'No name either; she just said he was a gentleman and very important.'

'And where exactly is the house?'

'All she said was that it was near Sattendorf, on the north side of the lake. I didn't think much of it at the time, not least because Frau Egger is prone to exaggeration and likes to make herself appear important. But when you asked me if I'd come across anything suspicious, I recalled what she'd told me. What do you think?'

Hanne said nothing as she tried to work out what she thought. There was no question in her mind that this could be important, but she wondered how far she could trust Frau Winkler. The alternative, she decided, was to return to Hauptplatz and put it in the hands of Captain Hart and his men, but she wasn't sure about that either.

'You say Frau Egger goes to clean the house every day?'

Frau Winkler nodded. 'Apart from Sundays.'

'Of course. And how does she get there?'

'By bus – I see her every morning around eight o'clock waiting at the stop by St Nicholas's church.'

'Which bus does she take?'

'I can't remember the number – they've all changed since the buses started again – but it's the Bodensdorf service. It starts on Hauptplatz, crosses the river, then stops outside the church, as I say, before heading through the town and along the north side of the lake. It stops at Annenheim, Sattendorf and Deutschberg before Bodensdorf, if that helps you: Klaus and I used to enjoy that trip, it was a lovely outing…'

Hanne leaned forward and took the old woman's hand. She said she hoped she'd understand if she asked her not to utter a word about this to anyone.

Frau Winkler nodded with the eagerness of a child let in on a secret.

'Can you tell me how I can identify Frau Egger?'

Frau Winkler described someone of medium height who always wore a dark brown coat and a black beret. It could have been any woman in the town in their sixties.

'Is there anywhere I could see her, perhaps?'

'She returns from the house in the middle of the afternoon and goes straight to the bakery across the road from here. There's usually quite a queue when they reopen at four o'clock, and she's invariably in it, pushing her way to the front.'

Hanne asked if Frau Winkler could walk past the bakery later on in the afternoon and approach Frau Egger so Hanne could identify her. 'Perhaps stop and speak with her – maybe put your hand on her shoulder?'

Frau Winkler said that would be no problem. In fact she'd buy some bread while she was at it. 'You make yourself comfortable: you'll have a good view from here.'

–

Hanne left Frau Winkler's just after four thirty, after watching her hold what appeared to be a friendly conversation with Frau Egger in the queue, placing one hand on her shoulder as they parted. She held it there for slightly longer than Hanne would have liked, but it didn't seem to bother Frau Egger, and when Frau Winkler glanced up at the window, Frau Egger didn't notice.

She walked back through the town to Hauptplatz, pausing on the Draubrücke to watch the Drava flow urgently beneath it on its long journey east from Italy. She was mesmerised as the water changed colour and speed by the second, and by the trees arranged like small forests on both banks, encroaching into the river itself.

She felt satisfied as she continued walking, pleased that she'd got somewhere and relieved that she didn't have to involve the FSS at this stage. Once she was certain about the house, she'd tell Captain Hart. Until then, she was on her own. It felt safer that way. She couldn't wait to tell Richard.

She'd been so taken with the river and so busy thinking through her plan for the next day, she didn't spot either of the two men who'd been following her since leaving Frau Winkler's – not the older one, tall with a short leather jacket, or the younger one, who looked like a boxer waiting for the bell to ring. It wasn't entirely her fault that she didn't notice them: both men were skilled at ensuring they weren't detected – they'd grown used to their lives depending on it.

She didn't spot them when they followed her as far as the FSS building on Hauptplatz, or when she emerged from the same building early the following morning and walked the short distance down the icy street to the bus stop. Nor did she notice them getting on the same bus as her when it pulled in before heading north, next stop St Nicholas's church. By now the older man was accompanied by a woman.

Frau Egger was waiting at the bus stop outside the church, shoving aside a mother and child to ensure she got a seat. She was wearing the dark brown coat and black beret of the previous day, and looked dumpier and less elegant than Frau Winkler, untidy silver-grey hair poking from under her beret and a pair of spectacles held together by tape. She sat towards the front of the bus, a few rows in front of Hanne.

The bus made noisy progress through the town, and soon the lake came into view. A few passengers alighted at Annenheim, and when they passed a sign for Sattendorf, the vehicle slowed down and Frau Egger stood up and slowly made her way to the door. Hanne waited until it had stopped, not wanting to get too close to the woman she was following.

There wasn't much to the village, which lay on the north shore of the lake: just houses, and what appeared to be a hotel or two close to the water. More houses were dotted on the hill rising on the north side of the road, with mountains looming high above them.

Frau Egger crossed the road from the bus stop and stopped to put on her scarf and gloves. She walked faster than Hanne would have expected, up a road with large houses arranged on either side, then turned right up a narrower road with only the occasional house on it. As the road became steeper, she paused once or twice but didn't turn round. Hanne slowed her own pace, allowing the distance to increase between her and the older woman. It was bitterly cold; the air fresh from the lake and the mountains, and the sun cast the area in an almost blinding light. At one stage Hanne turned round and noticed a couple behind her, clearly hikers out for a day on the mountains. They didn't seem to notice her.

Frau Egger stopped outside a high metal gate and appeared to press a bell. As Hanne walked past, a young man opened the gate and hurried the housekeeper in. In the brief moment before the gate closed, she spotted a drive leading to a small but smart-looking white house. She carried on walking up the hill. The house had been the last one on the narrow road, and now she was in the countryside, the wind sweeping down from the mountain. The hikers walked past her, wishing her a good morning.

She waited until they'd disappeared and then walked through the gorse to circle round until she had a view of the house. She noticed now that the trees on the lower slopes of the mountains reached as far as the rear of the house. Despite not being dressed for the rough terrain and the biting cold, she carried on. At the start of the treeline, a well-maintained wooden fence barred entry into the woods. She managed to climb over and felt safer once in the cover of the trees. She moved through them, closer to the house. Soon parts of a white building with a red-tiled roof became visible. As she paused to catch her breath, she noticed a wire fence just a few feet ahead of her; the top strand was barbed wire. Avoiding the fence, she moved further round towards what she guessed was the rear of the house. It was then that she spotted a tree with a long branch just four feet from the ground. She pulled a log across and managed to haul herself onto the branch, from where she had a much better view of the house.

She could see a high fence surrounding its perimeter, and beyond that a glimpse of snow-covered grass leading to the house. The windows were all shuttered. As she craned her neck, she caught a movement: a man carrying what appeared to be a sub-machine gun walking along the side of the house with a large black dog by his side.

She glanced at her watch. It was nearly ten o'clock. It would be some hours before Frau Egger would leave, but her visit had served its purpose. She was sure she'd identified the house. She had no doubt this was a stopping point on the Kestrel Line. She would return to the town and brief Captain Hart, and they'd return in force once it was dark.

At that moment, she became aware of a noise beneath her, and before she could look down, she felt a tap on her ankle and heard the click of a safety catch being released on a gun.

'Climb down very slowly, please.' It was a man's voice, speaking German.

'And when you reach the ground, keep your arms in the air.'

Chapter 20

Berlin, December 1945

It was the great paradox of Kommissar Iosif Gurevich's war, and more particularly its aftermath.

He'd spent over four years either in enemy territory or fighting them every day. It was reasonable to assume that once the war was over, there'd be a sense of absolute relief and of pleasure at life returning to normal.

And for the first few weeks – perhaps until the end of June – this had indeed been the case. He'd relished the absence of danger and enjoyed the considerable trappings of victory. But as the summer took hold of Berlin, the city began to shake itself down and the Allied powers staked their various claims, his feelings began to change. It dawned on him how much he missed living with danger. He realised how the unique sense of exhilaration that came from risking his life had become an urgent physical desire.

Sometime in August, a young officer from one of Marshal Konev's mechanised brigades had gone mad, climbing onto the table in the officers' mess and shouting about peasants and Nazis as he fired his revolver at the ceiling before blowing off his own head.

Konev had been persuaded that this could well have been a direct consequence of the psychological effect of the war, and he realised the Red Army couldn't risk a recurrence. As a result, a group of psychiatrists had been dispatched from Moscow with orders to interview all senior officers.

Kommissar Iosif Gurevich had been blasé about his own appointment. There was, after all, nothing wrong with him. He'd survived the war and had since been promoted, and he was absolutely fine, especially since he'd tracked down the SS officer who'd murdered his family in Minsk and wrought his revenge. Seeing the psychiatrist would be a mere formality, something he was only doing because he'd been ordered to. It would be like the visit he'd made to the dentist the previous week.

The dentist had turned out to be a rather beautiful woman from Leningrad who he was convinced had allowed her hands to brush his face: he'd even arranged another visit. The psychiatrist could not have been more different: a tiny man with thick spectacles and a slightly startled expression. But there was an unspoken connection between the two of them: the Jewish psychiatrist from Moscow, the Jewish commissar from Minsk.

'Tell me about your family, Comrade.'

It was Gurevich's turn to be startled. He'd only mentioned in passing that they'd been murdered by an *Einsatzgruppen*, and he was hoping the session would shortly come to an end with the psychiatrist assuring him he was fine.

But instead he found himself talking about his family's murder, and how he had no one left other than a brother, and how much he regretted ditching a fiancée many years ago in order to save his career. By now he was pouring his heart out, and tears were running down his cheeks.

He stopped talking and apologised and assured the psychiatrist he had no idea what had got into him, but the man from Moscow said not to worry, it was good he was talking, and assured him this would not reflect badly on him at all.

'It's the ones who don't react with any emotion that I worry about. You need have no concerns about my report, Comrade.' He'd smiled: the unspoken connection.

Then Gurevich mentioned how he missed the sense of danger he'd experienced during the war, the sheer exhilaration of facing down death every day: was this... odd?

'Not at all: it was your way of coping with the stress of war and with the personal traumas in your life. Subconsciously you felt you had little to lose and therefore you were able to be reckless: it was as if you were finding a way of redeeming yourself. But a consequence of this behaviour was that this sense of risk and the excitement became like a drug. You became addicted to it.'

'I miss it dreadfully sometimes, like I'm drawn to danger.'

'Of course you will be – it's an addiction, as I said, and you are experiencing what we call withdrawal symptoms. It will take time to get over; you will need to be patient. If you occasionally flirt with danger, that may help, though do be careful.'

Iosif Gurevich said this all made sense and thanked the psychiatrist very much. As he prepared to leave, the psychiatrist came over and spoke quietly in his ear.

'On a personal note, Comrade, if you want my advice, stay here as long as you can. Things are really not good for us in Moscow.'

–

Now Kommissar Iosif Gurevich was taking the doctor's advice and flirting with danger. He'd crossed into the British sector, the risk increased by the fact that the British knew who he was but mitigated by not having shaved for a few days and being dressed in shabby civilian clothes. To add to his cover, he was accompanied by a female NKVD officer called Yulia, who provided a useful extra set of eyes and ears as they walked arm in arm through the city.

'Don't worry,' he assured her, 'our papers are very good. We're Polish Germans, a married couple from Poznań, trying to escape the damned Russians!'

He laughed, but she looked nervous: even jokes could be dangerous. Just look down, he told her. 'Avoid eye contact; look for cigarette butts on the ground. Keep coughing: they'll think you're ill and will want to move you on.'

Their destination was on Cornelius Strasse, just south of the Tiergarten. He told Yulia to wait in the shell of a bombed-out building opposite. *Lean against the wall, look exhausted; if any British soldiers say anything, ask them for money. They'll soon leave you alone then!*

Of course he could have asked them to come to him in East Berlin. It would have been more of an order than anything else and they'd have been obliged to do as he said. It was like that with these people: you were meant to be on the same side, but when one was a master and the other in effect a servant, relationships were more fraught.

The main reason he'd crossed the city to see them was that he didn't want his own people to know what he was up to. They'd benefit in the long run – possibly – but in the meantime it was best to be discreet. That familiar sense of excitement, which had been building up all day, was now even more pronounced. His heart beat faster and his senses sharpened, and he felt more alive.

He told the guard on the door who he was, and a senior officer was called who spoke good Russian. He was led up to the top floor, through part of the building that seemed to have taken a direct hit from a shell and had no windows and little in the way of walls.

The man whose office he was shown into was someone he'd met since they'd captured Berlin, and although there was an atmosphere of distrust, it was one born of uncertainty more than anything else.

They were, after all, meant to be on the same side.

Kommissar Gurevich said he didn't have long; he wanted to cross back into the east before it was dark. He explained the purpose of his visit. 'Come closer, come round here and have a look. This is them, and here… look at this map… and this photograph too.'

As he explained in more detail what he wanted, the other man remained expressionless, giving the impression that he understood what Gurevich was saying but wasn't too sure what it was that he was asking.

Kommissar Gurevich had spotted this and took two large cigars from his jacket pocket. They were intended as bribes at difficult checkpoints, but he decided this was as good a time as any, and they had the desired effect: the man looked very impressed and asked where he'd got them from, and Gurevich said it was a good job the Nazis were like magpies, and both men laughed heartily, the tension now broken.

Gurevich explained again what he wanted, and when he had finished, he took out another cigar and placed it on the desk between them.

'What I'm saying is that it's as much in your interests as it is in ours.'

The other man had already pocketed the cigar and was nodding. Both he and Gurevich knew full well that if anything, it benefited him even more.

Chapter 21

England, December 1945

In the shocking moments immediately after Tom Gilbey had spoken, Richard Prince felt himself reeling, his instinct to find something mundane to concentrate on as he absorbed the appalling news. Outside, flurries of snow that had appeared beautiful and almost balletic just minutes earlier as he'd walked through St James's now had a decidedly violent quality to them. They looked like they were in conflict. He knew how they felt.

It occurred to him that he wasn't sure how much more bad news he could take. His first wife and daughter had been killed a few years back in a car crash; then his son had gone missing, and Hanne too. He chewed hard on his knuckles in an attempt to retain some kind of composure.

Pop in for a chat, would you, Richard – later this morning, perhaps?

On reflection, Gilbey had sounded far too casual. And 'Richard': he should have remembered that the man reserved the use of his first name for serious matters.

'Did you hear what I said, Richard? That I'm terribly sorry to say that Hanne has disappeared in Austria – that town in Carinthia.'

'Yes, I heard you the first time, sir.'

'I didn't see you react.'

'And how would you like me to react, sir?'

He watched Gilbey move awkwardly in his chair and felt an odd sense of indestructibility: his boss could hardly discipline him for insubordination when he'd just announced his wife was missing.

Gilbey shrugged, looking at his desk as if that would provide him with something to say. 'It might not be such bad news; it's possible it's not as sinister as it sounds.'

'Oh really, sir – in what way exactly? That it turns out Hanne was having such a good time that she decided to go and explore the countryside and her postcard telling us is delayed in the post? She was in Villach to try and pick up the trail of the Kestrel Line. By the sounds of it, she may have done just that, and now the Nazis have captured her.'

Gilbey nodded. It was hard to disagree.

'What about the Field Security Section – weren't they meant to be looking after her?'

'They were, Richard. In fact it was Captain Hart from the FSS in Villach who raised the alarm. He—'

'I mean, shouldn't they have been with her all the time? It's not as if she was looking for a jewel thief: she was hunting for escaping Nazi war criminals, for Christ's sake!'

'Come on, Richard. One realises this is distressing news, but perhaps a sense of calm might be helpful. I can assure you Hart's commanding officer in Klagenfurt, Major Stewart, is hopping mad about this, though he does say that apparently Hanne showed a tendency to operate on her own.'

'Well she was hardly going to drag the Home Guard around the town with her, was she, sir?'

'Somewhat unfair, Prince.'

'What do we know?'

'Evidently on the Tuesday afternoon Hanne went to see a Frau Winkler, who may have had information about recent suspicious Nazi activity in the town. According to Frau Winkler, she told Hanne that a Nazi acquaintance of hers called Frau Egger was working at a house overlooking the Ossiacher See, which is a lake just outside the town. She said she'd been hired by a man from Vienna and the house had armed guards. Hanne never told Hart about this. Early the following morning, one of Hart's chaps spotted her getting on the bus to Bodens-dorf, which would have stopped close to the house.'

'And nothing from then on?'

Gilbey shook his head. 'And before you ask, yes, the FSS are combing the area around the house, but they need to be discreet – they don't want to alert whoever's holding Hanne. The feeling is that if they know we're looking for her, it may blow whatever cover she was using.'

'Jesus Christ.'

'You'd better get out there as soon as possible.'

'That goes without saying, sir.'

'Shame, though, Prince, what with you making such good progress with the gallery.'

—

The accountant's name was Slater, and with his stooped stance, common in tall men, along with a miserable expression, he was the kind of person one had to resist the urge to tell to cheer up.

As one of MI5's specialist accountants, he'd been investigating the two business accounts of Bourne and Sons and the personal accounts of Bourne and Ridgeway. That morning, just a matter of hours before Prince had been summoned by Gilbey, he had followed Prince into his office looking almost excited.

'Mind if I pull up a chair?'

He noisily dragged one across the floor and sat slightly closer than Prince felt comfortable with. Despite the heaters being on, and everyone else in shirtsleeves, Slater was wearing a heavy suit and a thick pullover. Prince couldn't help noticing that his nose had a perpetual drop hanging from the end of it, which he occasionally wiped with the cuff of his shirt.

'I think we may have a development.' He coughed and laid some curled sheets of paper on the desk.

Prince glanced at them and told Slater it might be easier if he explained.

'You remember that our examination of the various bank accounts – business and personal – associated with Bourne and Sons was not fruitful? Well, we have been keeping an eye on all four accounts, and the people with whom we liaise in those banks know to contact us as a matter of urgency if any approach is made from their clients or if there are any unusual transactions.' Slater paused and coughed noisily before pulling a large handkerchief from his top pocket.

'The London clearing banks have to adhere to wartime regulations, which are still in force. For cash withdrawals over twenty pounds, one full working day's notice is required in writing, along with the name of the person who will be making the withdrawal. That person is required to bring their national identity card and further proof of identity. For withdrawals over fifty pounds, the requirement is for three working days' notice. However, there is an exception to the latter requirement...' Slater shifted his chair even closer to Prince and licked his thumb prior to turning over one of the sheets of paper. 'If the withdrawal is to be made from the main branch of a bank in the City of London, then only one day's notice is required, whatever the sum.

'Last Thursday, the main branch of Martins Bank in Lombard Street was informed that a Miss Myrtle Carter would be making a withdrawal of one hundred pounds in cash from the Bourne and Sons account the following day. Unfortunately, by the time we were informed of this, that withdrawal had already been made. As a consequence, we contacted the Midland Bank, who hold the other Bourne and Sons account, and instructed them to be especially alert to that account. Just fifteen minutes ago, I received a telephone call from our contact at the bank to say that a request had been received for a Miss Myrtle Carter to withdraw the sum of one hundred pounds in cash from their Threadneedle Street branch tomorrow.'

Slater looked pleased with himself and leaned back in a manner inviting a gesture of gratitude from Prince.

'No other details – like this woman's address?'

Slater shook his head. 'Looks like the ball's in your court, Mr Prince.'

Fortunately Bartholomew was in the office and they began to make plans. Bartholomew would have a team watch the Midland Bank in Threadneedle Street and arrest the woman once she had withdrawn the cash. He'd make sure every exit was covered. He'd even have people behind the counter.

Prince went to the records department in the basement and asked them to check on a Miss Myrtle Carter. A friendly woman with a Welsh accent told him she'd recently reorganised all the watch lists and they now had a centralised record of all the names on those lists. 'When I took over, there were more than two dozen separate lists, would you believe: lists of people wanted by the police, deserters from the armed forces, people who'd applied to travel abroad now that it's possible, political extremists... It was utter chaos, my love. Those individual watch lists still exist, but what I've done is create an alphabetical list of names of everyone on them. It's been invaluable. We've even spotted people on as many as three different watch lists! It's made the work of this section so much more efficient, but naturally my senior officer has taken all the credit. Now then, what did you say her name is?'

It took her less than a minute to find Myrtle Carter on her centralised list, along with a reference to where to find her in the original watch list.

'Here we are: Carter, Myrtle – she's applied for a permit to travel by ferry to France, accompanied by a Mr Harold Hamilton, both of them with an address in Bayswater. Looks like my system works a treat, eh, my love? Try and make sure I get some credit.'

But when Prince returned to his desk, there was the message to call Tom Gilbey and then the summons to St James's.

Pop in for a chat would you Richard – later this morning perhaps?

–

Prince was persuaded to return to MI5 that afternoon while arrangements were made to fly him out the following day. In the time he'd been away at MI6, Bartholomew had made progress, and now they were in Hugh Harper's office and Sir Roland Pearson had joined them. Bartholomew spoke first.

'The address in Bayswater is a large house with a dozen or so bedsits. No sign of either a Myrtle Carter or a Harold Hamilton: they've never been there as far as we can tell, nor do they receive mail there. It's what we call a postbox, which means it was probably used solely for the purpose of providing an address for registering their national identity cards. Once these came through, their contact in the house would have moved on. It's not used as a safe house or as a place to receive messages. We won't find where she or this Hamilton chap are through this address, and there's no record of her anywhere else.'

'Harold Hamilton rings a bell,' said Prince, frowning.

'Not for me, I'm afraid,' said Harper.

'The forger who was arrested in Manchester: didn't he provide a list of false identities he'd provided and try to have his charges reduced by telling us that one of his clients bore a striking resemblance to Edward Palmer – the Nazi agent code-named Milton?'

'Good Lord, Prince, you're quite right. No one believed him at the time, did they? We thought it was just an attempt to curry favour. What was the identity he said he provided for Palmer?'

'That's the point, sir – it was Harold Hamilton: the forger said he sold it at a premium.'

It was the time of year when darkness descended in the afternoon with a suddenness that turned day into unexpected night. When Hugh Harper turned on his desk light, all four people in the room looked shocked. They had now established a connection between Edward Palmer, the fugitive Nazi spy who'd worked in the War Office, and a woman associated with the group of Nazi sympathisers apparently helping to fund the Nazi escape line. For a few moments they sat in silence as they absorbed this.

'We shouldn't arrest her tomorrow, Bartholomew.'

'Whatever do you mean, Roly?' Hugh Harper looked confused.

'I agree with Sir Roland,' said Prince. 'We know that this Myrtle Carter and Edward Palmer are planning on travelling to the Continent with at least two hundred pounds. If we arrest her at the bank, we lose him. If we follow her to wherever they're living, we might arrest them both but...'

'...we lose the trail of the Kestrel Line,' said Pearson. 'Prince has got it. Bartholomew, you need to have a top team on this, and even then we're running an enormous risk. We need to keep an eye on her as far as possible, but the priority is to find out exactly when and where they're crossing the Channel and then follow them to wherever they're headed. With some luck they'll take us to Turin – and maybe even Martin Bormann.'

'And Hanne,' said Prince, his voice quiet. He was clearly upset. 'With some luck they'll lead us to Hanne.'

–

By the time Prince left MI5 that evening, his journey to Austria was taking shape. He'd be on an RAF flight in the morning to the US Air Force base in Munich, and would travel on to Villach from there.

He was staying at a MI6 safe house in Holland Park, and as it was a dry and not too cold evening, he got off the Underground early at Notting Hill Gate to walk the rest of the way. He wanted to clear his head: he ought to return to Lincoln to see Henry before travelling to find Hanne, but as much as he felt drawn towards his son, he felt he couldn't risk delaying his search for her by even one day.

He turned into Addison Road, which despite its size felt as quiet and isolated as a country lane. He stepped aside to allow a couple walking their dog to pass, and was annoyed when they slowed down in front of him. He was about to cross the road when a man came alongside and positioned himself between him and the kerb. Prince turned round: another man was close behind him, a hand menacingly inside his coat pocket.

'Don't worry, my friend.' It was the man walking next to him who spoke, his accent foreign. Prince sensed that the couple in front and the man behind were now even closer: it felt like a trap.

'I have greetings for you from my colleague Iosif in Berlin. He hopes you are well.'

'I hardly think—'

'I have limited time, so it will be best served by you listening to me. Iosif assumes you are travelling to Austria to look for Hanne.'

'How the hell do you know that?'

The man shrugged. He was a big man with a neat beard, a hat pulled low over his face. He kept his head down as he spoke. 'Please listen. Iosif says to go to Vienna first. He'll meet you there: don't worry about finding him, he'll find you.'

'I can't go to Vienna. I have to go south; I have to find Hanne.'

'That, my friend, is why he wants to meet you in Vienna!'

Chapter 22

Austria, December 1945

'It's wonderful, isn't it?'

The man who'd appeared beside him was pointing at the Hofburg Palace as if Prince hadn't noticed it. Prince had been standing in the drizzle on Heldenplatz in front of the enormous edifice for a few minutes, and had begun to feel thoroughly miserable. He now felt an enormous sense of relief.

'In what way?'

The man concentrated on finishing his cigarette. 'You'd do well to find a more impressive symbol of imperialism still standing in Europe, and now it's under the control of the Soviet Union! So when I said "wonderful", I meant the irony of us controlling what was once the heart of the Habsburg Empire.'

Prince laughed. 'But you don't control it, do you? The centre of Vienna's an international zone. We control this place as much as you do, and we still have an empire – though by the sounds of it, you're starting to acquire one!'

Iosif Gurevich laughed, then turned to embrace Prince and told him it was good to see him. 'I didn't think you'd get here quite so soon.'

They'd started to walk and were now on Löwelstrasse, the drizzle turning into heavy rain. 'I was told you might be able to help me find Hanne. You can't imagine how desperate I am, Iosif.'

'Is that what they told you?'

Prince recounted what had happened the previous evening in Holland Park.

'I said not to be so heavy-handed. Four of them behaving like that is ridiculous: it sounds as if they were planning to abduct you! That's the problem with London station. They have no sense of proportion. You look dreadful, by the way.'

'I feel it. I can't remember when I last slept.'

'Come, I have somewhere we can talk.'

–

Prince certainly hadn't slept the previous night. After his encounter with the Russians in Holland Park, he'd returned to the safe house, the message that Gurevich could help him to find Hanne occupying his every thought.

He should have reported what had happened straight away, but decided against it. He didn't want anything to jeopardise his chances of finding Hanne, especially now the Russians seemed to be offering some hope.

At the safe house there was a message from Gilbey. *Change of plan: there's a flight to Munich at three in the morning and you're on it. A car will pick you up in half an hour.*

He was driven to RAF Benson in Oxfordshire and flew from there on an RAF DC3 to Neubiberg airport just outside Munich, where he was met by a harassed British liaison officer called Cuthbert who assured him he was working on getting him to Klagenfurt. 'Shouldn't take terribly long.'

'To get to Klagenfurt?'

'Uh, no… to work out how to get you there. We're rather dependent on the Americans here. No rush, though, is there?'

Prince explained that actually there was a rush, but knew better than to rely on this man to expedite matters. He wandered around the airbase until he found the officers' mess, where he joined a table of USAF pilots to whom he explained his dilemma. *I need to get to Vienna.*

'Is this official British business?' The man who asked the question was young and wearing dark glasses, and spoke with a long cigarette clamped between his front teeth. Prince assured him it couldn't be more official.

The pilot stood up, towering over him. 'Follow me.'

He'd arrived in Vienna just before noon, and in the eight hours since then had wandered round the city knowing he'd only see the Russian when Gurevich was ready to be seen.

Don't worry about finding him, he'll find you.

And now Gurevich was ready. They made an unlikely pair as they walked through Vienna's First District, one in a British Army greatcoat, the other in a Red Army one. They walked past the magnificent St Stephan's cathedral, which seemed to throw shadows even in the dark. Gurevich's pace quickened as they turned into Dominikaner Bastei, seemingly heading towards the Danube Canal, and Prince wondered what would happen if they crossed from the neutral First District into the Soviet zone.

Gurevich stopped just before the junction with Schweden-platz. He looked round as he lit a cigarette, pausing to allow two Austrian police officers to pass. Moments later, Prince found himself in the basement of a bar, furniture piled high at one end, the bare room lit by a single bulb. Gurevich sat down opposite him at the solitary table.

'Hanne's safe.'

Prince gasped and stared intently at the Russian in an attempt to work out whether he was telling the truth.

'You look like you don't believe me, my friend. Why would I lie?'

Prince coughed and realised tears were forming in his eyes. 'It's not that I don't believe you, but... maybe this is just what someone has told you... maybe they're wrong... How do you know she's alive?'

'Believe me, I know.'

'Has she escaped from the Nazis, or been rescued?'

'Who said she was with the Nazis? In our business we shouldn't make assumptions, should we?'

'Don't play games with me, Iosif, I need to find my wife. Where the hell is she? I need to know if she's safe!'

'I told you she's safe. What happened to her may be my fault, but from what I gather, we probably saved her life. She'd got herself into a very dangerous situation.'

'Is she here in Vienna?'

'No, she's still in Villach. Don't worry; you'll be taken there tomorrow.'

'What do you mean, it may have been your fault?'

Gurevich undid his greatcoat and from an inside pocket produced a flask, which he put down on the table, indicating that Prince should drink first. 'The war was very straightforward in many ways, wasn't it? I'll admit that our alliance with Nazi Germany was awkward, though of course Comrade Stalin was correct to try and buy time. Had the Nazis invaded in 1939, we would have struggled to resist. Once they did invade, in 1941, it was clear exactly who our enemy was: we could see them, we were fighting them every day. But since the war ended, matters have become complicated. We're meant to be friends with the British and the Americans because we were on the same side, but everyone knows that it is hardly a friendship. Even within the Soviet Union the comradeship and unity that was there during the war has been replaced by a degree of mistrust.'

He wiped his mouth with his sleeve and lit a cigarette. 'And then we have our other allies, in countries where the Soviet Union is trying to exert its influence. You yourself made reference to us acquiring an empire, which of course is unfair, but it is true that there are countries in eastern and central Europe that we are trying to bring into the embrace and protection of socialism, with the Soviet Union at the vanguard showing strong leadership. We believe this is absolutely in their interests and we have no doubt that in time they will understand this too.'

He stopped and looked hard at Prince, wanting him to understand that as urbane and amenable as he was, there could be no doubt as to where his loyalties lay.

'There's an old saying I remember my grandfather using: your enemies appear in the light, your friends in the dark. The enemy is easier to spot than a friend. A friend can become an enemy before you realise it. But with some of these countries – our friends – the relationship is, how shall I phrase it… complicated. They too have fought a long and hard war and they have a desire for independence that is not necessarily compatible with our interests. So we need to work hard to extend our influence. One way of achieving this is by doing favours for them; making them feel indebted towards us.

'The country presenting us with most problems at the moment is Yugoslavia. Their partisans fought an outstanding war against the enemy, but now there are indications that they wish to follow their own path. So we need to increase our influence with them.

'After you left Berlin, I discovered that in the summer of 1944, Friedrich Steiner was transferred from Amsterdam to Maribor in Slovenia. He operated from the Gestapo bureau there under a different name, and he did not use his nickname of the Ferret. His brutality in Maribor was particularly appalling, and the Yugoslavs too are hunting for him. So I went to see them at their mission in Berlin on Cornelius Strasse. I told them about the Kestrel Line and Steiner and about Villach and you and Hanne and… hang on, hang on, hear me out… and in return I can expect favours from them: it will help make them well disposed towards us. They will understand we're on the same side.

'I was told they had sent a team to Villach. But it is important that you know I instructed them that under no circumstances should any harm come to you or Hanne: I made it very clear that you're both to be treated as comrades… Why are you shaking your head?'

'Because how do I know we can trust them?'

'They will know not to upset someone like me, but if there are any problems, you can contact me on this telephone number. Someone here in Vienna will answer. If necessary, I can come back here and sort things out.'

–

Well before her husband had arrived in Vienna – indeed, some time before he'd left London – Hanne found herself in the small wood outside Villach, standing against the base of the tree with her hands in the air as she'd been instructed to do. The man who'd given the order stood in front of her. A woman was next to him, and Hanne recognised them as the couple she'd assumed were hikers when they'd passed her minutes earlier.

Neither of them said a word, and when Hanne began to speak, the woman put a finger to her lips. The three of them stood still as the couple listened carefully. There was not a sound to be heard other than a light wind brushing the tops of the trees. Eventually the man nodded, and the woman stepped forward and searched Hanne then indicated she could lower her hands.

'Are you alone?'

The man spoke quietly but firmly and Hanne thought she detected a lack of menace in his voice. She replied that she was, and when he asked what she was doing here in the woods, she said she was out for a walk.

'You walked up a tree?'

She shrugged and said something about looking round, and when the man asked why she was looking at the house, she said she didn't know what he was talking about, realising as soon as she said it just how unconvincing it sounded.

'We can talk later, it's not safe here – but you probably know that. Come.'

They started to walk through the woods, Hanne behind the woman and in front of the man. When they reached the wooden fence, she noticed a younger man crouched by it with a pistol in his hand. He spoke quietly with the couple in a language she couldn't place before heading off. Hanne waited in the woods with the couple, the three of them sitting down between the trees. She asked what this was all about and said she needed to return to the town, but they shook their heads and said 'later'.

After about an hour, the younger man returned and they followed him to a car parked on the nearby lane. As far as Hanne could tell, they drove past Villach and ended up somewhere to the south-east of the town. On the outskirts of a village, they pulled onto a rough track and then into a farmyard. The farmhouse was bitterly cold and sparsely furnished.

'We aren't Germans,' the older man said as the four of them sat around the kitchen table. 'You should understand that we are on the same side as you. I will tell you what we know and then you will tell us what you know.'

He opened a packet of cigarettes and placed it in front of him. Hanne reckoned he was in his fifties, his eyes red with exhaustion.

'We know you're on the trail of a Nazi escape line – the Kestrel Line – which is connected to Villach. We know the Kestrel Line is organised by an Austrian Nazi called Wolfgang Steiner and that his son Friedrich is one of the fugitives on it. We know too that there is a possibility that Martin Bormann is also on it. We're aware that you're working for the British. We've been watching you since you arrived here and we believe you may have a lead – we suspect you think the house you were watching in the woods may be connected to the Kestrel Line. This is all correct?'

Hanne said nothing. A younger woman had come into the room and sat down. All four now watched Hanne closely. 'Can I ask who you are?' she said eventually.

'I'll tell you who we are and you will answer our questions.' It was the woman who'd just come into the room. Although she was the youngest of the four, she had an air of authority about her. 'My name is Marija, this is Branka.' She pointed at the other woman and then towards the two men: 'Edvard and Jožef. Your name is Hanne, isn't it?'

Hanne nodded.

'Are you on your own in Villach?'

'Not quite.'

'With your husband?'

She shook her head.

'We're Slovenian partisans – members of Osvobodilna Fronta Slovenskega Naroda, the Liberation Front of Slovenia, which is part of the Yugoslav National Liberation Army. You may have heard of our leader, Tito: the Yugoslav partisans were the most successful resistance organisation in Nazi-occupied Europe.'

The others nodded and Marija paused as she lit a cigarette. 'The Nazis divided Slovenia into three zones – one controlled by the Germans, one by Italy and the other by Hungary. It was a brutal occupation, especially in the German area. The centre of that was Maribor, which is the second largest city in Slovenia and is where we're from. Maribor traditionally had a large German-speaking minority and the Germans wanted to turn the area into a German one. The oppression of the Slovenes was dreadful.

'The Gestapo in Maribor was based at Kersnikova, and I don't think I need to tell you how cruel they were. Many civilians were murdered. In the summer of 1944, a new Gestapo officer by the name of König arrived at Kersnikova. There is no question he was the worst of the lot.'

'The man was a psychopath.' It was the first time the younger man, Jožef, had spoken.

'Every Gestapo and SS officer who served in Maribor was a war criminal, and those who were still alive at the end of the war are now in our custody.'

'Apart from König,' said Jožef.

'And he's the one we want most.' Marija paused and angrily stubbed her cigarette out on a saucer. Edvard leaned over the table and spoke in a quiet voice.

'In November, König arrested three seventeen-year-old girls he spotted walking on the street. He claimed they were involved with partisans – this was quite untrue, but he concocted some flimsy evidence against them and used that as a pretext to keep them in custody and interrogate them. The girls were all very pretty, and we're convinced that was his motive for arresting them. From what we gather, he raped all three of them over a three-day period and then shot them.'

The room was silent but for the sound of a dripping tap and the wind whistling through a cracked window.

'Their bodies were found in a wood outside the town. At around the same time, König left Maribor,' said Branka, her German more hesitant. 'So you can see why we want to catch him.'

'Once the war was over, a Yugoslav mission was established in Berlin, and through them we've tried to find König, but we could discover no trace of him. As far as we could tell, König was an assumed name. But recently there was a breakthrough: our mission in Berlin was told that König was in fact Friedrich Steiner, who'd served as a Gestapo officer in France and the Netherlands and was wanted by the British for the murder of their agents.' Marija nodded as she finished talking.

'Which brings us here,' said Edvard. 'Tell us why you were interested in that house.'

Hanne didn't think she was in a position to hide anything. She told them how they knew the Kestrel Line had some connection with Villach, and about Frau Winkler and the house near Sattendorf. 'I needed to check it was the right place; when I saw it was guarded and looked very secure, I realised it must be. My intention was to return with British troops. Then you came.'

'Then we came indeed. But what you did was very reckless, Hanne. We have spent the war fighting the enemy, risking our lives every day. We know how dangerous it can be. You were on your own, you were exposed, and had we not found you, the Germans would have done.

'Edvard, please don't lecture me about the dangers of oper-ating in enemy territory!' Hanne's voice was raised and the four looked up at her. 'I worked for the British in Denmark, then I was a prisoner of the Gestapo and spent two years in a concentration camp. I know what danger is, thank you. I knew what I was doing. You may well have alerted the Nazis yourself turning up like that. You should have left me to it.'

The Slovenians apologised one by one.

'All we want is the man Steiner: in return, we'll help you to find where the Kestrel Line ends. Who knows who else you'll find there – maybe even Bormann himself?'

'Where do you think the Kestrel Line goes from here?' Hanne had calmed down and the atmosphere in the room had changed. It was clear they were now on the same side.

'Look...' Jožef pulled a map from his pocket. 'We're here, just south of Villach. The Nazis chose this place well: we're only five miles or so from the Slovenian border, but more importantly from their point of view, maybe seven miles from Italy. My guess is that the Kestrel Line ends there.'

'Across the Gailtal Alps,' said Edvard, 'the natural habitat of the kestrel.'

–

Prince left Vienna as dawn broke over the city, a muted light filtering through the black clouds as the sun rose from the east. The rain was so heavy it felt as if the waters of the Danube had been whipped up and were being sprayed over the southern suburbs as the Red Army staff car picked its way through the bomb-damaged roads. Gurevich sat in the back with Prince, toying with an unlit cigar and wiping the condensation from the window with a leather-gloved hand.

'It still looks like a battlefield, doesn't it, my friend? I'm told the campaign to take the city was particularly bitter – our offensive was mostly from the south, round here. It would explain why the place looks like Berlin. I almost feel at home!'

They picked up the pace as they drove through Wiener Neustadt, continuing south through the Soviet zone. Just after the small town of Friedberg, the car turned off the road, driving along a narrow track through a wood and pulling into a small clearing, where it parked alongside an unmarked black Daimler. Iosif Gurevich told his driver to leave the car and turned to look at Prince.

'I do what I can to help you, I hope you understand that. I feel an obligation to you – we are friends, I can trust you.'

Prince said he was very grateful, but the Russian hadn't finished. 'I'm not naïve; I'm a Red Army officer – a commissar. I know that politics matters and dictates the relationship between our countries, and of course my loyalty will always be to the Soviet Union. But I see no reason not to help you as a friend when I can – when our interests happily coincide. I don't know if we'll ever see each other again: I will return to Berlin, but my future may be uncertain. I just want you to know that you can trust me, and all I ask is that maybe one day you will ask after me.'

'Of course, I—'

'But use your discretion, please – it may not look good if people know I have a British friend!'

They embraced, and Gurevich told Prince the other car would drive him to Klagenfurt; he'd better get a move on.

Just before noon, the Daimler stopped in a side street in the centre of Klagenfurt. The driver – a heavily built man with notably thick eyebrows and bloodshot eyes – turned round and spoke for the first time, in a deep voice: *walk along this block, take the first left and then turn right – the building you want will be ahead of you. You'll spot your flag.*

The building was the headquarters of the Field Security Section, and within minutes of announcing himself at the guard post, Prince was in Major Stewart's office.

'Where the hell have you been, Prince?'

Prince said he'd taken a roundabout route.

'I don't think people like you appreciate quite what havoc you wreak. Poor old Cuthbert at Munich has had something of a nervous breakdown. He's being blamed for losing you. What's this about you hitching a ride on an American plane to Vienna?'

Prince said that was for another time. His priority now was to get to Villach and find Hanne.

'Oh, don't worry about her, she's fine – turned up at the FSS headquarters there very pleased with herself and with a group of bloody Slovenes in tow. She wants to be damn careful – these Slovenes think Carinthia is theirs by right, and we can't be seen being too helpful to them. She thinks she may have found a house being used by the Nazis, but once she heard you were on your way, she decided to wait for you. I'll go with you, Prince; can't have you going freelance again, can we?'

'We'd better get a move on then.'

'Hang on. There's a telegram for you from a chap called Bartholomew. Seems it's urgent.'

Chapter 23

Germany, December 1945

Wolfgang Steiner had planned to remain in Berlin for a few days after meeting his contacts there in October. His intention was to leave no stone unturned in his search for Martin Bormann. He still believed there was a good chance the Reichsleiter was alive: Bormann was smarter than most people he knew, and he wouldn't be the least bit surprised if it turned out he was hiding in a cellar somewhere, being protected by a sympathiser, patiently biding his time until it was safe to make his next move.

He remained convinced that the absence of any news on Bormann's whereabouts had to be a good sign. If he'd been captured by the Russians, the Americans or the British, they would quickly announce it – as they would if his body had been found. In Mitte and elsewhere in the Soviet sector, they sold a newspaper called *Deutsche Volkszeitung*, which was a communist publication but seemed to devote a good deal of coverage to the fate of important Nazis. Steiner scoured it daily but saw no mention of Bormann.

But his meeting with Willi Kühn had unsettled him. The schoolteacher had asked too many questions, and there was something about his manner that had made Steiner suspicious. Kühn may well have been a childhood friend of Bormann's, but Steiner hadn't detected much sympathy: he'd seemed curious about Bormann rather than concerned. As a result, Steiner had left Berlin the following day, travelling by bus and by foot and arriving three days later at the farm near Eggenfelden. He was relieved to find that Ulrich and Friedrich were no longer there.

'They left perhaps two days after you did,' Frau Moser assured him. 'The younger one, he didn't even say goodbye or thank me. Manners don't cost anything, do they? Their parents should teach them manners.'

Steiner said nothing: they'd been gone for a week, so he reckoned they'd be a safe distance from the farm by now.

'Did my cousin Jens telephone, by any chance, the one from Essen?'

Frau Moser assured him he hadn't. There were no messages for him.

Steiner was exhausted after his journey, and all he wanted was to have a bath and go to bed, but he had something more important to do first. He unlocked the cellar door and moved the crates and old bicycles out of the way. Then he lifted the boxes of empty bottles and placed them on the floor, and removed the four leather suitcases from under the large tarpaulin, checking them thoroughly to make sure they each had the right number of notebooks and rolls of film in them.

Once he was satisfied that everything was in order, he locked them again, replaced the tarpaulin and put the boxes back on top.

He'd give it a few more weeks, and if there was still no sign of Bormann, he'd put his own plan into operation, as he'd intended all along.

–

As October had turned into November, Wolfgang Steiner had begun to have mixed feelings. Of course he still wanted Martin Bormann to be alive, and he felt a duty to help him escape on the Kestrel Line. There was no doubt that with Bormann safe, some kind of victory could be salvaged from humiliating defeat, although he also knew that rescuing the Reichsleiter would be perilous in the extreme: he would be putting himself in enormous danger. And as November moved on and a harsh winter gripped the farm, he wondered how much he really wanted to risk his life. He knew it was likely that Friedrich and Ulrich had made their way to safety. He questioned how much of an obligation he now really felt to Bormann.

And then there was the question of his original plan, the reason why he'd photographed so many documents and compiled the notebooks in the first place, and why he'd gone to the trouble to find the farm. He'd put the plan on hold until he knew about Bormann, but now he didn't want to wait much longer.

On a dirty Monday afternoon in early December, he locked himself in the cellar and took out the leather suitcases again, counting the 218 rolls of film that he'd meticulously logged in a ledger. He selected a handful of films, writing a list of their contents on a separate sheet of paper:

> *Roll 12/41: persons convicted of sexual offences, Berlin area, Jan. – June 1941*
>
> *Roll 8/42: senior personnel, Luftwaffe Intelligence Directorate*
>
> *Roll 22/42: names and addresses of senior NSDAP officials, Düsseldorf*
>
> *Roll 6/43: names and address of clients arrested at (male) brothel, Spandau*
>
> *Roll 17/43: General Staff and Senior Army Group F (Bayreuth)*
>
> *Roll 20/43: NSDAP members: details of bank accounts with Bank Leu, Zurich*
>
> *Roll 6/44: names of officers, II SS Panzer Corps*
>
> *Roll 19/44: list of scientists, Peenemünde rocket development facility*

He checked that each film was properly sealed in its small metal canister and then sowed them all into the hem of his overcoat. He thought about taking a couple of the notebooks but decided they'd require too much explanation. If these films didn't interest them, nothing would.

From the lining of one suitcase he retrieved his old identity papers, including his Parteikanzlei pass. In Munich he'd be Wolfgang Steiner once more.

—

He left the farm early the following morning, walking across the fields to Eggenfelden and catching a bus from there to Mühldorf.

He arrived in Munich early in the afternoon, the journey not having taken as long as he'd expected. It meant he had more time to kill than he'd anticipated, which at least allowed him to find a bed for the night.

He found a bar on Landwehr Strasse, north of the Theresienwiese, where Friedrich had stayed. It was the kind of area where the right amount of money would mean that the requirement for a guest to register could be overlooked. The bar keeper told him he had some rooms upstairs. *Do you want one on your own or are you prepared to share?*

Steiner said he'd prefer one on his own and handed over what he considered to be a small fortune. The room was on the top floor, more of an attic than anything else, with bare floorboards and a cracked window. The bed was hard and dusty, the sheets looked as if they'd not been changed in a while and there was a smell of mice. The bar keeper must have sensed Steiner's disapproval. *At least you'll be safe; no one will know you're here.*

He remained in the room for an hour, but the mice got the better of him, and in any case he wanted to eat. He headed south, and on Lindwurm Strasse found a café, though that was a generous description of a gloomy, hollowed-out shell of a building with a few tables set amongst the rubble.

He sat in the corner and avoided looking at the other customers. He made a bowl of soup and some chunks of black bread last an hour before deciding to leave. His plan was to walk around, making sure he kept on the move and hoping to reach his destination once it was dark. He began to brood: it wasn't too late to abort his trip, and the more he thought about it, the more he wondered whether he was actually insane. It was as if he was surrendering for no good reason. A plan that had been so carefully thought through in Berlin during the war – which had seemed to be so clever, and even flawless – felt very different here in Munich.

As he walked the short distance from the café to Sendlinger Platz, he felt uneasy, putting that down at first to nerves before becoming aware of a presence behind him. When he turned round, there was a man no more than a foot or two from him.

'Wolfgang, you devil! What the hell are you doing here?'

Steiner stepped back and blinked. The man looked very familiar, but he couldn't for the life of him recall his name.

'Don't you remember me – it's Gustav, Gustav Wagner. Surely you know me!'

'Of course – Gustav: how are you?'

Wagner gripped Steiner's hand and shook it enthusiastically. 'I can't believe I've bumped into you of all people: talk about this being my lucky day!'

Wagner was one of Steiner's former 'clients', as he liked to call them. He'd been the *Gauleiter* of the area north of Bremen – the local political leader, a role with a good deal of influence – but had spent too much of his time abusing the privileges of office. He'd made contact with Steiner when he was accused of stealing party funds. Steiner had negotiated a solution: Wagner would admit to an accounting error, pay back the money and then accept a transfer to Poland, always an unpopular posting. The last time he'd seen him had been in February in Berlin. Wagner had told him he'd been in Budapest: *I helped organise the transports to Auschwitz, I signed a lot of death warrants.*

'What are you up to, Wagner?' Steiner pulled his hand away from the other man's.

'I'm on the run, Wolfgang – surely you are too? I can't return home, and apparently my name's on wanted lists in Poland and Hungary. They say I'm a war criminal – can you believe that? I never fired a gun, not once! I'm desperate for money. I thought Munich might be safer, but Christ, Wolfgang… it's like the whole world's changed.'

'It has, Gustav.'

'How come you're in Munich?'

'Same reason as you, I imagine.'

'Please – can you help me?' Wagner was holding Steiner's arm with both hands. He looked as if he was on the verge of tears, his face lined and unshaven, his eyes hooded and blood-shot. 'If I had money, I could buy papers to get me to Spain. I've heard there are people there who can help us; I even have an address in Bilbao.'

Steiner began to pull away from him, but stopped as a thought occurred to him. 'I can help you, Gustav, of course I can… a loyal comrade, a good National Socialist. You see that bar there?' He was pointing across the road at Bar 1860, the '6' hanging at an odd angle. Most of its windows were boarded up, but the lights were on inside. 'Meet me in there at four tomorrow afternoon and I'll have money for you – enough to get you to Spain, and I think I may have the name of someone who can help get you there. I may even join you!'

'That would be wonderful, Wolfgang. Imagine, just like old times!'

–

Steiner waited until eight o'clock before arriving on Neuhauser Strasse, where one of the few buildings in the street unscathed from Allied bombing had become the Red Cross Club for US Army officers.

He joined a couple of dozen other Germans strung out along the street either side of the entrance to the club. Some were begging for money, others selling cigarettes or themselves. Steiner felt his heart pounding as he watched the officers entering. Most arrived in groups, busy talking to each other and ignoring the Germans.

He moved away from the others, and after half an hour an officer approached on his own, pausing close by to light a cigarette. Steiner moved fast.

'Excuse me, sir, but I have valuable intelligence here for the United States Army!'

The officer looked startled and stepped back, but not before Steiner had handed him an envelope.

'What the hell is this?'

'Films, sir, photographs of important documents that will be of interest to the United States. Please hand it to a senior officer.'

'Hang on, pal, how the hell do I—'

'Your intelligence people will want to evaluate the films first. I will come to your headquarters tomorrow morning.'

'Wait, who are you?' The American looked at him as if he was mad.

Steiner was already moving away. 'I will be there tomorrow morning. The name I will give is on the envelope.'

–

Wolfgang Steiner had thought long and hard about the best way to approach the Americans. His original plan had been to turn up unannounced at their headquarters, but he'd worried they'd ignore what he had to say and would either send him away or arrest him. He decided the best way to be taken seriously was for them to somehow be aware of who he was and what he had to tell them before he arrived.

The American headquarters in Munich was in the south of the city, in the old Reichszeugmeisterei building on Tegernseer Landstrasse. Within moments of arriving there the following morning, Steiner knew his gamble had paid off. No sooner had he given his name at the guard post than he was taken aside and asked to wait as an officer made a telephone call. Within five minutes he was sitting in a carpeted office on an upper floor facing a smiling American officer who introduced himself as Major Tom Barrow. He'd even been asked if he'd like coffee.

The major's desk was covered in photographs, Barrow tapping them as he spoke. 'Where did you get these from?'

Steiner showed him his identity papers and his Parteikanzlei pass. He explained that he was a senior Nazi Party official who had had access to thousands of documents. 'I realised early in the war that should matters not turn out in our favour, I would need something to protect myself, so I began to photograph documents that I believed might turn out to be of interest to the Allies in the event of their winning the war. I saw them as my insurance policy. The four films I handed over last night, which I'm pleased to see you've had developed, are just samples. I have more.' He took out the other four rolls of films from his pocket and passed them to the officer.

'Is that all you have?'

Steiner laughed and leaned back in his chair. 'No! I have another two hundred and ten rolls. Each one has thirty-six exposures and each film covers at least three documents, so you can work out how much material I have. And I promise you it's all valuable intelligence: look at what you already have – a list of scientists at Peenemünde, Nazi Party members with accounts at a Swiss bank... there's much more just like that and even better. There are notebooks too, filled with information. I think it's what you call a treasure trove, isn't it?'

'And where is this treasure trove, as you put it, Steiner?'

'If you're interested in it, then we can come to an arrangement.'

Major Barrow watched him carefully, clearly trying to work out whether to believe him. 'You're taking a hell of a risk, aren't you?'

'Of course I am, but it's a calculated risk – I'm confident you'll be interested enough in what I have to give you.'

'From what you tell me, you were a very senior Nazi official.'

'I was, and I don't deny I was a member of the Nazi Party, but I can assure you I'm certainly not one of those war criminals you seem to be so interested in. I was a bureaucrat – a senior one certainly, but no more than that.'

'And I'm to believe that you're now prepared to turn against the people you worked for and were clearly so loyal to?'

'The war's over, Major: I think the saying is "every man for himself", is it not?'

'And what's in it for you, Steiner?'

'I want money, obviously, and I also want a guarantee of immunity from prosecution for anything in connection with my work for the Reich. I also want a guarantee of anonymity with regards to this material.'

The major was busy making notes.

'There is something else. I have a son, Friedrich. He worked for the Gestapo and is wanted by the British: they're hunting him across Europe. I'll only hand over the rest of the material if I can have an assurance in writing from the British that he is no longer wanted by them. I have also been involved in an escape route called the Kestrel Line, which they are also investigating. I want them to stop doing that.'

Barrow carried on writing and said he was sure he could sort that out. They discussed arrangements for handing over the rest of the films and the notebooks and for Steiner to receive his assurances.

'I just hope I can trust you, Steiner.'

'I guessed you'd say that, Major. I can offer you a war criminal as proof. Go to Bar 1860 on Sendlinger Platz at four o'clock this afternoon and you'll find a man called Gustav Wagner waiting there. Look him up: you'll find he's wanted for war crimes in Poland and Hungary.'

Chapter 24

Austria and Italy, December 1945

GENEVA, WEDNESDAY

PRINCE EYES ONLY

CONFIRM MYRTLE CARTER & HAROLD
HAMILTON CROSSED CHANNEL
MONDAY. TRAIN CALAIS TO GARE DU
NORD, PARIS. MOVEMENTS
OVERNIGHT UNCLEAR BUT SPOTTED
GARE DE LYON TUESDAY. TRAIN TO
GENEVA WHERE THEY REMAIN. WILL
ADVISE RE ONWARD JOURNEY. STOP.

BARTHOLOMEW, GENEVA

KLAGENFURT, THURSDAY

BARTHOLOMEW, GENEVA ONLY

ACKNOWLEDGE RECEIPT OF
COMMUNICATION WEDNESDAY RE
CARTER/HAMILTON. AWAIT ADVICE RE
ONWARD MOVEMENTS. CAN BE
CONTACTED THROUGH FIELD
SECURITY SECTION VILLACH. STOP.

PRINCE

It was, in Prince's opinion, a classic case of overkill.

As a non-military man, he'd not voiced his opinion at the time, but it seemed clear there'd been far too many men involved in the raid on the house just north of Sattendorf. Major Stewart was in charge, and he'd brought half a dozen of his Field Security Section along from Klagenfurt. They joined the dozen men from the FSS base in Villach plus a company of ninety New Zealanders from one of their infantry battalions. When you added in the Slovenian partisans who'd insisted on coming along, as well as Hanne and Prince, it was well over one hundred people.

And they found nothing.

The house was empty.

Major Stewart stomped around it muttering, 'I see the birds have flown,' and Prince had to explain the historical reference to Hanne.

'May I make a suggestion, Major?'

Stewart glared at him, giving the impression he'd very much rather he didn't. 'If you must, Prince.'

'I am a police officer, as is Hanne. We ought to treat this place like a crime scene. Now that we've established no one is here, having so many people tramping around the house will get in the way of our investigation.'

'So what do you suggest?'

Prince suggested that a platoon of New Zealanders remain to guard the property and its perimeter, while he and Hanne would examine the house with the help of half a dozen men from the FSS. The others should search the grounds of the house and the woods and fields beyond it.

They spent the rest of that day and most of the following one combing through the house. It was evident that at least two people had been staying there and had probably left the day before the raid. There were no other clues.

Frau Egger was questioned, insisting she'd been hired as a cleaner and had never met anyone at the house. It was something she'd made up. She'd been trying to impress people, she said.

'I wanted people to see me as more than a cleaner. Now the war's over and I'm no longer a *Blockleiter*, I feel… humiliated.'

'What about being approached by a man from Vienna, and your story that very important people stayed at the house?'

Frau Egger shrugged. 'Who told you that?'

'You seem to have been telling half the town. You also said there was an armed guard at the house.'

'That's nonsense, of course there wasn't.'

'I saw armed guards there.' Hanne had moved closer to Frau Eggers, who looked nervous and picked up her handbag as if preparing to leave. Hanne made it clear she wasn't going anywhere. 'Either you start telling the truth or you'll be charged with aiding a fugitive, and the only place you'll be cleaning then is your prison cell!'

After a little weep, Frau Egger assured Hanne and Prince that she'd been forced into the job and she wanted them to understand she was as much a victim as the Jews claimed they were.

'Two men stayed at the house: one of them had just one arm and was German, though I've no idea where he was from other than he wasn't Bavarian – I'd recognise that accent. He never gave me his name. The other one was younger and he had that Viennese accent that sounds as if they're giving you instructions. He even asked me if I had a daughter who'd want to come and work there, can you believe that?'

She stopped and had another weep. 'You promise I'm not going to be arrested?'

'I don't know, Frau Egger, you've still not told us very much. What about the guards?'

'Two of them, also Germans. What else can I say?'

'Far more than you've done so far, if you want to stay out of trouble.'

Frau Egger dabbed her eyes with a crumpled handkerchief, which she then used to wipe her nose. 'One day I heard the man with one arm call the younger one Friedrich: they didn't realise I was in the next room. Just Friedrich, no other name. Is that good enough?'

'What happened to them? How come the house was empty?'

'You won't find them, you know.'

'What do you mean?'

'All four of them left: the man with one arm, the younger one he called Friedrich and the two guards. One afternoon they told me they were leaving that night and I was to give the place a more thorough clean the next day and that I'd have to let myself in. They were wearing mountain clothing and special boots. That's why I say you won't find them: they've gone over the Alps!' Frau Egger leaned back defiantly and allowed a thin smile to cross her face.

—

'But Richard, you heard what that woman told us – they've crossed the Alps. Why are we sitting here in Villach drinking tea? You English are so… cautious!'

'Because another telegram has come through from Bartholomew – look.'

TURIN, FRIDAY

PRINCE EYES ONLY

ADVISE CARTER & HAMILTON
TRAVELLED THURSDAY GENEVA TO
TURIN, ITALY. CURRENTLY STAYING IN
APARTMENT IN VANCHIGLIA DISTRICT.
FIELD SECURITY SECTION TURIN
ASSISTING. SUGGEST YOU JOIN TEAM IN
TURIN URGENT. STOP.

BARTHOLOMEW, TURIN

'When did that arrive?'

'While we were with Frau Egger. So we were right all along: their destination is Turin. Maybe the idea is to hold them there until they can arrange their escape by sea. We'll set out first thing in the morning.'

Prince woke early the following day and noticed that Hanne was sitting on the side of the bed, her head in her hands.

'Are you all right?'

She turned to face him. In the half-light he could just make out a smile and the glistening of perspiration on her brow.

'I don't feel too good, Richard. I think it may be something I ate last night.'

'We hardly ate anything last night.'

'Maybe that's the reason.'

'Don't forget you had typhus not that long ago. Have you been remembering to take the tablets?'

She responded with the irritated look she always used whenever he asked her that question and told him to go back to sleep and not worry. *I'll be fine.*

His head had barely hit the pillow when there was a knock at the door and a voice announcing that there was a telegram for them, marked urgent.

VERONA, SATURDAY – URGENT

PRINCE EYES ONLY

CARTER & HAMILTON LEFT TURIN
LATE FRIDAY NIGHT. ROUTE
UNCERTAIN BUT NOW MOVING EAST
FROM VERONA. STOP.

BARTHOLOMEW, VERONA

Hanne frowned. 'They're moving away from Turin? But that makes no sense… Maybe they're heading to Genoa.'

'Wrong direction: we'll have to stay here and wait to hear from Bartholomew. Let's hope his men don't lose them.'

'What about asking the Slovenians to help us?'

'Stewart's not keen on them: apparently the official British line is that they're a nuisance. And I'm told we don't trust Tito.'

'Tell me, Richard, if we catch Friedrich Steiner, what will happen to him?'

'I imagine we'll put him on trial somewhere.'

'The Slovenians would kill him.'

'Do you approve of that? As police officers we're meant to believe in the rule of law.'

Hanne laughed. 'I think those rules were suspended during the war, don't you? I just think it would be… cleaner to let the Slovenians deal with him. They seem smarter than our lot, to be honest. They know this area. We may need their help.'

'Let's decide when we know where we're heading.'

'We need to hope Friedrich and the other man are making for the same place as Carter and Hamilton.'

The answer came on the Sunday morning.

TRIESTE, SUNDAY – MOST URGENT

CARTER & HAMILTON ARRIVED
TRIESTE EARLY SUNDAY MORNING.
LAST SEEN ENTERING BUILDING ON
VIA DELL'ISTRIA. CURRENT
WHEREABOUTS UNCERTAIN. REQUEST
YOU TRAVEL TO TRIESTE
IMMEDIATELY. MEET FSS BASE VIA SAN
LAZZARO. STOP.

BARTHOLOMEW, TRIESTE

VILLACH, SUNDAY

FOR: BARTHOLOMEW, TRIESTE ONLY

266

ADVISE WE ARE DEPARTING VILLACH
IMMEDIATELY TO MEET YOU AS
INSTRUCTED. STOP.

PRINCE

–

Hanne had made her way to a bombed-out building close to the banks of the Drava. The floor was covered in mud, debris and the remains of dead birds. Marija and Jožef were leaning against a wall, the glowing ends of their cigarettes moving up and down in the gloom.

'Are you sure?' Marija asked.

'Yes, I'm sure. I told them I needed a few minutes to clear my head. I'm taking a big risk telling you all this, so I want you to promise you'll be careful and make sure you're not spotted, all right?'

The cigarettes bobbed up and down. 'What about Steiner?'

'You get Steiner, but whoever else we find you leave to us – even it's Martin Bormann.'

'Very well, but your husband – what does he make of this?'

'I think he understands. It's just that he doesn't want to be told too much.'

'What do you know about Trieste, Hanne?' Marija said.

'Not much, other than looking at the map yesterday. It's an Italian port and it isn't too far from here.'

'It's as much a Slovenian city as it is an Italian one. From the centre of Trieste to the Slovenian border is just five miles.' Jožef had moved out of the gloom and was now standing in front of Hanne. 'We Slovenes suffered terribly there during the war. The Italians treated us badly enough, but it became far worse when the Germans occupied the city in September 1943. The bastards even built a concentration camp there, you know.'

'Risiera di San Sabba,' said Marija. 'Thousands of Slovenes, Jews and political prisoners were murdered there. Many more were sent from there to the death camps.'

'Our partisans captured the city on May Day,' continued Jožef. 'Marija and I fought in that battle. But the Germans would only surrender to troops from New Zealand. They knew what we'd do to them.'

'We got our chance, though.' Marija had moved out of the gloom too. 'They handed over the city to us and we controlled it for forty days until it was given back to the British. We got our revenge, especially against the traitors.'

'So we'll be at home in Trieste, Hanne, we consider it to be our city. And you don't want to worry about us being spotted. We know every shadow.'

'And you never know – you may be grateful we're there.'

–

It was one hundred miles from Villach in Austria to Trieste in Italy, all of it across territory controlled by the British Army. They crossed the Gailtal Alps into Slovenia just north of Kranjska Gora, heading south before entering Italy at Gorizia.

The final part of the journey was over a stretch of rocky terrain called the Carso, and it was the middle of the afternoon when they arrived at the Field Security Section on Via San Lazzaro. Bartholomew was in a top-floor office with the windows wide open despite the cold. It was close to dusk, the twinkling lights of the Adriatic just visible through the mist.

'They're mercurial, this bloody pair, I can tell you that.' Bartholomew looked as if he'd not slept in days. He was in the same raincoat he always seemed to wear. 'They must be important, because they seem to have plenty of local help. I can't believe we lost them in Paris, but fortunately we counted on them moving on and we're not exactly short-staffed there so we had every station covered. We almost lost them in Geneva too, which would have been a disaster, but they were collected from the station in a green Renault and we were able to follow that to where they stayed overnight and from there to Turin, but I can tell you we've been stretched to the limit. This Italian coffee is remarkable, you should try it... you don't need to sleep!'

'What happened in Turin?'

'The apartment they stayed in had links to fascists and we thought that was where they were going to stay...'

'So did we.'

'...but then they did a midnight flit: fortunately the FSS chaps in Turin were on the ball and we managed to track them to Verona. Following them to Trieste turned out to be the easiest part, actually. This place certainly makes sense: big port and easily accessible from Austria, and it's full of all types, not just Italians. It's the kind of place where it's easy to be inconspicuous.'

'Where are they now, Bartholomew?'

'We followed them to a building in the south of the city. I've got the local Field Security Section chaps watching it now, and two of my men are there too. I'll go down later. You're welcome to join me.'

'Is anyone else with them?' Hanne asked.

'That's what we don't know: I would recommend keeping an eye on the place for at least another twenty-four hours. By then we ought to have an idea.'

'If this place is the end of the Kestrel Line, we need to know if Friedrich Steiner's there too.'

'And Martin Bormann.'

'I understand.'

'And the port – where could they sail to from it?'

'I asked the same question of the senior FSS officer down-stairs. He pointed to a map of the world and said to take my pick.'

'They've been in there all night, sir.'

It was ten o'clock on the Monday morning. Hanne and Prince were huddled in the back of a Fiat truck with Bartholomew and a Field Security Section officer, a well-built Welshman called Evans who'd been on duty all night. The truck was parked next to a large cemetery on Via dell'Istria on the opposite side of the road from the building Myrtle Carter and Edward Palmer had been seen entering.

'You've got the rear covered?'

'Yes, sir – every angle is covered.'

'And do we know what the building is?'

'Are you a betting man, Mr Prince?'

Prince shrugged. 'The occasional flutter, I suppose: the Grand National, you know...'

'Well I'd have bet a tidy sum on the Catholic Church being involved in a Nazi escape line: all the intelligence we're getting is that they're up to their ears in it – organising the fugitives' passage into Italy, hiding them, arranging new identities and then helping them escape from Europe. And sure enough, this place belongs to the local Catholic diocese: apparently it's some kind of hostel for people connected with the Church to stay in when they're visiting or passing through Trieste. A couple of parish priests live here too. Carter and Palmer went in yesterday when they arrived in the city and haven't been seen since.'

'So we don't know if Friedrich Steiner's in there, or anyone else?'

'No idea, sir.'

'You know about Martin Bormann?'

Evans nodded and pointed to a photograph of Bormann taped to the side of the truck. 'No sign of him either, sir.'

They watched and waited for the rest of Monday and into the night. The uneasy silence was broken only by the occasional sound of other vehicles passing. There was a discussion about whether to raid the hostel, but they agreed to wait until they saw Friedrich or anyone else of interest in the building.

At midnight, Hanne and Prince slipped away to a hotel the FSS had taken over on Via San Nicolò. They'd only been asleep a few minutes when there was a knock at the door.

'I'm sorry to wake you, but they're on the move,' said Bartholomew.

Evans met them outside the hotel. He'd been on duty when a van had pulled up in front of the hostel on Via dell'Istria and a small group had hurried from the building into the back of the vehicle.

'Carter and Palmer were definitely among them, and I'd say from the description you've given me that Steiner was too. One of the men could have had just one arm, but it was difficult to tell. There was another man too.'

'Who do you think he was?'

'Could have been Bormann: he was dressed as a priest. I've been staring at his bloody photo all day, but I can't be sure it was him, but neither could I be sure it wasn't him, if you see what I mean.'

'Do we know where they are?'

'Fortunately two of our motorcyclists were able to follow them: this is quite an easy city to find your way around, as it's laid out in a grid pattern. They're not far from here – at the port. Jump in.'

They drove to a warehouse on Porto Vecchio. It appeared to be deserted, but Evans said one of his motorcyclists had spotted movement in the first-floor offices when they first arrived.

They waited huddled in the back of the truck as the port came to life. A salty wind whipped in from the Adriatic, but other than a rusty sign swaying in the wind, there was no movement in the warehouse.

'Do we know anything about the building?'

'The sign on the door says *De Luca e Figli* – De Luca and Sons.' Evans was looking at the building through binoculars.

'And underneath that it says *Fornitore Navale*, whatever that means.'

'Ship's chandlers,' said Bartholomew.

'I think we should go in now,' Prince said.

'No, not yet,' replied Hanne. 'If we have the place surrounded, we can afford to wait and see what's going on.'

Bartholomew agreed. In his experience, he said, it would be better all round to wait for them to come out rather than raid the place too soon.

'I must say, though, it's a damn clever location: close to the port and the railway station, and there's even a seaplane base over there,' said Evans.

They agreed to wait until the morning. In the meantime, the Field Security Section said they'd check all the ships in the port and see if any had imminent plans to set sail.

–

Hanne woke before dawn and left the room without waking Richard. She spotted Jožef in a doorway in a side street with a view of the hotel. He stepped back into the shadows and nodded to her, and she spoke quietly, avoiding looking in his direction.

When she returned to the hotel, her husband was waiting for her looking agitated.

'Where've you been?'

'I wanted some fresh air, our room's so stuffy. Is something the matter?'

'I'm not sure… Bartholomew's called: something's up. We're wanted immediately at the FSS place on Via San Lazzaro.'

–

Fifteen minutes later, they were in an office in the Field Security Section, the two of them looking at each other, stunned, before Hanne glared at Bartholomew in an almost accusing manner.

'Look, I'm sorry – I'm as surprised at this as you are. Please understand this is London's decision, not mine. You know how it is, orders are orders.'

Prince held up the telegram once more, he and Hanne reading it at the same time, both shaking their heads angrily as they did so.

LONDON, TUESDAY

FOR: RP/HJ, TRIESTE – THROUGH BARTHOLOMEW

BE ADVISED OF NEW ORDERS: OPERATION TO ARREST STEINER TO CEASE FORTHWITH. UNDER NO CIRCUMSTANCES IS HE TO BE APPREHENDED. INVESTIGATION INTO KESTREL LINE TO END NOW. PLEASE ACKNOWLEDGE RECEIPT IMMEDIATELY AND RETURN TO LONDON. STOP.

GILBEY

'It's ridiculous: if we let Steiner go, then the same will apply to the others… Carter and Palmer, bloody traitors… And Bormann, what about if he's there?' Prince looked on the verge of tears.

'But if we don't acknowledge receipt, there's nothing to stop us going ahead and arresting Steiner and the others, is there? We could just say we didn't see it until it was too late.'

'I'm afraid it's not as easy as that, Hanne.' Bartholomew looked awkward, loosening his tie as he spoke.

'Why's that?'

'Because I've already told London we've seen it.'

Chapter 25

England, December 1945

'Good try, Jenkins, but I'm afraid what you ask is completely out of the question.'

Tom Gilbey stared long and hard at the overweight American sitting opposite him in his office in St James's. He barely knew Joseph Jenkins, so had asked Sir Roland Pearson to join him. In his role as Churchill's intelligence adviser, Pearson had enjoyed many dealings with Jenkins during the war, though neither man would have chosen the word 'enjoyed' to describe their encounters.

Joseph was a senior liaison officer in London for the Office of Strategic Services, the American version of MI6. Except that it seemed he no longer was. He'd been the one to request the meeting, and he began it by looking quizzically at Sir Roland.

'I thought you'd been sacked, Roly?'

Pearson bristled, not least at the presumption of the American in calling him 'Roly'. Jenkins was not in one of the limited categories of people he permitted to use that name.

'I was most certainly not sacked. Mine was a personal appointment by Winston Churchill, so when he left Number Ten, I quite properly tendered my resignation. In fact I had always intended to leave once the war was over.'

'And now you're working for Mr Gilbey here?'

'Not for, with: I'm working *with* Tom. I was also at school *with* Tom.' He emphasised the word as if he was instructing the American in the correct use of a preposition.

'All you guys seem to have been at the same school. If I meet someone else from Missouri, it's a big deal. I have some news for you: I have a new job!'

'Many congratulations, Joe,' said Pearson after a short period of hesitation. It was now Jenkins' turn to bristle: he hated being called Joe – he didn't want people to associate him with Stalin. 'Does this mean a move away from London, perhaps?'

'Ha! If I didn't know you better, Roly, I'd think you wanted me to leave. No, for the time being, I'm going to continue to be based here at the embassy. Have you heard of the Counter Intelligence Corps?'

'It's an intelligence section within the United States Army, isn't it?'

The American nodded his head, and Pearson asked him if that meant he was now a soldier.

'No, I'm still with the Office of Strategic Services, but I'm attached to the Counter Intelligence Corps for a few months. They want to use my expertise.'

'Do you get to wear a uniform now, Joe? I can recommend an excellent tailor in Jermyn Street if you have difficulty in finding one the right size.'

Jenkins glared at Sir Roland.

'Well, jolly well done,' said Tom Gilbey. 'It's always nice to be wanted, to have one's achievements recognised. After all, you've been in the same post for an awfully long time as I understand it, eh?'

Jenkins bristled once more.

'And it's so nice you came all the way here from Grosvenor Square to give us the good news in person.'

'That's not the sole reason I came, Tom. It's connected with it, though.' The American pushed his chair back and smiled at both the men opposite him.

'Do please tell us.'

'One of the current operations of the Counter Intelligence Corps is to identify senior German officials who are wanted by various Allied countries but who in our estimation can in the long run be of assistance to the United States of America.'

'I think you may need to explain that more clearly, Joe.'

'I prefer Joseph, if that's all right with you. There are thousands of senior Germans in custody in Germany and elsewhere in Europe, with many more still at liberty. Some are war criminals and must face Allied justice. But at the same time we'd be foolish to ignore the fact that there are some amongst them who can be of better use to the United States by working for us.'

'You mean you're recruiting Nazis?'

'They're not all Nazis, Roly.'

'Well who are these new recruits of yours then?'

'You know as well as I do that the focus in Europe has shifted dramatically. We now have to turn our attention to the Soviet Union, which is already extending its influence in eastern and central Europe in a way that represents a threat to the United States. One way of combating this is by having an effective intelligence operation in Europe, and there will be a small number of Germans who may be ideal operatives for us in this respect. Likewise we should acknowledge that the Germans have a considerable degree of expertise in many areas. For example, their tanks were superior to ours, their aircraft technology was first class, and the V1 and V2 rockets they developed meant that their scientists are the top guys in this field.'

'So you want to recruit them?'

'In a word, yes.'

'And how many people are we talking about?'

'Hundreds rather than thousands.'

'Hundreds! You want to release hundreds of Nazis from prison and give them some kind of amnesty just because it helps the United States?'

'It would be the low hundreds, Tom, but yes – and I'm surprised that you're so surprised. In fact I'd imagine you guys are doing the same. It makes sense, don't you agree? Sure, we can let some well-placed former general rot in prison for a few years, or sentence a brilliant rocket scientist to hard labour, but wouldn't that be cutting off our nose to spite our face when we can harness their expertise to help us?'

'I'm not sure I—'

'Look, Roly, hundreds of years ago, one country would conquer another and they'd sack their cities and help themselves to whatever they could find – including the women. This is a modern-day version of that.'

'From what I understand, the Soviets are doing just that, and transporting whatever they can lay their hands on in Germany back to Russia. Even whole factories, I'm told, right down to the light switches, would you believe!'

'Exactly,' said Jenkins. 'So the Soviets are helping themselves to factories and we're helping ourselves to spies and scientists. I think we'll benefit more in the long run. Meanwhile, you guys are thumbing through the rule book to check if this is cricket!'

'Well do keep us in touch with how it goes, Joe. Presumably at some stage we'll have sight of a list of who you've recruited?'

'That's why I asked to see you today, Tom.'

'You've brought a list, have you?'

The American shook his head and looked from Gilbey to Pearson and the back again, deciding which man to address his remarks to.

'There's a Counter Intelligence Corps section in Munich run by a Major Tom Barrow. A few days ago, Tom had a walk-in and...'

Sir Roland Pearson sighed and looked up at the ceiling.

'I know what you're thinking, Roly – you don't trust walk-ins. You don't need to worry, we're quite aware that they can be set-ups. We're as sceptical about them as you are, but some of our best intelligence has come from walk-ins; they just need to be checked out even more thoroughly.'

'So do tell us about the chap who walked into your office in Munich.'

Jenkins put on a pair of thick-lensed spectacles and looked at his notebook. 'According to Barrow, an American officer was approached by a German man outside the US Army officers' club on Neuhauser Strasse. He handed him an envelope that he said contained information our intelligence people would want to see and said he'd turn up the next day at our headquarters.

'The officer handed the envelope to our intelligence people first thing the next morning. It contained four rolls of film, which they had developed straight away. What they saw was so interesting the photographs were handed to Major Barrow, and when the man arrived in the morning, he was brought to see him. He was able to show he'd been a senior official at the Nazi Party headquarters, and had been photographing important files since sometime in 1941. We've checked him out and he is who he says he is.'

'Why would a senior Nazi do that?'

'Self-interest: to give himself some kind of protection once the war was over. Barrow realised straight away how important the material was, and the man gave him another four rolls of film and said he had a further two hundred and ten hidden away.'

'Presumably he was after money?'

'Yes, and he also asked for immunity from prosecution. Barrow says the material is excellent – he has details of some of the other documents the man photographed: lists of senior Nazi Party members, serious crimes committed, SS officers, names of scientists... The Nazis destroyed so many of these records that to have these copies is remarkable. It's perfect material for the Counter Intelligence Corps, like we stumbled across a gold mine.'

'How do you know this chap's genuine? The films he gave you could be all that he has, assuming they're not fakes.'

'Our assessment is that both he and the films are genuine. He's smart, too. We have to get our hands on those films. And there's something else: as a way of showing we could trust him, he told us where we could find a Nazi war criminal high up on our watch list, a man called Gustav Wagner, a former *Gauleiter* wanted for war crimes in Poland and Hungary. He was exactly where he told us he'd be.'

'So what's stopping you doing the deal with him, Joe? You give him some money and immunity from prosecution and he gives you the rest of the films? I hardly think you need our permission, though it's awfully nice of you to ask.'

'It's not as straightforward as that, Tom. There's a further condition he's set before he hands over the rest of the films, and we need your cooperation.'

Jenkins looked more nervous now, running a hand over his cropped hair and wiping perspiration from his brow.

'The man has a son who's wanted by you guys. As a condition of him handing over the rest of the films, he wants you to abandon the hunt for his son.'

'What's the man's name, Joe?'

'Wolfgang Steiner. His son's name is Friedrich. We want you to call off the hunt for Friedrich Steiner and forget about the Kestrel Line. Letting a minor Nazi go free is a very small price to pay for us getting access to such invaluable intelligence.'

Which was when Tom Gilbey responded by telling the American it was a good try but was completely out of the question. Sir Roland Pearson let out a weary sigh. Jenkins sat defiantly with his arms crossed.

'Leaving aside the not inconsequential fact that Friedrich Steiner is a war criminal who murdered British agents, there's also the issue of the Kestrel Line. Not only do we think we'll find the traitor Edward Palmer on it, but there's also a distinct possibility that it could lead us to Martin Bormann!'

'You're not going to find Bormann, Gilbey; I don't know why you guys believe that story.'

'We have it from an excellent source.'

'Russians – you trust the Russians?'

'More than I'd trust a Nazi!' Gilbey was shouting now, red-faced and clearly furious, and on the word 'Nazi', he slammed his hand on the table.

'Bormann's probably dead.'

'There's no proof of that, Joe' said Sir Roland, speaking softly in an effort to calm things down. 'We hear what you say regarding Friedrich Steiner, and my advice to Tom, should he seek it, would be for us to refer the matter up, but I would suggest you don't hold out a lot of hope: we have a first-class team on the trail of Steiner and the Kestrel Line, and they're very close to finding them.'

Joseph Jenkins shook his head and gathered up his papers. 'It's too late for that; I'm afraid. I was trying to be courteous. Ambassador Winant has already met with Foreign Secretary Bevin, and he agreed to our request. I think you'll be ordered to call off the hunt any minute now.'

–

Messrs Bourne and Ridgeway had reached the limit of their endurance. They struggled to regain their breath as they crouched by the high laurel hedge while at the same time not taking their eyes off the side door of the large Victorian house.

They'd spotted a thin line of light behind a curtained bay window, and another light in a top-floor room, but the house was otherwise dark, its broad shape just visible in the half-moon, its array of chimneys silhouetted like turrets against the mottled sky. The world around them was as silent as the churchyard they'd crept through some twenty minutes earlier. An animal scurried behind them, and high above came the soft call of an owl.

Bourne was still breathing heavily and Ridgeway was concerned. 'Are you all right, Bourne – you sound in difficulty?'

'It's the asthma. Spending the best part of an hour creeping through the countryside in the bloody damp isn't good for it.

Christ knows why people live in the middle of nowhere. And I've cut my hand on the brambles.'

'I have too, and I fear I may have torn my trousers. Do you think we should go in? We've been waiting long enough. He said to be here by eight, and it's already a quarter past.'

'Our instructions were very clear, Ridgeway: to park at the back of the village pub and work our way through the woods, then take the footpath by the side of the field and enter the garden through the back. We're to wait here until we see a light go on over that side door. We have to be patient, and in any case, it gives me a chance to get my breath back.'

Ten minutes later, a weak yellow light flickered into life above the side door and the two men walked nervously towards it. The door was unlocked as they'd been told it would be, and they moved carefully along a dark corridor until they came to a door opening into a kitchen area. Their host was standing there, nodding but saying nothing by way of greeting. They followed him into the library, where the heavy curtains were drawn. The room was lit by two lamps, one at either end.

'I've given my man the evening off, so we're alone until…' their host glanced at his wristwatch, 'ten thirty. That gives us two hours − more than enough time. You followed my instructions to the letter, I hope?'

'Yes, Admiral, absolutely.' Bourne's breathing was still heavy.

'And I trust you didn't go anywhere near the front of the house or onto the lane? The bastards are still watching me, you know: I don't know whether it's MI5 or Special Branch, I think they maybe take it in turns. In the two years since I was released from prison, I don't think they've missed a day.'

Bourne and Ridgeway both tutted and shook their heads. The two men had known the Admiral for some time and admired him enormously. As Bourne had said to Ridgeway during their otherwise silent drive up, the man was remarkable. To have someone of his stature and vision still involved in what remained of their movement had been an inspiration. Had it been a lesser person, they doubted the movement would have lasted much beyond 1939.

As it was, his loyalty to the cause had survived the test of the outbreak of war and indeed the difficult few months leading up to it. After the destruction of the synagogues in Germany in March 1938, many lesser folk had left the movement, but the Admiral had set a steadfast example for those resolved to stand by Germany. His network in Britain was impressive, as was people's loyalty to him. Even more impressive were the contacts he had in Germany, which he'd managed to maintain both before and after his imprisonment.

They'd discussed the injustice of his imprisonment too. Defence Regulation 18B was a scandal, far worse than anything Nazi Germany was being accused of. It was used to throw patriots like the Admiral into prison – in his case for two years – without trial. It did rather vindicate though what the Admiral always said: that the war had been engineered by the Jews and the communists for their own benefit, and Germany should have been seen as Britain's ally.

'Notwithstanding the risk inherent in you coming here, I thought it would be useful for us to be clear as to where we are: we cannot afford any misunderstandings, can we?'

Both men said 'No, Admiral' at the same time, and jumped as a grandfather clock noisily struck nine o'clock.

'Don't worry about that; it's five minutes fast. Well done for getting Palmer out of the country – and with all the money too.'

'Much of that credit is due to Myrtle: for a woman she is remarkably calm and well organised. As far as we understand, they've left Turin and should be in Trieste any time now.'

'And no sign of them being followed on the journey?'

'Not as far as she's aware. As you know, the plan is that once they get to Trieste, they'll meet up with Friedrich, Ulrich and whoever else is there, and then catch the boat, which we understand you know more about than us.'

The Admiral stood up and straightened himself in the manner of someone with a painful back. 'Sailed into Trieste once, strange place – one wasn't too sure what country one was in. I've come across other places like that: Salonika, Barcelona, Odessa and Istanbul – too many bloody Jews if you ask me, though I doubt there are now!'

Bourne and Ridgeway laughed dutifully.

'I have good news and bad news to impart. Prince and that Danish woman seem to have caught wind of what's going on and have turned up in Trieste. Hang on, hang on… Overriding that is the fact that my very good friend Wolfgang has somehow managed to persuade the Americans to put pressure on MI6 to call off the hunt for Friedrich and forget about the Kestrel Line.'

'Really – how on earth did he manage that?'

'Don't ask me, but I'm not surprised. When I first met Wolfgang in Berlin in 1938, I realised he was one of the most intelligent men I'd ever come across – and that's saying something: the whole city was full of impressive and clever men. I'm just pleased I've been able to maintain contact with him and that we've been of some help to him and the cause. He's still optimistic that he'll find Martin Bormann alive, you know – imagine that, eh?'

'And do you think we can count on Palmer to behave?'

'You'll know that I've had my doubts about him, even though I had a hand in his recruitment. I know he was a first-class agent for the Reich during the war, but once he disappeared, I thought that either they'd catch him or he'd be found dead, and I have to say it would have been safer for us had it been the latter. I was most surprised, as you were, when he turned up at your gallery in August. My instinct was to finish him off, you know – I realise that would have been ungrateful after everything he'd done, but I felt he knew too much, and there can be no room for sentimentality. I asked Myrtle to see to it, but she took the view that it would be too risky. She thought there was a possibility he might have put something in place to protect himself, something that would have come out if he was killed – you know what I mean: a solicitor being instructed to forward an incriminating letter from him to the authorities after they'd not heard from him for an agreed period of time.'

'So sending him on the Kestrel Line makes sense.'

The Admiral nodded and checked his watch. 'Yes, gets him away from here. The ship's going to South Africa, you know. Most of the German escape lines end up in South America, but I know a chap in Durban who'll look after them. He'll send the Germans to Windhoek, which is pretty much a German city, and he'll sort Palmer out too.'

'And Myrtle?'

The Admiral stood up and walked towards the door, making it clear to his visitors that their time was up. 'Myrtle will stand on the quayside and wave them off. Then I want her back here.'

Chapter 26

'Gilbey wants you back as soon as possible.'

Two pairs of eyes scowled at Bartholomew. Hanne sat red-faced, her nails drumming on the table, while Prince was very still with his back to the open window: behind him the early-morning mist had lifted and the blinking lights of a ship on the Gulf of Trieste was just visible over the rooftops, the muffled sound of its horn breaking the silence.

'You heard what I said? You're to return to London. Please don't look at me like that; I'm simply the humble messenger here.'

Prince said yes, he understood, and he was sorry for his reaction but this did feel rather personal actually, and after chasing all over Europe and putting one's life at risk, well... it was rather a kick in the stomach for the hunt to be called off at the last minute.

Bartholomew said he understood too. It was always a disappointment when something like this happened, but he was well used to operations being called off just as they reached their conclusion.

'You'll fly back from Klagenfurt. The RAF has daily transport flights from there into Munich, and there are plenty of flights home from Neubiberg.'

'When do we leave?' Hanne sounded less conciliatory than her husband.

'Straight away: London isn't keen on you hanging around in Trieste.'

'They obviously don't trust us,' said Prince. 'And what about you, Bartholomew: staying behind to check we don't sneak back in?'

Bartholomew said he'd follow them in due course. Evans would look after them on their journey to Klagenfurt.

'And you've no idea why they've called the whole thing off just when we have them in our sights?'

'I've told you, Prince: it's not my decision. I daresay Gilbey will enlighten you when you're back in London, but…' Bartholomew hesitated and adjusted his tie. He was a man who chose his few words carefully.

'But what, Bartholomew?'

'It doesn't matter, Prince. This is Gilbey's show.'

'I think we have some role in it, don't you agree, Mr Bartholomew?' Hanne sounded less obviously angry than she had been. She even smiled at Bartholomew.

'Look… this may just be gossip, and I'm only sharing it because I admire you both enormously and because…'

'…because we are on the same side?'

'Exactly. You didn't hear this from me, understand?'

They both nodded and moved closer.

'There's talk that the Americans have signed up Wolfgang Steiner.'

'What do you mean, "signed up"?'

'Recruited him.'

'To work for them?'

Bartholomew was still playing with his tie. 'They're up to it all over Europe, seeking out Nazis they think can help them: senior military types, rocket and aircraft scientists… From what I've been told, even before the Germans surrendered, the United States were clear that their enemy was now the Soviet Union and started recruiting Nazis to work for them on the basis that their enemy's enemy is their friend.'

'That's outrageous! So because the Americans have recruited Wolfgang Steiner, they're leaning on Gilbey to call off the chase for his son? Steiner's a bloody Nazi, and his son's a…'

Bartholomew said nothing, but did raise his eyebrows. 'I know, Prince, I know… But as I say, once you're in London, Gilbey will tell you more.'

'By which time it will be too late.'

Bartholomew shrugged and made a gesture with his hands to indicate he'd said enough.

'We'll need to go back to the hotel to collect our things,' said Hanne. She was standing up and buttoning her raincoat.

'Evans will meet you outside the hotel in, what… ten minutes?'

'Make it twenty,' said Prince.

'Fifteen – and nothing clever, understand? The Field Security Section is still watching the warehouse, in case you had any ideas. And one other thing…'

'Go on.'

'Don't take it out on Evans. This isn't his fault either.'

—

'We're being followed, Richard.'

'Of course we are. What should we do, Hanne? We can't just allow Friedrich to go free… and what about Bormann? You don't seem to be as angry as I'd thought you'd be.'

The rain had now turned into sleet, and Hanne linked her arm into her husband's and moved closer to him. 'The Slovenians are here.'

'Who?'

'The Slovenian partisans, the ones who were in Villach: they followed us to Trieste. When I said I went out for some fresh air this morning, I actually met Jožef and told him the Germans were in a warehouse in Porto Vecchio and we were going in this morning. I didn't want them to stop us arresting the Germans, but of course now… If I can somehow get a message to them, maybe they can…'

'What are you saying, Hanne?'

'You know full well.' They'd reached the hotel entrance and watched as the two men who'd been following them carried on past.

Prince nodded. Hanne said he should go up to the room and collect their things. 'I'll meet you down here. I just need ten minutes.'

'Hanne, be...'

'What Richard – careful? Come on, we don't want Friedrich Steiner to escape, do we?'

'I don't want your Slovenians to be too rash. In any case, I have another plan.'

–

The journey to Klagenfurt was a largely silent one, other than the near-constant sound of Evans blowing his nose. Hanne and Prince were in the back of the British army car, Evans in the front next to the driver. When Hanne had returned to the hotel, she'd just had time to whisper to her husband that everything was fine and he wasn't to worry before Evans bustled into the reception area.

They crossed the Southern Alps from Slovenia into Austria on the precarious Loibl Pass. An hour later, they stopped to refuel at the British base in Ferlach, south of Klagenfurt. When Evans went to find a toilet, Prince and Hanne left the car and made sure they were out of earshot of the driver.

'I was thinking during that drive, Hanne.'

'Thinking? I thought you were sleeping!'

'We agree we can't let these people get away with it – Friedrich Steiner, Palmer, Myrtle Carter, Bormann... maybe. I know who can help us.'

'Who?'

'Remember I mentioned before we left Trieste that I had another plan? When I met Iosif in Vienna, he told me about the Slovenians and how he'd tipped them off about Villach. He also gave me a telephone number in Vienna to use if I needed to contact him. Now we're in Austria, I should call that number.'

'I thought he was in Berlin?'

'I don't know – I just need to be able to get to a telephone. If the Russians hear the British are letting Nazis go free just to please the Americans, they're bound to intervene.'

'How?'

'Iosif will think of something.'

'Won't Gilbey realise we're behind it?'

'How could he prove it?'

Hanne nodded: what Prince said made sense. In the distance they saw the large figure of Evans ambling towards them, a handkerchief pressed to his face.

'Bad news, I'm afraid.' He was struggling to light a cigarette in the wind while still clutching his large white handkerchief, which was blowing horizontally from one hand like a flag of surrender. 'The plan was to take you straight to the airport for this afternoon's flight to Munich, but apparently the area's cloaked in fog and all flights are cancelled until tomorrow: damned shame.'

They agreed it was indeed a terrible shame, and when Evans said they'd have to stay in Klagenfurt, Prince said that was a pity but not the end of the world. Evans replied that he wasn't sure, Klagenfurt seemed very much like the end of the world, and the car rocked as he laughed out loud. He repeated the joke periodically until they arrived in the town. They could see what he meant.

Major Stewart couldn't hide his annoyance at having unexpected charges thrust upon him. He adopted the manner of a schoolteacher who'd had a disruptive pupil brought before him once again.

'I suppose we'll have to find somewhere for you to spend the night. Just do me a favour and stay inside Innere Stadt. I know you're both prone to wandering off, but not here, please. The town's still a bloody mess and there's a good deal of resentment towards the Eighth Army.'

Half an hour later, they were in a small hotel just off the Alter Platz. As soon as they were alone, they left by a rear door and hurried through the narrow streets. Dusk was beginning to fall on the old town centre, and with half the buildings damaged and empty, it felt like a journey into the dark. Some of the streets were impassable, blocked with piles of rubble that reached as high as the first floor of those buildings still standing. In the shadow of the cathedral they turned a corner and spotted a pharmacy with its lights on: *Wörthersee Apotheke*.

'You speak, Hanne, your German's much better than mine. Remember to say that—'

Hanne stopped and turned to face her husband. 'You asked me to speak, Richard, didn't you? So leave it to me!'

There was almost an apologetic air to Wörthersee Apotheke, as if the shop was embarrassed to be the only one left unscathed on the street. An elderly couple stood behind the counter, clearly grateful at the prospect of customers.

Hanne stepped forward to the counter and Prince closed the door, standing in front of it. The couple looked at her expectantly.

'We are sorry to disturb you, but we need to know if you have a telephone?'

They nodded, their heads moving in unison.

'We need a telephone for a private matter, and if we could use yours, that would be very much appreciated.'

The pair looked anxiously at each other, trying to work out whether there was a catch.

'Of course it goes without saying that we would pay for any inconvenience.'

The man began to say of course, but the woman stopped him. 'How much?'

Prince stepped forward and spread some Alliance *schillings* on the countertop. The occupation currency was much in demand, and he had calculated he was offering them a generous sum. The wife raised her eyes in surprise and quickly gathered up the notes.

'The telephone is here in the back, in our little office.'

'When do you close?'

'In ten minutes,' said the husband.

'Close now,' said Hanne, clearly giving an order. 'Lock the door and turn out the lights. I'd be grateful if you could allow us some privacy.'

They left them alone in the office, explaining that they'd be upstairs in their apartment.

Prince rang the Vienna number he'd memorised.

'Ludwig.'

The deep voice had answered far more quickly than he was expecting. He hesitated slightly before giving the response Iosif had instructed him to. 'It's Horst: I need to talk with Joachim about a problem with a package.'

'Is this to do with the watches?'

He hesitated once more. He knew that unless he replied correctly, the man would terminate the call. 'No, the boots.'

'Very well – and you can be reached on this number?'

'Yes, but not for very long.'

'There'll be a call from Joachim within the hour. Make sure you're there.'

Hanne called up to the couple, who quickly emerged onto the first-floor landing. There was a family problem, she explained, quite a distressing one and of a confidential nature, and her husband had to wait to be called back. Would it be possible to have use of the office and the telephone for another hour – and of course we will pay for your troubles?

Iosif Gurevich rang back within half an hour. Through the static it sounded as if he was shouting into the phone from the other side of a room.

'I'm in Berlin – this call is being connected via Vienna. I'm not sure how it works and nor am I sure how secure it is, so you'd better be quick.'

Prince explained everything: how they'd tracked the Kestrel Line to Trieste, where they were convinced Friedrich Steiner was hiding in a warehouse by the port, and how they'd been instructed to call off the operation and had been driven to Klagenfurt, where they were waiting to be flown back to England.

'Who is with Steiner?'

'Another German – we think he escorted Steiner from Frankfurt – and an English couple, one of whom is an important Nazi spy I was hunting last year: a traitor. It's outrageous that they're being allowed to escape just to please the Americans.'

'It doesn't surprise me.'

'You don't sound too shocked, Iosif.'

'Of course I'm not shocked, my friend – we're up to it too! It's only you British who are shocked by this kind of thing. What about Bormann?'

'He could be with them, we're not sure.'

'So what are you asking me to do?'

'Tell the Slovenians they can do what they want with Friedrich Steiner, but we don't want the others to get away: they must be detained somehow.'

There was no immediate response from Iosif, just the static down the line, but then he came back and asked how long they'd be in Klagenfurt, and when Prince replied until the next day, Iosif said something that was hard to make out and then told him to leave it with him. He couldn't promise, but… and then the line went dead.

–

Kommissar Iosif Gurevich put the phone down and gazed out of his office window high on Behrenstrasse over the jagged and ruined roofscape of Berlin. The few minutes between the end of dusk and the start of night were now ticking past, and he knew he had little time. The prospect – however remote – of capturing Bormann was a tantalising one: it would certainly secure his next promotion. Apprehending the English spies would be a good career move too, Moscow liked the idea of having the British in their debt. And the fact that he'd be helping his English friend was pleasing, though only a secondary consideration.

He shouted for his assistant to come through. 'You look as if you're ready to leave.'

'I was hoping to, sir, but if you—'

'We're going to be here all night, Yegorov. It will be like the old days. Get hold of Fyodorov, I think he's still based at Hohenschönhausen prison.'

'And what should I say to him, sir?'

'Tell him I want to see him now, immediately. Oh, and get a pot of coffee, the stronger the better.'

Kapitan Fyodorov was a bag of nerves when he knocked tentatively on Gurevich's door just half an hour later. It was best to assume a summons from a commissar was something to worry about, though for the young NKVD officer, almost everything was something to worry about these days. Gurevich shouted for him to come in and sit down and not look so nervous.

'For heaven's sake, Fyodorov, take your coat off. You're not cold, are you? Here, have some coffee.'

He waited as Fyodorov sorted himself out. He noticed that the younger man held his coffee cup with both hands, and he remembered the days when he too would shake in the presence of such a senior officer. He didn't think he came across as that harsh.

'I hear very good reports about you, Leonid.'

'Thank you, sir. It is an honour to serve the Soviet Union and to—'

Gurevich held up his hand to stop him. 'I'm sure. There is an urgent matter that needs to be dealt with. You remember Willi Kühn?'

'You mean Paul Hoffman's contact?'

'That's him, the schoolteacher – former KPD member. I need him to do something for us, but I'm not sure how far we can trust him.'

Gurevich swivelled his chair round, and when he'd completed a full circle to face Fyodorov once more, he lifted his feet onto the desk and closed his eyes in thought.

'Let me put this another way: if we were to approach Kühn, how do you think he'd react?'

'He's not the trusting type, sir.'

'What's Hoffman up to these days?'

'Since the Volkspolizei was formed in October, he's become a very effective officer in it, sir: I understand he is even trusted to investigate political crimes.'

'So we could use him to approach Kühn?'

'That would be a better approach, sir.'

'I thought so. Very good, get Hoffman here now.'

An hour later, Paul Hoffman swaggered into Gurevich's office without any of the nervousness shown by Fyodorov.

'I want you to bring Willi Kühn here, Hoffman.'

'When, sir?'

'Ideally, an hour ago, but I'll settle for some time tonight.'

Hoffman coughed and looked less confident now. 'There is a slight problem with that, sir.'

Gurevich looked up in the manner of a man who had enough problems already. 'Go on.'

'He's in Wedding, sir, in the western part of the city. I think that's in the French sector.'

'In that case, I'll allow you two hours to bring him here.'

–

The war had been over for more than seven months, but that didn't stop Willi Kühn breaking out in a cold sweat and his heart missing a beat or two when he heard knocking on his door so late at night.

At least he was alone. His daughter was working as a nurse at the French hospital, and his son-in-law was in a Soviet prisoner-of-war camp, where frankly Kühn hoped he would remain. Through the frosted glass he saw the shadows of two still figures.

'Who is it?'

'You don't need to sound so worried, Willi. It's me, Paul – Paul Hoffman.'

Kühn undid the chain. Hoffman's face was just inches from his. He couldn't make out the slightly shorter figure standing behind him.

'What is it – am I in trouble?'

'You will be if you don't let us in,' said the other figure. It spoke with a Russian accent. 'It's fucking cold out here.'

The three of them stood in the doorway, the light from the lounge spilling into the hall. Kühn peered at the Russian, trying to work out whether he recognised him. Fyodorov held a card in front of him and said he was NKVD.

'Get your coat on, you're coming with us.'

'I can't, I…' His heart beat faster and he felt nauseous.

'Really? It must be a very important social occasion if it's preventing you from doing what you're told.'

Hoffman cleared his throat. 'You're not in trouble, Willi, but your cooperation would be very much appreciated.'

'Where are we going?'

The Russian reached into his inside coat pocket and Kühn backed against the wall. He relaxed when some papers were handed to him. 'If we get stopped, this is the pass you show, but let Paul do the talking. We should be all right, though; we'll take a longer route, but it's a safer one.'

'I need to know where you're taking me.'

'You're going on a trip to the east, Willi.'

–

The events that night in his office on Behrenstrasse reminded Iosif Gurevich of a play he'd seen in Moscow before the war. He remembered little of it other than that it was predictably earnest, with long periods of silence punctuated by speeches that sounded like editorials from *Izvestiya*, though without the jokes.

A recurring scene saw a series of workers at a collective farm summoned to the party chairman's office, each eager to take the blame for some unspecified misdemeanour. The succession of people coming through his door that evening reminded him of those hapless workers: the put-upon Yegorov; Fyodorov; Hoffman, and now Willi Kühn, who stood in front of him blinking in the bright light. Gurevich felt like the party chairman on the collective farm, studying his most recent visitor as he stood nervously in front of him, twirling his hat round against his chest.

'Kühn, I understand that when you met Wolfgang Steiner in October, he gave you a telephone number to contact him in the event of you having a message from Bormann. That is correct?'

'Yes, sir and I gave that number to Herr Hoffman when I met him and a very charming lady colleague of his on Kurfürstendamm. Do you not remember, Paul?'

'I know you gave him the number, Kühn, I'm not disputing that: I have it here in front of me. What I want to know is whether Steiner gave you any idea as to where he was?'

Kühn shook his head. 'I did ask him where he was based – I think that's how I put it – but he didn't tell me. That's when he gave me the telephone number. Why don't you try and trace it?'

'Thank you very much, Kühn, I had no idea you'd make such a brilliant detective – maybe you could join Hoffman in the Volkspolizei. Yes of course we've tried to trace that number. Fyodorov...'

'It's untraceable sir: obviously we checked it out as soon as we got it. The Nazis had a sophisticated telephone system in many respects, and it seems they were able to set up numbers and then remove any record of where they were located. Our engineers suspect they may have used some kind of shadow system, where a property has a primary telephone number and then a secondary number operating from the same line that no one knows about.'

'And there's still no way of tracing it?'

'The only possible way is if we were to intercept the number on an outgoing call, but the chances of that happening are so remote as to be impossible.'

'Thank you, Leonid – I'll give you the benefit of the doubt and assume that makes sense. So you see what our problem is, Kühn? We want to discuss some matters with Herr Steiner and it looks like the only way we can make contact with him is through you. So take your coat off and come over here – in fact, you can sit at my desk.'

'And what do you want me to do?'

'To make a bloody telephone call!'

–

Frau Moser was on the landing before him, standing by her bedroom door in her enormous flannelette bed dress with a blanket wrapped around her shoulders.

'It's all right, Frau Moser, let me answer it.'

'Who calls at eleven o'clock at night?'

Wolfgang Steiner told her – a bit too sharply on reflection – to go back into her room, and hurried downstairs into the draughty hall.

'Hello?'

'Hello… it's Willi.'

Steiner rubbed his brow. He'd been woken from a deep sleep and was still a bit dazed. When it suddenly registered who Willi was, he was shocked, not least that he was using his proper name. He should have agreed a code name. 'Willi, yes… Don't use my name… Is everything all right? Where are you?'

'I'm in Berlin. Look, I'm sorry to call you so late, but I thought you ought to know I've heard from your friend Graf – you'll recall he was a former colleague of mine… Graf?'

'Yes, yes, Graf… I know… Where is he?'

A pause: Steiner wondered whether Bormann could be with Kühn. It sounded as if someone was.

'He's here in Berlin – he made contact with me yesterday and I saw him today and he instructed me to contact you: he wants you to come and rescue him. He says you have to, only you, and—'

'How do I know this is true? Is there any proof?'

'Do you think I'd have called you if it wasn't true? Our friend – Graf – is desperate: he was seriously injured in May and has been recovering, but the place where he was staying is no longer safe and now he feels well enough to travel. He insisted I call you. Where he is now, he can only stay for another day or two.'

Steiner felt all his anxieties sweep back. He leaned against the wall and tried to gather his thoughts. This was either a trap and he should ignore it, or it was true and at last he had an opportunity – an honour indeed – to rescue the Reichsleiter. If only this had happened before he'd gone to Munich. If he hurried, there'd be time to get Bormann on the boat from Trieste to South Africa: it would be the most enormous act of service to the cause. But he realised that whatever he decided, he needed to do it now. He took a deep breath.

'I'll set out for Berlin first thing in the morning. You remember the place we met in October?'

'Yes. You mean the—'

'Don't say where it was: be there at four o'clock tomorrow afternoon. Wait for half an hour, and if I don't show up, return at eight o'clock the following morning. Again wait for half an hour, and if you've not seen me by then, return at two that afternoon.'

'And if you're not there then?'

'Then I won't be there at all.'

–

When Willi Kühn replaced the receiver, sweat was pouring from his brow and his hand felt quite numb from gripping the phone so tightly. He breathed an enormous sigh of relief and looked up at the Russian, who nodded and said well done.

'And what happens now?'

'We wait to see if he shows up at four o'clock tomorrow. You could have asked him where he was coming from.'

'I doubt he'd have told me. What if he suspects something is up? He could try and shoot me.'

'I don't imagine a wanted Nazi is going to shoot someone in the middle of Berlin, not even in the French sector. In the morning, you'll show us where it was you met him, and then we can make arrangements. In the meantime, we'll find you a bed for the night.'

'Can't I go home?'

Iosif Gurevich laughed. 'No, Willi, that wouldn't be a good idea.'

Chapter 27

According to the luminous dial on his bedside clock, it was around a quarter to three. It was pitch dark, and no sound crept into their hotel room from the ruined streets of Klagenfurt. Prince assumed he'd been woken by an inevitably complicated dream in which he'd been running with his son through the fields near their home in Lincoln and for some reason had hidden in a copse, ignoring Henry's increasingly disturbed cries.

His absence from Henry was clearly on his mind, and he realised he ought to make his son his absolute priority. They'd soon be on their way home. He'd make sure they returned to Lincoln as soon as possible. No one would be able to accuse him of not having served his country.

But it soon became apparent that there was another reason why he'd woken. From the narrow landing outside their room came the creaking sound of movement on the uneven floorboards. There was only one other room on that landing, and the manager had assured them it was unoccupied. They were, he told them sadly, the only guests in his hotel.

Prince turned round to face Hanne. A tiny shaft of half-light caught her hair splayed over the pillow. He gently touched her face, and she moved as he slowly slipped his hand over her mouth and tapped her shoulder at the same time. Her eyes opened wide and he placed one finger on his lips before pointing to his ear and then to the door.

As Hanne turned over to face the door, there was the sound of a lock being turned. Both of them sat bolt upright, and as

Richard rose from the bed, the door opened and a large figure squeezed into the room. He closed the door and stood with his back to it.

'You don't need to worry,' he said in German.

Prince recognised the voice as the deep bass tones of Ludwig, the man he'd telephoned the previous evening in Vienna to send the message to Iosif.

'Comrade Gurevich sent me to help you. Maybe put the small light on.'

When Prince turned on the bedside light, he recognised the heavily built man as the one he'd met in the woods when Gurevich had driven him from Vienna, who'd then taken him into Klagenfurt in his Daimler. The three of them looked at each other, Ludwig's bloodshot eyes blinking from under his thick eyebrows.

'You know they're watching the hotel?'

'Who are?'

'Your people – the British.' He shook his head in a derisory manner. 'They're not very good: two of them in a car at the front, one of them asleep. There's a man in the alley at the back too – an amateur: all he does is smoke. He may as well be waving a torch around.'

'How did you get in?'

'It's my job. In any case, your people paid the hotel owner to let them know if they heard anything or if you went anywhere. Once they do that, it's easy: we just pay more. You'd better get ready.'

'Where are we going?'

'Comrade Gurevich says he's more or less sorted everything out, so you need to get back to Trieste. You'd better get a move on, or you'll miss all the fun.'

–

The Allied Kommandatura met three times a day: at seven in the morning, noon and seven in the evening. The Kommandatura was the body that brought Berlin's four governing powers together, and since July it had met at a building on Kaiserswerther Strasse in Dahlem, opposite Triestpark.

There was a certain predictability to the meetings. The Western Allies had four representatives each, the Soviet Union eight. The meetings would begin with discussions on non-controversial matters – power and water supplies, for example – although in the fetid atmosphere of December 1945 Berlin, nothing could be described as non-controversial. There had once been a lengthy and heated row over who was responsible for cleaning gutters. They would then move on to more difficult matters, and as the meeting came to an end, if any party wanted to raise a matter directly with another, they would then do so.

It was bitterly cold, with a wind building up, when they gathered for the meeting at seven o'clock that Wednesday evening. No one was in the mood for a long meeting, and in any case the evening meeting tended to be the least difficult one of the day.

As the meeting closed, one of the Soviet representatives asked to meet with an American representative about a delicate matter. The senior American officer present was a colonel, who carefully studied the Red Army officer who'd made the request. He was a one-star NKGB commissar, young for such a senior rank, and the colonel had met him before but couldn't recall his name. The colonel nodded to one of his colleagues, an affable Italian American in civilian clothes who was responsible for what were euphemistically called 'sensitive issues'.

The commissar was smiling and seemed relaxed. 'I need to give you a message and I wanted to be sure you received it and understood it.'

The colonel didn't like the way the Russian behaved, as if he were at a social event. He narrowed his eyes, resisting the urge to tell him to get on with it. The man looked like a Jew: he was amazed how many of them there were in the Red Army in Berlin. It was as if they'd come there to gloat. He nodded for him to continue.

'I would be grateful if you could pass this message on to a Major Barrow of the Counter Intelligence Corps in Munich.'

The Italian American began to cough.

'I am not sure if you'd wish to write this down. Major Barrow recently established a relationship with a Wolfgang Steiner. That's W–O–L—'

'I know how the hell to spell Wolfgang, thank you.'

'Wolfgang Steiner would like you to know that he has reflected on his decision to work for the United States. He has decided that peace in Europe is best served by cooperating with the Soviet Union. He is now resident in the Soviet sector, where he intends to remain.' Iosif Gurevich smiled and removed a pack of cigars from his pocket, offering them to the two Americans. It took all the colonel's willpower not to accept one.

The Italian American said very well, he'd pass the message on just in case anyone had had any dealings with this gentleman, whom he'd never heard of.

'You think we're fools, do you?' The colonel was red-faced, squaring up the Russian, who was noticeably taller than him.

'In what way, Colonel?'

'You think we'll believe that crap about this guy deciding to work for you? You abducted him, didn't you?'

The commissar smiled and lit his cigar, blowing a cloud of brown-tinged smoke above the American's head as he announced that the meeting was over and he hoped they'd have a good evening.

–

Wolfgang Steiner had turned up at the patch of wasteland in Wedding close to four thirty that afternoon.

Willi Kühn had been in a terrible state: at one stage on the Wednesday morning he had refused to go through with it, and Gurevich had told him that in that case he would be arrested for assisting the escape of a Nazi. It had all turned very unpleasant until Kühn said he'd do it if they told him what precautions they'd be taking.

Gurevich had decided not to risk sending too many Russians into a western sector of the city. Fyodorov would be there to keep an eye on things from a distance, but otherwise they were relying on one of their German teams.

He'd very much enjoyed Fyodorov's subsequent account of what had happened. Kühn had been so nervous as he paced around the wasteland that at one point he'd stumbled over, and Fyodorov had been worried he might leave. Two of their German team were disguised as old ladies collecting firewood in the distance. When they'd checked the patch of ground that morning, they'd discovered a cellar in the middle of it covered in rubble, and had managed to clear it enough to conceal three of their men there.

Wolfgang Steiner had emerged from the east and walked slowly towards Kühn, who looked terrified, frozen to the spot. From where Fyodorov was, he could tell how nervous Kühn was and he was convinced Steiner would realise something was up, but the German carried on oblivious, holding out his hand in greeting as he approached the schoolteacher.

The two men were standing close to the cellar, and Fyodorov thought Steiner must have heard something, because he peered over towards it. That was when he gave the order, and in a matter of seconds two men had leapt out of their hiding place and bundled Steiner into it.

From then on it was very straightforward. After a brief struggle, Steiner was subdued and searched before being given an injection to knock him out. His coat was replaced with a shabby one that smelt of alcohol, and he was carried to a car that had pulled up nearby. If they were stopped, he'd be a drunk being helped home by his friends.

Half an hour later, he was strapped to a metal chair in a cellar in Behrenstrasse, the effects of the injection now wearing off. Gurevich was sitting in front of him assuring him he'd be fine, though he understood he might have a headache for a while.

When Steiner asked where he was, Gurevich said he was surprised that he hadn't worked it out. 'The main thing, though, is that you're no longer working for the Americans!'

Steiner looked stunned as the truth dawned, then he burst into tears, sobbing for quite a while, which Gurevich found disconcerting at first, though when it came to men realising their fate was sealed and their days were numbered, it was quite unpredictable how they'd react.

He'd left the German in his cell and returned to his office, where he rang the general in charge of that evening's meeting with the Western Allies on Kaiserswerther Strasse and said he'd very much like to attend.

He had, he said, an important message for the Americans.

Chapter 28

England, December 1945

It was noticeable how unwell Joseph Jenkins looked. His normally florid complexion had been replaced by a greyish pallor, and he appeared to have lost weight, though Tom Gilbey thought that could have been a trick of the lighting. He thought it best in what were obviously awkward circumstances not to remark on Jenkins' appearance as they gathered in a low-ceilinged windowless room at the American embassy in Grosvenor Square.

But Sir Roland Pearson showed no such inhibitions. 'Are you under the weather, Joe?'

Jenkins glared at him. He was sitting between a young officer clearly there to take notes and the deputy head of station for the Office of Strategic Services, a man Sir Roland had met on numerous occasions over the past two or three years but whose name he couldn't for the life of him remember.

'I've brought you here to share a very serious development.' Jenkins' voice trembled, adding an odd timbre to his Southern accent. Neither Pearson nor Gilbey replied. They waited for the American to continue.

'A few days ago I came to your office to inform you that the Counter Intelligence Corps had recruited a Wolfgang Steiner as an agent. I also informed you that a condition of Steiner's recruitment was that the British abandon the hunt for his son Friedrich and stop investigating the Kestrel Line. You remember this – it was just a day or so ago?'

Neither Englishman reacted.

'I requested that you issue an immediate instruction to your agents in Trieste to drop everything. This had been authorised at the highest level: Ambassador Winant discussed the matter with your Foreign Secretary.'

Still no reaction from Tom Gilbey, but Sir Roland said that all this rang a bell and he hoped they were getting some decent intelligence from this Steiner chap after going to so much trouble.

Jenkins slammed the table so hard that the young officer's notebook fell to the floor. 'I'm sure there are some people who find your boarding school sarcasm amusing, but I'm not one of them. I'm here to tell you that Steiner has gone missing. Maybe "missing" is the wrong word. To be more precise, we were informed last night by the Soviets that he was now working for them: he's apparently in their sector of Berlin.'

'I beg your pardon?'

'We want to know what the hell you guys have to do with this, Gilbey. One day we tell you about Steiner, the next he defects to the Russians.'

'Defected may not be quite accurate.' It was the man from the Office of Strategic Services. 'My feeling is that Steiner was lured to Berlin and then abducted by the Soviets. There is no way he'd have gone over to them voluntarily: it was in his interest to work with us. He had nothing to gain from becoming a Soviet agent. My guess is he won't be in East Berlin for very long. The bastards will take him to Moscow and finish him off there.'

'Well I'm obviously sorry to hear all this; it's a damn shame.' Gilbey was sitting up straight and doing his best to sound genuinely concerned. 'But I do hope you're not implying we were somehow involved.'

'I'm saying,' said Jenkins, some of the colour now returning to his cheeks, 'that it's one hell of a coincidence.'

'Well it's nothing to do with us, I can assure you, Joseph. I fear it is just that, a coincidence. Maybe Steiner was careless, who knows?'

'According to our guys in Berlin, an NKGB commissar called Iosif Gurevich came to the Allied Kommandatura last night to tell them about Steiner. Does that name ring a bell?'

Tom Gilbey shook his head and said he was awfully sorry and only wished he could be more help.

–

'You know him, don't you, Tom?'

'Know who, Roly?'

They were back in Gilbey's office in St James's. The departure from the US Embassy had been a swift and uncomfortable one. The man from the Office of Strategic Services had ended the meeting by saying they'd not heard the last of this matter. He'd be discussing it later that day with the ambassador.

'The Russian commissar he mentioned.'

'Gurevich?'

'Exactly – I noticed you didn't even write the name down. Who is he?'

'He's the NKGB officer who helped Prince in Berlin back in May, when he was looking for Hanne. Prince has kept in touch with him and he was the source for the information that gave us the Steiners.'

'So…'

'So it's entirely possible that Prince somehow got a message to Gurevich and he organised Steiner's abduction.'

'So quickly?'

'It would be a big error, Roly, to underestimate Prince's resourcefulness. Do remember that he operated in Nazi-occupied Europe. He and Hanne are first-class agents.'

'Good Lord.'

'My view is that they were so appalled at being ordered to let the Nazis go that they took this course of action.'

'But that's appalling, Tom: disobeying orders like that… working with the Russians!'

'That's as may be, but knowing Prince and Hanne, I doubt there'll be any evidence of that. I'm not sure if Bartholomew's still in Trieste: I'll have to see if the Field Security Section chaps there can resume the operation and arrest the Germans. Talk about shutting the stable door after the horse has bolted. Bloody hell, Roly – and to think I took the view life would be less complicated after the war, eh!'

They were interrupted by a knock at the door. It was Bentley, Gilbey's boss, who nodded his head by way of greeting and glided into the room as if there was someone he didn't want to wake up.

'You've heard the news, I imagine.'

Gilbey said they had; in fact they'd only just returned from the American embassy, where an irate Joseph Jenkins had told them about the disappearance of Wolfgang Steiner into the Soviet sector.

'I think we may be talking at cross-purposes here, Tom. I didn't mean that news – which is news to me, in fact. I meant about Prince.'

'He and his wife are on their way back here.'

Bentley shook his head. 'That's the thing, you see. They arrived in Klagenfurt on Tuesday afternoon and were due on a flight to Munich yesterday.'

'Please don't tell me they've been causing trouble?'

'I'm afraid they have. As far as we can gather, they disappeared from their hotel in Klagenfurt early yesterday morning and there's been no sign of them since.'

'Yesterday morning – and we're only being told now?'

'I think the FSS chaps who were meant to be keeping an eye on them rather hoped they'd turn up before they had to break the bad news to London.'

–

It had been a particularly busy morning at the Bourne and Sons art gallery in Cork Street. Since the end of the war, business had been picking up, and that very morning they'd had a most promising meeting with an RAF officer who'd brought in a seventeenth-century Flemish baroque painting he'd inherited from an aunt. The impression gained by both Bourne and Ridgeway was that he wanted to sell it quickly and had little appreciation of its real value, aesthetic or financial. Ridgeway – who knew more about Flemish painting than Bourne – thought it was certainly from the Antwerp school, and with some judicious wording they could attribute it to a student of van Dyck.

By the time the man left and Bourne and Ridgeway had worked out the considerable profit they could make on the painting, it was close to one thirty. They decided they would close the gallery until three o'clock and have a decent lunch. Their plans were thwarted by a rapping at the steel-reinforced door that led on to the alley at the back of the gallery. Bourne peered through the security glass and it took him a moment to realise that the man in the bowler hat with a scarf wrapped round the lower half of his face was the Admiral.

He stepped back in shock: it went without saying that the Admiral had not been expected. In fact he hadn't visited the gallery since before the war. After his release from internment two years earlier, he'd rarely left his home in the country, and had even given up his rooms in London.

Bourne opened the door a few inches.

'I walked past the front and saw that the gallery was open. Is anyone else in there?'

'Just Ridgeway and myself, sir.'

'Close the gallery and let me in.'

Once inside the cramped office, the Admiral removed his hat and unfurled his scarf. He took the seat behind Bourne's desk, still wearing his overcoat, though he did unbutton it. Only when he'd removed his leather gloves did he look up at the two men standing obediently in front of him.

'We may have a problem, gentlemen.'

Bourne and Ridgeway looked anxiously at each other, unsure whether to remain standing or to sit down.

'May I ask the nature of that problem, Admiral?'

'The messages one gets from the Continent are of course by definition sporadic and often imprecise.' He paused to straighten his gloves. 'But there would appear to be two developments, both of which are a cause for concern. Why don't you sit down?'

He waited for Bourne and Ridgeway to arrange their chairs in front of the desk.

'Wolfgang has disappeared and there are reports that he may now be in East Berlin.'

'The Soviet sector?'

'Obviously, Ridgeway – but remember, this isn't confirmed. If it is true, I have absolutely no idea why he's there or how the hell he got there, but I do know that he's not been heard from in a while. And the news from Trieste is even more confusing. The ship is still in port, but according to its master the passengers: have moved from the warehouse to another location and he's getting very nervous. He was meant to sail tomorrow and he's now agreed to wait until Monday, but no later than that. I'm suspicious about the whole business…'

'What about Palmer?'

'Exactly, Bourne – what about Palmer indeed? It wouldn't surprise me in the least if we're in the process of being outsmarted by that menace Prince and the bloody Danish woman. If they catch Palmer, I don't trust him to keep quiet, and that means all of us are in serious trouble. I knew we should have got rid of him as soon as he turned up out of the blue in August. I regret letting Myrtle talk me out of it. One can only hope she knows what to do if they're in danger of being caught.'

'May I ask what that is, Admiral?'

'She will ensure Palmer does not pose a problem. In the meantime, gentlemen, my advice to you is to disappear for a while, at least until we know what's happened.'

'But Admiral… the gallery…' Ridgeway's voice trembled. He looked petrified, and Bourne was little better, anxiously wiping his forehead and apparently on the verge of tears.

'Pull yourselves together and forget about the bloody gallery and your miserable paintings. I presume you made arrangements for such an eventuality, as I told you to?'

The pair nodded uncertainly.

'You're to leave now. Call me in the middle of next week and I'll let you know if the coast is clear.'

'And if it's not?'

The Admiral stood up and started to button his overcoat. 'If the coast isn't clear, then I very much doubt I'll be answering the telephone.'

Chapter 29

Italy, December 1945

They slipped away from Klagenfurt at around a quarter past three on the Wednesday morning, not long after Ludwig had appeared in their hotel room. He'd waited in the corridor while Prince and Hanne dressed, during which time they had an urgent whispered conversation, with Prince worried that defying orders like this could be regarded as desertion – or even treason. 'What do you think, Hanne?'

'If you're so concerned, then let's call the whole thing off. Tell him we're not going.'

'But do you think we should go?'

'Of course I do! There's a group of Nazis in Trieste and we shouldn't allow them to go free. I just hope it's not too late.'

'But going off with the Russians like this…'

'Richard – how are we going to get into trouble for trying to catch Nazis?'

Ludwig led them to the end of the corridor and up a small flight of stairs, where a ladder attached to the wall led to a trapdoor to the roof. Klagenfurt was quite still and eerily silent, with just enough moonlight for them to see where they were going. They followed him over the rooftops until they were well away from the hotel, and only then did they descend: a precarious climb down a drainpipe, a short drop onto a terrace followed by a six-foot jump onto a pile of rubble, from where he led them the short distance to an alley where his black Daimler was parked.

He told them to sit in the back of the car and pointed to two large blankets. 'Cover yourselves, pretend to be asleep.'

'But there's a curfew: don't you think we're going to be a bit conspicuous?'

Ludwig shrugged and said not to worry: *Mach dir keine Sorgen*. When he started the engine, the sound seemed to reverberate throughout the town.

They drove through the dark streets, Ludwig appearing to be quite relaxed as he hummed a tune. He kept muttering *Mach dir keine Sorgen* over and over to himself, and then chuckling.

On the outskirts, they came to a British Army checkpoint. Ludwig stopped humming and reminded them to pretend to be asleep. The checkpoint was remarkably straightforward. Prince and Hanne clutched each other tightly, their hearts banging so loudly they were sure the soldiers must have heard. They heard a voice ask in English-accented German for papers, which Ludwig must have had ready, because the soldier quickly said everything was in order and they could carry on.

Ludwig wound the window up and slipped the Daimler into gear, accelerating away from the checkpoint. He resumed humming whatever tune it was and turned round to address his passengers again with a smile: *Mach dir keine Sorgen*.

Once they'd passed Ferlach – and another oddly trouble-free checkpoint – Ludwig slowed down. He told them he didn't want to cross the Alps before daylight, so they waited by the side of the road and watched dawn break in spectacular fashion over the mountains. He shared a flask of brandy with his passengers, but said little until the landscape in front of them had turned from black to grey then to white and he said it was time to go. The Loibl Pass was as good as could be expected at this time of year, he added, in between humming, and then he chuckled.

Mach dir keine Sorgen: don't worry.

–

The Daimler pulled into the courtyard of a large house in Trieste later that afternoon. Hanne and Prince were hurried in and taken to a large dimly lit basement where a dozen armed men and women were sitting on the floor, apparently uninterested in their arrival.

Hanne gripped Prince's hand tightly as the steel door slammed shut behind them and the sound of it being bolted from the outside reverberated. For a few moments they both worried this was a trap, but then a tall figure moved towards them, and when he spoke – enquiring about their journey and the weather over the Alps – his voice was familiar and they realised it was Edvard, the oldest of the Slovenian partisans.

He pointed to the others sitting around the room. They were comrades from the Liberation Front of Slovenia, he said, and reeled off their names. 'They've come to help us. We want to get Friedrich Steiner and catch the others for you.'

'I thought you'd have done that by now.' Hanne sounded angry.

'We have to be very careful. The British have increased their patrols around the city, and especially the port area. And in any case,' Edvard moved close to them, a strong smell of tobacco on his breath, 'we've been told by our mission in Berlin to wait until we get the signal from them to mount our operation. The British stopped watching the warehouse on Porto Vecchio yesterday, and that same night the Germans must have moved out of it, but we don't know where to. We're searching the area, and Jožef and Marija are talking to our contacts on the docks.'

'Where are we now?'

'Scorcola. We have to wait here until we find where the Germans are hiding.'

'And then get the go-ahead from Berlin.'

'Of course.'

Once it was dark, Edvard took them into a room on the top floor of the house, where Jožef and Marija sat in a cloud of cigarette smoke either side of a short man in oil-stained overalls and heavy boots. His dark face was deeply lined and the black hair sticking out from under his cloth cap was flecked with grey. It was hard to estimate his age, though when he spoke, it was with the rasping voice of an older man.

'Giuseppe is a docker at Porto Vittorio Emanuele.' Jožef placed an arm round the Italian's shoulder as he spoke. 'He's Italian but his mother was Slovenian, so he helps us.'

Giuseppe spoke. He sounded as if he was arguing with himself, emphasising some point or other by hitting an open hand with his fist.

'He's explaining that his job is to help prepare ships for their departure, making sure the cargo and all the supplies are loaded. On Monday he was allocated to a South African ship, the MV *Ankia*, which is due to set sail for Durban on Friday,' said Marija.

Giuseppe stopped her and spoke again.

'He says he's the foreman on this job, and yesterday the master took him into his cabin and asked him if he spoke German, which he does – a little. He said he'd agreed to take some passengers from Trieste to South Africa but they didn't have any paperwork. He knew he was breaking the law but he'd been offered a lot of money and now he was worried about how he was going to get them on board, especially as the authorities were looking for them.'

'Did he say who these passengers are?'

Marija translated for Giuseppe. 'He's not sure, but he thinks they're Germans or something to do with Germany. The master said that if Giuseppe could find a way to smuggle them on board, he'd reward him very generously. Before he left the port this evening, the master gave him the address of where the passengers are – it's on Viale Miramare, which is between here and Porto Vittorio Emanuele. His instructions are to go to the building at first light tomorrow morning and discuss with them how he's going to get them on board: he said they only speak German or English. Giuseppe speaks no English.'

'He definitely mentioned English, did he?'

'Yes, he's sure of that.'

'Good,' said Edvard. 'So we have the address of where the bastards are hiding. Now we just need to hear from Berlin.'

–

They heard from Berlin in the early hours of the Thursday morning, long before the sun rose over the city and began to glint off the Gulf of Trieste, long before the first shouts of the workers and clashes of metal disturbed the peace of the port and even longer before the curtains of Trieste were drawn and yellowy lights illuminated the homes of its stirring population.

When Edvard entered the room where Hanne and Prince were asleep on a sofa, he told them it was time to get dressed, and dropped two Beretta semi-automatic pistols at their feet.

Downstairs, the kitchen was crowded, but other than the occasional muttered word, no one spoke, the tension preventing anything in the way of conversation. The only noise was of the dozen people in the room checking their weapons, the placing of ammunition in barrels and magazines, the clicks of safety catches, and a few nervous coughs. The room was diffused with the smells of gun oil and coffee: on the stove, two large moka pots were brewing.

As the strong coffee kicked in, the room became busier: snatches of conversation began and a slight easing of the tension was apparent. One or two of the Slovenes slapped each other on the back, and there were brief snatches of laughter. This all stopped suddenly with a knock at the door: everyone fell silent and the lights were turned off.

Moments later, the door opened. Jožef and Marija bustled in and nodded at the others in the room, and were greeted warmly. Jožef went over to the wall and pinned up a large sheet of paper: a map showing a road and the area around it. Edvard stood between Hanne and Prince and translated as Marija spoke.

'The building is here, on the east side of Viale Miramare. The west side of the street is the railway line, and beyond that

Porto Vittorio Emanuele, where they'll be heading. Behind the building are courtyards: Branka's unit will cover the rear... Any questions so far?'

She barely paused before continuing. 'We think there are at least five in the group, and the plan is for them to sail on Friday on a ship currently docked in Porto Vittorio Emanuele. Giuseppe is to meet them later tonight to plan how to smuggle them on board. The group are in an accountant's office on the first floor – the name on the door says *Mariani: Ragioniere di Costo*. From what we can tell, the office is self-contained: we think it only has the one door. Giuseppe was told the entrance on the ground floor is unlocked, and when he gets to the first floor he's to knock four times and then announce he has a parcel for a Signor Giordano. Can someone give me a coffee, please?'

She lit a cigarette and drank the coffee in one go, then handed the cup back for someone to give her another one.

'We don't think the British are aware of this building – yet. We must assume the group will be watching the front from where they are on the first floor. We've found a back door that leads to the basement and then up into the entrance hall. Our plan is that Jožef takes his unit down to Viale Miramare now while it's still dark and waits in the basement. When Giuseppe enters the building, they'll follow him up so they can burst in when the door is opened.'

'Does Giuseppe know this?'

'He'll know what he needs to know Edvard. At that point I will follow in with my unit, which will include our comrades from England.' She pointed her cigarette at Hanne and Prince.

Edvard stepped forward and tapped the crudely drawn map. 'My unit will secure the front of the building: two of you here at one end of the block, and two at the other end. We'll have two at the entrance and three across the road, then—'

'That's nine in your unit, Edvard?'

'Plus me, yes.'

'And there are how many of us here – eighteen including the English?'

'Don't worry, we have some Italian comrades helping us: I've been promised at least half a dozen. Are there any other questions?'

'What do we do when we enter the office?'

'Don't worry Marija, Jožef knows what to do.'

'We need to know too, Edvard.'

'The German, the one called Friedrich Steiner – the one we know as König – he's ours. And the English Nazis and Bormann… Maybe you explain?'

Hanne stepped forward and said they were looking for a man and a woman, both English, both Nazi sympathisers. 'The woman is involved in a group helping to fund the Kestrel Line – we need to know who else in Britain is involved in that group. The man is called Edward Palmer: he was a very senior Nazi spy – Richard?'

'I've been hunting for Palmer for a while now. He was a British officer who was working in the intelligence department of our War Office and gave the Germans military information about the Allies' offensive in Europe. He disappeared in April in London, just as we were about to arrest him.'

'So we want them alive, and Bormann too, if he's there,' said Hanne. 'It's essential they're interrogated and put on trial.'

–

Myrtle Carter was utterly exhausted: she looked back on the journey from England as a succession of places they'd hurried through, like stations flashing past a speeding train. It had been a perilous journey. Paris had been fine; Geneva she was less sure about and had been glad to see the back of, and Turin had felt so hostile she'd insisted they head for Verona sooner than planned. From there they'd made it safely enough to Trieste. She doubted she'd slept more than a dozen hours since leaving England.

Once in Trieste, they'd met Friedrich Steiner and the man called Ulrich in the Catholic hostel. She found Steiner deeply unpleasant: an entitled, spoilt young man with few manners who thought everything revolved around him – insisting on the best revolver, the most comfortable place to sleep, the most food… The man called Ulrich was little better. He didn't mask his hostility to them, even though she'd explained how she and Palmer were in a minority of English people – albeit a very small minority – whom he must regard as friends rather than enemies. And then there was the other German, the older one dressed as a priest who said he'd been a senior official in the Reich, though she doubted he was as important as he gave the impression he was.

Two younger Germans had turned up to move them from the hostel on Via dell'Istria to the warehouse on Porto Vecchio, and for the very first time on the journey, Myrtle wondered if they were being watched. Until then she'd been sure they'd not been followed, but now she wondered about the odd movements she'd caught sight of outside the warehouse, the strange vans that had appeared, the people hurrying past the building and glancing up at it, holding their gaze for a second or two too long.

A message had appeared under the door sometime on the Tuesday – quite late in the day, just after dusk – telling them that they'd be moving that night, and sure enough, the two young Germans had turned up again. When they left the warehouse, there was definitely no one watching them: no suspiciously parked vans, no one strolling past, no sudden movement in the shadows. They made their way safely to where they were now: an accountant's office on what she was told was the Viale Miramare, which was close to where the South African ship would sail from on Friday.

The office was actually quite comfortable, and at the back of it she and Palmer found a sofa and an easy chair where they could avoid the Germans for much of the time. The latest message had come this evening: an Italian man would arrive early the following morning saying he had a parcel for a Signor

Giordano, which to her sounded like a line from one of those dreadful cheap novels her mother used to read. He would be there to make arrangements to take them to the ship later that day.

And now Myrtle realised she had decisions to make. She knew full well the Admiral expected her to return to England: her task had been to distribute the money to the Kestrel Line, to escort Edward Palmer to Trieste and to ensure he and Friedrich Steiner got on the ship and out of harm's way.

'I want them to disappear,' the Admiral had insisted, more than once.

But Myrtle had begun to wonder whether she wanted to go back to England after all. It no longer felt like her country: she detested the place after its victory in such an unjust war. She hated the way people gloated about their triumph, and to cap it all, there was now a socialist government to make life even more intolerable. South Africa, she understood, was at least somewhere white Christians could still lead a decent life. And Palmer would be an agreeable companion. He was an intelligent man and an accomplished lover, even if he didn't seem aware of that himself.

She'd withheld some of the funds for the Kestrel Line and had brought a couple of pieces of valuable jewellery with her. They'd get by in South Africa, and by the time the Admiral realised she wasn't coming back, she and Palmer would have disappeared.

But before that, there was a further consideration, an unpleasant matter but an unavoidable one: what would happen if they were caught? The Admiral had been very clear about this: under no circumstances was Palmer to be captured alive. *You know what to do, Myrtle.*

But would she be able to go through with that? And what about herself – could she bear to be taken alive?

–

When it was over, it took Bartholomew a good while to make any sense of what had happened.

He was woken up by the Field Security Section duty officer to be told that something was happening on the railway line by Porto Vittorio Emanuele. By the time he appeared in the FSS office, it turned out that whatever was going on wasn't on the railway line but on the road running parallel to it – Viale Miramare. Over the next few minutes, confusing reports came in from the British patrols on the scene. There'd been shooting in a building on Viale Miramare: a number of people were dead and some Slovenians had been arrested. He was putting on his coat and preparing to go to see for himself when another report came in: at least one British person had been arrested – and one more, possibly, was dead. It was then that Bartholomew muttered the word 'Prince'.

–

They'd left the house in Scorcola while it was still dark and walked in small groups down the road, each group climbing into their allotted van or lorry. Hanne and Prince followed Marija into a small van; half a dozen of them squeezed into the rear. Marija explained that Jožef was already in position, and once Edvard had secured the front of the building and Jožef had followed Giuseppe to the first floor, then they'd follow.

By the time the van parked a block away from the building, dawn was rising over Trieste. In the few minutes between the van stopping and the order to move in coming over the radio, the sun had risen. They'd watched the short figure of Giuseppe head into the building, and now they hurried in too.

From the entrance hall they heard shouts upstairs. Hanne and Prince had both drawn their Berettas and now they ran up the stairs after Marija.

The office door was wide open: on the floor inside was the body of a one-armed man, his blood turning the pale brown lino flooring dark red. Prince shouted to Hanne to go the left, he'd go right.

The first thing Hanne saw was the terrified figure of Friedrich Steiner on his knees by the window with his hands tied behind his back and a deep gash across his forehead. Lines of blood ran down his face like a spider's web as his body trembled violently and he whimpered something about being innocent and needing to leave. He was surrounded by Slovenians, who appeared to be arguing with each other about what to do with him. One of them held a knife to his throat and the blade had already drawn some blood.

Hanne spotted one of the Slovenians release the safety catch on his pistol, and she stepped forward. 'Not here – don't kill him here!'

There was a shout from the back of the office, and Prince called her over. Slumped on the sofa was the body of Edward Palmer. He was on his back, gazing at the ceiling with a surprised, unblinking stare. His jacket had fallen open, revealing a white shirt with a growing patch of blood and the hilt of a knife protruding from the centre of it.

Sitting in a chair alongside the sofa was a woman, her hands gripping the sides. She was bloodstained but appeared uninjured. Her face was pale and there was a nervous look on her face alongside the trace of a smile.

'It's Myrtle Carter, isn't it?' Prince was leaning in front of her, his hands on his knees so that he was at eye level. He was still holding his Beretta. 'We've met before. That's Edward Palmer – did you kill him?'

The woman shook her head and said something in a voice so quiet Prince asked her to speak up, and she replied that she didn't have the faintest idea who he was and what he was talking about.

'I'm a prisoner,' she said.

There was a commotion from outside the office and a lot of shouting inside it.

'This is her, Hanne – this is the woman.'

'We need to handcuff her.'

'We don't have any cuffs.'

'Then we need to tie her up. Have you searched her?'

Hanne walked over to the woman and told her to stand up, then started to frisk her. 'Get some rope or something, Richard. You – put your hands down!'

Myrtle Carter held out her left arm but moved her right hand towards her mouth. Hanne grabbed it, and a struggle followed. By the time Prince realised what was happening, the two women were wrestling on the floor.

'Oh my God, Richard – look, grab her arms!'

Myrtle Carter was writhing on the floor in agony, her hands clutching her throat, her eyes bulging and her face turning a shade of blue as she appeared to choke.

'Get some water or something!'

'It's too late, Richard – I tried to get it out but it was too late. It must have been a suicide pill.'

–

Bartholomew and the FSS men entered the first floor office on Viale Miramare with their guns drawn and a scene of chaos and carnage laid out before them. Had Prince not been at the entrance holding his hands up and shouting who he was, he was sure there'd have been more shooting.

He was aware of Bartholomew asking what the hell was going on, and Evans from the FSS shouting and threatening the Slovenians, and Hanne saying something about them all being dead.

A few hours later, they were in the Field Security Section office on Via San Lazzaro, and Bartholomew – still wearing his raincoat – thrust the headphones and microphone at Prince.

'Mr Gilbey wants to speak with you.'

'I struggle to see how you're going to manage to come up with a plausible explanation, Richard, but I imagine you're going to attempt one?' The line was surprisingly clear, and Prince noticed that while Gilbey sounded annoyed, he didn't sound furious. His tone was more one of resignation, and he had called him Richard.

'In what sense, sir?'

'In the sense, Prince, that I ordered you and Hanne to return to London and you chose to disobey that order, and now we have a bloodbath in Trieste to try and sort out.'

'An opportunity presented itself to catch Friedrich Steiner, sir, along with Myrtle Carter and Edward Palmer. That was our original mission. I know it would be preferable for them to have been captured alive, but at least they've not escaped. I don't know about Bormann...'

'Bartholomew said the man dressed as a priest isn't Martin Bormann – he doesn't look remotely like him. He's dead too, isn't he?'

'So I believe, sir.'

There was a long pause, and as the line filled with static, Prince asked Gilbey if he was still there.

'And I daresay if I ask where the hell Friedrich Steiner is, you'll say you have no idea, eh?'

There was a long pause. Enough time had elapsed. Prince remembered they'd told him Slovenia was just five miles from Trieste, so they'd almost certainly be there by now. It was probably safe to tell the truth.

'Actually, sir, I believe some of our Slovenian friends may have captured him. I saw them dragging him away just before our chaps—'

'So Bartholomew tells me – and you didn't try to stop them?'

Prince laughed. 'I think you'll find that even had we wanted to, Hanne and I would have been outnumbered.'

'So you just let them take him.'

'He'll face justice, sir, I think we can be sure of that.'

'And the others? A bloodbath by the sounds of it.'

'The woman killed Edward Palmer before we got there, and then killed herself.'

'Poison, I understand?'

'I'm afraid so, sir.'

There was a long silence during which Prince heard Gilbey cough and possibly say something to another person.

'I think, Prince, it would be safer all round if you and Hanne returned to London immediately.'

'Of course, sir.'

'Let's just hope no more opportunities present themselves before you get here, eh?'

–

They stayed in Trieste that night. Bartholomew didn't want to leave the city while it was dark, but he made a point of ensuring that Prince and Hanne were never left alone. Either he or someone from the FSS was with them the whole time, and when they went to bed, the door was locked and a guard remained outside.

But there was one lapse, and it came the following morning. They were already awake and were beginning to pack when there was a knock on their bedroom door and they heard the FSS guard tell them to open it for the chambermaid. When the young woman came in, she closed the door behind her and went over to the sink, where she turned on both taps before turning round and beckoning them towards her. It was only then that they realised it was Marija, barely recognisable with a scarf tied round her head.

'Come closer, I don't have long.'

The three of them huddled together.

'We took Friedrich Steiner straight to Maribor and interrogated him all night. It was so easy – the man's terrified and showed no courage whatsoever. He gave us the details of all the safe houses he stayed in – in the Tyrol, near Munich, Salzburg, all of them. He was truly desperate to tell us as much as he could, anything to save himself. We've written those addresses down for you – here.' She handed them a piece of paper. 'He pleaded for us to spare him and he betrayed everyone he could think of. I've given you those names too; the only ones we are interested in are those in Slovenia, and he gave us the names of some informers from Maribor. He even told us, would you believe, all about his father – how he's a senior Nazi and where we can find him.'

'And where is that?'

'Apparently he's been hiding at a farm in Bavaria, near the town of Eggenfelden. Friedrich said that he and Ulrich stayed there for a few weeks ago, and while he was there, he discovered that his father had hidden notebooks and rolls of film in the cellar. He said he's sure they're full of top-secret material. He told us exactly where to find it. You can have that information – the address of the farm is on that piece of paper, and there's even a helpful diagram Steiner drew of where to find the films. In the—'

There was a sharp rap at the door and they heard Bartholomew's voice telling them to get a move on. Marija gathered her things and leaned close to them.

'Today my comrades are taking Friedrich Steiner to the place where he buried the three girls outside Maribor. He'll then be handed over to their families.'

Epilogue

Bartholomew didn't think there was much damage left to be done by Hanne and Prince in Trieste, but he still wanted to get them out of the city and back to England as soon as possible. But before they left, there were one or two of what Tom Gilbey euphemistically termed 'loose ends' to be tied up.

Chief among these was what to do with the dozen or so Slovenians and Italians they were holding in custody – as far as they could tell, around a dozen more had managed to get away. The commander of the British garrison in Trieste was all for throwing the book at them and was minded to ignore the view shared by Gilbey and Bartholomew that imprisoning former partisans for killing a Nazi might not play terribly well at home or anywhere else for that matter. In the end, Sir Roland Pearson had to have a word with Field Marshal Alexander, who as far as he could make out was now in charge of the Mediterranean area, and fortunately he agreed with him. The Slovenians, he said, should be released and told to make themselves scarce, which they seemed more than happy to do.

–

The Admiral began to worry when the news from Trieste of the deaths of Edward Palmer and Myrtle Carter and from Berlin of the disappearance of Wolfgang Steiner filtered through in the dark days just before Christmas. He was fearful of what would happen to him. His man left after lunch on Christmas Day and he spent the afternoon in his library, the room lit only by a candle and the fading embers of an untended fire.

As darkness wrapped itself around the isolated Victorian house he found himself in a depressed mood as he wandered into the dining room he rarely used and gazed at photographs of long dead family members on top of a piano which was never played.

But once he'd turned on the lights and drawn the curtains he took a grip on himself. There was no point allowing himself the indulgence of worrying about what was to happen to him. He needed to do something about it.

His man wasn't due back until the day after Boxing Day so he applied himself to the task in hand, going through the house and especially the cellar and removing everything that could be regarded as incriminating. By midnight on Boxing Day all; the evidence had been burned. He now turned his thoughts to Bourne and Ridgeway.

Since being ordered to make themselves scarce they'd moved furtively around the country, three or four days at a time in cheap bed and breakfasts, travelling coast to coast, county to county and calling him at the isolated telephone box twice a week for brief, coded conversations.

But now it was clear British Intelligence were closing in on them. The art gallery in Cork Street had been raided, as had their homes. It was only a matter of time before they were caught and the Admiral doubted either of them would hold out very long under interrogation.

He assured them he would look after them: they were to travel by train and bus and on New Year's Eve meet him at a wood some five miles from his house from where he'd take them to safety.

When he arrived at the wood at eleven o'clock that night they'd clearly been waiting for a while, both drenched and looking thoroughly miserable. The Admiral told them they'd walk through the wood to where a car was waiting. They appeared confused but did as instructed and it was, the Admiral reflected later, like leading lambs to the slaughter. Along the route he'd carefully prepared, the two men breathed heavily behind him until he stopped and told them to rest and would like they like a drop of whisky and they both nodded as he made to remove a flask from his jacket pocket.

Ridgeway spotted the pistol first but before he could utter a sound he was hit just below the throat and when Bourne spun round the Admiral shot him on the side of the head. He finished both off with shots to the temple and allowed himself a minute or so to regain his breath before dragging their bodies down the small slope to the pit he'd dug earlier that day. He retrieved the spade from the undergrowth and covered them with earth and then re-arranged the surface.

To his surprise the Admiral caught himself whistling a jolly tune as he made his way through the densely packed trees and out of the woods.

–

Kommissar Iosif Gurevich was apprehensive when a week after Wolfgang Steiner's capture he was ordered to meet Marshal Zhukov. Any concerns Gurevich might have had about meeting the commander of the Soviet zone in Germany seemed to be allayed when the hero of the Battle for Berlin nodded as he entered the room and said the operation to lure Wolfgang Steiner to Berlin had been most clever.

'May I ask about Martin Bormann, sir?'

'What about him, Gurevich?'

'There seems to be some unresolved questions as to his fate. The other man they found in Trieste – the one dressed as a priest – wasn't Bormann, so I understand.'

'No, he wouldn't have been. Bormann is almost certainly dead. If the Americans and the British want to believe he's still alive, then that is fine with us – we can use the prospect as a way to confuse them for many years.'

'But the information we got from Willi Kühn suggested he could be alive?'

Zhukov stared at Gurevich, letting him know he was deciding whether to share a confidence with him. 'Bormann escaped from the bunker on the first of May and reached Friedrichstrasse station, and was then seen on the railway line near Weidendammer Bridge, so if people want to believe he's alive they have that to cling on to. But there was a very heavy artillery attack on the area where he was last seen, and we have good reason to believe he was killed there. We don't have the body as such; you know how it is after an artillery attack...'

Gurevich nodded.

'It serves the interests of the Soviet Union to leave a question mark hanging over his fate.' Zhukov clapped his hands to signal there was to be no more talk of Bormann. 'And Wolfgang Steiner... his interrogation was a serious disappointment. Did you carry it out yourself?'

'Kapitan Fyodorov was the main interrogator, sir, but of course I supervised it and take full responsibility for it. I have to admit that once he'd recovered from the shock of being captured by us, he proved to be remarkably resilient, which was quite unexpected. Fyodorov is an experienced interrogator, but it took him a long time to break Steiner.'

'And that information he eventually divulged – about the films and notebooks he'd hidden in a farm in Bavaria – he held out for how long until he gave us that?'

'Five days, I'm afraid, sir. I think he was hoping to keep it to negotiate for his life, but even when Fyodorov resorted to more physical methods of persuasion, he still gave us very little. But once we told him his son had been killed in Maribor, he appeared to give up; he seemed like a broken man. After that, he was quite forthcoming.'

Marshal Zhukov nodded and looked carefully at Gurevich, clearly not quite satisfied. 'By which time it was too late.'

'I'm afraid so, sir. We managed to get a special unit to the farm, which was no mean feat given that it's in the American zone, but there was nothing there.'

'The incompetence!' Zhukov slammed his fist on the desk and was now shouting, his face red.

Kommissar Gurevich said he could quite understand how the marshal felt; indeed, he shared his anger, his frustration…

'It's more than anger and frustration, Gurevich. We've been made to look like bloody fools, and by the British of all people. What was it that woman on the farm said?'

'That only two days before we got there, some British troops had arrived at the farm and searched it. Apparently they went straight to the cellar and removed some suitcases. They turned the farmhouse upside down but didn't take anything else. They knew precisely what they were coming for.'

'She's sure they were British, not Americans?'

'She's certain, sir.'

'So it would appear that English friend of yours, Prince—'

'He's hardly a friend, sir.'

'It would appear he beat you to it. From what Steiner told us about the content of the films and notebooks, this is a disaster for us and a major intelligence coup for them!'

Zhukov shook his head and looked up at the ceiling. Gurevich could hear the marshal's boots tapping loudly on the floor.

'Sir, I propose we put Steiner before a war crimes tribunal – it needn't last more than an hour at the most – and then execute him.'

Zhukov sat very still and said nothing for a while, then shook his head again. 'He'll go to Moscow. He can be dealt with there: he may provide more intelligence under interrogation, and then he can be disposed of.'

Iosif Gurevich said he understood, and when Zhukov stood up, he did too, realising their meeting was now over. He was unsettled by how it had gone and was relieved it had ended. There was no doubt he'd made an error in underestimating Steiner.

He was in the doorway when Zhukov called him back.

'Oh, and Gurevich – you'll return to Moscow with Steiner.'

Kommissar Iosif Gurevich left in a daze, and as he walked down the corridor; he realised he now had an escort. It wasn't a total surprise, but it had still come as a most dreadful shock, like when he'd heard of the murder of his family in Minsk.

Zhukov had made it sound like a routine matter, but to Gurevich it was a death sentence.

–

'I have to admit that I was ready to give both of you a very hard time. A severe reprimand would have been considered lenient in the circumstances.' Tom Gilbey was looking at Prince and Hanne, who were sitting opposite him, innocence personified. He'd hoped to sound as severe as possible, but feared he'd not managed to do so. It was very rare for him to be outman-oeuvred, but when it had happened in recent years, Richard Prince was usually to blame, as was the case on this bitterly cold afternoon close to Christmas, where a few limp decorations in the corridor outside his office in St James's were the only hint of approaching festivities.

'Disobeying orders, collaborating with the Soviets – and the Slovenians – and going off on your own freelance operations… that's not how we work, is it?'

Neither Prince nor Hanne replied. Gilbey thought he detected a hint of a smile on Prince's face.

'So I was going to throw the book at you, though I'm not sure what book it was going to be.' He laughed at his own joke, but was the only person to do so. He caught a glimpse of Sir Roland slowly shaking his head.

'However, Prince, as usual, you've come up with the goods, eh? What is it they have in that game Monopoly – a "Get Out of Jail" card, isn't it? Well, that intelligence you acquired about the farm in Bavaria – it was spot on, absolutely spot on. I can't tell you how invaluable it is for us; it will keep us going for some time. We've already recruited some Germans to work for us on the basis of what we found. Apparently the Americans are absolutely furious about it: they were after that haul themselves, and Joe Jenkins has made such a nuisance of himself about it that they're sending him back to the States. Are you going to tell me how you found out about it?'

'Sources, sir,' replied Prince.

'The main thing, surely,' said Hanne, 'is that it proved to be correct. Is that not good enough?'

Sir Roland Pearson pulled his chair forward and said that of course it was good enough; indeed, from what he'd heard, it was more than good enough.

'And the Soviets, sir?'

'They turned up at the farm two days after us, didn't they? It would appear they're as furious as the Americans are. You look concerned, Prince…'

'I'm concerned about Kommissar Iosif Gurevich, sir: he's been very helpful to us. He could continue to be helpful to the Service. You said you'd enquire about him.'

Gilbey drummed his fingers on his blotting pad and slowly moved his fountain pen from one side of the desk to the other. 'I got Bemrose to ask some questions. He managed to nail a NKVD officer at the Allied Kommandatura last night.'

'And?'

'And it would appear Gurevich has been transferred back to Moscow. That could be good news or it could be bad news, but…'

'…it's most likely to be bad news, sir.'

'Perhaps if our chaps in Moscow put in a good word for him – resolute ally against the Nazis, that type of thing?'

'I think you'll find, Tom, that our putting a good word in for him may well have the opposite effect.'

'Maybe you're right, Roly.'

Prince looked downcast and Hanne put her hand in his. Tom Gilbey cleared his throat and said something about it being a shame neither Edward Palmer nor Myrtle Carter had been captured alive, but on balance it was probably better not to have the awkwardness of a trial.

'And what will you two do now?'

Hanne and Prince looked at each other.

'I'll continue as a police officer, sir. You may recall that when you asked us to take on this mission back in September – when you said it would last just a couple of weeks – I did mention I was in line for promotion to chief superintendent. I understand that is now very much a probability. And in any case...' He hesitated and blushed, and looked at Hanne.

'What Richard was about to say, Tom, is that I'm pregnant. Our careers as spies have come to an end.'

–

Tom Gilbey and Sir Roland Pearson watched from the upper-floor window as Prince and Hanne emerged from the MI6 building and crossed the road before hailing a taxi.

'Nice to hear they're having a child, after what they've both been through. Doubt we'll see them again, though, Roly, eh? Pity, both good sorts and first-class agents. We could do with more of them rather than the usual Oxbridge classics scholars.'

'I wouldn't be so sure, Tom.'

'So sure about what?'

'About not seeing them again.'

'What makes you say that?'

'They're addicted to espionage – and they have an instinct for it. The only people in this game who are any good are people like that. And more to the point, they know Europe; they have a feel for it. I've heard you say more than once how the rules of the game have changed and you're not sure you understand them.'

Gilbey nodded.

'Well those two do, Tom. They understand.'

Author's Note

End of Spies is a work of fiction, so any similarities between characters in the book and real people are unintended and should be regarded as purely coincidental.

There are of course references to obviously non-fictional characters such as Winston Churchill and Hitler, along with others such as prominent Austrian Nazis Ernst Kaltenbrunner, Arthur Seyss-Inquart, Odilo Globocnik and Adolf Eichmann. Other real people mentioned include John Winant, the US Ambassador to London, Heinrich Müller, the head of the Gestapo, Field Marshal Alexander, and Fritz Suhren, the camp commandant at Ravensbrück.

I've tried to stick as closely as possible to what was known at the time about the fate of another non-fictional character – Martin Bormann, Hitler's deputy. It was known he escaped from the bunker on 1 May and was seen later that day nearer Lehrter station. Over the years the hunt for Bormann continued and there were reported sightings of him around the world, with some people believing he'd escaped to South America, and others convinced he was a Soviet spy in Moscow. In 1972, what were thought to be Bormann's remains were discovered near Lehrter station, and this was confirmed in 1998 as a result of DNA testing.

The fate of Max Stein in Chapter 15 is based on an actual deportation of Jews from Berlin. Osttransport 33 left Hamburger Strasse on 3 March 1943, and all sixteen hundred people on board are believed to have been murdered at Auschwitz.

The book is set in Europe in 1945 in the immediate after-math of the Second World War and is factually based in many respects: a lot of the locations and events featured are genuine. This is the case with, for example, the Gestapo headquarters in Dijon, Paris, Amsterdam and Maribor, and with the US Army headquarters in Frankfurt and Munich. The Red Cross Club for US Army officers in Munich was indeed located on Neuhauser Strasse. Many of the Berlin locations actually existed, including Hohenschönhausen prison and the Allied Kommandatura on Kaiserswerther Strasse.

Trieste suffered badly in the war under first the Fascists and then the Nazis, with the city's Slovenian and Jewish populations being especially badly treated. The concentration camp referred to in the book – Risiera di San Sabba – did exist. Thousands of prisoners were murdered there, and many more were sent from there to Nazi death camps.

At the core of the plot is a plan for Nazis to escape from Europe from Trieste. It's very well documented that the Italian ports (especially Genoa) were used as part of the various Nazi escape lines. Italy was the destination for many fleeing Nazis, and there is no doubt that their escape was often facilitated by the Roman Catholic Church.

In Chapter 2, reference is made to the particular problems the Special Operations Executive had with the Netherlands, and this is also based on fact. The Nazi occupiers of the Netherlands managed to penetrate the SOE N Section agents to such an extent that British undercover operations there were suspended for a while.

The Counter Intelligence Corps was an intelligence branch of the United States Army, and after the war it was involved in recruiting Nazis – especially scientists – to work for the US. There is no question that as the Second World War ended, both the United States and the Soviet Union quickly switched their focus to each other, hence both sides' recruitment of Nazis to work for them.

Likewise, the Field Security Section existed during and after the Second World War as part of the British Army, with a security and intelligence function in areas occupied by British forces.

Readers may wonder whether I have stretched credulity with apparently respectable British citizens aiding the Nazis during and after the war. They may feel that in particular the character referred to as 'the Admiral' is especially unlikely. In fact there was an Admiral Sir Barry Domvile, a former Director of Naval Intelligence and such a prominent Nazi sympathiser that he was imprisoned under wartime regulations for three years from July 1940 to July 1943. Domvile was involved in shadowy organisations such as the Link and the Right Club, which were characterised by their pro-Nazi sympathies and virulent anti-Semitism. Together they claimed thousands of supporters, only a small number of whom would have been detained under Wartime Regulation 18B.

Cork Street in London's West End – where the fictional Bourne and Sons is located – is the centre of the capital's commercial art galleries. There is no known connection between the street and Nazi spy rings.

There are frequent references in the book to sums of money in pounds sterling. To get an idea of the value of these sums today, I rely on the Bank of England website. As a ready reckoner, £5 in 1945 would be worth approximately £217 today, equating to €243 or US$275. Other currencies are, as they say, available.

I'd like to express my sincere thanks and appreciation to the many people who've helped bring about the publication of this book, not least my agent Gordon Wise at Curtis Brown, who has been enormously supportive over a numbers of years. My publishers Canelo have done a fantastic job with the Prince series, and also in republishing my Spy Masters novels. *End of Spies* was the second book in the Prince series that I wrote during the COVID-19 crisis in the UK, but Michael

Bhaskar and Kit Nevile and the whole team at Canelo remained attentive, professional and helpful throughout. Thanks too to Jane Selley for her skilful copy-edit, and to the many people who helped me with aspects of the book and answered seemingly odd questions as I was writing it.

And finally to my family – especially my wife Sonia, my daughters and their partners and my grandsons – for their encouragement, understanding and love.

Alex Gerlis
London, January 2021